FROST AND SUNSHINE

MAGIC IN MYTH BOOK ONE

J.S. ALEXANDRIA

SHADOW RAIN PUBLISHING

Frost and Sunshine is an 18+ romance novel that contains adult themes and graphic scenes. Content warnings include: graphic sex, violence, kidnapping, foul language, and parental death (off-page).

To us.

"A million dreams is all it's gonna take... Oh a million dreams for the world we're gonna make."

THE CITY OF WONDER

"Papa... tell me a bedtime story."

He sat on the edge of the small bed and smiled at her. "Well, what would ya like to hear tonight, *iníon*?"

Her small face crinkled in thought. "Somethin' magical."

"Magical, ya say?" He raised an eyebrow.

"With faeries and magic."

He nodded slowly. "Did ya know that the people say we live in a *magical* city?"

She gasped, green eyes wide in her freckled face. "We do?"

"Maybe." He shrugged.

"Tell me, tell me!"

He smiled and tugged the sheets to her chin. "Once upon a time," he whispered, "the land stretched far and wide, empty and lonely."

"That's sad..." she whispered.

He tapped her on the nose with a finger. "Then, the Goddess of the Wood and Wild swept out her hand and created the Great Forest of L'el, a magical Forest that rests between France, Belgium, and Germany."

"We live in Germany!"

He frowned. "I thought ya wanted to hear a story?"

She giggled and snuggled deeper into her blankets. "Sorry."

"The Goddess filled that Forest with all *kinds* of creatures. Magical creatures and people. Fae and werewolves, vampires and witches."

He paused dramatically. "She even made *faeries.*"

"The faeries are my favorite..." she sighed.

He chuckled. "The Goddess is the mother of all these beings, the mother of Lorekind. And it was her fae that made a great city at the edge of the Forest on the banks of a wide, lazy river. And what do ya think they named this city?"

She took a breath, then paused, crinkling her face again. She smiled, big and bright. "I dunno!"

"*Faerloch*, because it belonged to the faerfolk."

"We live in Faerloch now!" she exclaimed.

"We do. They say the fae made this city and gave the city magic. It is a City of Wonder. And they lived here happily for many, many years."

"Do the fae still live here now?" she asked.

He shook his head. "No. As more and more humans moved into the city and brought their iron with them, the fae moved deep into the Forest, into a valley made of silver and starlight."

"Silver and starlight? Did they take all of Faerloch's magic?" She furrowed her copper brows.

"No, because the magic of Faerloch can't be stolen. The fae left, but they say many other magical beings stayed, right under our noses." He poked her nose again.

"Like faeries?"

He smiled, smoothing back her red hair. "Aye, like faeries. And dwarves. And witches, werefolk, even gnomes!"

She giggled, wrinkling her nose. "Gnomes?"

He nodded. "Some people say they can still feel the magic in the city. And some people say there is no such thing as magic, and that the fae and the vampires and the werefolk are just superstitions and bedtime stories for wee children."

Another bright smile, but her lashes fluttered, fighting sleep. "Do you believe in magic, papa?"

He gave her a mysterious shrug. "I think if ya know where to look, ya can find magic in anything, *iníon.*"

Her lashes dusted her freckled cheeks, her voice soft. "Maybe people... forgot how to... look..." And then she was asleep, her soft breaths filling the quiet room.

He leaned down to brush his lips over her hair. "Maybe indeed, *iníon*. Sleep well." He stood and headed for the door, but paused to look back once more. "But..." he whispered to his sleeping daughter, "those of the Lore do not forget. And so... the magic remains."

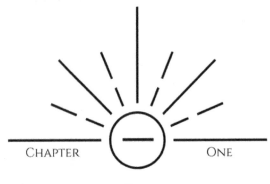

CHAPTER ONE

AVOID THE WITCHING HOUR

Preceding other well-known Lore Metropoli by over five centuries, Faerloch is touted by the Acolytes of the Goddess to rest above the birthplace of the Great Mother Goddess. The city predates human settlements by an estimated 1,000 years...

- Gherald Schmidt, Faerloch Historical Archives

"Are you *fucking* kidding me?"

He ground his teeth together to prevent a growl from escaping as he watched the last bus of the night round the corner and drive away.

Slate Melisande shifted his gear bag across his shoulders and over his back. He supposed he could hoof it from here—it's not like home was far, really. Maybe a mile. Thankfully, the night air of April was balmy and clear, and most of the walk home would take him through the nice, ritzy neighborhoods that lined the river.

Besides, there was a late-night cafe on the way home. He could get some tea.

He tightened the strap on his bag and started walking, crossing the street and following the route along the edge of the Loch River. Just over it, he could see the lights of the Eastern District—where he called home. At the slight bend in the river, he could even see the faint red lanterns illuminating the pedestrian bridge that was the main vein leading into the district. From there, it was just a block or two to the apartment he shared with his father, located above the martial arts school they owned and operated.

Slate pushed open the door to the small cafe nestled on the first floor of some ritzy condominium. Even though it was the witching hour, there were a handful of patrons here, and most of them recognized Slate at this point. They tipped their chins in silent welcome, and some of them laid their hands over their hearts in greeting. None of them ever spoke to him, though. Slate guessed they didn't speak German—they all looked a little foreign to him anyway, what with their silvery blonde hair, narrow faces, and large eyes above high cheekbones.

Not that Slate was one to talk, really. He was half-Japanese.

"Slate! I was wondering if I would see you this evening! Or, perhaps, it's more early morning."

He grinned at the owner of the cafe and tipped his chin. "Hey, Andreyas."

"Another fight tonight?" The gentleman beckoned him to the counter. Slate guessed the man was older, but he didn't necessarily appear that way. His longer platinum hair was pulled away from a distinguished face that seemed young except for the eyes. He had old eyes, but Slate couldn't explain why he thought so.

"Yep. Missed the damned bus." He didn't mind making small talk with Andreyas. "Again..."

"No twins tonight?"

Slate shook his head. "Nah, they were busy with the family tonight." Usually, his two best friends Jian and Kari came with him to all his pro fights. They practiced martial arts with him at his gym and usually came to support him in the circuit; the three of them were thick as thieves. "Just me burning the late-night oil."

Andreyas chuckled lightly. "Well, we do enjoy seeing you from time to time, boy. Just the same for you, then?"

"Please."

"Did you win your match this week?" Andreyas asked as he tooled around the little barista counter.

Slate scoffed. "Of course. Hoping to make it to the finals again."

"Dangerous sport, pro fighting."

He shrugged nonchalantly. "I'm good enough at it, I suppose."

Slate leaned an elbow on the counter and pinged his crisp, rich blue eyes around the cafe. He liked it here; the vibe was nice, but sometimes the patrons gave him furtive glances as though they were watching him closely. But their gazes would skitter away if he made eye contact with them, and sometimes they'd whisper in low voices in a beautiful, lilting language that part of him recognized, but couldn't place.

Andreyas returned with a paper cup. "I added a secret ingredient to help give you a little energy boost."

Slate raised his brow in suspicion and opened the lid of the cup. "What secret ingredient?"

The man chuckled. "It's not poison, just a dash of a different herb. Old family recipe."

Slate sniffed it, then sipped it cautiously. Tasted like plain old green tea to him. "Well, I appreciate it," he answered. He dug his wallet out of his gear bag. "What do I owe you?"

"Oh, just the same."

Slate raised a dark eyebrow over his bright eyes. "Nothing here is free, my friend."

Andreyas laughed. "Let's add an extra buck."

Slate smirked and thumbed out the cash—including the extra. He handed the money over, and Andreyas printed the receipt.

"There you are, my boy." He handed Slate the slip. "How is your father doing these days?"

Another shrug of his shoulders. "Hanging in there."

He offered nothing else. Some people cared, most didn't. Slate was in such a habit of fielding the niceties around his father that he just didn't elaborate anymore. In essence, no one understood exactly what was wrong with his father. Sickness had overtaken him one day, and he hadn't been the same since.

Slate bid Andreyas farewell and left the cafe, heading back through the neighborhood once more. He shifted his gear bag to the other shoulder and stretched his arms as he walked, careful not to spill the tea. Hopefully, his father would be sleeping when he got in—the man didn't exactly approve of Slate's nighttime recreations.

But the money was good. Excellent, even, and Slate was good at it.

"The studio was always enough to put food on the table and pay the bills," Ebisu would say. *"Martial arts is meant to teach you how to avoid the fight, not seek it out."*

All true points. But Slate was hardy, and when you could take more hits than the other guy and pack a better punch, the money just rolled in. And the extra cushion in the bank account was a warm security blanket.

But his father was traditional. Martial arts was for cultivating the spirit, honing the body, and tempering the mind. Using martial arts for amateur fighting circuits was something thugs did, people who just wanted to overcome others until they were black and blue. Those were the people that drifted in and out of seedy bars and boasted cauliflower ears and thick skulls. Those were the people that couldn't hold a job any more than they could hold their tempers. They were not martial artists.

Slate was a martial artist to his core—he wasn't out to pick fights with people. He softened his wild, hot fuse of a temper with diligent training. More accurately, his father had raised him on a diet of self-control and discipline. Martial arts focused him. His father focused him.

But something about getting in the ring and fighting someone... Something about it satisfied some deep, primal urge in him, a little piece of him that always wondered what it would be like to just *let go*.

His footsteps halted and stuttered for a moment.

Something was... off.

His eyes darted around. He half-turned his head to scope out the street behind him, though he knew better than to turn around. You never turned to look behind you when walking at night. Just like you never listened when the wind whispered through the Forest of L'el to the west of the city. And you never stepped in circles of mushrooms or flowers.

You didn't do certain things in the city of Faerloch.

He shifted his bag and picked up the pace, but he couldn't shake the feeling of disquiet. Once or twice, he was certain he could hear the whisper of laughter, or someone calling his name. He even thought he saw the briefest sparkle of lights out of the corner of his eye.

But he knew better than to look or listen for these things—there was never anything there. Nothing real, anyway.

He was nearing the end of the neighborhood, where the fancy high-rise condos petered out to more trees, when he realized he wasn't alone on the streets—a rarity at this hour. He suspected he hadn't been alone for some time now.

Slate crossed the street casually and went down a little side street that would pop out a little further along. The other person... followed him.

A shot of panicked adrenaline flooded his system and made his heart rate jump. An icy flush slithered over his skin, and his mind zipped through a couple of self-defense scenarios. This wasn't the first time he'd had to defend himself, and it wouldn't be the last. His phone was in the side pocket of his bag. He could smoke this guy if he needed to and call the police. It was probably a street thug looking for trouble. Which seemed so unusual in such a nice community.

Slate stopped and did something that went against superstition.

He turned around.

"What's up, man?" he called to the figure twenty paces behind him.

Silence met him.

"You need something? You lost?" Slate tried again.

Self-Defense Logic Number 1: Verbally engage the threat to try and de-escalate a situation.

"Are you Zlaet, son of Aredhel?" Finally, the figure spoke. Their voice was deep but lilted, and somewhere in his mind, Slate recognized—but couldn't place—the accent.

Zlaet, son of Aredhel?

"Nope," Slate answered. "Not me."

"You are mistaken." Haughtiness dripped from the guy's words.

"I'm really not. What do you want?" Slate demanded.

"I have heard tell of your training in the warrior arts, Zlaet."

"What?" Slate frowned. "Warrior arts? Man, just tell me what you want with me, seriously." This guy was giving him a bad vibe, especially from the way he spoke.

"I have been tasked by the Council to bring you in," the figure—who sounded like a man—said. "It is recommended you come quietly. None of your warrior arts will compare to one such as I."

... what the actual what?

Was this guy for real? "Whoa, wait, wait, wait," Slate said. "Are you a police officer? Am I in some kind of trouble?"

Some instinct told him this guy was *not* a police officer. Like a warning or a red flag. It was the same kind of feeling Slate got when someone lied to him. He could just tell.

"Trouble is a relative term and will be determined by the Council," said the man. "Now, if you please, Zlaet, let us go."

"Look, man." Slate adjusted his bag. "I dunno what you're on about, but it's late, and I got places to be."

He turned and started walking away.

"Zlaet," the man called.

"That's not my name!" Slate waved his hand over his shoulder.

Suddenly, a glowing golden circle appeared on the ground, about the size of a child's hula-hoop, so fast he couldn't stop himself from stepping in it. Stunned, he stared at the faint glint surrounding his sandaled feet.

His feet were stuck as if they were glued to the concrete. He inhaled sharply, pulling desperately. What the hell was happening?

The man came into his line of sight. He wore a hood that obscured most of his face in the dark, but once he was close, he folded the material back. He appeared to be a young man, maybe mid-thirties, certainly not much older than Slate. He had a sharp face, gray eyes, and his silver hair was pulled back into a low ponytail.

A cool anger burned through Slate, an anger that manifested itself when he was put into a position to defend himself. He dropped his bag heavily onto the ground and leveled a burning look at this individual.

"What do you want?" he growled.

"I am to bring you into the Council. Do not resist. I do not wish to duel with a *faeling*." He procured something from beneath his cloak with long, gloved fingers. It looked like… were those restraints?

Oh, hell *no*. He didn't have any clue what was actually happening, but one thing was certain—he wasn't going *anywhere* with *anyone*, especially not in restraints and *especially* not with this guy.

His fists still worked and when the man came within critical distance, Slate clocked him—palm heel to the nose, jab to the solar plexus, hook punch to the floating ribs.

The hits were enough to shake his assailant—the golden circle under his feet vanished, and he had mobility in his feet again. Slate snatched up his bag and booked it.

He had to get out of here.

He got maybe a dozen solid steps before he tripped. He tried to tuck his shoulder to roll, but his feet were stuck again. He fell flat on his face, scraping his cheek and the heels of his hands. Slate twisted, eyes zeroing in on his legs. His calves were wrapped in some kind of wire.

"My first request was polite." The man's form cast a shadow over Slate. "I will not ask you again. You are to accompany me to the Council. Do not resist."

"Get lost," Slate growled. He grabbed at the wire catching his legs... and yanked his hand back with a sharp gasp.

The wire had burned his hand.

"What the fuck?" Angry red streaks crisscrossed his palms.

The man reached for him, and Slate slid backward out of reach, assuming a ground-fighting stance.

"You have proven yourself to be a feisty warrior," the man stated, pulling out the restraints again. They glinted in the low streetlight as they dangled from his gloved fingers. "But it is in vain. Your mortal warrior tactics are useless against the fae."

Faster than Slate could follow, the man hauled him up by the front of his shirt and slapped the unforgiving restraints over his wrists.

The instant they touched him, his skin burst with heat, a slow, angry burn.

"A relief to see your human nature has not affected your tolerance to pure iron." The man almost smirked. "How you can tolerate the city air is beyond my comprehension, but that is neither here nor there. Let us go, *faeling*."

He grabbed Slate by the elbow and did something with his hand. A circle appeared on the ground in front of them.

Slate struggled, throwing elbows—his last weapon—but his feet were still bound and his cotton pants were shifting up, exposing skin, and the wire was burning him. And the handcuffs too, were sending unlocalized pain up his arms, acute and intense and never-ending.

"Do not resist," the man said.

CHAPTER TWO

MORTAL MYSTERY

Many claim it is their short lifespans and the great passage
of time that has resulted in mortals outside of Faerloch
forgetting the rules of faeries, kobolds, kelpies, will-o'-
wisps, and other such mischievous sprites. Interestingly,
humans within Faerloch have allocated such knowledge to
superstition, and as a result, human deaths are
proportionally lower...

- Gherald Schmidt, Faerloch Historical Archives

"The Den is lame tonight," Dani muttered under her breath.

Immediately, a low growl rumbled across the dim-lit room. Dani straightened swiftly
from where she'd been slumped in the booth and shot a grin at the bartender. Loraine's
eyes were more golden than brown right then, glinting under her snowy white brows.

"No offense meant, Loraine!" Dani called to the *dirndl*-clad bar matron, using a voice
much louder than was necessary for the werebear to hear her.

As Loraine snorted, holding a stein to the beer tap, Dani muttered, "There's no privacy in this place." She gazed into her own stein, nearly empty, and sighed through her nose.

"One doesn't frequent a bar for privacy, Daniella," Roger's smooth voice remarked from where he sat across the table from her. His long, elegant fingers were wrapped around a glass of dark red liquid. She never bothered to ask what he was drinking.

After all, vampires usually favored one particular type of drink.

Dani scowled at him, summer-green eyes narrowed playfully. The cool—and often-times sarcastic—male was one of her best friends, aside from Selene. "And yet somehow, *you* still manage to be one of the most private people who ever come here," she teased with a smile. She leaned across the table to tug at the lock of mahogany hair that draped over his shoulder from the neat queue tied at his nape. He had eyes the color of dark chocolate, with a long nose in the middle of a handsome, somewhat aristocratic face. He appeared to be in his mid-thirties, but Dani knew he was much, *much* older.

With the barest movement that was difficult for the mortal eye to follow, Roger shifted back enough to avoid the tug. "I don't flap my business around like some people I know."

Dani rolled her eyes, picked up her beer, and drained the last bit of it. "As if I need to 'flap it' around here. I could just *whisper* my business, and most people in here would *still* hear me." She dropped her stein heavily onto the tabletop and flipped her red-gold hair over her shoulder.

"Then you needn't come to a bar full of Lorefolk and such," Roger reminded her, placing his wineglass on the table. Currently, there were only a handful of individuals in the pub at the moment, but after the witching hour, it would pick up again.

Dani grinned, licking the beer foam at the top of her lip. "Well, that would be boring. Plus, Loraine has the best beer around." She threw a radiant smile at the pub's bartender. Loraine snorted without looking up from the glasses she was polishing, a wisp of snowy white hair drifting down from her severe bun.

A bell tinkled through the pub as the door opened. Dani glanced over her shoulder out of instinct, and she did a fast double-take as panic spiked through her throat and her muscles tightened.

Fae.

Both had pale hair, one almost silver, the other a platinum blonde, and they had delicately pointed ears. They spared a glance around the pub and began to weave their way through the tables with an eerie grace native to their race.

"Did I tell you about my date the other day?" Roger's voice sounded like it echoed from far away.

"What?" Attention split, she dragged her eyes back to Roger. "Wait, your date with Peter?" It was a deliberate effort to focus on his reply, to hear past the buzz that had started in her ears. Despite herself, her gaze slid sideways, tracking the fae across the room. She noted the haunting beauty of them, the sharpness in their facial features, large eyes, slender frames...

Nightmares could highlight the smallest details.

"Indeed. It was disastrous."

That was enough to yank her attention back. She blinked at him. There was a grim knowing in his eyes before his lips curled into a smile. After a beat, she smiled back. She knew what he was trying to do. She was grateful for the effort.

"Yeah, right, like you'd do *anything* disastrous." Her voice sounded stiff, so she cleared her throat and tried to relax her shoulders. Forced herself to focus on Roger and Roger alone.

"I would never lie." A solemn nod.

"Uh-huh..." Her stomach tensed as the fae stepped past their table...

... and continued to one of the booths on the other side of the bar.

The fear was irrational, a cold coil that writhed and twisted in her belly unpleasantly. It wasn't often that fae made an appearance in the Den, one of the other reasons she enjoyed frequenting this establishment. Fae were uncommon in this part of the city. The few who lived in Faerloch preferred little pockets closer to the Forest, where there were fewer steel and iron components.

Dani did her best to avoid those parts of the city.

"Indeed, the establishment he brought me to had UV lights."

Her cold fear stumbled. "Wait, what? Can't those hurt you?" She blinked at him, suddenly concerned.

Roger cracked a rare real smile this time, and she realized he was messing with her. She glared at him, but her lips wanted to twitch into a smile. "You jerk."

An amused shake of his head was her answer. His gaze flicked to where the fae sat and like a magnet, her gaze followed. There was half a room between them, and yet it was like they were in the booth next to her.

"Daniella."

Her eyes jumped back to Roger, finding him watching her now.

Busted.

Dani dropped her gaze, shame blooming out of the fear in her stomach. It wasn't his fault his brown eyes could make her feel her fear more acutely, could make her see her own cowardice twice as easily.

He offered her a half-smile. "It is rather late, is it not? I'm certain Selene is anxious to depart."

Dani was grateful for the valiant excuse he provided for her. It might make her cowardly, but she clung to it just the same. It was too late to muster anything else, to try and wrestle with demons that had somehow grown larger the older she became.

While there are many creatures in the Lore more fearsome and lethal than the fae, none of them caused the bone-deep chill in Dani that these graceful beings did. They were powerful, certainly—she'd seen some fae warriors who were built sturdy as trees—but they lacked the wild ferocity of the werefolk. Fae magic, too, was powerful, and yet she had seen witches do incredible feats of magic. All the same, they didn't cause the knot of ice in her gut quite like the fae.

For a moment, memory and reality blended together. Crystalline blue-gray eyes replaced brown ones. Pale skin became a rich mocha, rounded and sweet. A peaceful smile clashed violently with the silent horror in familiar, beloved eyes while long fae fingers curled over the girl's slender shoulder.

That ice inside her grew razor edges that prickled along a stomach suddenly too small to contain it.

Kat...

Dani pulled in a breath, shoving the memory aside, and nodded her head. "Yeah, I think it's time I get home," she agreed with a smile she hoped didn't look too forced. "It *is* almost three in the morning."

Which wasn't terribly unusual for her, if she was being honest, considering she didn't get out of work at the clinic until midnight.

Roger inclined his head and drained the remaining contents of his wine glass. The speed and grace with which he slid out of the booth marked him for his race, entirely more fluid than the grace of the fae, like a slinking shadow. "I'll walk you to the door. I wouldn't want Loraine thinking I've forgotten my manners."

"Because manners are more important today or something?" she teased him, appreciating the light banter. Bantering was normal, easy, something familiar to cling to rather than the fact that Roger was subtly angling his body to block her view of the fae. Not subtle enough for her not to notice, though.

Coward...

She smothered her inner voice, voting instead to give herself a break. It had been a long day at the animal clinic, and they'd nearly lost a patient. She should cut herself some slack.

It was a mental conversation she'd had with herself so many times now it was starting to sound rehearsed, even in her own head.

"Manners are what separate civilized folk from utter chaos. Have you ever seen a monkey use a napkin? Utter barbarity." His smirk was almost as dry as his tone, which was at odds with the absurdity of his words.

She couldn't help herself; she giggled, and his smile grew. The vampire slid his hands into the pockets of his charcoal slacks, the motion tightening his crisp white dress shirt around his biceps, lean but corded with muscle. He wore an elegant vest of black silk with gold buttons, but no tie; the top button of his dress shirt was undone, revealing smooth pale flesh. He looked more like a young entrepreneur, or even a hipster, rather than the lethal vampire he was. "At least, mortals seem particularly concerned about manners, and we must mind what mortals say."

"Since when do you care about what mortals say?" She cocked a reddish-blonde brow.

"I'll have you know, little *lorekissed*, that I make it a point of personal interest to know what mortals say."

"So you can blend in?" She grinned, gesturing to his outfit.

He ignored the gesture in the haughty way Roger did when he deemed a topic too beneath him to address. "Only in the 'manner' that it counts." Another hint of a smile.

She let out a little laugh. "You're just full of humor today, aren't you?" They were at the door. She turned to face him, and with a hand on his arm to steady her, she rose on her tip-toes to brush her lips over his cheek. "Thanks, Roge," she murmured, once more grateful to have such a good friend.

Dani dropped back to her heels and leaned to the side to peek over Roger's shoulder. "Thanks, Loraine! I love your bar!" She offered the bartender a smile and a jaunty little wave.

The female werebear let out a small growl, but Dani had a feeling she was pleased.

She turned back to Roger. "Text me later. We can grab coffee with Maddie or something this week."

He gave her a nod of agreement. "Good evening, Daniella. Be safe." He turned back towards his booth as she stepped out into the night.

The crisp air of late spring was refreshing after the stuffy air of the bar.

Within three steps, Dani heard a soft croon and the ruffling of feathers from above. She smiled, casting a brief glance skyward to search for Selene, but the night sky was empty. Around the corner and tucked into the alley was her motorbike, a gleaming white Vespa. A GTS Super Model, to be precise.

She was digging out her key when there was a gentle thump behind her. Selene leapt down from the roof of Loraine's building. She had a roost there for whenever Dani was at the Den, much to Loraine's chagrin.

"Sorry to keep you, my girl," Dani said, slinging one leg over the bike and angling her head to glance over her shoulder at her friend.

Selene, or Sellie, was breathtaking, to say the least. And a far cry from a normal house pet. She was a snowy owl and snow leopard griffin, extremely rare even among the endangered griffin population. Dani had rescued her from a pack of hellhounds when she'd been just a chick, escaped from some rare creature dealer from the Dark Market District. Female griffin feathers were exceedingly valuable, and a single griffin, especially one with the coloring Sellie had, would have made whatever merchant had smuggled her a *lot* of money.

Dani, however, wasn't interested in money when an animal's life was on the line. She shared a special relationship with animals. When she'd been younger, she didn't realize how different she was, but it hadn't taken long for her to realize her knack with creatures wasn't like other people's.

After all, no one else could talk to animals.

More accurately, Dani could speak to the core of the animals, directly into what she referred to as their *heartfire*—the fire of life she could feel inside all beings. She could feel the heartfires in people as well; after all, people were a type of animal. Mortals had little more than embers at their cores. Animals and Lorefolk, however, had brighter heartfires, depending on their breed and race.

Dani would've been alone in her uniqueness if not for Katarina. Kat, who had been her first friend after Dani had relocated from Ireland to Faerloch at the delicate age of five. Kat, who could move objects with her mind. Kat, who had also been a victim of the cruelty of children because of her dark skin, unusual steel-blue eyes, and crinkly hair.

Humans could be monsters too.

Kat had been so much more than what others had seen; she'd been confident and sassy, and she'd cared little for what others thought of her. Kat had shown Dani how to embrace her abilities. Their 'powers' had been their little secret, the glue that bonded them together, thicker than thieves and closer than sisters.

Then Kat had been kidnapped by the High Fae when Dani had been 11.

A fate that had almost been Dani's a few years later. But she'd been rescued by a sarcastic vampire with a flair for fancy clothes who'd decided on a whim to be a good samaritan that night. She'd learned, a few short weeks shy of seventeen, that she was what Lorefolk called *lorekissed*. A mortal with a drop of magic, diluted over generations from some distant magical ancestor. In Dani's case, her drop of magic gave her a gift with animals—the ability to speak directly to the heart of them, to understand them. According to Roger, it was a fairly unusual ability to pop up among the lorekissed.

Dani assumed Kat had been lorekissed as well, which was probably why the fae had taken her away.

Next to her on the sidewalk, Sellie ruffled her feathers with annoyance, succeeding in tugging Dani's thoughts back to the present. The griffin projected images to Dani that conveyed that she was tired and had wanted to go home an hour ago. Dani didn't need her magic for Sellie to get her message across—unlike most creatures, griffins could project thoughts to whomever they pleased, but Dani usually understood her better than most. Griffins were almost as smart as people, but their priorities made their thought processes confusing to some.

"I lost track of time," Dani answered the griffin. Sellie snapped her beak in a retort. She crouched low before launching herself into the air, her enormous wings creating a gust of wind that buffeted Dani.

Chuckling at the griffin's imperious nature, Dani swept her waist-long hair into a loose bun, zipped up her jacket, and pulled out into the street with a rev of her Vespa's engine. Like all adult griffins, Sellie was able to glamour herself from those she didn't want to notice her, which was why none of the few cars passing by at this hour swerved or crashed, despite the fact a mythical being flew above them.

The streets of Faerloch were not completely abandoned at this hour of the night, even though it was 3am on a Thursday. But as she got further from the Pub District, the streets became increasingly deserted, especially as she skirted the city's major highways in favor of taking the scenic route along the river.

She enjoyed taking the scenic route; it allowed her to admire the city even under the blanket of night. Faerloch was unique in all of Germany, all of Europe, in fact. Not that Dani encountered many tourists these days, but without fail, someone would ask why a *German* city had a *Scottish*-sounding name. They couldn't know that Faerloch was older than both Germany *and* Scotland, and the beings who created this city might have also been responsible for much of Scotland.

Dani had a feeling Lore history books looked *very* different from the human ones when it came to European History.

The humans who came with grand plans fueled by politics and money to change the city and the Forest around it always changed their minds once the magic-soaked earth was beneath their feet. Human minds were much more malleable than those of Lorekind.

She wasn't entirely sure how it worked if she was honest. What she did know, however, was that the city and the Forest were old, and the magic was even older. Roger told her the magic had long protected the city from the casual cultural whims of humankind.

The result? A modern, vibrant city like no other, filled with citizens like no other. Few cities in Europe were such a melting pot of cultures. Faerloch drew in people from all over, from the farthest reaches of Asia, all the way from Africa and the Americas. Magicfolk and non-magicfolk alike.

Sometimes Dani wondered if the magic of the city wasn't sentient, cleverly manipulating the humans within her domain into not noticing the strangeness. To keep humanity from looking too closely, lest they see the magic.

A piercing whistle cut through the warm April air to reach her ears. Instantly, Dani slowed to a halt, casting her gaze skywards. She held herself perfectly still until Sellie's image shimmered into existence in the air, back the way they had come. Her fluffy white wings, dusted lightly with ashen spots, were dead silent as she alighted on the edge of the building further down the road, where a small side street deviated from the main drag.

The hair on Dani's arms pebbled. Something over there had caught Sellie's attention. The griffin commonly alerted Dani if a creature was in trouble and needed Dani's help, but from the way all of Sellie's feathers stood on end, Dani knew it wasn't an animal.

Silently, Dani slid off her bike, pulled it over to the side of the road, and dropped the kickstand. She pulled a very small, very illegal handgun out from her jacket pocket—a specially designed gun meant for her personal self-defense, with specially crafted bullets designed specifically for her brand of nightmare. For a moment, she held still, facing the direction of the side street. Was this the moment she would finally need it?

"Please don't be fae..." she whispered and drew in a deep, centering breath before advancing on the mouth of the street on silent feet. The gun was loaded with bullets that contained a high content of pure iron, a substance dangerous to the fae, but it wouldn't help her much if it was a werefolk or a renegade witch.

She was being ridiculous. Why had she even stopped? She stuttered in her steps, second-guessing herself. She should leave. Just... leave. Go home. It was late.

But now that she was here, she couldn't bring herself to turn around and walk away. Something inside her urged her forward—magic, instincts, whatever it was, it told her she needed to see what was down that street. Needed to *know*.

She slowed when she reached the intersection and flattened herself against the brick siding of the building. She gripped her gun in both hands, arms fully extended and muzzle aimed at the ground. With a deep, fortifying breath, she cautiously peered around the corner.

She whipped her head back almost immediately, breathing deeply and silently. Two people in the middle of the side street. She'd seen it. She'd seen the magic on the ground—the glowing gold of a portal.

Fae. They were fae. She needed to leave.

Right now.

The hair on the back of her neck rose, and a shiver of apprehension raced down her spine. She should run, run before she was caught. Something tugged at her still, and Dani steeled her nerves, berating herself for being cowardly. She peered around the corner once again, this time really looking.

Two people. Fighting.

She squinted through the dim light offered by the streetlamps. She was too far away to sense their heartfires. One of the two moved with eerie grace, and coupled with a slender build and glint of silver hair, she was almost certain they were fae. Not all fae had silver hair, but it was common enough.

The other person was a... well. She couldn't be sure. A man. Young, broad, dark hair, but that was about it. Judging from his movements, she had the sinking feeling he was human.

The scene was eerily familiar. A portal on the floor. Piercing eyes with silvery hair and pointed ears flashed in her memory.

"Come, you must come with us..."

That man was going to be kidnapped by the fae.

How was her luck so bad that she was involved in *three* different fae kidnapping attempts? She must be a magnet for trouble where they were concerned. Inhaling slowly to help steady her, Dani shifted around the corner, keeping to the deep shadows as she silently inched closer.

The scuffle was intensifying, and their voices reached her ears.

"... that is neither here nor there. Let us go, *faeling*."

A *faeling*?

Was he fae? She was still too far to tell, but he didn't act fae, didn't move like one. A lorekissed with fae blood? After her own attempted kidnapping, Roger had encouraged her to exercise caution, as lorekissed had become increasingly targeted by the fae in recent decades. No one knew exactly what the fae wanted with lorekissed, only that they would go missing occasionally.

Even with her insides a knot of fear, Dani couldn't abandon this person. She'd been that lorekissed once.

What if they just take you again, too? her terrified mind argued, but Dani grit her teeth and continued slinking through the shadows, slowly closing the distance towards the two figures.

The fae grabbed the other man by the elbow, and a circle appeared in front of them. Another portal.

Fear choked up her throat, but she locked her knees and forced herself to stay still, focusing her attention on the human male. Without her, he would be taken. Without her help, he would know the terror she currently grappled with.

She couldn't allow that.

She leveled her small handgun up and exhaled slowly. She had to act fast and without warning. If she called out, the fae could simply step into the portal, and she'd have no chance of saving the human. No, her only chance was to catch them by surprise.

Dani stretched out her senses, feeling Sellie's heartfire like a burst of wind and feathers and with it, a mental connection.

Now... Dani urged.

Sellie let out a piercing shriek, the loud sound echoing off the brick walls of the street, stunning the two figures who were unprepared for the vocal assault.

She used their brief moment of confusion to step out of the shadows. She swung her gun up, arms straight, stance firm.

She shot the fae right in the shoulder.

The fae let out a startled yell and released the other figure. The young man jumped, ducking at the sound of the gunshot. There was a heavy thump as Sellie landed directly behind Dani. She knew without looking that the griffin had fluffed up her feathers to look more intimidating, looming above Dani's head threateningly.

The young man's wild eyes turned towards her, and she briefly noted their uniqueness, a bright blue that seemed to glow from within. He gaped up at Sellie, panicked confusion overtaking the anger on his face.

Dani shot again. Her bullet missed, but it singed the High Fae in the face, leaving a scorched streak along his sharp cheekbone. She lunged for the man, and he tried to take a step, but he wobbled unsteadily. Her gaze dropped, and she saw his legs—his legs were wrapped with wires. He couldn't even run.

She hooked her arm through his just as he stumbled. His weight was substantial, and he took her down with him. She squeaked, tripping, falling nearly on top of him. Her eyes flew to the fae, her one hand tightening on her gun even as she untangled her body, terror and adrenaline pounding through her, a drumbeat in her ears.

Sellie stepped forward, positioning her body protectively above them, making it clear the assailant would have to go through her to get to the other two. Her appearance began to shimmer, becoming less solid as she drew her glamour around her, attempting to camouflage Dani and the man.

The silver-haired fae removed his hand from his shoulder, blood coating his palm, shiny and dark under the yellow street lights. Pale eyes assessed them with almost cool boredom; from Sellie snapping her beak at him, to his quarry effectively protected by the angry griffin, and to Dani's surprisingly stable grip on her gun, still pointed at him.

"I see..." he mused. He shifted, stepping back once more, angling his head to peer beneath Sellie at the man half-crouched by Dani's side. "I shall have to return. You have only delayed the inevitable, Zlaet, son of Aredhel."

The fae turned on his heel and casually approached the glowing circle on the ground. Without a backward glance, the fae stepped into the circle and vanished. The portal blinked out of existence, and the street was quiet once more.

For a moment, the only sound was their heavy breathing and the quiet ruffling of Sellie's feathers settling.

"Are you alright?" Dani asked, whirling around to face the man. She flipped the safety on her gun and tucked it into her jacket pocket.

His eyes shifted from the spot on the ground where the fae had disappeared to Dani, then to the griffin over her shoulder, then back to Dani. She had noticed their uniqueness before, but now up close, even in the weak light of the street lights, she could see they were a remarkable shade of blue. Stunning, in fact, and rather unusual paired with his faintly Asiatic features.

"Yeah. Yeah, I'm good." He nodded, swallowing hard.

"Here." She reached down and quickly yanked the wire off his feet, tossing it off to the side, and leaned forward to gingerly unwrap the metal from around his wrists. He hissed through his teeth. Angry welts—red and bleeding in places—marred his skin where the cuffs had touched him.

She felt the itch against her skin almost immediately. Which meant the metal was made of iron. She wasn't nearly as susceptible to iron as many fae-based lorekissed. The worse she experienced were hives and redness.

Her eyes darted to his face again, particularly to his ears. Smooth and rounded, as a mortal's should be.

Nothing else about him seemed remarkable in the magical sense. In the dim light, it was impossible to tell the exact color of his hair, but it appeared black on the top half, long enough to be pulled back into a tie. It was shaved close on the sides and down his nape, and the short hairs there gleamed silver even in the dark. He was clean-shaven and dressed in what looked like warm-up pants, a tee-shirt, and ratty straw sandals. His Asiatic ancestry was evident in his smooth golden skin, high cheekbones, and almond eyes. He couldn't have been much older than she was—if she had to guess, he was maybe thirty.

"Thanks..." he rumbled, his voice rough.

Sellie shifted behind her, angling her head to peer over Dani's shoulder at them, and let out a disgruntled squawk.

The man's eyes cut swiftly from Dani to the griffin.

"Well, *you're* the one who wanted to play hero," Dani said accusingly to the griffin, shifting to stand next to her.

The young man rose to his feet slowly, but with a grace that belied his size. He stood a full head taller than her, easily six feet to her five foot three. She noticed he continued to rub at his wrists, angry red welts marring the otherwise smooth, taut skin.

Is he mortal? Or is he lorekissed? Dani asked her griffin, stepping back to rest a hand on Sellie's feathered neck. His heartfire was as weak as a human's, and yet... the heat from it wavered like a small flickering flame. Perhaps it was from his adrenaline?

The griffin blinked, one eye closing before the other, then cocked her head curiously as she peered at the man. The reply Dani got was a wavering, uncertain confirmation. Dani frowned and shifted her eyes away from the guy to stare at her friend.

"What does that mean?" she asked irritably, but Sellie's answer made no sense to Dani.

The man gingerly grabbed for his duffle bag, not removing his breathtaking eyes from Sellie, a distinct wariness about him. He took a calculated step back.

"What does what mean?" He whipped his gaze to her.

Dani offered him a smile and slid her hands into her back pockets. "Sorry. So, rough night for you, Mr...?"

He watched her silently for a moment—she recognized appraisal when she saw it—and he shifted his gaze distractedly back to Sellie, who continued to peer at him in her imperious way.

"Slate," he said slowly, and Dani wondered if the guy was in shock. He bounced his eyes around, taking stock of his surroundings like more fae might jump out of the shadows. His eyes flicked down to where she'd stowed her gun in her pocket, then back to her face. "My name's Slate."

"Slate." She nodded. "Listen, you look confused, but you were almost nabbed by the fae, and..." she glanced around, "... in a reasonably nice part of the city, which is odd. Lucky for you, Sellie and I were passing through to help."

"Sure," he muttered. "Sure, lucky, yeah."

"Any idea why the High Fae have a reason to target you?" she asked, once more looking him over. He seemed ordinary enough to her, except for the obviously *not* normal iron burns on his skin. She gestured a hand towards his wrists. "You can't be a mortal, with burns like that from iron wires. You're lorekissed, right?"

He dropped his eyes back to hers again. "What?" He rubbed his whole face. "No, what? No. I'm not... I'm a martial artist—You know what, never mind. I'm going home now. It's been a weird night. Thanks."

He turned on his heel and started walking away.

She arched a brow at that, then frowned at his retreating form. *Was* he mortal? Either he was a good liar, or this guy really had no idea about the supernatural beings who resided in this city.

Which on one hand, was totally normal. Thousands of people in Faerloch didn't know shit about magic, despite the fact the city was one of the magical hubs in Europe.

But on the other hand, the way his skin had reacted to the iron... and how his heartfire wavered, stronger than a mortal's, but not *quite* as blazing as a lorekissed.

Where to begin? Sellie hadn't concealed herself, allowing him to see her—and the griffin had been driven to save him. He seemed physically mortal in every aspect she could discern in the darkness of the alley, and he had no idea what had just happened to him.

He turned out of sight. After another long moment of contemplative silence, she huffed out a sigh. "Let's go home, shall we, girl?" she asked Sellie. She didn't need to get involved or worry about it anymore. She'd done her good deed for the day.

Not her circus, not her monkeys.

The griffin ruffled her feathers and preened Dani's hair affectionately before soaring into the sky with a graceful pump of her wings.

CHAPTER · THREE

CHANCE ENCOUNTERS

It was during the human World War II that the Forest and city's magic became noticeably weaker, having had to expend much energy on such an influx of human minds. Through magical misdirection, Faerloch was spared much of the devastation, culturally and physically, that spread across most of Europe. Tensions between Lore races reached a peak, and the Dwarven Coalition pushed for...

— Gherald Schmidt, Faerloch Historical Archives

The studio was just beyond the bridge, nestled along the river. The Melisande family had owned the building for generations, having been drawn to the city sometime after the Second World War. The bottom was a spacious martial arts studio, complete with an office, two decent-sized locker rooms, and three training floors. Slate had the place renovated two years ago, with some of the earnings from his first big ring fights. Above the studio was the spacious apartment he shared with his father. And on the roof, a splendid garden with equally spectacular views of the Faerloch skyline.

Slate turned down a narrow alley and punched in the key code for access to the studio's back door and hallway. It took him three tries to get the code right, his hands were shaking so hard from post-fight adrenaline. He slipped off his sandals and headed up the stairs to the apartment. He had to be crazy. This whole night had to be something concocted out of his imagination.

He didn't expect his father to be awake, but he also wasn't surprised to find the man in the kitchen brewing some tea. Slate dropped his bag by the door, dumped his keys and wallet into the basket on the table, and joined his father in the kitchen.

Ebisu had once been a powerful force to be reckoned with and despite the age and stress, his body still held ghosts of that. But his strength had waned, his body hunched a little more, his gait slowed, and his fine motor skills suffered.

In the last five years or so, Ebisu's health had taken a serious nosedive. He'd once been ageless in Slate's mind, a demon of a martial artist, a brick shithouse of a man who could stare a hole in your soul. But one day, a few years ago now, Ebisu had collapsed in the kitchen. He'd been ill for days. And once he'd recovered, well, he hadn't quite been the same. He hardly ate or drank anything anymore, claiming food and beverage tasted like ash in his mouth. He slept fitfully at best. And lately, Slate had been noticing his father talking to himself, carrying on whispered conversations with seemingly no one, particularly in the garden on the roof of their building.

He still had dark eyes that could pierce right through you, and it was with those that he pegged Slate with a look. Hardly a glance up from his tea, but it was enough to send a bolt through him, even though Slate was a grown-ass man now.

"Do I even want to know?" Ebisu asked steadily, carefully pouring himself a cup of tea.

Slate dropped his aching body into a bar chair and studied his reflection in the back of a teaspoon. "I was mugged on my way home," he answered.

That got his father's attention. He paused mid-grab for a second cup. "Mugged?"

Slate shrugged. "Some crazy *gaijin*." And not like any foreigner Slate had seen before. He touched his face gingerly, feeling for a scrape. "Tried to kidnap me or something, I don't know."

His father gave him a long, unreadable look. "Kidnap you?" His father finally grabbed the second mug and poured Slate some tea. "Why would someone kidnap you?"

"I dunno. I told you, he was crazy."

"You are fortunate to have escaped with so few injuries," Ebisu replied slowly.

"I guess." Slate gave another shrug. "I can't even say for sure how I shook him." What was he supposed to say? *Oh, some woman and her giant, predatory cat-bird rescued me?*

The further he got away from it, the more bizarre the whole thing seemed. As if it were slipping from his memory like a forgotten dream. Or a nightmare, actually. Just the impression of real, bone-deep fear for one, maybe two heartbeats.

He must've knocked himself out for a moment when he hit the pavement.

His father was quiet for a moment, stirring his tea slowly. "The city can be a dangerous place at night," he commented.

Slate sighed and leveled a tired look at his father. "I know, if I didn't do the fight circuit, I wouldn't be out so late, and I wouldn't have set myself up to be attacked."

"The studio is thriving by itself. It is enough to keep us."

"And those winnings helped us renovate the studio two years ago."

Ebisu sighed. "I don't love it." He cocked a brow, not unlike his son. "But if you must fight," there was a sharpness around the older man's eyes, a sharpness Slate recognized. He himself saw it in the mirror sometimes, "then you must win."

Slate chuckled. "I'm good at that, at least."

The next morning was Friday. Slate didn't teach any martial arts classes on Friday mornings.

He found himself entering Jian's house a bit after nine. Decades of coming and going had him knocking only out of politeness before opening the door. "*Ohayo...*" he drawled as he slipped off his shoes.

"*Yo,*" came a deep voice from the kitchen

Slate rounded the corner. There was Jian, his best friend, dressed in a colorful *happi* and a pair of cloth basketball shorts, cooking something. His rich copper hair was distinctive and incredibly mussed from sleep. Unusual, that color, given their Asian ethnicity. But it was a natural color, something they inherited from their mother.

"What a good *waifu* you are," Slate teased. "Where's your partner in crime?"

"Getting her beauty rest, naturally."

Slate rolled his eyes. Karisi Meho did not need beauty rest. She was drop-dead gorgeous, with long hair a shade lighter than her twin's—almost a strawberry blonde threaded with rose gold—and a perfect, thick hourglass figure packed into a muscular five-foot-nothing.

He remembered how she'd pretty much paid her way through university by modeling for the art department.

To be fair, Jian was no slouch either. An inch or two shorter than Slate, Jian was a ball of fast-twitch muscle fibers. Sculpted, stocky, and rock-steady. His shock of copper-brown hair stood thick and straight off his head, and his gunmetal gray eyes were alert and clever. He was a doctor, after all.

Those gray eyes finally looked up from the stove and immediately caught sight of Slate's bruised face and his wrapped hands. Jian frowned. "What's that?"

Slate shook his head. "Nothing, just a little something from last night."

"That's right! Your fight. How'd that go?"

He perched in a chair at the little eat-in kitchen table. "Easy. Guy kept telegraphing with his back leg."

Jian lowered the burners and rustled around for a minute. "Let me see your hands."

"It's nothing, dude, seriously." Even though every flex of his hands caused a jagged spike of pain through his fingertips.

"I don't care. I wanna see."

"Fine." Slate humored him, carefully unwrapping his hands to reveal the angry red welts.

Jian studied them for an uncomfortably long time. "What?" Slate finally asked.

"Nothing," his best friend said with a little shake. "I have just the thing for this."

"'Course you do." Jian had everything. He'd attended Faerloch University for a degree in medicine, but his real love was more towards the homeopathic shit, taking after his father. He was pretty much a magician with healing herbs.

"You get that in your fight?" Jian asked, procuring a pestle and mortar from a cupboard. Another cupboard yielded a plethora of jars, and Jian began parsing through them, studying each one carefully before selecting it.

"No," Slate replied, gingerly running a finger over one angry red slash. "Would you believe a fucking *gaijin* tried to get a piece of me while I was walking home?"

"*No.*"

"Yes."

"On Aster Way?"

"Yeah. Just passed that little cafe there, the Lights and Stars Cafe or whatever. He was crazy, seriously. Spewing all kinds of mad shit at me. Cut my hands or something." The more he tried to remember exactly what had happened, the more insane it sounded. The idea of someone trying to kidnap him? Insane, right?

And what happened to the woman?

"That's such a nice neighborhood..." Jian mashed something in the mortar. "You kick the shit out of him?"

"Yeah..." Slate held his hands out and Jian rubbed the ointment on it. It smelled like lavender and sterile drugs. "And there was a woman there..."

"A woman?" a light voice echoed.

Slate turned and tipped his chin at Karisi—Kari for short—as she walked into the kitchen. She was dressed in tiny sleeper shorts and a tank top, showing a generous amount of skin, but both Jian and Slate were indifferent about it at this point. Kari always showed a lot of skin. Her hair was in a loose braid, messy from sleep. "What about a woman? You seeing someone new?"

"No," Slate laughed. "Hardly. I was telling Jian someone tried to jump me after my fight last night. Over on Aster."

Her large gray eyes widened. "No way. Wait, a woman?"

"No. No, the guy was scared off by the woman..." How crazy would he sound if he told them the entire story? Including the cat-bird. No, he must have imagined that last bit. Maybe he dreamed it and his memories were melding with his dreams.

"A pretty woman?" Kari purred, peering curiously over the stovetop where Jian's breakfast concoction was simmering. Kari reminded Slate of a cat, the graceful way she moved, the curious way she investigated things. Even the way her eyes were set into her face—Japanese, but larger somehow, tilted more. A *kitsune-gao*, a fox-faced woman. Witty, mature, but piercing.

"Don't touch that, it's not done yet," Jian drawled idly.

"I mean, I guess she was pretty?" Slate shrugged as Jian wrapped his hands again. "A tiny thing. Long hair, I think it was red? Freckles all over her face. I didn't get a good enough look at her. It was dark."

"Damn it, we should've gone with you last night," Kari sighed. "What'd the guy look like, anyway? I have friends in that neighborhood, maybe they've seen him hanging around."

"I dunno. Blonde? Silvery blonde, actually. Almost white. A bit of an accent."

Kari made a thoughtful noise in the back of her throat. "Not much to go on, there, Slate. Oodles of those types hang around, what with the cafe there."

"It was dark, it was late, and I was in fight-mode. What do you want from me, a detailed police report?"

Kari and Jian made eyeballs at each other. There was some truth to the old adage that twins had a secret language between them. He'd asked them once, and they both just laughed and made those same eyeballs at each other, as though they shared a twinny secret.

"There's been a lot of crime lately in the city limits," Kari said slowly, continuing her prodding through the pans on the stovetop. "People going missing and stuff."

"You nervous, Kari-*baa*?"

She chuckled richly. "No, I'm rarely nervous." She closed the lid to a pot and grabbed a mug from the cupboard above her head, standing on her tiptoes. "When's your next fight?"

"Not for a couple of weeks."

"Excellent!" Jian breathed, sealing off the wraps. "Can't wait. We'll go with you this time, *ne, baa-chan*?"

"Of course," Kari answered with a saucy grin.

Slate stayed for breakfast, entertaining the twins endlessly with perhaps a slightly embellished retelling of his match last night. Both Kari and Jian were martial artists like him, and the three of them had been closer than friends since nearly birth. Well, at least Jian and Slate—they'd both gone to preschool together. Kari had had to stay home because she was apparently 'too shy' to handle preschool.

Which was difficult for Slate to grasp because she was incredibly social now. Social, smart, strong—she was a triple threat. She handled most of the business side of the studio for Slate, allowing him to teach full-time and allowing his father to more-or-less retire.

Jian did a little teaching here and there as well, but his life was consumed by his medical practice. He and his father saw clients here at their home for homeopathic remedies, and Jian worked part-time at Faerloch General Hospital as a regular physician and sometimes a general surgeon.

Breakfast was nearly over by the time Jian and Kari's parents popped into the kitchen. Anzu and Joon were like Slate's second parents. Slate's own mother wasn't in the picture, so Anzu had stepped in to fill that gap in his life. She often joked that she had three children.

"What happened to you, Slate-*kun*?" she demanded sharply, cupping his chin with one hand and studying the scratches on his cheek with shrewd hazel eyes.

"Just a little love mark from my ring fight last night," he replied.

She continued to assess him as if she could discern his well-being on looks alone. Anzu had given her coppery hair to her children, as well as her sharp tongue and wit.

"You fuss, *ai-chan*." Joon laughed. "Slate-*kun* is strong and supple."

She released his face. "I am a mother, it's my job," she answered. "Plans today, my children?"

"I have to run into the city," Jian said. "Gotta pick up that thing we ordered, *to-san*, for the exam room."

"Ah, yes, I remember." Joon nodded.

Some days, Slate looked at the twins and thought they looked like Anzu, with their matching hair and the angular, wide shape of their eyes. Some days, though, like today, he thought maybe they looked more like Joon, with his easy, charming grin and his dark, thundercloud gray eyes. Just enough of each parent to look like them at any given moment.

But regardless of the parent or the day or the moment, Jian and Kari were unmistakably twins, nearly identical, from the shape of their eyes, their noses, their mouths. Even the way they interacted with the world around them, how they watched people, the ticks they had. Perhaps it was eerie to some, even uncomfortable to others, but Slate didn't see it that way. It was neat to be so in tune with another person.

Anzu and Joon left, off to do whatever it was parents did. Kari cleaned up breakfast—Jian cooked, so Kari cleaned—and Jian asked Slate if he wanted to join him for his little adventure into the city.

"Always," Slate replied instantly.

"Don't get into trouble, you chuckleheads," Kari called after them as they headed towards the front door.

Jian and Slate grinned wickedly. "We never get into trouble, *baa-chan*..." Jian said innocently.

The Eastern District was too clustered and the houses didn't offer a ton of space for parking, so neither Slate nor the twins owned their own personal vehicles. Jian borrowed his father's car, and the two of them zoomed off into the city proper. Jian said he had placed an order for specific medical equipment and supplies, and it wasn't something that could be delivered to his house.

"I have to go through Faerloch General to get it," he explained, peeling off the highway. "And they won't even deliver it to the hospital. They said I can only get it through their warehouse in the Market District. So stupid."

The Market District was a tightly-packed community of businesses that ran along multiple blocks. Anything and everything could be found there, from clothing to toys to adult entertainment and, clearly, medical equipment.

Jian parked at the garage, and the two of them wandered around the streets. The day was glorious and crisp, and the streets were packed with teenagers on spring break, loitering and shouting and laughing. Slate loved people. He loved to people-watch. He was a self-proclaimed social creature—sometimes humanity sucked, but in general, people were attracted to him, and he to them.

He and Jian stopped to admire the kittens and puppies in the window of the pet store, drumming the glass gently and chuckling.

"If I had the schedule for a dog..." Jian sighed.

"Your folks would flay you alive," Slate reminded him.

"But the idea is nice, sometimes."

Movement in the store caught Slate's attention. There was a flash of red, then a burst of green.

The hair on the back of his neck stood up in awareness, even before the tinkling of the door announced someone exiting the little shop. Slate turned.

There, with a bag of dog food under one arm and a cloth bag bursting with toys, was the woman from the night before.

She pulled up short when she saw him standing in front of her, clearly recognizing him as much as he recognized her. His heart clogged up into his throat. In the daylight, she was stunning. Long red hair with streaks of blonde and copper in it that shimmered in the sunlight, freckles speckling her nose and cheeks and along her forehead a little. The color of her olive jacket set off the color of her eyes, which was probably the most alluring part of her. They were a strange shade, as if green, gold, and emerald had a love child.

Eyes like that could drown a man in their splendor trying to decipher what color they exactly were.

"Well." She smiled and dropped the heavy bag of dog food to her side, the sound startling him out of his daze. "If it isn't Mr. I-Was-Almost-Kidnapped... Slate, right?"

"That's right..." he replied thickly.

Jian turned beside him, and Slate saw his best friend's expression narrow in assessment, giving the woman a once-over.

Her eyes—those *eyes*—flitted from Slate to Jian, then back to Slate, down to his hands still wrapped in bandages.

"Well," she said again. "I'm glad to see you have recovered from your adventures last night." She picked up her bag of food, offered him a cheerful grin and a wave from the hand that held the bag of toys, and turned on her heel. She disappeared down a side alley.

Slate blinked, clearing his head, before turning to Jian. "What are the fucking *odds...*?"

His best friend shook his head. "That the woman? From last night?"

"Uh-huh, yeah. That was her."

Something about Jian's posture though, something about how his shoulders were tense, made Slate's hair stand on end. Jian was rarely tense, always easy-going, quick to laugh, slow to temper.

Slate took off down the sidewalk, ignoring Jian's sudden yell of his name. It was an impulse, something he normally kept under tight wraps, that had him pounding pavement. He didn't stop to question it. He whipped around the alley where the woman disappeared, only to find her still there, straddling a small, sleek, white Vespa. She turned and gave him a look, cocking her head to the side like an animal might.

"What's your name?" Slate asked breathlessly.

She grinned, tucking her red-gold hair behind an ear. "Why should I tell you?"

"Because I asked nicely."

"I didn't hear anything nice. What's the magic word?"

"Please."

Her smile widened, and something inside him lit up, like some primal instinct reached out with insistent tethers towards her.

"Daniella," she said. She turned the ignition over. "But my friends call me Dani."

With a rev of the engine, she burst out of the alley, and she was swallowed quickly by the traffic and the crowd.

CHAPTER · 四 · FOUR

LOREKISSED

... a recent rumor of lorekissed abductions was investigated and dismissed by the Silver Valley, but...

- Gherald Schmidt, Faerloch Historical Archives

This was a bad idea.

She was crazy, clearly.

But she couldn't stop thinking about that guy. Slate.

After a long night at work, Dani found herself laying in her bed, staring at the ceiling, unable to fall asleep. Even after a week since she'd seen him at the pet store, he still lingered in her mind. It had been a week and a day since the night with the fae. Images swam before her—the portal on the ground in the street, the sound of the bullet from her gun, Slate's wide, startled eyes in the dark. The images mingled with ones from another night, years ago; voices in the night, a cloth over her mouth, the weakness in her limbs, the warm suction of a portal...

She snatched her phone from its charger. She remembered seeing a logo on the back of his tee-shirt that day in the Market District. *Melisande Martial Arts.* A quick Google search came up with a small, privately owned martial arts school in the Eastern District.

She should not get involved. This was madness. Clearly, the man had some magic in him. He was probably lorekissed of some kind, targeted by the High Fae Council. She shouldn't even bother.

Roger would scold her. She could almost hear his voice: *Daniella, remember the last time we dealt with High Fae...*

Madness. But as she drifted to sleep, that Slate guy drifted around in her dreams, all vivid eyes and broad shoulders.

And all through the following day, he skirted her damned thoughts as well.

She couldn't help but remember how he was almost kidnapped. How scared he might be. What questions he might have. How if someone only warned him, he might be able to defend himself, watch his back...

She wished someone had warned her. She might have seen the warning signs.

Morning bled into early afternoon, and she still told herself this was a terrible idea as she opened the garage and started her bike. Even as she drove through the city towards the Eastern District, Sellie gliding along above her, she knew this was a bad idea. Why was she getting involved? Stupid, stupid, *stupid*. What was it to her if the High Fae were targeting this guy?

Roger would have words with her about this.

She pulled to a gentle stop right before the bridge over the river that led into the Eastern District. She'd never really had a reason to enter this district, and had only been once, as a young teenager when she'd attended a festival with her parents. It had been like a whole other world, with its lanterns and curled, smiling roofs, clusters of little houses, and open-air markets. She supposed there was a certain charm about it, something romantic about the memory.

On a whim, she parked her bike in the car park and walked across the bridge, using the pedestrian walkway alongside it. She didn't need the attention of the engine as she wandered around looking for one random man in a sea of thousands.

Her search was remarkably short. The place she was looking for was two or three blocks into the district, a straight shot from the bridge. A big glass window displayed the exact logo she'd seen on his tee-shirt, though it seemed closed at the moment. She spent another five minutes debating turning around, but in the end, she cautiously peeked through the window into the dark interior. She saw blue foam puzzle flooring, neatly organized materials, and a couple of kicking bag stands in the corner. She tilted her head to try and see the rest—it looked like there was a darkened waiting room to the side of all those blue mats.

Seemed as though no one was around.

She knew this had been a bad idea. Turning from the window, she reached out her mind to Sellie, sending the image of returning home, but the griffin had found a lovely rooftop garden she wanted to explore. And when that female put her mind to something, hell and high water would have to come before she moved.

Heaving a patient sigh, Dani turned down the street. She'd spotted a little tea shop a street over, and she'd always heard Eastern tea was divine.

The tea shop was quiet when she stepped inside, light music playing in the background. A couple of the patrons glanced up at her arrival, but no one said anything as she approached the counter and placed an order. She'd just taken a cautious sip of a sweet jasmine tea when there was a rush of air as the door opened.

She turned and nearly choked.

There he was.

Slate.

He stopped short at the sight of her. He was dressed in a gray tee-shirt and shorts, with worn-out flip-flops. She would never mistake those eyes, a bright sapphire, unlike anything she'd ever seen before. The kind of color that needed to be bottled and sold. She'd thought they were stunning before, but in the light of the tea shop, they practically glowed.

A few people called out to him in Japanese, and he tipped his chin in greeting as he approached the counter.

"Taking to stalking me, have you?" he asked when he reached her.

She sipped her beverage, grinning cheekily over the rim of the paper cup. "Maybe I think you're hot."

He let out a startled laugh. "Sure, that's not creepy or anything." Leaning towards the counter, he ordered himself a green tea. She noticed his hands were no longer bandaged, but angry red lines lingered around his wrists. She swallowed the unease that crept up her throat, studying him, from his very human ears to his very human physique. Almost everything about him was ordinarily human—all except for the striking color of his eyes and the silver on the shaved sides of his head that contrasted against the dark hair on top.

Plus, there was that thing with his heartfire, an occasional flicker of warmth when most mortals were mere smoke and embers.

He had to be lorekissed of some kind, right? Lorekissed were vastly different from fae. Lorekissed were mortals with a drop of magic in their veins.

This was such a bad freaking idea.

"So, what does *Dani* do for a living?" Slate asked her, leaning against the counter. He gave her a once-over, and she was incredibly aware of the fact that she was dressed in short, frayed jean shorts, showing a generous amount of leg above her black boots.

"Asking the real questions now, are we?" She smiled at him, teasing a finger along the rim of her cup.

A casual shrug of broad shoulders. Good Goddess help her, he was incredibly attractive. Dangerously attractive. He was a perfect marriage of beautiful slanted eyes, smooth skin, and olive complexion with a tall, broad body.

"I'm a vet tech," she replied, yanking her mind out of the gutter. "I work second shift over at Kingstreet Animal Hospital in the South End." There was no harm in sharing a little bit of information about herself. It might be good to build a little rapport before she yanked the rug out from under him. "What about you? I saw you were wearing a martial arts tee-shirt the other day?"

He nodded. "My father and I run the school down the street—Melisande Martial Arts. And I fight in an amateur fight circuit at night."

Her eyebrows shot up. "Unconventional and risky."

"Maybe I like a little risk."

Dani grinned, and his answering smile had more than a hint of wickedness to it. His tea arrived then, and when Slate inclined his head towards a nearby table, Dani joined him. They talked about little nothings for a few more minutes. He lived with his elderly father, he was thirty years old, had no siblings, and the man she'd seen with him in the Market District was his best friend named Jian, but he didn't seem to have any clue about any magical underpinnings. He liked to watch bad martial arts movies and teach and train. Dani liked to think she was a pretty good judge of character and decided he was witty and sassy, but genuine as well.

And he was utterly, dangerously clueless.

Because one good turn deserved another, she told him she lived in a house in the suburbs with a variety of pets she'd rescued over the years, including a red fox named Dash. She told him that she, too, had no siblings, and that she originally hailed from Ireland.

"Really?" A curious light sparked in his eyes.

She grinned. "Like my hair and freckles weren't a big enough hint?"

He laughed, and his eyes dipped to said freckles. Warmth erupted in her chest. "Huh. I wouldn't have guessed, honestly. You don't have an accent, like, at all. When did you move here?"

Dani shrugged, looking at her tea. "I was about five, so I don't really remember much ..." She offered him a lopsided grin. "You lose an accent fast when it's the topic of ridicule in school."

Slate winced and hissed between his teeth. He ran his fingertips over the silver hair at his temples. "Love, I feel you."

Dani laughed, feeling lighter. "I imagine you got lots of fun names as a kid."

"Kids are cruel." His grin was sharp, and it pulled an answering smile from her. "That's why I learned to beat them all up in martial arts."

"Pretty comfortable defending yourself?"

A lift of his shoulders. "Most of the time."

There was a beat of silence. Dani sipped her tea, watching him as he also watched her in return; an assessment. Once again, she questioned whether she should be getting involved with him at all...

"I can't decide what color your eyes are," he said finally, breaking the silence.

"Green..." She cocked a brow. "Obviously."

He studied her. "Nah, not just green. Green and gold, maybe. Like sunshine in summer."

Dani let out a laugh, and Slate's lips curved into an answering grin. "Aren't you sweet and poetic," she mused, finishing her tea.

"Would you prefer if I said you were hot?"

She chuckled, unexpectedly charmed. "Do you think I'm hot, Slate Melisande?"

He gave her a silent once-over and boy, didn't that look send a shot of fire through her. She suddenly had the impression he was a wicked soul between the sheets.

A tiny part of her whispered that she should find out.

Goddess above. She should not be getting *involved*... He had the High Fae after him!

"I think... you didn't come here just to flirt with me," he finally said.

She sighed. The moment of truth. "Is there somewhere we can go to talk?"

He cast her a wary look, but he clearly wasn't too put off, because he jerked a thumb over his shoulder. "Studio's just down the block."

"Will we be able to speak privately?" She slipped a slender finger around the rim of her cup.

He stared at her in silence for a moment, and she wondered if he was debating the intelligence of inviting a perfect stranger into his space. A perfect stranger who had a giant griffin for a companion; a fact she couldn't imagine he'd forgotten lightly. Finally, he nodded and stood. "Private as you can want."

She pushed herself to her feet. "Let's go there, then."

The studio was dark and comfortable compared to the slight chill of the spring afternoon outside. Slate unlocked the front door and gestured for Dani to step inside. She paused, then slipped off her boots in the entryway, before padding into the waiting room, glancing around.

"In case you turn out to be a creep after all," she said, running a hand along the side counter with a teasing grin, "my griffin is nearby in someone's garden, and she's got no qualms about disemboweling you."

He would've laughed, but his mind got stuck. "Garden?"

"Yes, on a roof nearby."

His eyes widened. "We have a garden on the roof."

"Does it have a vegetable patch in the middle?" she asked, glancing at him with a raised brow.

"Yes." Shit, if this wasn't some fucking bizarre-ass dream he was concocting, was she saying there was a giant predator-cat-bird on his fucking *roof*? In his *father's* garden...

If he didn't already know that his father was at the temple this afternoon, he'd have already been storming up the stairs.

She tilted her head for a moment, eyes going unfocused. "Hmm, yep, seems like it's this roof then, according to Sellie. She likes it. She's complimenting your taste. The faeries are a nice touch. She likes those pesky little things."

Slate didn't think he was a stupid guy, but he was struck stupid standing there between the entryway and the waiting room. "Wait, what?"

She turned, eyes wide and innocent and such a mesmerizing shade he couldn't draw a full breath when they collided with his own. "My griffin, Sellie, she likes your garden."

"Yes, but... like, how do you know that?"

"Oh, that's my thing, animals." Dani grinned at him. "I have a touch of magical affinity with them—"

"Magic?" He could taste the disbelief in his own voice.

She nodded slowly. "Yes. Magic."

She perched on the edge of one of the chairs along the wall, glancing around the room again. He cautiously joined her, feeling his own heartbeat in his ears, the same feeling that had overtaken him the other night when she'd shot that guy. "Why do I have the distinct feeling I'm getting in *way* over my head right now?"

She shrugged. "Because you are, unfortunately. But if you've attracted the attention of the High Fae, then you're already in deep shit."

"You keep saying 'fae' like I'm supposed to know what that means. Like, faeries? Elves? Fucking Harry Potter and Tolkien? What are we talking about here?"

Dani took a deep breath. "I'm about to blow your mortal mind right out of the water..."

She started talking. Every word out of her mouth was wilder than the last. Magic. Magic was *real*. Based on what she was saying, fairytales were not just bedtime stories that parents told their children, but hints towards a hidden reality. Fae... witches... vampires... magical beasts... werewolves... *magic*...

It was utter lunacy. Had he not experienced it for himself firsthand, he'd have kindly escorted her out.

He honestly didn't know too much about Western folklore other than what he'd studied in school. He'd grown up with Eastern bedtime stories. Great tales like *The Bamboo Cutter* and *Momotaro the Peach Boy* and *Journey to the West*. Stories embellished with samurai warriors, feudal magicks, demons, *kitsune*, and fickle *kami*.

What he knew about Western fairytales was limited to a short unit of study from middle school. They'd studied classic short stories from around the world and read a few novels. All he remembered were lots of fairy godmothers, magic, and princesses.

From what this woman was telling him, there was a whole lot more to it than that. It also brought up an uncomfortable thought: if Western fairy tales were true... were Eastern ones true too?

It had to be impossible. Surely, he'd know otherwise.

Right?

Then, she started getting into this idea of *lorekissed*—people who were completely mortal in every aspect but for a tiny drop of magical blood in their genetic code. They had certain affinities with things: plants, sweet speak, a drop of some kind of telepathy, telekinesis, or even advanced senses or physical prowess.

"I'm lorekissed," she said. "I have a touch of magic from some distant relative. Probably fae. I can talk to animals and influence them a bit. I can sense a kind of heat from inside them. I call it a heartfire. It varies a little creature to creature and between magical and non-magical people. It's pretty useless though." She laughed lightly. "I have to be pretty close to feel it. If I'm paying attention, I can feel if someone is using magic, because their fire gets a little hotter when they're using it."

A silence fell between them. At some point, Slate had gotten up from his chair and started pacing the waiting room, his brain turning over information rapidly. Overwhelmed, disbelieving... none of this could be real, right?

But his memory locked onto the glowing circle that had tied up his feet the other night, the angry burns that crisscrossed his hands, the memory of her griffin coming into sharp focus now with context.

"What are you thinking?" Dani asked, still perched on the edge of her chair, though she seemed pretty relaxed, even as his world was a turbulent storm of thoughts.

"That this is the most insane fucking thing I've ever heard in my life," he answered, pulling his hair out of its tie to shove his fingers through it. "But I also know you aren't lying to me, so..."

She frowned. "How do you know that?"

He glanced at her, and for one, horrifying moment, something crawled up his throat like a memory long buried and long forgotten. "I just... I know. I've always been able to tell when people lie."

"Always?"

He nodded slowly before returning to his pacing. He could tell she was giving him time to process, giving him silence and space to do that.

"Why are you telling me all this?" he asked, whirling to face her.

"Because you should know. You deserve to know if you have the attention of the High Fae Council...."

"But *why?* You don't know me from shit."

She regarded him silently for a moment. "Because I was you once. Unprepared and caught off guard. You just... you deserve to know, okay? That's it."

"What do the fae want with someone like me? I'm nobody."

"I don't know. I've heard rumors. Lorekissed have been targeted by the High Fae for a little while now, but usually, it's females. No one really understands why. Maybe they are branching out to male lorekissed too?"

"I'm not lorekissed."

She cocked a slender brow. "You have to be something. Normal people's skin doesn't usually react to iron that way. And your heartfire wavers and pulses. It's... not mortal but not Lorefolk, either. And you said you know how to tell if people are lying to you? Maybe that's your thing. My thing is animals."

Slate watched her for a moment. "You have someone watching your back, then? Since you're a lorekissed or whatever?"

She smiled cheerfully. "My two best friends are a vampire and a griffin. I'm good."

Well shit. "Fair enough."

She rose from her seat with more grace than he'd have expected from her, like a cat leaping effortlessly to a countertop. "Listen, I know this is a lot to process." She picked up one of the pens scattered by the clipboards on the counter, then snagged his hand. Flipping it over, she scribbled something on his palm. "But I kind of like you, I think you're nice, and you don't seem like a creep. If you need to talk, I'm around."

"Okay, sure."

And as loudly and wildly as she'd stormed into his life, she was slipping her boots on at the entryway and ghosting out the door.

Slate stood rooted to the spot for gods only knew how long, feeling the tatami mats under his toes, the lingering sting from the pen scratching into his skin. The scent of her shampoo still fluttering in the air around him.

He glanced at the ink on his hand. A name and a phone number.

Slate tipped his head back to look up towards the roof garden, where apparently there were faeries and a freaking *griffin.*

Holy *shit.*

Like, holy fucking shit.

Magic.

CHAPTER · 五 · FIVE

FAERIES AND FAMILIARS

... faeries, often mistaken as glimmering insects by humans, are known to spread gossip and news at alarming speeds, but without enough consistency or reliance to be used as messengers for the fae...

– Gherald Schmidt, Faerloch Historical Archives

Slate sank into the desk chair in the little office attached to the studio waiting room and jiggled the trackpad on the laptop. He stared at it—for minutes, hours, he wasn't sure.

Where was he even supposed to start?

His brain was burning with questions. He clicked open Google and started searching for the first thing that popped into his mind: *Western Fairy Tales.*

And he began.

His search led him to Wikipedia, which he supposed was good—he needed a baseline to get started. Words and websites blurred through his vision as he read, popping open new tabs as different trains of thought led him on a frantic search for answers.

He could've spent years in front of that screen. At some point, his eyes began to itch, and he noticed the sun was setting, but there was no way he could go upstairs and face his father. Not with all the information, questions, and concerns swirling through his head. He had to know everything he could. What were the fae? What were faeries? Witches? His search brought him to websites about magic and music, to tales of Peter Pan and Little Red Riding Hood. Some stories were relevant, others seemed to lead him off on a tangent, but he took it all in.

Pieces began to come together. The concept of a circle stood out. Circles were sacred to the faeries, but they were a bad omen to people in Faerloch. The general reluctance to make promises, which was often remarked upon by tourists, the propensity for people to plant gardens on their rooftops...

He'd known Faerloch was *unique* compared to other cities in Germany, even around Europe. He hadn't focused too deeply on it; he was accustomed to the strangeness. Everywhere else had always been a bit of a culture shock, like the time he'd gone with the twins to the Alps, or up to Munich for Oktoberfest one year, but he'd never really given much thought to just how unique Faerloch was.

But if he looked at the city through the lens of *magic*, perhaps the strangeness was intentional.

His mind was still swirling with information late into the night when he finally dragged himself up to the apartment above the studio. He didn't see his father—a small blessing—and when he passed out on his futon, his dreams were a blur of magic; fae with pointed ears, griffins, glowing circles, and a hazy mirage of a beautiful town tucked into a mountain valley.

Slate's father was at the temple again the following morning, attending to Slate's witch of a grandmother. She wasn't the magical kind of witch; she was a literal angry old woman. She was also ancient, a *miko* at one of the temples, and she hated Slate with a vengeance. Didn't like that Ebisu "ran away" with some *gaijin* woman and had Slate.

With this new context for magic, though, Slate supposed his grandmother had always known something was different about him.

Maybe he *was* lorekissed like Dani. *Shit.*

How? Why? Questions consumed him.

Slate found himself on the roof of the warehouse, staring at the beautiful expanse of garden. It was less of a garden and more of a paradise, as if the garden simply grew out of the roof, the bamboo and teakwood boxes beautifully and gracefully camouflaged by draping flowers and budding fruits and vegetables.

His father loved this garden. And aside from the studio two floors below, this was Slate's favorite place as well.

He felt like he was exploring the garden through a new lens, as if somehow a veil had been removed. Vibrant flowers stood out in harsh relief—sunflowers, snapdragons, pansies, petunias, foxglove—all flowers he assumed were to attract the bees and the butterflies. But those weren't butterflies flitting between the flowers.

Slate crouched next to a vibrant patch of tulips and edged his way closer. No, definitely not butterflies. How had he not noticed them before, with their gossamer wings and tiny, humanoid bodies that seemed more nature than human? Browns and greens and yellows with bright, shimmering wings that caught the sunshine and seemed to vanish at odd angles.

They zipped and twittered between the flowers. At first, they didn't seem to notice him, but one of them caught sight of him and dipped into a flower. The others followed suit.

"No, no," he said softly. "Come out so I can see you. I won't hurt you."

Whispers emerged from the flowers, and it occurred to Slate in a dizzying rush that his father must know about the little faeries. On several occasions, Slate had come up here and could have sworn up, down, and sideways that his father was carrying on whispered conversations with the flowers. He'd dismissed it as musings of an old man, but now... he wondered.

One bold little thing peeked its head out of the flower and gave him a small but deliberate appraisal. Slate waved his finger at the faerie, and it disappeared with a whispered squeal back into the flowers. He changed his approach, pulling a few errant weeds from the garden, one eye on what he was doing and the other watching, waiting for little heads to peek out. He didn't know much about faeries, per se, but he knew about children, having taught kids martial arts classes for decades now. If faeries were part of children's stories and sometimes referred to as *the little folk*, he wondered if they behaved like children as well. Children were notoriously curious about new things.

So he weeded and waited. He held his breath when one head peeked out. Two heads. He heard them whispering to each other in delicate voices, and soon, a dozen of them were cautiously flitting about the flowers again, skirting him in the curious, wary way of small creatures. He didn't dare deviate from his motions, keeping his rhythm predictable, approachable, and non-threatening.

One of them touched his tee-shirt sleeve. Another ghosted by his head to touch his hair. He went predator-still, not breathing, willing his heart to slow its rapid beating against his sternum. Faeries. Little tiny three-inch high *faeries*. Gingerly, Slate uncurled his hand and held it out. A couple of them skittered away. But then... one, two... five... fluttered into his palm and walked their delicate little bodies across his hand. They touched tiny hands to the angry scars that crisscrossed his skin, carrying on in whispered conversations. One bold faerie chanced a look at him and said something in a high, delicate voice.

It spoke *to* him.

He didn't understand what they'd said, but he knew they were asking about the scars. "I got them in a fight the other night," he whispered, "with... a High Fae."

Dismayed sounds, fidgety bodies, and more faeries dove for cover in the flowers, some recoiled visibly from the scars, as if they could still feel the iron that had wrapped his skin.

Two little faeries came back and laid a sprig of lavender across his palm, and the gesture softened his anxiety. Lavender was a healing plant.

He spent the better part of the next fifteen minutes weeding in the garden—a mindless task. The faeries grew accustomed to his presence rather quickly and continued on with whatever their jobs were within the garden. He watched them. There was a feminine grace and shape to them, but also androgyny and ambiguity as well. They were exactly like tiny, dutiful little children. Easily startled, and highly curious, but they loved the plants. He watched one faerie sob over a dead tomato leaf while their friends comforted them. They sprinkled pollen—and something that looked too sparkly to be pollen—around the budding plants and generally flitted about, gossiping in their tiny, high voices. He didn't understand a word of it, but they were awfully cute so he pretended.

Eventually, a new visitor made his way into the garden. Old Tom was their house cat, more specifically, his father's cat. Tom was *ancient* to Slate's memory; he didn't remember a time when the cat wasn't part of their lives. His black fur was still sleek and smooth, and he was agile as a cat should be. But he had to be close to 30 years old now...

Tom slinked through the flowers, low to the ground, and Slate watched him, a nagging suspicion pulsing through his mind. The cat paused, still as stone, before skulking with more enthusiasm. Playful squealing. Slate tipped his head. The cat was chasing the faeries.

... *chasing the faeries.*

Tom could *see* the faeries.

> ... *In European folklore, familiar spirits—sometimes referred to simply as "Familiars" or "animal guides"—were believed to be supernatural entities that would assist witches and cunning folk in their practice of magic... typically, Familiars take the form of a cat or a raven.*

He'd read that last night, one of the many, *many* web pages about European and Western Lore he'd scoured to familiarize himself with the culture and the stories.

Casually, Slate brushed himself off and disappeared back into the apartment. He swiped his phone off the counter and called the number he'd programmed into it last night.

She answered after two rings. "Hello?"

"Hey, it's Slate."

She let out a low laugh. "Ah. I was wondering if I'd ever hear from you again. What's up?"

"I know we aren't really like, friends or anything, but I need you to come over."

"Ooh, shouldn't you buy me dinner first, Slate Melisande?"

He chuckled. "Can you come over and have a look at my cat? You're the animal person, right? Come over and tell me if I'm crazy."

"What's wrong with your cat?"

"Just... come look. Please?"

"Sure. I'll be over in a few minutes."

Fifteen minutes later, Slate tugged Dani up from the fire escape onto the roof of the apartment. She gasped softly, eyes bouncing around. "Wow. This is..."

"Right? My father's pride and joy, this garden."

"I bet. Sellie tried to describe it to me, but this is far better than I imagined." She wandered forward a few steps. "It's beautiful here." She turned back around and cocked her hip out. "So? What did you need? Something about your cat?"

"Yeah... hang on..." He made the kitty-come click with his mouth. Like a sleek black shadow, Old Tom trotted out from between the bushes and flowers.

The cat stopped dead at the sight of Dani, his luminous chartreuse eyes peering at her. Dani gasped. Tom hissed. He turned tail and disappeared once more through the flora.

"He's a Familiar..." Dani whispered. She slid wide eyes to him. "A Lore Familiar..."

Slate ran his hands over his face. "I was hoping you'd tell me I was crazy."

Why did it feel like his whole life was crumbling at his feet? As though his whole perception of the world had been viewed through a warped glass and now everything was straightening out and he was thrown off-kilter.

When he glanced up again, Dani was gazing into the garden, but her head was cocked slightly to the side, as though she were listening. "He refuses to speak to me," she whispered, "which, I mean, I'm not surprised—cats can be 'one-person' creatures."

"He's talking to you?"

She nodded slowly. "Oh yes. Familiars are incredibly sentient, perhaps the most sentient of all animal species. Though, there are rumors of dragons being the *most* most—"

He decided to shelf the dragon comment for now as he listened to her. "—but Familiars, particularly feline Familiars, are bred for human speech capabilities as well."

"Human... human speech? Like, talk, talk?" The words stuck in his throat.

"Yes. Out loud talk talk. Extended life span and the ability for human speech make them ideal companions for witches, and some werefolk and fae families even have Familiars." She made a face and draped her hands over her hips. "How do you have a Familiar?"

"I dunno. He's my dad's cat. For as long as I can remember."

"And how did your dad come across a Familiar?"

"I dunno."

"Does your dad know the cat is a Familiar?"

"I don't know!" Slate threw his hands up and rubbed his whole face again. "Sorry," he muttered softly. "I feel like I could explode with all the shit happening." He had a headache when he woke up this morning, and now it was coming back.

A soft hand touched his arm. "I totally get it," Dani said, smiling. "I was totally you once. Blew my mind. My entire life... completely uprooted."

The feeling of her hand on his arm steadied him, like breathing in the warmth from a cup of tea. Or sitting in the sun. A lazy, steadying warmth.

"Listen," she continued. "Why don't we go out next weekend? I have some friends you could meet—some Lorefolk. It might be good for you to just jump in it. I'm still convinced you're lorekissed."

"My father is very normal."

"What about your mom?"

Slate opened his mouth, then shut it. He didn't know anything about his mother. When he was little, he and his father would get letters sometimes. But Ebisu only said she had a prestigious and important job that didn't allow her to be with them. Slate didn't even know her name, really. *Ari.* That's what his father called her.

Not a picture of her existed. Anywhere.

The letters stopped when he hit his teenage years. By the time he was 20, there was little mention of her in their home. Not long after that, Slate's father collapsed from sickness and his health had been a roller coaster since. Slate hardly thought about his mother. He didn't have any feelings towards her—nothing, no anger, bitterness, longing. Nothing. He had his father and he wanted for nothing.

Which meant he knew nothing about his mom; for all he knew, she could've been *magical* and that's why she "couldn't be with them".

"I dunno," he answered. "I don't know anything about her. Hardly a name. My father refers to her as *Ari.* That's all I know."

Dani cocked a brow. "Then part of you remains a mystery. Just... let's go out next weekend, alright? Next Saturday."

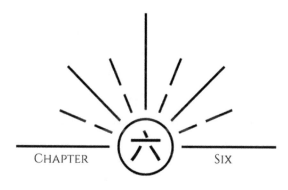

CHAPTER   六   SIX

DENIZENS OF THE DEN

... a summer retreat for the royal family, the Eas Manor is the crown jewel of Titan's Fen. The manor was designed by the sister of House Druidhil's Matriarch during the 2nd century AD, and construction...

— Gherald Schmidt, Faerloch Historical Archives

Unsurprisingly, Roger was skeptical of the idea that she was bringing someone to the Den. Dani knew he'd have words with her over the whole 'playing hero' facade she'd been doing with Slate. She could practically *taste* the dry yet cynical words of warning he'd fired at her over text.

Roger: *Do explain why you desire my presence for your date.*

Dani: *It's not a date. I'm just trying to explain magic and the Lore to this guy.*

Roger: *...*

Roger: *The young male who was almost kidnapped last week?*

Roger: *Daniella.*

Roger: *It is unwise to get involved in anything pertaining to the High Fae.*

Dani glared at her phone, before tapping her fingers rapidly against the screen.

Dani: *Are you coming or not?*

There was no immediate reply, and Dani wondered if the vampire was sulking, which made for an amusing enough sight in her mind. Then her phone vibrated.

Roger: *This is unwise, but I know you well enough to understand the futility of attempting to stop you. So be it.*

Roger: *I shall be present.*

Satisfied Roger would indeed show, Dani turned her attention back to the mirror in her bedroom. Why she was bothering at all was a mystery even to her. It wasn't like it was a date at all. She hardly knew this man.

Still, she studied her profile, spinning this way and that, and finally deemed her dark skinny jeans and forest green halter top passable. She'd even put some product in her hair and a little mascara on, and she opted for strappy sandals instead of tennis shoes or boots.

This wasn't a date by any stretch of the imagination, despite the fact Slate Melisande was *exceedingly* attractive and a little part of her wanted him in her bed.

Perhaps under different circumstances... no.

Get your hormones under control, Dani.

She'd agreed to meet Slate at the pedestrian bridge that separated the Eastern District from the ritzy Riverside District. As she rounded the corner on her Vespa, she saw him sitting on the railing of the bridge, feet dangling precariously over the water. He turned his head when he heard the engine, watching as she pulled right onto the sidewalk, ignoring the honking of annoyed drivers at her rather reckless and unconventional entrance.

"Hi!" she greeted.

He tipped his chin at her, and she didn't miss his gaze shifting over her. "Hi, yourself." He spun around and leaped gracefully off the railing.

Something about the smoothness of the motion alerted her senses. *Lorekissed, lorekissed...* he said he could tell when people were lying to him, which could totally be a lorekissed thing. And she'd met some lorekissed who had no magic whatsoever, but they were sturdier than mortals. Maybe that was Slate. A... sturdy lorekissed.

She couldn't stop her eyes from assessing him before recentering on his face. He was dressed nicely, compared to the last few times she'd seen him. No warm-up sweats or basketball shorts in sight. Dark jeans, a light gray button-down with cuffed sleeves, and a black tee-shirt underneath. It fit him like a dream; she could see corded muscles shift under his clothes at every movement.

The whole look was completely ruined by his ragged flip-flops.

"Are you prepared to take a step into the Lore? You won't be able to take it back if you do," she warned him, but her eyes were dancing with amusement. "Once you get into this world, you won't be able to forget it exists."

"If I wasn't prepared, I wouldn't be here," he answered simply, smirking. "It's probably in my best interest to not ignore it, if I got people tailing me. 'Keep your enemies closer' and all that."

"Not sure I'd want to keep these particular enemies closer, but whatever floats your boat." She waved her hand. "You ready to go, then?"

"Ready when you are." A little crease appeared between his brows. "You expecting me to get on that thing with you?"

She laughed lightly and gestured to her helmet. "If you're nervous, you can try to fit your head into my helmet," she told him with a grin.

"Ah, no, you keep that," he replied.

"Listen, just know that this beauty has more enchantments on it than a teenage witch, and she can handle your weight." She gave him a cheeky grin. She scooted forward so there was plenty of room for him. She revved the engine and gave him an expectant look.

He hesitated for a moment, eyes tracking from her to the Vespa then back to her.

"What? You want me to slide in behind you?"

"Where else you gonna go? In the boot?"

He eyed the space again, and his face split into a wide, sharp grin that did nothing to quell her hormones. *Goddess help her.* "Shouldn't I buy you dinner first?" His eyes were a little too sharp around the edges.

Her mouth popped open, her heart doing a little kick in her chest. "You are a wicked thing, aren't you?" She laughed. "Get on, and maybe if you're really nice and buy me a *very* nice dinner, we can discuss our next steps."

"Shit, love, I was just kidding," he chuckled. He swung his leg over the back of the bike, and she felt him gingerly test his weight. "Are you sure about—"

She didn't give him time to finish before she revved the engine once more and accelerated back out into traffic. He cursed and his hands flew to the little bars on the sides of the bike designed exactly for a handhold.

Within seconds of weaving dangerously and expertly in and out of traffic, she heard a low, mischievous laugh right near her ear. It sent her heart thumping against her ribcage again.

"So," he said in her ear. She could feel his breath, "you can enchant inanimate objects? Like, with magic?"

"Of course," she called over her shoulder. "I bought a bunch from the witches. They work with elements and can enchant objects, depending on their magic. Water for illusions against thievery, earth to keep the wheels grounded and anchored in bad weather, stuff like that."

Dani was a bit of a speed-demon. It was one of the many charms she'd bought for the bike; any law enforcement who spotted her speeding quickly forgot about seeing her the moment they blinked or took their attention off of her. On her days off, she'd sometimes drive off into the countryside—the opposite side of the city from the Forest of L'el—and zip along the smooth, winding country roads.

As her speed kicked over the limit, Dani shifted her body forward to lean into each turn she made. A grin of delight spread over her lips, and she let out a whoop of pleasure as they sped between two cars, then slickly crossed in front of another car to take a speedy turn into a side street. Several honks faded into the distance behind them.

About ten minutes of speeding and weaving later, Dani pulled up to the front of The Den, cutting the engine to drift the last few meters before bringing the bike to an easy halt.

Dani let out a satisfied sigh. "We're here!" she announced. She twisted her torso to glance back at him. "See? You survived."

He grinned, and she was decidedly impressed that he only looked a *little* green around the gills. "I didn't think I wouldn't. I'm a lot tougher than I look, love."

Dani laughed, shaking her head. Her gaze flipped over to their destination. From the outside, the pub looked like a dive. A faded sign above the door read *The Den*. A couple stood outside the door, and Dani eyed them surreptitiously. The male's heartfire had just enough chaos to maybe indicate some werefolk, but the female...

The female was fae. Stunning silver hair, beautiful, almost hauntingly so, with tipped ears.

Her moment to swallow hard was interrupted when Slate's face peered around at her, and his hand touched her shoulder. "We going in or did you suddenly lose your nerve?"

She blinked, her discomfort dispelling as her mind focused on his eyes and his hand, anchoring her to the here and now. She grinned. "Oh, no way. The Den is like my home away from home. Come on."

Dani led the way up the few steps to the door of the Den. From outside, Loraine's bar seemed quiet, but the moment Dani opened the door, a cacophony of sounds spilled out. The Den was heavily warded, especially to keep normal people from wandering in accidentally. It was part of the reason Lorefolk liked the Den; they could be themselves without worrying about normal folk.

The place was packed. Dani reached behind her and slipped her fingers loosely around Slate's wrist. "Stay close," she warned, smiling.

Dani led him towards Roger's booth, expertly side-stepping and weaving through the crowd. Some of the folk here knew her by name, most at least recognized her, and all associated her as Roger's friend, and they parted out of her way.

Dani glanced back. Slate's head was on a swivel, but his eyes weren't wide in wonder. No, they were narrowed, watching, observing, lighting on faces and booths, exits and dark corners. Her lips hitched in a wry smile. So the martial arts and fighting weren't just for show—he actually knew what he was doing. She could practically feel his wariness pulsing through her from where her hand gripped his wrist.

But there wasn't any fear. He didn't seem scared in the least to be in a room of supernatural beings.

"Daniella," Roger's smooth voice easily cut through the din around them, and Dani's smile widened into a true grin as she reached the table. A glass of dark red drink sat in front of him, and as usual, he was dressed immaculately. The vampire offered her a small smile, but that smile cooled as his eyes shifted to Slate.

"Hey, Roge," Dani greeted. She gestured with a hand towards Slate and gave Roger a little warning look that said *Play nice, please!* "This is my new friend I was telling you about. Slate, this is Roger." She didn't tell Slate what Roger was, partly because she wanted to see if he'd be able to guess it himself, but also because she hadn't exactly been sure how keen Slate might be to meet a vampire. They had a fairly rough reputation, if you didn't count sparkly vampires.

Roger rose from the table, his eyes drifting over Slate from head to toe, and back again. Dani saw the way Slate's shoulders tensed, and he gave Roger the same assessment.

She barely controlled her eye roll. *Men*. Honestly.

"Roger Addington, a pleasure." The vampire held out a hand for Slate to shake.

"Slate Melisande," Slate replied, taking his hand. He gave Roger a pointed look. "You're a vampire, right? Where're your fangs?"

Dani's brow shot up—well that was fast.

Roger's lips curled into a wry smirk, baring a hint of his teeth. "They come and go when I see fit." As he spoke, his canines elongated ever so slightly into discernible fangs, before sliding back up into a normal, mortal-like smile. An aloof, haughty smile.

"What gave him away?" Dani asked, studying Slate curiously.

Slate tipped his chin. "The dark wine, the paleness, and the fact you said the other day your best friend was a vampire." He gave Roger another assessing glance. "I might be new to the club, but I'm not dumb. Besides, something about you says *straight-up predator*." And he looked anything but daunted by that fact.

"So it would seem," Roger said smoothly, gesturing to the booth with old-world mannerisms as his eyes slid back to her. She offered him an optimistic grin and slipped off her jacket. From behind her, she heard an appreciative whistle.

"Nice tat," Slate said, approval in his tone, and Dani glanced over her shoulder, as if she could see her own tattoo that traced down the center of her spine, starting between her shoulder blades.

She smiled at Slate. "Thanks! It's Sellie's feather."

"Very cool," Slate nodded, and she noticed how his gaze lingered on her bare shoulders as she slid into the booth, sending flutters of warmth through her belly.

Dani's eyes caught on Roger as she slid into the booth. He was watching Slate with a skeptical perception only she recognized. She supposed it would take a while for his overprotective nature to simmer down, especially when he didn't quite approve of her making friends with someone who was being targeted by the Silver Valley.

She scooted over to the far side, and Roger's gaze shifted to hers. Once again, she urged him to be polite with a *Be Nice!* smile. Roger's eyes flicked to Slate, before he let out a quiet sigh, but the severity of his expression eased.

Progress! Dani smiled at both of them as she settled herself. Roger quirked a sarcastic brow at Slate before making the same gentlemanly gesture towards *his* side of the booth.

Slate raised a brow himself, and Dani had to smother another sigh at manly pride. "Thanks, I'll just..." and he plopped himself on the booth next to Dani and grinned wickedly at the still-standing vampire.

Roger's smile was thin, but he seated himself with a speed and smoothness that made Slate tense, just a little, and Dani kicked her foot at her best friend's shin with a little scowl. Roger ignored her and picked up his glass. "The naive and woefully ignorant do not last long among magicfolk," he said, sipping at his bloodwine as he watched Slate.

Slate returned the stare, a little smirk on his face. "Thank fuck I'm neither of those."

Roger gave Slate another assessing look. "Your eyes are a remarkable shade of blue. How did you come by those? Surely such a feature isn't common in your ethnicity."

Slate leaned back and lifted a shoulder. "My dad says my mother had blue eyes. She was a *gaijin*... a foreigner. You know like... not Japanese."

"Was?"

Slate nodded. "Was. My father raised me by himself."

"I see. And what does *Slate* do for a living?"

Slate cocked his head to the side, and his eyes narrowed ever-so-slightly. "*Slate* is a martial arts instructor and an amateur ring-fighter..."

Dani pinged her gaze back and forth between the two men, watching as Roger gracefully interrogated Slate, and Slate took everything and more. She was markedly impressed, honestly. Roger was... well, she loved the vampire, but he could be rather abrasive at times. Slate took him in stride, and something about it tickled her heartstrings.

She hadn't been expecting instant fast-friends, but she was hopeful they'd get along. And they were, for the most part. Roger even cocked a rare grin—the slightest tipping of his lip on one side.

But she could sense his wariness still, knew he believed Slate could tip the balance of their safe lives. If the High Fae were after him, he could bring them right to Dani's doorstep again. To Roger's.

She knew Roger would get involved when it came to her, but she couldn't guarantee Slate would be any safer by simply hanging around them.

"So, what are we drinking here, *mes enfants*?" A feminine voice cut in, and Dani sat up with a grin at the woman who appeared at their table. She was dark-skinned, with a rich figure to match the rich curls that tumbled from her ponytail. She had on a red button-down shirt that was tucked into a high-waisted skirt. On the back of her shirt was a large animal paw, a bear's to be exact, created from shimmering black sequins. The Den's logo that marked her as a waitress.

"Maddie!" Dani said in a delighted voice. "I forgot you were back from your trip! How was the beach?"

"Amazing as always, *cherie*," Maddie answered with a beaming smile, a slight French accent apparent in her melodic voice. "Tony is as red as a lobster and the twins made an enormous sandcastle! I had to destroy it because Leo was using a bit of *pizazz* to get it so tall, if you know what I mean..."

"And by pizazz, Maddie means magic," Dani said, turning her attention to Slate. "Maddie, unlike my small ability, is a full-fledged witch. She's a Coven Leader for the Silver Grace Coven, the largest one in Europe. Two of the enchantments on my bike are hers, and she only charged me a small fortune for them."

Maddie's gorgeous nutmeg brown eyes, soft under thick lashes, danced with intrigue and amusement as she studied Slate. She quirked out a hip and offered the man a friendly smile. "Nice to meet you, handsome. Too bad I'm married, *n'est pas?*"

Slate let out a chuckle, looking surprised but delighted, and inclined his head toward the short, curly-haired witch. "Too bad," Slate said with a smirk. "It's nice to meet you too, Maddie. I'm Slate. Largest coven in Europe?"

Like he knew for all the world what he was talking about. Dani couldn't help but grin.

"She's exaggerating my greatness, *cher*." Maddie winked at Slate. "And her enchantments? I gave her quite the discount for talking all the mice out of our basement. Where's your formal introduction for your new friend here, Daniella?" Maddie chided good-naturedly.

Dani laughed, scooting back in the booth to lounge against the corner where the booth met the wall. "Maddie, this is Slate, a martial arts instructor from the Eastern District. Slate, this is Madeline Adeleye. Happily married, two children, twins, part-time waitress and full-time badass witch." She grinned at Slate, who raised a brow at her before he offered another smile to Maddie.

"My best friends are twins," Slate said, seeming to relax more into the booth at such a normal-ish conversation. And, of course, ignoring the even stare of the vampire across from him.

"Magical twins?" Maddie asked.

"No," Slate laughed. "No magic. Just lots of regular twin trouble."

Maddie made a little noise in the back of her throat. "My own children will be the death of me one day, certainly. Not Sara, maybe. But Leo, especially. We learned on our vacation he has another element... water." She rolled her eyes and brushed a stray curl off her face. "So, Slate, how did you and Dani meet?"

Dani glanced at Slate, and his eyes widened slightly as he hesitated. "Well..." Dani started, "someone's got the Silver Valley Council looking closely at him."

Maddie's body tensed. "The Silver Valley?" she whispered, leaning closer so as not to be overheard.

"Apparently I offended some fae," Slate added. "The last two weeks have been... chaotic, to say the least."

Maddie cupped his chin with one hand and frowned with a little tsk. "Not the most glorious way to be inaugurated into the world of Lore Magic. Beer is on the house for you, *cher*. And you!" She pointed her pen at Roger. "You be nice to this poor man."

Roger had the grace to look mildly offended. "I am capable of niceness, Madeline."

"Then be gentle."

"Don't, actually, please," Slate said. "I'll take honesty over bullshit any day."

Maddie laughed richly and cupped his face again. "Oh, you will fit in splendidly here, *cher*. I'll be back with your drinks."

"Thanks, Maddie," Dani answered with a smile and glanced at Roger. "I guess I'm not sure where to begin, really."

"What do you want to know, Slate Melisande?" Roger asked in an even, almost bored tone. He sipped his wine glass delicately.

Slate leaned forward, his arms resting on the table. "Is that blood?" He didn't look horrified, but rather intensely curious.

Roger's lips curled up slowly, and his eyes glinted with a hint of the monster that lay behind the smile. "Mostly, yes. But fear not, I didn't harvest this myself. These days, Loraine gets most of her stock from donations."

Slate regarded him evenly for a moment, and Dani shifted in her booth. "It's donated, Slate, I promise," she assured him.

Slate nodded once. "I see. So," he moved on without another blink, "tell me about the goddamned fae, and how I can get them to leave my ass alone."

CHAPTER SEVEN

LEGENDS AND LORE

... calling for an abolition of the term 'High Fae' and insisting it promotes class division among an already weakened population. The motion was dismissed by the Fae Council shortly after Zeyphar Titania replaced his sister as...

- Gherald Schmidt, Faerloch Historical Archives

Roger placed his wine glass down deliberately, gaze trained on the spot where the glass met the table. "I can tell you about the fae. But you cannot simply get them to 'leave your ass alone.' Once the fae—once the Silver Valley Council—wants you," he lifted his eyes to Slate, "they will stop at nothing until they *have* you."

Dani felt the blood rush from her face, but Slate didn't look scared. His eyes narrowed and his mouth pinched slightly as though he were annoyed or angry.

"They have me confused with someone else," Slate said. "The fae from the other night kept calling me Zlaet, son of... I dunno, some name I've never heard of."

"And that is not, in fact, your name?" Roger asked, voice as dry as paper.

Slate leveled him a stare. "No, it is not."

"Maybe it would be more helpful if you tell us what you know about the fae," Dani interjected, glancing between them.

Roger kept staring right back at Slate, but when Dani nudged him with her foot, the vampire let out a sigh through his nose. "I suppose." He dropped his gaze to study the wineglass he was swirling. "The fae are matriarchal—they prefer female leadership, but there is currently a male on the throne. He is known as the *Titania*."

"Are there *types* of fae?" Slate asked.

"Of sorts. You may have heard the term 'High Fae,' but it is simply a term for those fae who are part of the aristocracy, believing themselves to be 'better' than other faerfolk. It's hardly more than a social construct perpetuated by whoever holds the fae throne. It's a colloquialism and not much more. 'High Fae' are no more powerful magically than any other fae."

"There's fae nobility?"

"Yes. That's the political structure of the fae, since the creation of the Lore from the Goddess herself. Representatives from 13 High Fae Noble Houses, seated around a council table, making decisions. The *Titania* has the final say. Though, to my knowledge, the political structure in the Silver Valley is shifting rapidly, so the structure could be different these days." Roger took a delicate sip of wine.

"High Fae are usually silvery blonde," Dani added. "Due to 'purity' and inbreeding and all that. And High Fae don't live in Faerloch. The city has too much iron for them; out of all the Lorefolk, fae, in general, are the most scarce around here. Well, other than vampires, but they're scarce everywhere."

"So the High Fae live in this... Silver Valley place?" Slate asked, turning to look at her.

"Yep. It's an... it's an exclusively fae city, right?" She turned to Roger for clarification. The Silver Valley was little more than a mystery to her. An entirely fae city hidden in the Forest of L'el. She'd heard clips and phrases about the Silver Valley Council, but if she were being honest with herself, she didn't want to know much about the fae or the Silver Valley. Not somewhere she ever wanted to see, ever.

"Indeed. Nestled deep in the forest, away from the prying eyes of the mortal world. Everything within the Valley falls under the domain of the Titania."

"So... not the Council? I'm guessing the Titania are royalty or some shit, since that's who's sitting on the throne?" Slate asked.

"Correct. The Titania's word is law; as you said, they have become the Royal Family. As for how it became that way? I'm old, but I'm not quite so old as to know that detail," Roger drawled. "Perhaps once upon a time, the Titania Noble House was more powerful. To my memory—and you'll forgive me if I'm not terribly intimate with early fae political constructs—the Titania House used to put the interests of the faerfolk first, before the interests of the nobility. And the faerfolk adored them for it."

Slate sat back, and Dani watched him, his eyes flitting about the bar. Processing. He'd probably be pacing the room if he weren't so unfamiliar with the bar and the creatures in it. "And what's the political structure like now?"

"I cannot know for certain." Roger let out a short sigh. "It's nearly impossible to get close to the Silver Valley these days. Information is limited. My best guess is that it's chaotic."

"And the Silver Valley Council of High Fae wants a piece of me..." Slate mused. He ran a hand over his hair.

Roger turned to Dani. "You believe he is lorekissed."

She nodded. "I do. What do you think?"

The vampire turned and regarded Slate for a long moment. Slate matched his stare. "I believe..." Roger said slowly, "that you are not wrong, Daniella."

The Den always filled Dani with energy, which is why she rarely felt tired when she was there. It was totally possible Loraine had an enchantment on the place for that, but it was just as likely being in a room full of creatures that could easily kill her did the trick as well.

The room had emptied significantly in the last hour. Aside from their table, there were two tables full of werefolk—four large men and two stout women packed into the largest booths.

"My guess is Boar," Dani whispered into Slate's ear when she caught him watching them. "They snort when they laugh," she added with a grin as Slate shot an incredulous look at her.

There it was, some of that wide-eyed wonder in those rich blue eyes. She'd been waiting for it. For the better part of the night, they'd been tight with frustration and annoyance and confused processing. Perhaps she'd been hanging around Roger for too long, but

Slate had to be the most temperamental man she'd ever met—widely swinging across the spectrum of emotions, though he did so with grace and finesse. His expression hid nothing, and he didn't bother trying. He didn't seem to care much for subtlety.

Loraine gave the last call, then she came out from around her bar and made her way to their table. Loraine was tall and solidly built, which was at odds with the traditional *dirndl* of royal blue and white she wore. Dani could see Slate assessing the woman and trying to figure out what she was.

He opened his mouth, and Dani cut him a look, amusement dancing in her eyes. "Don't mention the dress."

Slate raised a brow, obviously making an effort to look away from the bartender. "Oh?"

"Not sure the last person to mention it survived," Dani said with a straight face, and she wasn't entirely kidding.

Both of Slate's brows shot to his hairline, and Dani cracked a little smile, which seemed to put him more at ease. When Loraine came to a stop next to the table, she towered over their seated forms. Roger looked up with a pleasant and warm smile.

"My dear, how has your evening been?" Roger inquired, lifting his glass and finishing the last of the blood-laced wine inside.

"Fine. Who's this?" Loraine wasn't one for pleasantries, and she trained her amber-gold stare on Slate, pinning him to his seat as effectively as if she'd held a knife to his Adam's Apple. Even when Loraine was being nice, she exuded a menacing air that allowed her to run an establishment like this without trouble.

"Ah." Dani smiled sweetly. "Loraine, this is Slate Melisande, my new friend."

Loraine inhaled deeply. "A mortal?"

"Daniella believes Slate is lorekissed," Roger supplied.

"There's no scent of magic." Loraine's voice was little more than a rumbling growl.

Slate opened his mouth to speak, but Dani pinched him under the table to keep him quiet as Loraine continued to stare at him. The matron's eyes shifted from his face to the sides of his hair, to where the shaved silver strands met the almost-black hair just above his ears.

"Not all lorekissed have magic though, right?" Dani looked at Roger questioningly. "Some are just... stronger or faster, right?"

Roger studied Slate, then tipped his chin into a slow nod.

Dani grinned and looked back at Loraine. "See? Could be that!"

Loraine took another deep inhale. "Fine. Don't let him die around here. Bad for business." She turned on her heel and headed back towards the bar, her steps amazingly graceful for such a large woman.

"I just lost a year off my life," Slate whispered. "Forget the fae, that's not a woman I'd cross at all."

Dani sighed, then smiled at Slate and patted him on his thigh under the table. "That's how Loraine shows you she cares."

"It is not frequent that non-Lorefolk make their way in here," Roger explained smoothly. "She is protecting you as well as her business interests, ensuring you can take care of yourself in a place where most beings could kill a mortal with their pinky."

Dani winced. "Yeah, Loraine was not a fan of me for a while, but I bet she might like me now."

A rumble rolled across the room, and Dani waved cheerfully at Loraine's glare. "Alright, time to get out of here." She tipped her mug of beer back and finished it off, then placed the mug on the edge of the table for ease of retrieval.

"Bring Slate back again sometime, Dani," Maddie said from the next table over, leaning across the surface to wipe a rag over the top. "Maybe on a night I have off, and I can show him some magic tricks, *oui*?" Maddie's eyes danced excitedly, her hands full of steins and cleaning rags. She came over to the edge of their table, leaned over Slate, and pecked Dani on each of her cheeks. "Goodnight, *cherie*, be safe." She pulled back just enough to administer the same kisses on Slate's cheeks.

She grabbed their empty glasses and left, sauntering over to the bar.

"Roger?" Dani asked, cocking a brow in question.

The vampire eyed her and shook his head. "I will remain a bit longer. Safe travels, Daniella." He inclined his head once towards Slate. "Slate."

Slate smirked. "Nice to meet you."

"I'm certain we will meet again."

"Alright, let's go." Dani patted Slate's shoulder and gave him a firm push. "Out. I have to pee, and then we can take you home."

When Loraine had come over to their table, Slate's first thought had been that this *was not a woman to be crossed lightly*. She was towering—and that said a lot because Slate was just over six feet himself—and her expression was so *savage*. Like fire and ice. She showed no emotion, but he knew she would burn his ass down and eat his ashes if he looked at her wrong.

Probably the most intense look he'd ever received, and he'd been on the receiving end of some of Ebisu's more... menacing moments.

But as they were leaving, Loraine rumbled, "Melisande. Come back again."

It came out like a command, and before Dani could police him with another pinch, he said, "Yes, ma'am."

And that was that.

"I can find my own way home, if you'd rather head out," Slate offered to Dani as they exited out onto the street. It was late—early—but time had moved quickly in the bar. Not one part of him was tired.

"Nah, I'll take you. Unless you're scared to get back on the bike with me?" Dani grinned, the freckles across her nose wrinkling rather attractively.

He chuckled. "No. Besides, fear is an illusion."

"Is it now?" She gathered her hair over her shoulder as they walked towards her Vespa, left untouched and parked on the street.

She grabbed her helmet and strapped it to the back.

"Not gonna wear it?" he asked, watching as she quickly braided her hair over one shoulder.

"I don't always," she replied, flipping the long, thick braid behind her. "Sometimes I like to feel the wind against my hair and face. It's freeing. Like flying." She tossed a leg over the bike and started the engine.

She paused for a long heartbeat, head cocked to the side, listening intently. Just as he took a breath to ask her what she was hearing, she stuck her thumb and first finger into her mouth and whistled sharply. A beat of silence, then a disgruntled squawk echoed, and Dani laughed, her face lighting up. The sight of it made his heart skip a beat or three.

She was... really pretty. All night, he could hardly stop watching her. She was a different kind of pretty than, say, Kari. Kari was a bombshell. Kari made men stop in their tracks on the streets so they could simply watch her walk.

Dani was... *adorable*. Slate wanted to put both his hands on her cheeks and squish her. Just hold her there and look at her, and look at those damned eyes and drown. Her pretty was found in her smile, in the way she tipped her head to the side, in how expressive she was, in the crinkle of her face when she was delighted or annoyed—

"Sellie isn't an early bird," she said. "Sometimes she doesn't wake up when I call for her."

"Call for her?" He swallowed his heartbeat, slow to the conversation as he refocused away from her eyes and freckles and on her words.

"Yes." She tapped a finger to her temple. "I can talk to animals, remember?"

"Oh. Yeah. Right."

She tapped a hand against the seat behind her. "She'll join us soon. You coming?"

He threw his leg over the bike and with a rev of the engine, she peeled away from the curb.

The spring air was cool, with the added wind of driving, it was near frigid. He loved it, the icy feel over his skin. He was a midwinter baby, born in a snowstorm, his father said, and he found a certain kinship with the cold. It was crisp and clearing, allowing him to think as Dani took a casual pace through the nearly empty streets of Faerloch.

It was like the veil had been lifted—he was seeing the city with new eyes. *Magic*. Magic was real. The city hummed with it. He almost thought he could feel it, an undercurrent running through the streets, a whisper from the Forest to the west...

And he'd suddenly and alarmingly fallen into it.

Lorekissed? Him? Impossible. But the more he sat with the idea, processing it, he supposed it made sense. He was a sturdy motherfucker, that was for sure. Strong, solid, fast, and certainly the top of his class physically.

But *how*? How was he, a half-Japanese kid from the Eastern District, son of a single dad, lorekissed? It begged the question—who was his mother? Did his father know? A better question, did his father *need* to know, if perhaps he didn't? Slate considered his father's failing health.

No, he'd keep this piece of information to himself for a while. He wasn't afraid of the High Fae. He was confident in his ability to take care of himself. These people sounded like pretentious, spoiled children.

He slipped a hand along Dani's waist and leaned forward to tell her to take the bypass along the river when she turned the corner and swore loudly.

In the dim light of breaking day and yellow streetlights, three figures materialized in the middle of the street.

High Fae.

CHAPTER — EIGHT

SHOWDOWN AT SUNRISE

... after the Great Conflict, vampire numbers plunged to such a rate that they sought magical assistance to boost their fertility rates, to no avail. Many believe they came close to extinction, and it was several centuries before vampire numbers shifted towards growth. It is considered the driving force behind their Highest Law, one that...

— Gherald Schmidt, Faerloch Historical Archives

Dani slammed on the brakes. Slate's body lurched forward as the Vespa went skidding. She yanked the steering, turning them abruptly, aiming for the side road.

Too late.

The front wheel of the bike hit a glowing circle in the road, and it stopped. Dead. Pavement hurtled towards Slate's face—instinct had him tucking his shoulder and rolling into it. Sharp, shallow pain burst across his skin, his thin button-down little protection between him and the pavement. He was aware of Dani's scream as she too, went tumbling.

His momentum slowed, eyes spinning in his skull. He pushed to his feet, orienting fast as lights and colors spun in his vision. He zeroed in on the High Fae not twenty paces ahead of them. All three had long silvery hair and delicately tipped ears, and all were distinctly martial. All three were staring at them like predators who'd caught a tasty mouse.

Slate didn't take his attention off them as he paced backward to Dani, who was struggling to stand. He grabbed her under her arm and hauled her to her feet. "You okay?"

"I'm alive..." she said shakily. "My jacket saved my skin, literally."

Indeed. The leather was chewed up, but intact.

She squeezed his forearm in a vise grip as her eyes landed on the barricade in front of them. Her freckles stood out in harsh relief against her suddenly pallid face, eyes too large for her features. They flashed to her bike, and he saw her free hand tap the side of her jacket in vain.

"Not sure a gun is gonna help us right now, love," he said.

She swallowed hard. "I don't know," she started, voice steady compared to her pale face. "I'm a decent shot."

"Do we run?" he muttered to her.

She shook her head minutely, and he felt a tremor vibrate through her. "You don't *run* from the High Fae..."

"Then we fight."

"We can't fight!"

"Well, we run, we fight, or we die. Pick your poison, love."

"Zlaet, son of Aredhel!" One of the High Fae called out to him. "This is our final request—the Council demands your presence."

"That's not my fucking *name*!" Slate hollered back. An icy anger settled over him. He gently shifted his body so he was slightly in front of Dani, blocking her from view.

"We know who you are, *faeling*. Accompany us. Quietly, this time, if you please."

That voice. He recognized it. This was the same fae from that first night, after the ring fight. Dani had shot him in the shoulder. But here he was—no sling, no outward sign of injury whatsoever.

The High Fae took a step towards him. Slate took three back, herding Dani.

"Sellie..." she whispered. "Sellie's getting backup."

"We're gonna run, then," he said, keeping his voice low. "Or, at least, you're gonna run."

"You'll never win against three of them alone."

"Yeah, well, I don't plan on being kidnapped, and I'm not taking you down with me. So you're gonna run when I tell you to run."

"Now, now, *faeling*." The High Fae—Slate assumed he must be the leader—beckoned with a long-fingered hand. "Come quietly and no harm will come to your female. It is you the Council is interested in."

"If you want me," Slate snarled, "come get me."

The leader sighed visibly and waved his hand at the others. "Restrain the female. Beware—she has a griffin companion."

"Go," Slate said, stepping backward. "Go, Dani, *run*."

He pushed her. She took three steps backward, looking from him to the fae and back again. In her eyes, he spotted a moment of sheer terror as she watched the fae approach, paling even more, her freckles stark against her face under the yellow street lights.

A surge of protective fury blazed through him, and he shifted his stance, ready to run with her, to fight all three of these fae if they caught up.

Dani turned a grim look on him once more, but then her shoulders squared. She nodded once. She turned on her heel and sprinted back the way they'd come.

He pounded the pavement after her, senses on high alert, the world shifting and narrowing as his adrenal gland worked on overload, pumping him full of an icy focus he usually found inside an arena.

The High Fae hesitated for only a second. Then they came in. And they came in fast. Dani darted into an alley, and Slate followed. A broken piece of two-by-four caught his eye at the mouth of the alley, and he seized it on an instinct, not a heartbeat too soon. One of the High Fae was in his critical distance and he swung that piece of wood as hard as he could.

A tingle shot up his arm, and the wood *exploded* on contact, sending the fae backward a half a dozen feet amidst a rain of wood splinters. Slate didn't stop. This was where he'd make his stand.

Keeping the alley at his back, he prayed he bought Dani enough time to run.

He hadn't lied to her—he had no intention of being kidnapped. But he wasn't stupid either. The fae were after him. Not her. He was prepared to fight and fight hard.

Stay out of the middle... stay out of the middle... He swept one off their feet and side-kicked the other, knocking his two fae assailants into each other. It bought him precious heartbeats. He gained ground, running. Dani was already at the other end of the alley, tearing off into the adjoining street.

The victory was sweet for barely a heartbeat. These were no amateurs he was fighting. It was two-on-one and he was starting to lose. Bad.

A scream. His heart dropped into the pit of his stomach in panic.

Dani.

He shook off his assailants and booked it down the alley, launching himself out into the street.

Dani was being dragged by the third High Fae, his hand fisting her braid, pulling her towards a glowing circle on the ground. A portal.

"Dani!"

"*Let me go!*"

The command was hardly more than an incoherent shriek, but the thrum of it resonated through his chest.

The High Fae froze as if stunned, and Dani wriggled free, hitting the ground and scrambling to get ground under her sandals. Even from a distance, Slate noticed her eyes—they were strangely reflective, almost glowing.

He was grabbed from behind.

More than grabbed. He saw the thin wires just in time and brought his hands up to his neck. The wire closed over his hands instead of his throat, giving him breathing room. The wire seared his palms, and he hissed in pain as he was dragged backward. He lashed out with a back-kick and was rewarded with a grunt. The wire loosened, and he yanked free from his assailant, flinging the burning wire away from him, and turned.

Two fae closed in.

Something pressed into his back, and he nearly clocked Dani in the head with an elbow as she pressed her back against his.

"I told you to run," he hissed.

"I..." She wiped her face. Her nose was bleeding. "I couldn't leave you like that."

He didn't understand her selflessness towards him, not when he'd seen how terrified she was. He wasn't anything more than a friendly inconvenience to her. If she didn't run, she was going to be taken down with him. "Dani—"

"You'd already be dead without me, so... at least I can watch your back if we're together."

The High Fae circled them. A little sound escaped her throat, and he felt her reach blindly and grab his hand. She was shaking like a leaf against a hurricane.

"Step aside, little she-fae," one of the High Fae said.

"No," she spat, her voice far steadier than her body.

One of the High Fae casually waved a hand. Slate went flying backward. Dani shrieked his name.

He tucked his shoulder and rolled, absorbing the fall. Wire wrapped around his knees, two little balls on either end as weights to tangle it thoroughly around him.

Another scream from Dani. She was tangled with another fae, arms twisted up behind her.

"Slate!"

"Dani!"

He was yanked violently to his feet. He threw elbows and fists at any target he saw. It was short-lived. He was no match against two fae without his feet under him. More burning wire found his hands, wrapping tight around his wrists, binding them behind him.

"We have entertained you long enough, Zlaet." The leader grabbed his chin and squeezed his face. "Now you will come with us. No more trouble from you, *faeling*."

Slate spat in his face.

The leader froze, then calmly reached into his pocket and pulled out a white silk handkerchief. He wiped his face delicately and tucked the cloth back into his pocket.

Then he punched Slate in the face. Hard.

He gasped, and his vision swam. His limbs went pliant underneath him for a heartbeat. Two heartbeats. Blood dripped along his cheek.

"Be thankful we do not plan to kill your female." The High Fae glanced over his shoulder at Dani scrambling against the strong grip of the third fae. "Though she would be a fabulous prize—"

"Touch her and I will beat you within an *inch* of your life," Slate growled.

"You *faelings* are so spirited—"

A screech split the air. Slate flipped his swimming vision towards the sky. Like a bolt of white, furious lightning, Sellie came in hot, claws extended, more bird of prey than cat. One ton of angry griffin slammed into the High Fae holding Dani.

The fae holding Slate swore, and the leader of the little trio turned burning steel eyes back to Slate. He grabbed Slate by his hair and flicked out his free hand.

A glowing circle appeared on the pavement not three steps away.

Slate's stomach dropped. This was it.

Darkness curled at the corner of his eye, and Slate's head snapped to the side. Next to him and the fae, unnatural shadows swirled and contorted, taking shape until Roger materialized out of the darkness and reached a hand out, wrapping it around the High Fae's throat.

A *clawed* hand.

"Leave my friends alone," Roger said, a deadly monotone to his voice.

The other fae yanked Slate backward, but someone else materialized out of the shadows. Maddie—the waitress from the bar—threw out her hands and a gust of violent wind ripped Slate free. He tripped and stumbled, tumbling to the ground, turning his face at the last minute to avoid his nose greeting the pavement a bit too hard.

Hands grabbed him, and he tensed, but a whisper of words told him who it was. Dani.

"Get up, Slate," she hissed frantically, pushing and pulling him. Sellie herded them back behind her, shrieking and hissing. Dani unwrapped the wire from his knees and hesitated for a moment with the wire on his wrists, eyes widening at the sight of scorched and bleeding flesh underneath.

He glanced at her fingertips and saw a rash of red where she'd handled the metal, far less severe than his own welts.

"You okay?" he asked breathlessly, gasping between his teeth as she peeled the wire away from his skin.

"I've been better." Her face was smeared with blood from her nose. "You?"

"Alive." The wires burst free, and she chucked them away. He pushed himself to his feet, eyes snapping around the scene.

The three High Fae were in a stand-off against Roger and Maddie. No one moved. Slate saw sharp eyes dart in his direction, as though the High Fae were trying to decide if it was worth it to go through a vampire, a witch, and a pissed-off griffin to get to him.

"You are forbidden to intervene, *vampire*," the leader spat, fury simmering in eyes that had darkened to the color of storm clouds. "This is not your concern. Nor yours, *witch*." The fae's face was full of disdain as they spoke towards to Maddie.

"I protect my own, Gelayeth. Stay away from my friends," Roger replied. Something was different about his face—longer, mouth slightly agape, teeth too large to fit properly. His eyes glowed. Were they red? Tinged with red, definitely.

The leader—Gelayeth?—flipped his gaze back and forth between Roger and Maddie, then to Slate, who stood his ground steadily, one arm out to keep Dani behind his shoulder.

"This isn't over, Zlaet," Gelayeth said briskly. "The *Titania* will see you in his court before Midsummer."

He used one pointed boot to make a circle on the ground, which began to glow with a soft golden light. He didn't take his eyes off Slate as he and his comrades stepped through, and vanished.

The silence left behind was deafening. Dani covered her mouth with her hand and pressed her forehead into his shoulder.

"Holy *shit*," she whispered.

He laid a palm on the top of her head. Holy shit was an understatement. He was still trying to regulate his heart rate, his adrenal gland still on overdrive. He swiped at the blood on his face with his free hand.

"That was close," he said quietly.

"Far too close," Roger said. The vampire's face had returned to normal, and he gave Slate another bodily assessment. Wariness. That's what Slate saw in those eyes. "Daniella, where did you leave your bike?"

She pulled her face out of Slate's shoulder. "Next street over," she said, gesturing with a shaking finger.

He nodded once and strolled towards the alley.

"Slate, *cher*," Maddie gestured. "Let me see your hands."

He stepped towards the witch and held out his hands. With the adrenaline starting to fade, he was aware of the pain in his palms. They were throbbing to the beat of his heart, and when he tried to move them, he found his efforts to be tight and painful.

Maddie whistled softly. "You have *quite* an allergy to iron, *mon garçon*."

"What, now?" he hissed as she prodded at his injuries.

"Iron. Pure iron is extremely dangerous to fae. It suffocates and absorbs magic. The more magic a fae has, the deadlier the iron." Her fingertips glowed a soft, peony pink, and there was a cooling sting over his hands. Slate flinched on reflex, but Maddie had a firm grip on his forearm.

"I don't have magic," he growled.

"Well, *cher*, you have something. This is an intense reaction for lorekissed, but not unheard of either." She traced his ugly wounds with those pink fingers. "Goddess knows how you lived your whole life with this reaction. Most full-fae avoid the inner-city limits."

"It's never happened before." He hissed through his teeth. "Wait. Actually, that's not true. I've—I've gotten rashes from jewelry and certain weapons." If he thought about it—which was a bit hard to do with the stinging in his hands—he realized he'd always been sensitive to certain metals, and he'd noticed it was getting worse as he got older.

"Very common." She nodded. "There. I've staunched a little of the bleeding, but I can't heal it. My magic isn't fine-tuned enough to handle that level of detail."

"Thank you," he said, flexing his hands. It would be tolerable until he got home. He had a fully stocked first aid kit in the studio office, courtesy of Jian.

"No worries, *cher*. Been awhile since I've been in some combat," Maddie said with a smile, brushing back a curl from her brow that had leaped free of her tight braid. "It was almost fun, now that it's over."

"No, thank you. Not my type of fun," Dani said as Roger returned, pushing her bike. Slate gaped at the fact that there was no damage on the little Vespa whatsoever. Dani continued, smiling at the vampire. "I'll leave the fancy fighting and magic to all of you... and you!" She turned to Slate. "Were you even scared?"

"'Course I was scared," he replied, brow furrowed in confusion.

"You were so confident and steady."

"I've been in a lot of fights, love."

"It will not be your last either, I'm certain," Roger said. "Daniella, I wish to escort you two home."

Slate's eyes darted back and forth between Roger and Dani. Slate prided himself on being able to read people and thought he was pretty observant. He was certain it was protectiveness he saw in the vampire's eyes, but he didn't miss how those same eyes soften a little when he looked at Dani.

Interesting.

"I need to get home myself, my little ones will be awake soon and wondering where I am. It's never a good idea to be missing when Leo wants to find me," she added with a maternal grimace.

"Maddie, how're you getting home?" Slate asked.

"Oh, Tony will find me, do not fret." The witch patted him gently on the cheek before placing a brief kiss there. "You fought well, *cher*. Stay safe." She turned to Dani and pulled the smaller woman into a brief embrace, before kissing her on each cheek. "You as well, Daniella. Please, for the love of the Goddess, text me when you get home."

"Thanks, Maddie. Be safe," Dani answered, giving the woman a weary smile.

Maddie moved over to Roger, gave him a kiss on his cheek and patted the vampire on the chest before she started walking down the alley.

"Let's go. I'm tired now, and I have a pounding headache," Dani sighed, slinging a leg over her bike.

CHAPTER ⟨九⟩ NINE

THE TEN-DATE RULE

... It is believed by some that the first influx of Mysticism into Europe predates the Dark Ages, but recent evidence points more conclusively to a minority cult of Mysticfolk who followed in Marco Polo's wake upon his return from the Far East. They grew attached to the City of Faerloch, and the now-named Eastern District became...

— Gherald Schmidt, Faerloch Historical Archives

The sun was starting to trace red and pink fingers across the sky, the fiery ball still obscured by the buildings all around them, when Dani crossed the pedestrian bridge into the Eastern District. Unlike the Pub District, people had already started to rise and get their day started. The sound of the engine was a menace to the early peace.

"There's a side access door for deliveries," Slate said, "in the alley."

She eased the bike into the alley and cut the engine. Her body hurt, tightening up from the fight. Slate was in no better shape; his face pinched as he swung his leg over and walked over to the side door.

Her mind briefly touched on Sellie and found her griffin was once more in the garden, delighted to play with the faeries. She'd found a nice little nook to settle in, somewhere that wouldn't crush any of the plants. She hoped Slate's father wasn't awake and working in the garden this early.

"Where's Roger?" Slate asked, his eyes catching in the awakening daylight.

"He finds his own way around," she offered, watching as Slate gingerly pressed the number code next to the door to release the lock. "Older vampires can do this cool thing—shadow travel. They just... materialize out of shadows and nothing."

"I saw that earlier," Slate said. The door released and he tugged it open with a grimace.

They entered a little back storage room. To the left was a set of stairs leading up, and to the right was a long hallway lined with shelves and stacked neatly with boxes. There was another door straight ahead.

"Don't vampires turn into ash from sunlight or something?" He raised a brow.

She laughed lightly. "No," she said, following him through another door and into the dark hallway. "Shoot, shoes off?"

"It's fine." He waved a hand.

"I mean, the sun isn't *good* for them," she continued. "But Roger's super tough. I know he doesn't *look* old, but he is. Disgustingly old, I'm pretty sure. Like, *ancient*. He can handle a good amount of sunlight. But he's nocturnal and prefers to be out at night. He turns into a grouch around mid-afternoon."

The room smelled like feet, a little tinge of sweat, and fresh bamboo. Her headache was intense, throbbing right in the front of her head. She pinched the bridge of her nose as she followed Slate through the waiting area.

Shadows materialized in the corner of the room. Roger stepped out of the deep, unnatural darkness, as unflappable as always.

"An interesting neighborhood you have here," he said softly by way of greeting. "I've not had business over in this part of the city in a very long time. Did you know there is a ward all around this district?"

"A what?" Slate dumped himself into a chair. Dani followed suit, grateful to be off her feet.

"A ward. A magical barrier."

"Cool," Slate sighed. Dani could hear the exhaustion creeping into his voice. Her heart panged for him—what a night they'd had.

"What kind of ward?" Dani mustered the energy to ask, stretching her neck from side to side.

"It's not Lore-based, but I'm not surprised. It's a Mystic ward, likely kept in place by *miko* or perhaps *manyeo*—"

"Wait." Slate held up a hand. "Wait. Wait, wait, *wait*. Hold up. *Mystic*?"

"Indeed. Eastern Mystics. Magic native to your ethnicity. You did not believe Europe had the monopoly on magic, did you, *faeling*?" Roger tucked his hands into the pockets of his slacks and gave Slate a long look. "Every major corner of the world has magic. Though, perhaps a more thorough education of magic will have to wait. The Mystic ward here keeps you safe; or at least, it keeps you concealed. Different magicks work differently against others, and this ward seems to suppress magical aura. Or *chi*, or whatever it is they call it here."

He said it with such confidence that it was hard to argue. Dani gave him a tired but bright smile, always amazed by Roger's vast knowledge, and Roger's lips curved up ever so slightly as he glanced at her.

"So we're safe here, indefinitely?" Slate asked.

"Well, so long as they don't come strolling along and happen to notice you. They can't track you here, so they would have to rely on fortune in finding you. It is no small district." The vampire shrugged. He slid his hands into his pockets, and after a dismissive look at Slate, he turned his attention to her. "I must take my leave now. Daniella, would you like an escort home?"

"No thanks, Roge. I have Sellie. Go home before the sun comes up."

Roger hesitated, studying her with an inscrutable face. Dani smiled encouragingly, banishing her own exhaustion for a moment. Roger shot another look at Slate and nodded reluctantly.

"A final suggestion for you, Slate Melisande." Shadows began to gather around the vampire. "Do not leave this district unaccompanied. It seems the High Fae are quite serious about their intent to apprehend you. They haven't yet begun to show their true power."

Slate shook his head. "I can't just stay here. I have a life, you know."

"Do what you will, but the fae will find you when you leave. The river marks the edge of the ward on the city side." Roger gave a small shrug. "Farewell." He melted into the shadows with one last look at Dani.

For a moment, they sat in silence, perhaps both of them a little shell-shocked.

"Do you have a first aid kit or something?" she finally asked, giving him an assessing look. One side of his face was a medley of dark, swollen colors, the split in his cheek creating a macabre ribbon of dried blood.

And his hands, Goddess, his poor *hands*. They were chewed up; burned and scorched, angry criss-cross patterns where his hands had saved his neck. The wounds were even worse around his wrists where he'd been bound. She'd never seen what iron did to fae skin before, and if he was only a tiny bit fae with this intense of a reaction...

"Yeah." He nodded. "Yeah, I'll get it—"

"You stay," she said, getting to her feet gingerly. She peeled off her leather jacket and draped it across the back of her chair. "I'll get it. Where is it?"

"In the office," he sighed. "Big red box on the shelf next to the door."

She found it easily and carried it back to the table. It opened like a toolbox, unfolding into many layered compartments that were carefully labeled. If she had the mental capacity to think clearly past her headache, she'd be impressed with the meticulous layout.

He huffed out a tired breath. "I can do it myself, love," Slate said as she dragged a chair over and sat, facing him knee-to-knee. "Not my first fight, not my first injury."

"Just because you can doesn't mean you have to," she quipped. "Vet tech here, not completely oblivious to first aid." She could tell how tired he was by the fact that he didn't argue with her, just huffed another sigh through his nose. She scooted closer, their knees interlocking, and held out her hands. "Alright, let me see them."

Slate held out his hands reluctantly, the fingers slightly curled as if it hurt to extend the digits fully.

"Oh shit..." she whispered in a long breath, wincing for him.

Having worked as a veterinarian's assistant for the majority of her adult life, she wasn't squeamish when it came to injuries. She asked for materials and he directed her—a towel, a large bowl—and she filled the bottom of the bowl with lukewarm water. Using the towels she'd found, she gently started to clean his hands and wrists, working the grit and dirt out of them.

"Big baby," she said, teasing him softly when he flinched and hissed out a breath.

"Listen, I need these hands. Important commodities."

She huffed out a laugh and lifted a brow. "I'm sure you do."

His grin was cheeky and a little wicked.

A quiet serenity fell between them as she continued working on his hands. The early morning light was beginning to filter in through the windows, the sound of birds starting to sing outside. The only other sounds were the gentle splash of the water and their breathing. It was a kind of peace that made Dani's muscles relax, finally, after the intense moments of the fight. Her headache, blessedly, started to fade.

"I have a personal question for you," he whispered into the silence between them.

"Hmm?" She didn't look up from her ministrations.

"Are you sleeping with Roger?"

She paused, the absurdity of the question filtering slowly through her brain. "Roger's my best friend," she answered.

"Doesn't mean you aren't sleeping with him."

She stopped and stared at him. No hint of a smile in his eyes, no sharpness. He was seriously asking her.

It wasn't any of his business, and part of her yawned open to tell him as much, but a larger part of her understood he wasn't asking to be a prying asshole.

"No," she replied, feeling her throat catch. "No, I'm not. I haven't. I—I mean, that's not the kind of relationship we have." Something about the intensity of that look made her want to answer him honestly, some deep part of her recognizing that the question wasn't entirely about Roger.

The words popped out before she could even think about it. "I'm not sleeping with anyone right now, actually. And Roger's not my type, anyway."

"What's your type?" A steady look with eyes that saw right *into* her. She blinked, looking away, and her insides pitched with a little roll of heat.

You, apparently.

Goddess help her. She needed to get a grip on her hormones.

Smothering the butterflies in her belly, she gave him a sly little grin. "Tall Asian lorekissed boys who are more trouble than they're worth."

He matched her grin. "Funny. I, too, like tall Asian lorekissed boys. Samesies."

She laughed, shaking her head slightly at his charm and cheek. She finished cleaning his hands and turned to investigate the first aid kit. She pulled out a couple of vials, checking the neatly handwritten labels. Finally, she settled on some purple liquid labeled antibacterial and grabbed a cotton pad. She shook a few droplets out and started gently dabbing the liquid over his cuts. Slate tensed, but didn't move. Offering him a little smile, she reached for another vial, this one labeled for cuts.

Slate exhaled slowly as she dabbed on the liquid to his wounds, face pinching, but the liquid was like magic. The angriness of the wounds started to fade almost instantly. Dani frowned a little but kept working as she wrapped gauze around everything, sealing it in.

"Better?" she asked.

"Better."

Was it the medicine that had healed him so fast? No way, it must be his lorekissed blood. To heal that fast though...

She glanced at his face, but all she saw was exhausted relief. She scooted closer to him, close enough that his scent filled her nostrils: musky, fresh, and with a hint of... frost? Like the first snow in winter. That familiar quiet settled over them again, comfortable, trusting. He held stone-still as she cleaned the cut on his cheek, and she focused all her attention on her task so she wouldn't be distracted by his eyes watching her.

It was likely a result of the adrenaline that still lingered in her system, but she was aware of the tiniest things. The soft scrape of her nails on the vial labeled 'for bruises' as she picked it up, the minuscule pop as she uncorked it. The slosh of the liquid as she dampened the cotton pad and dabbed the medicine on his cheek. The heat of his thighs on either side of her own. The scent of the medicine, the scent of him...

Even though the herbal remedies should've been the stronger scent, she found herself focusing on Slate's. It was almost meditative; the scent of him, the sound of their even breathing, nearly in sync. She was so close to him now that she could feel his lungs expand on every inhale, his chest brushing against her forearms.

She gently taped two butterfly stitches to his cheek, the crinkling paper alarmingly loud in the soft quiet. That sense of calm seemed to have enveloped them both, and she was reluctant to speak, to shatter the quiet that had wrapped them like a blanket, enclosing them from the rest of the world.

She turned his face back and forth, inspecting him. He let her, but his eyes didn't leave her face. She blinked, realizing she was done patching him up.

She realized, too, that she had abandoned her own chair. She was straddling his lap, his hands now resting on her thighs.

"Done," she whispered into the quiet, and she wasn't sure why she'd whispered.

"Thanks..." he replied, his voice equally quiet.

She sat back a little, resting her palms on his shoulders. It took a powerful amount of self-control to not stroke him, to explore the musculature under his shirt, the heat of him burning her.

Their eyes met.

He dropped his gaze to her mouth for a hot second. She did the same. Her stomach seized.

"I should go home," she murmured breathlessly. No part of her wanted to leave his lap. The inches between them closed.

"Not yet..."

His mouth was so close to hers, she could feel his breath. Her skin tingled as his hand crawled up her spine, not hesitating when he ran out of shirt and touched the bare skin of her shoulder blades, all the way up to the back of her neck...

The barest brush of his mouth against hers, softer than the edge of a butterfly's wing. Her throat closed up, insides pitching with sudden, fierce want.

And they were suddenly kissing. Kissing *hard*. As though they'd been riding a wave of sexual tension for months, years, instead of mere minutes. He looped one hand around her nape, trapping her to him. Dani pressed closer, one hand threading through his hair, dislodging the hair tie, and her other hand stroked his shoulder, his chest, feeling the strength and the muscles under his shirt. What she wouldn't give *right now* to have that be bare skin, to let her mouth follow her hands and see if he tasted as good as he felt.

A lot. *Goddess above*, she would probably sell her soul for it right in this moment.

He tugged her lower lip with his teeth. She sucked in a quick breath, and his tongue was in her mouth. He devoured her like a starving man and, holy hell, she wanted to be devoured. Wanted him to take her right down to the floor and eat her alive. She wanted—*needed*—to be skin to skin with this man in a way that was so achingly intense, it was almost frightening.

He slipped a hand under her shirt, the bandages a strange, soft texture against her skin. She ached for his hands, wet at the idea of the rough calluses stroking her, molding her body.

She tore her mouth from his, head tipping back, breathing ragged. He kissed down her neck, his tongue and teeth a fury against her skin.

"Oh my *god*..." she whispered. She undulated her hips against him, his erection a statement between them that was impossible to ignore.

He made it to her left shoulder, scratching his teeth against the sensitive muscle that lived between neck and shoulder, before she tugged his hair and pulled his head back up. She kissed him furiously, moaning into his mouth as she rocked her hips against him. It was on the tip of her tongue to demand he take off his clothes and bend her over the damned table.

They came up for air, and their eyes collided—green to blue—and they both paused, breathing hard.

The space between them swirled heavy and thick, yet tense, as if one miscalculation would send them both back in a furious spiral and they'd end up naked.

"That..." she whispered, her voice trailing off.

Too soon. They were kissing again. Hands grasping the other, touching, stroking, pulling at skin and hair and clothes, each pulling the other closer, unable to get close enough. Perhaps it was the adrenaline from earlier, the near-death experience fueling them both. There was no learning curve between them. He moved, she moved, as if she knew all his dance moves already, as if they'd done this a thousand times if they'd done it once. She might burn alive from sheer *want*—

They separated again, gasping.

"I think..." Slate said, voice thick and gravelly and ragged. "I think we should take things—"

"Slow, yeah," she murmured.

He bounced his gaze back and forth between her eyes, and she could see plain as day that he felt as intense as she did. He was as undone from the sheer intensity of them, the instant want, the zero to sixty in less than a heartbeat.

One stray hand and they'd both burn up.

It was like an out-of-body experience, the sudden loss of control. She knew that he knew—he could've asked anything from her in that moment, and she'd have given it to him, no questions asked. She *wanted* to. She would have had him right there, right then.

And it would be the best sex of their lives.

While Dani wasn't against sex, she generally didn't have sex on the first date; yet she *wanted* to, and that freaked her out a bit. Freaked her out because usually, her relationships didn't last long after sex.

And for some reason, she wasn't quite ready to be done with this man just yet.

"Slow," he agreed, his breathing stuttering a bit. "Uh, how about—how about a ten-date rule?"

"Yes," she nodded, a fast jerk of her chin, overwhelmed by this feeling. She swallowed a hard breath, and slowly, reluctantly, she released his tee-shirt and his hair. "Th—that's a good idea. Ten dates. Let's shoot for that."

Wait.

Wait.

Her mind instantly began to backpedal. Ten dates? The idea was almost as alarming as wanting to rip off his clothes here and there. Dani was a *casual* dater; the longest she'd dated a guy was a little over two months. Ten dates sounded like a huge commitment.

Just sleep with him and get over it, part of her mind whispered.

That was appealing, but men *changed* after sex. They became less fun and casual. They always wanted more, which didn't work for her. So while the idea of ten dates seemed like a lot, she also wasn't ready for all of *this* to be over yet. He was far too interesting, far too fun, let alone sexy as sin.

A cautious, nervous part of her mind shivered. Give a guy who made her this crazy the power of ten whole dates with her?

Walk away, get out of all of this mess... that same part of her mind whispered to her. *Easy peasy, no mess, no commitment. It would be easiest.*

Her gaze collided with his, and her thoughts scattered. She could give this ten-date rule thing a chance, right? She liked him, he was charming and funny, and without a doubt, their sexual chemistry was off the charts. If it didn't work, then whatever. She could walk away at any point during the ten dates.

A door shut somewhere in the studio. They both jumped. Dani flipped her head around as an older gentleman appeared around the corner.

Dark eyes flipped from Slate to Dani, then back to Slate. "I thought I heard you come in, my boy," he said, a ghost of a smirk dancing across his weathered face.

It was difficult to pull away from Slate, from the barest taste she'd gotten. But the voice behind her was an effective water bucket, so to speak, and Dani stood immediately, her legs sliding to the ground in a smooth gesture. She stepped back from Slate, the back of her legs pushing the chair back with her, nearly toppling it. She whipped out a hand to balance it.

Her lips burned with warmth, her breath a little uneven, and her heart was still racing in her chest. She could feel the lingering sensation of his hand against her back, in her hair, stroking her skin, tugging at her as though he couldn't get close enough.

Yes, ten dates was probably a good idea. This was intense and heady.

"Sorry, *to-san*, did I wake you?" Slate asked, and Dani was impressed by the level of calm he pulled over himself. She wished he could share some of that with her, get her damned heart under control.

"Not at all." The older man waved a dismissive hand. "I do not sleep much these days anyway." Even in the weak light of dawn, it was evident this man was Slate's father. Nearly identical besides the obvious age difference, but Slate's face was a little sharper and his eyes were wider, larger. "Who is your new friend?"

"This is Dani," Slate continued. Their eyes met and she saw his breathing stutter slightly. "Dani, this is my father, Ebisu. You can call him Ebisu or *jii-san*. Or old man, because he's old and likes the reminder."

"Cheeky thing," Ebisu chuckled.

"Nice to meet you, uh... Mr. Melisande," Dani said, interjecting some cheerfulness into her tone. She was painfully aware of her clothes, the state she and Slate were in, both from the fight and their hot makeout session. She was a bedraggled mess, which the older man picked up on with a small flick of his dark eyes. His gaze shifted immediately to Slate, looking him over with a narrowed expression as well.

"*Hajimemashite*," Ebisu answered with a small dip of his head.

"I uh... I'm going to go home now," she said, feeling awkward. She smiled, though, pulling up a good front. "Call me later, Slate?" She turned back to Slate. She was unprepared for the way her stomach sizzled merely looking at him. *It's just your heightened senses, Dani,* she berated herself.

"I'll walk you out—" He started to stand, and she saw his face flinch ever-so-slightly.

"I'll be okay." She laid a gentle hand on his shoulder.

They shared a look. An understanding went between them, and he nodded once.

"I will walk you out, Dani-*san*," Ebisu said, his tone cheerful. He held a hand out in the direction of the door, and after a moment's hesitation, she stepped away from Slate.

"Thank you," Dani told Ebisu, glancing over her shoulder at Slate one last time.

"Your evening must've been quite exciting," Ebisu said as they approached the door.

"What?" Her brain jumped immediately to hands tugging at her body, teeth against her neck, heavy breathing...

"Did the bar prove to be a bit more entertaining than you planned?" His dark gaze tracked over her clothing, lingering on the scrape on her cheek.

"Oh," she breathed. "Oh, yes. Well, yes. Some ruffians. Slate held his own."

"He does that well enough." Ebisu chuckled. "I do not particularly enjoy his thirst for fighting, but if he must fight, he must win."

"Sound advice." She laughed nervously, and she pushed open the door to step out of the studio.

A hand, weathered but powerful, stopped her with the barest touch on her arm. Dani glanced back, and Ebisu smiled at her gently.

"Your griffin is quite well behaved in my garden," he said softly, for her ears only. "She is welcome any time. *Sayonara, faeling*."

And Ebisu patted her on the arm once, turned, and closed the door.

Dani stared through the window of the door at the older man's retreating back, her mind reeling.

What.

Sellie sent impatient pictures of her nest at home, rousing Dani out of her stunned stance. Knowing she looked ridiculous, standing on the sidewalk and staring at the door, she turned on her heel, rounded the corner of the alley, and slipped onto her little Vespa.

She was halfway home when she realized what Ebisu had called her.

Faeling.

CHAPTER TEN

MAGIC, MYSTERIES, AND COFFEE

... human folklore has frequently taken aspects of truth from the Lore, leading to distorted...

– Gherald Schmidt, Faerloch Historical Archives

"Could you be any more intimidating?"

"What? I thought I was very pleasant."

Slate shook his head, rolling his eyes. Every step up the stairs was an an exercise in self-control to not growl and hiss. He felt like he'd been run over by a truck.

His heart was still attempting to come back into an even rhythm. That *kiss*. Hands down the most intense first kiss he'd ever had. Intense and heady and *god*, the feel of her under his hands—

Was it magic? Or something else? Was their chemistry simply that explosive?

He had no idea where the ten-date rule thing had come from. It had just popped out of his mouth. He needed *more* than just a quick fuck on the floor, especially with Dani. There was something different about her.

Slate knew if they'd had sex right there on the studio floor, it would have been explosive, like a match in a vat of gasoline, catching immediately and burning hot.

But fires like that burned to nothing *fast*.

No, one date and a fuck wouldn't have been enough, and he wasn't stupid enough to ask for a commitment, not when they barely knew each other.

Even though a small part of him had wanted to, as irrational as it sounded.

Ten dates seemed like a decent compromise.

He had a feeling ten might not be enough to sate him, because whatever had burned between them had somehow felt like more than good chemistry, more than just sex.

Besides, he *enjoyed* the process of dating, of getting to know someone, the flirting, the teasing, the slow burn.

Slate dumped his keys and wallet on the table by the door. He needed a bath like he needed oxygen.

"Dani-*san* said there was a fight." His father gave him a little glance before he moved into the kitchen.

Slate's already elevated heart rate jumped into his skull. "Yep. Just a little altercation that got outta hand. You know how it gets in those seedy places in the city." He didn't want to *lie* to his father, but he didn't want to give him the full truth either. That was the trouble with Ebisu though; he always knew when Slate wasn't being completely truthful. "You know how it goes—these types of guys that wanna take you on, *ne*? Overheard me telling some of Dani's friends what I do for a living. Wanted to test out my martial arts against their booze-addled brawling."

That sounded good. It wasn't exactly true but Slate and the twins had been in enough of those kinds of fights that it was believable, at least.

Ebisu huffed out a derisive laugh and turned on the kettle. "Did you win?"

"Of course."

"Dani-*san* had a scrape on her cheek."

"Oh... yeah, she tried to break it up. Got pushed."

The older man hummed. "I do not like it, all these fights." He sighed deeply and turned off the kettle. "Perhaps you should stay close to home for a few days, *ne*? The city is a dangerous place."

Slate thought about the ward that guarded this district—a *Mystic* ward. A ward that suppressed magical aura, or *chi*, according to Roger.

Slate understood what *chi* was. It was life force or the flow of energy. Some people had a lot of *chi*, some people didn't. Jian speculated that Slate had a lot of *chi*, that his life force and energy flow were strong and powerful, which contributed to why he was a talented martial artist and why he was healthy and strong.

Slate didn't imagine *chi* and magical aura were one and the same. Just... it didn't sound right. He had a powerful *chi*, but no magic. They had to be mutually exclusive. Right?

Either way, if the fae couldn't sense him when he was within his own district, maybe his father was right. Staying close to home for a few days sounded like a good idea.

After a long bath—spiced with herbs or whatever shit he had lying around from Jian to help with sore, tight muscles—Slate laid in his bed, staring at the ceiling.

"You did not believe Europe had the monopoly on magic, did you, faeling?"

Roger said there was more than Lore magic in the world. What an interesting concept. Eastern Magic. *Chi* in all living things. *Yokai. Kitsune. Oni.* Legends of great samurai, Jade Warriors... folktales he'd grown up with.

Was there truth to all that as well?

Slate fell asleep, his dreams filled with demons and *shikigami,* shapeshifting fox gods and *miko*—as well as a certain redhead woman with freckles like faerie kisses.

"What do you mean, he just said *hello*?" Dani asked irritably as she opened the garage door to allow the griffin inside.

Sellie strode past her with a regal tilt of her head, regarding Dani with a haughty expression. The imagery and meanings behind them translated to Dani as *It would've been rude to not greet him in return.*

"Yes, but that's not what I meant. He—" Dani was halfway in the garage with her bike when another voice, one not inside her head, interrupted her.

"Daniella! Are you just getting home?" The voice wobbled a little in age. Dani closed her eyes and counted to five for the patience to deal with her neighbor when she desperately wanted to sleep.

"Mrs. Mulhern, good morning!" Dani said in a cheerful tone, flipping down the kickstand on her bike. She walked back out of the garage, her hands in the back pockets of her jeans. "How are you? Out for an early walk?"

"The weatherman said it's supposed to be a beautiful spring day," the older woman said, her clothing a garish explosion of various colors. Though as far as Dani was concerned, when anyone made it to the ripe age of 79, they could dress however they wanted. "Were you out for a drive or another late night?" Mrs. Mulhern's eyes strayed to the scratch on her cheek, the chewed-up sleeve of her jacket, the tangled mess of her braid.

"Oh, uh, just... out late, I guess." Dani pasted on a smile.

In truth, she was endlessly grateful to Mrs. Mulhern and her now-late husband. The older couple had taken Dani under their wing after her parents died in a tragic car accident when she was 16 years old. Dani hadn't known the first thing about living on her own, and frankly, she hadn't been in the frame of mind to pull herself together. That had been a rough year for her. There was the death of her parents, followed by her kidnapping, which plunged her into the overwhelming world of magic. Plus school and therapy and court appearances...

The Mulherns had kept her fed, made sure she attended school, helped her balance her life out, and forced her to get out of the house.

She was absolutely one-hundred percent convinced that without their watchful eyes, she'd be in a far worse state.

Yet since Mr. Mulhern had passed away last summer, Dani was finding the roles had reversed. She reached out a kind hand towards Mrs. Mulhern and took her out into the world and made sure she got to the grocery store, the pharmacy, and whatever else she needed.

She was happy to do it, but right at that moment, all she wanted was a hot shower and her bed.

"I worry after you, Daniella." Mrs. Mulhern patted her affectionately on her cheek. "When are you going to find yourself a nice man to settle down with? Or woman, lord knows how you modern folk like to diversify."

Dani had to laugh. "Well, perhaps the one I saw last night will pan out this time."

She spotted an excited twinkle in the older woman's eye. "You coy thing, you, Daniella. Take care of yourself now."

"Let's go to the Farmer's Market next weekend, Mrs. Mulhern, does that sound alright?"

"You are a gem, dear. Yes, that would be alright." She turned and moseyed down the sidewalk. "Get some rest!" the woman called over her shoulder.

"Thank you, see you later!" Dani called back, swiveling around to put her bike back. Sellie was already asleep in her nest, which meant she wasn't getting the answer as to how the hell Slate's father could have seen Sellie... and why he had acted so calmly about it.

The mysteries surrounding the Melisande household kept getting deeper and deeper.

Dani made her way inside. A myriad of animal minds assaulted her, and despite the fact she was exhausted, she went about her normal routine. She lived in the suburbs to the south of the city limits, in what might be considered a 'gated community' of sorts—a series of rather nice, middle-class houses on a cul-de-sac. Her house was nestled towards the end, on the circle itself, with a patch of trees in the backyard that separated her property from the backyards of other houses. Other streets, other neighborhoods.

She fed her fish first, then headed out to the yard to lay out leftovers and scraps for the various wild animals in the backyard, as well as fresh birdseed. She had brief, reassuring conversations with all the animals, checking in on everyone—from the raccoon family that lived in the trees at the edges of her yard, to the birds with their fresh nests, to the deer with their new spring fawns.

At her heels, her red fox followed her happily. Dash was one of the many wild animals she'd rescued over the years, but he was one of the few whom she didn't re-home back into the wild. He'd been the runt of his litter, sickly and small, and after she'd rehabilitated him, he was too domesticated to return and survive, let alone thrive.

So he stayed.

Her house was small but modest—a standard two-bedroom two-story with an attached garage. It had taken her a while to move into the master bedroom after her parents had died, but some minor renovations and a fresh coat of paint had gone a long way towards making the bedroom feel more like hers and less like she was living with the ghosts of her parents.

It was small, but clean and earthy, and it was her landing place. The whole world could fall apart around her, but she had her little house with its cute backyard and her animals, and that's all she needed.

And after the chaotic night she'd just had, she was ready to separate herself from the world a little.

Her dreams were an unsteady mix of brilliant eyes, hot kisses, portals, and nightmares.

Slate found himself messaging with Dani constantly on Sunday. She was on his mind every spare moment of the day, and by the time Monday morning rolled around, he worked up the nerve to ask her out again. His heart pounded as if he'd just run a marathon at the idea of seeing her again.

He did not forget their ten-date stipulation.

They agreed to grab a drink at the little tea shop where they'd run into each other two weeks ago. Somewhere neutral, but also within the supposed ward that protected the Eastern District.

She was already there when he arrived, leaning her shoulder against the wall, scrolling idly through her phone. Her hair was down but pulled back away from her face in a loose tie, cut-off capris had replaced her jeans, and a light, loose oversized sweater replaced her leather jacket.

She was radiant.

"No bike today?" he greeted her.

She tucked her phone into her pocket and twisted the bulk of her hair over her shoulder. "Nope. Left it in the car park on the other side of the bridge today."

"And your..." he lowered his voice, "other friend?"

"Well..." She paused. "She's in your garden again."

Slate felt a prickle of ice; his father was spending the day getting the tomato plants in their beds.

"Oh *fuck me*," he breathed, and he whirled around, fully intending to go right back to the studio to fetch his father.

"Wait! Slate, it's fine, I promise." She snagged the back of his shirt. "Your father doesn't seem to mind, he says she's well-behaved."

Slate swiveled around to peg her with widened eyes and brows high, jaw slack. "My *dad* knows about your griffin?" His voice pitched a little, and Dani let out a little laugh, waving her hand at him.

"He must have seen through her glamour, or Sellie *let* him see, and she's an excellent judge of character. It's not a big deal, he seems to have accepted it quite well. I promise your father is safe with her. She'll probably just doze in the sun for a while." She appealed to him with a look. "You can go check on him, but Sellie says he's working on tomato plants and is quite content to let her sunbathe."

He sucked in a breath and held it, warring hard with the rational, logical part of him that trusted Dani, trusted what she said was true, and wanted to trust that griffin of hers who had protected his ass not once, but twice now.

"It's alright," Dani said again, softly, offering him a smile. "You've only experienced Sellie at her most fierce. She's quite lovely. Like an actual giant house cat, but don't tell her I said that."

Slate weighed his options for another minute—to go or not to go—before ultimately, he decided it was fine. His father was fine. He offered a short nod, and they stepped into the tea shop.

"Protective of your father," she commented lightly with a little grin. They sat at a table in the corner, near a window, where Slate had a full visual of the door and outside. It was an old habit.

"He's... tough in spirit, but his body grows frailer every day," Slate replied. "He had some kinda... episode a couple of years ago. Collapsed in the studio one day. Very random. And he was bed-ridden for a week. He hasn't been the same since."

"There's nothing the doctors can do?"

He shook his head. "Nope. He gets tonics and remedies from Jian's father Joon-*san*, but no, nothing." Slate had begged his father for months to go see a more Western-inclined doctor, but Ebisu had assured him every time that there was nothing that modern medicine could do for him. He was content with Joon-*san*'s herbal remedies, and to their credit, they seemed to work.

It would be the worst day in his life, the day he had to bury his father. The idea made him ill. Desperate to change the subject lest he vomit all over the table, he asked, "What about your parents?"

She paused mid-sip. All the hair on the back of his neck stood up. The way she didn't answer, how her eyes assessed him...

Something tragic had happened.

"Oh *shit*, love, I'm sorry. This is turning into a terribly depressing date."

She offered him a little smile with a shrug. "It's alright. My parents were wonderful people, and it was a long time ago. My papa was charming and sociable and my mama had a wild thirst for adventure and freedom. The two happiest married people you've ever seen in your life, always together. And that's how it should be."

She sounded calm and peaceful, like she'd made that bed of grief a long time ago and didn't let it bother her anymore.

He nodded. "Sounds like Jian and Kari's parents..."

Finally, the conversation began to turn to lighter topics. He regaled her with some wild stories about himself and the twins, and they chatted about favorite movies and books. She told him about when she was chased through the streets of Faerloch by a hellhound, cradling a baby griffin to her chest. She gushed about all her animal friends and he about martial arts. Slate noticed a confusion mixed with a strange light of awe on her face.

"I'm boring you with my fight-talk," he said, grimacing.

She leaned her chin in one hand. "No, no. I just know *nothing* about it, and you're so *passionate*. Tell me more." Her eyes—impossible, the color of them, emerald and gold—captivated his attention.

Back and forth, the conversation never stopped. It was easy and effortless, like they'd talked together a thousand times if they had once. Slate found himself absolutely hypnotized by her: the crinkle of her face, the sound of her laughter, the way she talked with her hands, how those same hands always found something to do like hold onto the cup or play with the lid or twist her hair.

What got him though, was how *bright* she was. Like a sunlit day. Radiant and bright and kind. The sort of woman who would do everything within her power to help her friends.

She excused herself to go to the restroom, and he took a second to check his phone. Nothing from his father—Slate had yet to decide if that was a good thing or a bad thing—but he had a couple of rather demanding messages from Kari.

He called her.

"What do you want, *baa-chan*?" he greeted without preamble. "I'm *out*."

"You should bring your date to the shrine today."

"And *why* would I do that?"

"Because I'm here, and I want to meet her."

"No," he replied emphatically. "Why are you at the shrine anyway?"

His eyes followed Dani as she came back to the table. She cocked her head to the side, tipping her chin slightly at his phone, a little frown on her face. He shook his head, the universal sign of *Don't worry, it's not an emergency.*

"Doing my civic duty."

"Bullshit."

"*Fine*. I'm helping out. All the damned university students are coming around, praying to the *kami* for luck on their exams," Kari drawled. "It would be *fun*. Just do it."

Slate tipped his phone away from his face. "What time do you have to work today?"

Dani checked her phone. "Not for a while. I go in at four."

"Wanna go to the shrine today?"

She shrugged. "Sure. I've never been to one."

He turned his voice back to Kari. "You win today, *baa-chan*."

CHAPTER ⊕ ELEVEN

A GREAT MANY THINGS

... three tails will give these creatures a great power, but historically, many died before then, leading to their modern-day scarcity. It is unknown if the Jade Emperor intentionally...

- Gherald Schmidt, Faerloch Historical Archives

The Inari Shrine of Yousei was the pride and joy of the Eastern District. Set along the river to the north, it was a slice of serenity amidst a busy, overpopulated city. It was large and sprawling, hugging the lazy path of the Loch River, with a few vendors, koi ponds, and statues to honor the *kami*. It was picturesque.

Slate glanced at Dani, watching as her head swiveled around, absorbing everything as they approached the short set of stairs that would take them into the shrine. Her wide-eyed curiosity made his throat stick shut. He was torn between wanting to squeeze her face or kiss her.

"What is this archway?" she asked, pointing to the vermillion and black arch at the bottom of the stairs. "There's one on the pedestrian bridge too."

"It's a *torii*," he explained. "It denotes a sacred space. There are hundreds of them here at this shrine in particular because it's an *Inari* shrine."

"Explain it to me like I'm four years old," she said with a laugh. "Because I have *no clue* what any of that means."

"Umm, well okay." Slate floundered for a moment, gathering his knowledge and his mind to explain something so normal to his daily life. "*Inari* are... like deities? It's part of Shintoism—the idea that gods or spirits, or *kami,* are in everything. Some places are more spiritual than others, hence the shrine. *Inari* are the gods of rice and foxes and general prosperity. That's why all the university students are visiting. Luck for exams. And businesses donate *torii* to the shrine, if they're successful and shit."

They reached the top of the stairs. The courtyard opened before them, with winding and sprawling paths, gardens, and ponds—all overlooking the river. Several buildings dotted the space, but none as large and majestic as the shrine itself at the other end of the courtyard.

"See? There?" He pointed. Two statues flanked either side of the shrine. "*Inari* statues shaped like foxes. Two. A male and female representation. Those are rice stalks in their mouths."

"Wow..." she whispered. "This place is magical—in the completely figurative way, of course," she added with a crinkle of her nose.

He chuckled. "I got you, love. I understand."

"Slate!"

He turned, and his face broke into a wide grin as a small woman raced up to them to launch herself at him, linking her arms around his neck while her feet dangled off the ground.

After a tight squeeze, Kari released him and dropped back to the ground, flipping her long rose-gold ponytail over her shoulder. "I didn't think you were actually going to come."

Slate gave Kari a once-over, frowning. She was dressed as a *miko* today—red *hakama* and a white *kosode*. He gestured to the outfit and raised a brow. "Little out of character for you."

Her grin was positively devilish. "I have many characters, pumpkin, this is just one of them." She turned thundercloud gray eyes to Dani, and Kari's eyebrows shot up. "Oh *my*, aren't you a pretty thing. I'm Kari." She stuck out her hand. "One of Slate's best friends."

Dani pinched off her immediate jealousy of the woman when she stuck out her hand and introduced herself. Slate had tried and failed to explain Kari Meho to her, and she could immediately see why. Kari was a *bombshell*, even in the strange outfit that engulfed her small frame. Long rose-gold hair spilled from the tie that secured it at her nape, hanging in rich waves down to her waist. She had wide almond eyes, high cheekbones, perfect skin, a full hourglass shape, full mouth, straight teeth, straight nose—if Dani were to look up what an Asian model was supposed to look like, she'd see Kari's picture.

But Kari also *oozed* soft sexuality, and Dani could tell instantly she was a big personality. She liked the woman immediately.

"Dani," she replied with a smile, taking Kari's outstretched hand. "Slate's friend."

"Friend with a capital F." Kari winked.

The moment their skin touched, Dani sensed it. She nearly gasped but managed to hold onto her breathing.

Dani's magic allowed her to feel the heartfires of animals in her immediate vicinity. There was a distinct flavor about animals, each one as unique to her as a color along the spectrum. She sensed heartfires in people too—after all, people were, on some base level, animals as well—and lorefolk, but her magic wasn't as sensitive to them as it was to animals.

Kari was a little flame of life on Dani's radar, triggering her magic. Small and subtle, the flavor of her *extremely* unique, but startling all the same.

She saw the slightest shift in Kari's eyes, a minute dilation, a ghost of something skittering through her irises.

"So!" Kari said cheerfully, and whatever Dani saw was gone in an instant. But the feeling remained. "Dani, have you ever been to a shrine before?"

"No," she replied, pulling herself together in the space between her heartbeats.

"Well!" Kari hooked her arm through Dani's, and started to drag her away. "You *must* get the whole tour!"

"Kari," Slate drawled, trailing along behind them.

"I've sabotaged your date, Slate, sorry." Kari waved a hand flippantly over her shoulder. She didn't sound sorry at all.

"It's alright, still counts." And when Dani turned over her shoulder to glance at him, he grinned at her.

Kari didn't miss the exchange. "What are we counting?" Her eyes bounced back and forth between them a couple of times, and a devilish, almost foxy grin appeared again. "Oh! I see. Counting dates, are we, darlings? It was that good already, huh?" She laughed, the sound as rich and stunning as the rest of her. Dani found herself fascinated with the little woman.

Kari took her on an entire tour of the shrine property. Dani washed her hands in some water-filled basin to cleanse herself before heading into the shrine. Everything was foreign and beautiful, and Kari was an avid storyteller, explaining what the *miko* did, who ran the shrine, and why people came. Any question Dani asked, Kari had an answer for. She was vibrant and vivacious.

Kari disappeared at one point to go help and take pictures with people who were visiting the shrine, so Dani sidled close to Slate.

"I have a personal question for you," she whispered.

Slate chuckled. "No. I have not slept with Kari. Never have, never will."

"Not your type?"

Slate's gaze shifted from her face to where Kari was laughing with some tourists. "Kari is as close as I'll ever get to a sister," he said. "And her twin brother is my absolute number one best mate. Brother from another mother."

"Jian, right? The man I saw you with in the Market District?" She twisted some of her hair over her shoulder and forced herself to stop staring at Slate. She'd decided that he was probably the most beautiful man she'd ever met, but not just because he was conventionally attractive and slightly exotic with his ancestry. There was a sharpness to him, a wickedness to his smile, a transparency to his emotions that encouraged her to study every line about him, like a thirst to learn every nuance about him.

"Yep, that was him." Slate's eyes slid her way again and lingered on her face, and Dani hoped her cheeks weren't as red as they felt. Out of the corner of her eye, she saw him grin, and she swatted him gently with a scowl, but her lips tugged upwards despite herself.

Kari returned, and her sensual voice tugged Dani's attention away from Slate's playful mischief. "Whew, you two are seriously going to keep counting? This is painful to watch. You should just get it over with, though preferably not right here."

"Kari," Slate growled at her.

Kari grinned, and Dani couldn't keep herself from laughing. Kari had a point, and the temptation was strong, but now that they'd started this ten-date rule, she found herself enjoying it. Things were casual and fun. Dani liked casual and fun.

Draping her hands over her generous hips, Kari tilted her head at Slate. "So! Slate!" she said. "You have your fight on Thursday?"

"Yep."

"A fight?" Dani glanced back at him, russet brows raised. "Like, a professional fight? Or a date with an asshole kind of fight?"

Slate's wicked grin was dazzling, and Dani was glad he didn't have super hearing, or else he'd hear how her heart accelerated every time he smiled at her. "Depending on who I'm up against, it could be a bit of both."

"Dani, you should come!" Kari exclaimed, clapping her hands together with a grin. "It's so fun. And we can go out afterward, if it's not too late."

Dani bit her lip. "Well, I can get off early that night, but wouldn't that...?" She trailed off because it would be ridiculous to imply she'd distract him.

Right?

"Totally fine, love. If you wanna come, come. But it counts if you do." He smirked.

"It'll be fun!" Kari quipped. "Jian will be there too. He's always ring-side with Slate though, so you'll have to slum it with me in the arena seats." Kari's smile was beautiful and perfect as she looked back and forth between them.

"Okay," Dani agreed, her own lips tugging wide as she slipped her fingers into the back pocket of her capris. "I'll get out of work early, or maybe I'll just take the day." She rarely asked for time off; she doubted anyone would mind.

They were nearing the end of their tour when both Kari and Slate pulled up short and winced. Dani glanced between them, then followed their stares. An older *miko* ahead of them paused in her assistance with some young university students. Dark eyes slid to Slate and stayed. Then a withered hand beckoned him.

"Fuck," Slate muttered.

"Who's that?" Dani asked.

"My grandmother." His expression was stony, and Dani had to fight the urge to reach out and touch him, as instinctual as breathing. She resisted and glanced back at his grandmother. She didn't seem particularly pleased to be seeing her grandson.

"Go," Kari hissed. "And when she's done boxing your ears, come find us."

Slate heaved a sigh. "Fine."

Kari looped her arm through Dani's once more, and guided her towards the shrine. It was beautiful, with its intricate red wooden lattice-work and roof with uptilted corners of a rich black tile.

Inside was stunning and quiet. People milled around, admiring various statues and scrolls.

"Slate and his grandmother don't get along?" Dani asked softly.

"No," Kari said with equal softness. "She's... traditional, and Slate's not. If his eyes weren't a dead giveaway that he's not all Japanese... well, she's a little too traditional for my taste too."

Kari stopped at a scroll and sighed dreamily. It was a painting of a beautiful woman in elaborate and colorful robes, a shrine painted in the background. She had a mask in her hand—white with ears and red lines and a clever, pointed face.

"This," Kari said, laying a gentle hand on the scroll, "is my favorite."

"What is it?"

"Well," Kari started. "The woman in the painting? She's a *kitsune*. A..." She rolled her hand, as though she were trying to find the proper word. "A fox monster? No. A demon! A fox demon."

"A fox?" Dani could scarcely breathe.

That.

That was what Kari's inner flame, her heartfire, reminded Dani of. It wasn't the same, but it was similar enough now that she'd connected it... *Fox-like*. Distinctly different, but still a sort of... echo of her little fox, Dash.

"Mhmm. They say *kitsune* know a great many things about the world, that they are the eyes and ears for the gods, for the Jade Emperor himself."

"Really?"

"Really. Kitsune are shapeshifters, masters of disguise. They disguise themselves as a beautiful woman to blend in with everyday folk with illusions and trickery."

"Like, magic?"

Kari cut a sharp look towards her and smirked. "Sorta, I guess. Who knows if it's real or not. Magic within myth, perhaps. Do you believe in magic, Dani?"

"My father used to say you could find magic in anything if you knew where to look."

Kari was watching her, expression carefully neutral. "Most people don't look." Gray eyes slid towards the entrance of the shrine, to where they could see Slate speaking to his grandmother in the distance. "It's for the best sometimes, wouldn't you agree?" Kari's gaze snapped back to her, one brow arched gracefully.

There it was again. A flicker of something like blue fire in Kari's eyes, there and gone in a blink.

Kari was most definitely not a normal human. Dani's gaze dropped down to the illustration that Kari continued to stroke with delicate fingers, before jumping back up to meet Kari's gaze. The corner of the woman's lips curled, ever so slightly, and she murmured, "Don't you think so, Dani?"

Dani glanced back towards Slate, who was staring straight ahead as his grandmother wagged a finger at him. "I think... some people might have already gotten a peek. What then?"

Kari gave her a long, inscrutable look, then turned back to the painting. "I see..."

Dani watched her, wondering if she was reading between the lines correctly. One of Slate's friends didn't seem to be human, and seemed to know that Dani could sense that, and was asking her not to tell Slate.

Before she could get her thoughts in order, Kari snaked her arm through Dani's with an enigmatic wink. "Things will work out, I know. I also know that we are going to be good friends."

"Do you?" Dani asked, a little fascinated by this wild woman.

Kari gave her another grin. Foxy and sly. "I do. And I know a *great many things*."

CHAPTER · TWELVE

RATTLING THE CAGE

... able to connect their condition with the Full Moon. The curse of this Clan has led to one of the most stubborn of human superstitions, and it came up frequently in the debates held at the 18th Gather as to whether or not intervention was necessary...

- Gherald Schmidt, Faerloch Historical Archives

Dani eased her Vespa into the alley by the martial arts studio just before 8pm that Thursday. She cut the engine and sat for a few moments, her mind a whirl and her stomach in knots.

She hadn't seen Slate since their little tour around the shrine. As the days bled together, she'd heard less and less from him. But he'd told her as much when they'd parted ways on Monday.

"Just... letting you know my nerves start to peak hard around a fight-night," he said as he walked her to the car park where she'd left her Vespa. "I eat, sleep, and breathe competition."

And then he'd kissed her and made her toes curl in her shoes, and they'd both somehow walked away from each other.

Her stomach pitched at the thought of seeing him again. What date number would this be? Four?

She was so endlessly curious about him as well. For a seemingly clueless human, he had a father that was comfortable with a griffin in his garden, and who had called her a *faeling*. Slate also had a best friend who was... what *was* Kari?

Regardless of what she was, the conversation between them had told Dani two things: Kari was aware that Dani knew something was different about her, and Kari didn't want her spilling the beans about it to Slate.

Which was fine, of course. It was faux-pas in any magical community to out someone without their consent.

Not for the first time, Dani worried she was getting in over her head. The new guy she was seeing was utterly clueless about magic, being targeted by the Silver Valley Council, and seemingly surrounded by magical—or at least knowledgeable of magic—folk, and he himself was potentially lorekissed and didn't know?

It was all so strange. More than once this week, she'd told herself she ought to just tell him good luck and wash her hands of him. She didn't need this kind of excitement in her life. She liked her job and had a solid friend group. She was good.

And yet something inside her refused to walk away from it. From him. Maybe it was the way he kissed her so thoroughly and melted her insides, or maybe it was how easy and comfortable everything already felt with him. Maybe it was how sinful and charming he was on the outside, but with an undeniable goodness on the inside. Maybe she just *really* wanted to see what he was like between the sheets.

It certainly made her nervous, how much he seemed to get under her skin. Sometimes, she could almost picture things between them as... more than casual.

Which scared the shit out of her.

But for now, it *was* casual. Casual and fun. She liked casual and fun, she reminded herself. Silver Valley and maybe-magic friends aside, things between her and Slate were great. For now.

I can always walk away... after I get him to blow my mind in a bed somewhere, she reminded herself, and that calmed some of her nerves.

She strapped her backpack to her bike and headed around to the front door. As she passed the big windows, she saw light pouring out. She peered inside for a moment. Slate was in there, his back to the window, gloves on his fists, punching some hand pads held by another man with a shock of copper hair. Dani recognized him as Kari's twin; she could certainly see the resemblance he had with his sister even through the window.

She entered the studio and slipped her shoes off at the door. "Hello?" she called inside.

"Dani!" Kari burst into the waiting room. With a saucy grin, she sauntered up to Dani and kissed her on the cheek. "How are you?"

"Fine, thanks. How are you?" She smiled at Kari. As it was the first time they'd met, Dani's awareness of the little heartfire within Kari—a hint of something animal-like—tickled at Dani's senses.

"Stoked for fight night! Come on." Kari angled her head, and Dani followed her into an open training floor with bright blue mats. Dani's heart flipped four ways over when she saw Slate—wearing a black tank top and a pair of loose, black cotton pants—nailing the hand pads in a blaze of moves she could barely register with her own eyes. Muscles bunched, flexed, and tightened with every movement. His face was a mask; he was totally focused.

Even more impressive, perhaps, was the dance the other man was doing, moving the hand targets perfectly in response to Slate's movements—up, down, sideways, down for a kick, back up for a punch. Dani didn't know anything about the nuances of fighting, and she'd barely seen Slate in action the other night with the fae, but she was certain she wouldn't want to meet this man in a dark alley.

He might not be able to handle more than two fae, but she was pretty confident he'd fuck up most mortals.

"Hey, Dani," Slate said in a huff of breath, not deviating slightly from his combo.

"Hi," she replied. "You're looking pretty ready for tonight." She couldn't help but grin as she watched his moves, almost like a vicious dance.

"Uh-huh."

"I'd shake your hand, but mine are busy," said the other man. He barely spared a glance at her, yet she noticed his eyes were the exact shade as Kari's. In fact, everything about his face was nearly the same—the shape of their eyes, the tilt of their noses, the fullness of their mouths. This man was no slouch either. As beautiful as Kari, but in a decidedly masculine way. Though, he didn't quite have the same sensual aura about him that seemed to be

Kari's second skin. Neither did he have a wild-touched heartfire that tickled her senses. "Name's Jian, Kari's better half."

"You wish," Kari quipped back. "That's my dumbass twin. He's a doctor."

"Oh? I didn't think many dumbasses became doctors." Dani grinned at Kari before glancing back toward the male twin. "It's nice to meet you." She gave him a little wave. "Are both of you martial artists like Slate?"

"Oh! Yes!" Kari laughed. "I guess that didn't come up the other day, huh? Yep. All three of us, bred and bled here on this very floor. Slate's the senior student, even though he's the *baby*."

"By six months," Slate growled, drilling the pad with a kick hard enough to send Jian careening backward a couple of steps, a rich laugh bursting out of him.

"Senior student?" Dani perked a brow.

"Yep. Slate's a fifth degree black belt, Jian and I are fourth degrees."

Dani's brow rose even higher. "That's... a lot of black belts. Is that why you like to fight, Slate?"

"Hmm?" Slate looked up distractedly, bouncing back from a kick, then shifted stances as he faced off with Jian.

"Slate just likes to *fight*," Jian answered, seamlessly picking up where Kari left off. "And he's not allowed to around here or else Ebisu-*jii-san* will kick his ass."

"Martial artists aren't supposed to pick fights," Kari informed Dani with a grin and a shrug.

"No," Slate agreed with a growl. "But we'll finish them."

He knocked one hand pad with a fist that sent Jian's shoulder reeling backward.

"That's it, that's the money shot right there," Jian laughed with an easy grin, rolling his shoulder.

Slate pulled in a deep breath, yanked his hair tie out, and shuffled his fingers through his hair, pacing the training space. He resonated energy, nervous and fidgety, yet with a cool facade to mask the restlessness. She had the insane urge to stroke her hands up his chest and hold his face, to make him stay still and look at her for a second, to try and get him to focus and calm down.

Even more insane? She had the strange feeling that if she did that?

It would work.

The arena wasn't far from the Eastern District, and the walking seemed to give Slate something to do with his body. He was restless and jittery—almost chaotic. A mania to him she hadn't seen yet.

"He's always like this before a fight," Kari said softly. The boys strode ahead of them by a few paces, talking shop. *Hook punch* this and *side kick* that. "His nervous energy is contagious. I can hardly stand it sometimes. Once he gets in the ring, though... you'll see. Totally different animal. Cool and collected."

Dani nodded, watching him. She'd seen that side of him, as they'd faced the fae the other night. He'd told her to run, to try and buy her time. He'd been rock steady. Angry, *furious* even, but rock steady. She hadn't seen fear in his eyes. Only fury.

Slate said goodbye to them in the foyer, giving Jian a fist bump and kissing both Dani and Kari on the cheek.

"I'll meet you ring-side!" Jian called after him. Slate simply waved over his shoulder and disappeared through the double doors.

Inside, the arena was packed, and she was surprised by how legitimate it was. Honestly, she'd imagined Slate participating in back-alley fight clubs, not an actual circuit. For some reason, he seemed the type to participate in something barely legal.

Maybe it was that wicked smile.

The energy was a living, pulsing, breathing thing inside the arena. Jian disappeared the moment they entered, saying he needed to go ring-side with Slate. Kari held Dani's hand, leading the way as she navigated the throngs of people to get a seat toward the front and close to Jian.

"What does that entail, being ring-side?" Dani asked as they dropped into seats.

"Means Jian is in Slate's corner—like a coach. Most of these fighters here have professional coaches from local clubs, but Slate likes Jian with him. Jian doesn't like to fight, but he's pretty observant, you know? He can pick up on stuff. Weaknesses and tells of Slate's opponents, stuff like that." Kari tipped up a shoulder in a casual shrug. "Plus, Jian's good to have on your side in a fight, since he's a doctor."

"I see. This is far more legitimate than I'd imagined." She offered Kari a lopsided grin.

Kari laughed. "Lady, what did you think this was? Fight Club? That we'd be taking bets and it'd be a riot in here?"

Dani shrugged innocently. "I don't know! I feel like when he said he 'fought in an amateur fight circuit', that was just code for something *not exactly legal*."

Kari laughed so hard, she had to take a couple of deep breaths to regulate herself again. Dani grinned back, giving another little shrug. Kari's eyes danced as she smirked at Dani. "Ah, girl, you are too funny. No, this is very legal. Very legit. Slate actually makes a *lot* of money doing this. Which is surprising because most amateur MMA fighters make *nothing*. He's been scoped out a few times for the pros."

Dani blinked at Kari, taken aback. "What? Pros? As in *professional* MMA?"

Kari nodded. "He's won the Faerloch Championship title two years running. He's currently undefeated. Looking at another Championship title this year, too." Kari's grin faded a little. "But... his father's health keeps him from venturing too far away from home. This is something to... take the edge off, I guess? I don't know." Kari's eyes bounced around the room, before she glanced back at Dani. "Slate's been restless lately."

"Lately?"

"I mean, I say lately, but it's been a couple of years, really. I think his dad's sickness bothers him a lot. Ever since then, he's been kinda different. Not in a bad way! Just... different."

The topic was cut short when the lights dimmed. The crowd went absolutely insane. The commentator announced the contestants for the preliminary matches and then read out the roster for the main events. When Slate's name was called, the number of female shrieks in the stadium was deafening. Kari smashed a hand over her ear, wincing.

"Good, Slate's up first tonight. Means we won't need to stay longer if we don't want to," Kari said. "Sometimes these events can go *late*. We've had some nights where we don't get home until 4am."

Dani's brows rose at that, but working the late shift, she was used to getting home early in the morning. The first of the preliminary matches began a moment later. Two gentlemen were in the ring, wearing nothing but tight shorts, gloves, and mouth guards. Kari didn't seem impressed, but Dani was enthralled, watching their match with rapt attention.

"You wait," Kari told her, grinning. "This is nothing."

The preliminary matches finished and the crowd became visibly more charged. When the lights dimmed again and the announcer came back, the crowd lost their minds. Even Kari joined in the hooting and hollering, pumping her fist in the air.

"Ladies and gentlemen... It is now time for the event you've all been waiting for. In the red corner, weighing in at 208 pounds, we have Connor 'Lightning' Laraway!"

A monster of a man came out of the doors on the left, running and skipping down the aisle and up the stairs into the arena, pumping his fists in the air, holding a single finger up. The crowd began chanting *number 1* again and again.

"This is hilarious," Kari laughed. "So much showboating. It's all about who can make the crowd think they have the biggest dick." She wiped imaginary tears out of her eyes. "Just wait and see how Slate is." Her grin was sly, and her eyes danced with sensual mischief.

"And in the blue corner..." the announcer paused with a chuckle when he was drowned out by female screams. "We have your champion from the last two seasons. He renounced his title, fought through the circuit, and now only two more matches stand between him and the championship title once again! Weighing in at 205 pounds... Slate "the Master" Melisande!"

The volume of the crowd roared to a crescendo, and there was more than one shrill declaration of love. Dani winced at the pitch, tempted to cover her ears as Slate emerged.

Slate didn't bounce down the aisle. He didn't even look at the crowd. He simply prowled towards the center ring, focused and stony. He wore nothing save his gloves, a pair of shorts, and shin guards.

Dani felt a shiver race down her spine, thinking his cool focus was far more intimidating than the showboating. This was not a Slate to be tangoed with. Her magical senses couldn't pick up on 'auras,' which were distinctly different than heartfires, but she didn't need magic at all to sense this kind of power. It was the kind of power and confidence that even humans could wear like threatening cloaks, making them seem larger than life. It was the cold set to his jaw, though, that had her stomach knotting. For the briefest moments, she was reminded of the fae; icy arrogance and an aura of power that was almost otherworldly. A flicker of fear whispered through her bones, her fingers curling in her lap.

He flipped his gaze to her, and they warmed, just for a heartbeat, and the fear in her stomach dissipated like smoke in a breeze, replaced with something much warmer.

Slate jogged up the stairs, his face a stone mask once more. Jian appeared beside the ring and handed Slate a mouth guard. He slipped it between his teeth and entered the cage with a last fist bump with the redhead.

As Slate faced off against his opponent, Dani caught it. For the briefest moment, she sensed a heartfire in him. A powerful one, something *big*.

It was gone as fast as it appeared.

Slate Melisande was a mystery she couldn't decide if she wanted to unravel, and yet she was helpless to take her eyes off him. She'd never encountered a person whose heartfire could appear and disappear. Of the few lorekissed she knew, their heartfires remained small but constant little flames. Lorebeings had stronger flames than lorekissed, like campfires instead of a candle flame. As for animals, their heartfires were distinctly less... organized? Chaotic and distinctive, instead of the groomed fires of lorebeings and lorekissed.

Slate was... none of these. What *was* he...?

The bell sounded, snapping her from her thoughts, and both men started bouncing around each other in a wide circle, like cats stalking their prey. 'Lightning' Laraway threw out a couple of quick jabs, one of which Slate absorbed in the ribs even as he danced out of reach of the other. The bouncing and circling resumed, reminding Dani of prowling panthers. The other guy threw out a couple more techniques, and once more, Slate either dodged, or blocked and absorbed it.

"Why isn't he fighting back?" Dani asked after a few moments, leaning towards Kari but unable to peel her eyes from the rippling sinew of a drool-worthy body.

Kari chuckled. "He's watching. Looking for tells. Just watch..."

Then, it happened. 'Lightning' Laraway threw out a couple more jabs and Slate blocked, dodged, and lashed out as fast as his opponent's nickname. Dani could barely follow the fast kick-combo as he caught his opponent in the solar plexus with one foot and in the head with the other.

The guy *dropped,* and the ref immediately stepped between them as a cheer erupted from the crowd. Slate paced the arena and shook out his hands while he waited for his opponent to get up. Five seconds... seven seconds...

The other guy got to his feet and stayed there, but his mouth was bleeding. Round one was over.

Both fighters retreated to their corners, before returning to the center of the ring to face off, and the fight continued.

There was more bouncing, but less need to jockey for position this time. 'Lightning' Laraway came in fast with fluttering kicks, catching Slate in the back of the hamstring. He dropped to one knee with a grunt. Slate caught the other leg that came barreling towards his face and swiftly redirected the energy, sending his opponent flying across the ring.

Slate got to his feet and waited.

Stomach in knots, Dani could scarcely breathe as she watched Slate move with unnerving smoothness and grace. She didn't know shit about fighting, let alone fighting *professionally*, but she could easily tell Slate was strong and talented. He was fascinating to watch; composed and powerful, and he didn't waste a single movement.

There were bursts of fighting, then backing off. Slate was focused and fierce. It was thrilling, even as that little knot of cold in her belly twisted. He was so *fluid*.

Like the fae... the back of her mind whispered. Dani ignored the thought and leaned forward, on the edge of her seat. *Lorekissed,* she reasoned with herself. *He had to be lorekissed.* Roger had said as much at the Den that night—Slate was likely one of those types that weren't kissed by magic, but had strength and speed instead. Roger was *old*. He would know.

While the tension in her shoulders eased, the cold knot didn't. It lingered around the edges of her insides like a phantom breeze.

Kari chuckled softly next to her. "Lady, you're drooling over there."

Dani shut her mouth with a fierce clank of her teeth. She hadn't even realized she'd been sitting here gaping like a fool. "Is this what it's always like?" she asked with a tilt of her head.

"Oh sure. And trust me, you aren't the only woman in this stadium who's gonna need to change her underwear after this match." Kari's smirk oozed coy sensuality. Dani had a feeling Kari wasn't ignorant to her own little fan-base building in the nearby crowd. More than one spectator, male *and* female, kept glancing at the petite woman.

The lull in the fight as the men prowled broke when Slate took a right hook to the face, and his lip split open, dripping blood. Dani gasped, hands flying to her mouth. Slate didn't even seem to notice his own blood dripping down his face. He was ready to jump back into it, but the ref separated him and his opponent, which Dani guessed meant it was the end of the second round.

"Don't worry," Kari said. "Slate takes hits on purpose... makes the guy feel like he's won something. People get sloppy when they start feeling emotion in the ring."

Dani nodded absently, eyes on Slate in his corner. Jian was right there, dabbing something on Slate's lip and talking to him. Slate was nodding. He looked like he'd barely broken a sweat. Sapphire eyes slid to her, and it was like a physical touch, a caress, gone in an instant as the bell rang once more.

Dani shivered, heat curling through her blood, all previous trepidation instantly forgotten as though scorched from existence by that glance.

Beside her, Kari let out a curious hum, and Dani blinked, glancing at her. The woman was watching her with open curiosity, but little of her thoughts were revealed in her gunmetal gray eyes—

There it was again.

She hadn't been imagining it in the shrine. Something like ghostly blue flames had definitely just shimmered over in her irises, just for a moment.

"Slate looked at you," Kari told her, interrupting Dani's mental speculation.

Dani blinked. "So?"

Kari's lips curled slowly into a decidedly foxy grin. "Let's just say that Slate's focus isn't so easily broken."

"What does—" Dani started to say, but then 'Lightning' Laraway scored a hit on Slate—a slap to his ribs—and her attention shifted back to the match. Slate took a couple more excellent hits, even getting pinned to the cage of the arena where Lightning started laying it on him, punching him whenever he could until the ref separated them. Connor paced around the ring, pumping his fists and cheering as if victory was closing in for him. Less than thirty seconds remained.

"Come on, Slate..." Kari growled. "Don't dick around... finish it!"

Slate shook himself out. He was a little red from the hits but he didn't outwardly look worse for wear, and both competitors approached the center of the ring.

20 seconds...

Slate dodged a deadly hook-uppercut combo, twisted his body like lightning and threw a fast jump spinning kick.

The back of Slate's heel collided with his opponent's head. Kari was out of her seat, cheering and screaming before the guy even hit the floor.

Instant knockout.

Dani's breath rushed out of her in a great gust. She was on her feet with the rest of the crowd, cheering and clapping.

"Ladies and gentlemen! Your winner by knockout—Slate Melisande!"

The crowd erupted, stomping their feet and cheering. Slate pulled out his mouth guard and offered a little wave and a smirk; the most emotion anyone had seen out of him during the whole fight.

"Yes! YES!" Dani could hear Jian shouting from ringside.

Kari grabbed Dani's shoulders and shook her a little. "We WON!"

Heart in her throat, Dani laughed. The matches had been much more enjoyable than she'd imagined, and watching Slate fight had been the most riveting of them all. He was exceptionally good at building the intensity in the room, making you hold your breath for his next move. She could see why he was so popular with the crowd, and not only because he was a pretty thing to look at. He was clearly a talented fighter.

"Sexy, isn't it?" Kari breathed dreamily as the two of them made their way out of the stadium and towards the foyer. "Used to be one of my favorite nights in university—all of us huddling around the TV to watch the UFC."

"Are you a good fighter?" Dani asked.

"Oh sure." Kari waved a hand. "But I'm too small to be a professional. Besides, I don't particularly like to fight, really. Martial arts isn't about *fighting*. It's more like... preparing yourself for a stressful situation within a controlled environment. I never want to be a victim, so I train." She shrugged. "But everyone trains for different reasons."

"What does Jian do it for?"

Kari stared at her for a long moment, head tilted slightly in thought. "Jian... Jian does it because he likes to help others, and he knows Slate's in it for life, and he likes to be close to Slate. Slate and I are best friends, but Slate and Jian are *best* friends, you know? It's different for boys."

Speaking of the devils themselves, Slate and Jian came around the corner. Dani's heart somersaulted in her chest. Goddess help her, the way he'd moved in the ring had been just... the whole experience had been sexy and exhilarating, despite her unease.

Now her earlier thoughts seemed silly; his little grin made it impossible to remember the icy fury that had come off him in the ring. He seemed utterly... mortal.

Kari exploded with squeals, and she launched herself into him. He caught her with one arm, laughing, and she kicked her feet in the air. He placed her back on the ground, and she twirled on the spot. "You were *amazing*! That hook kick KO." Kari fanned herself dramatically. "You could've killed him."

Slate shrugged. "I pulled it enough. He was coming around when I saw the EMTs wheeling his ass out. He'll be fine."

His eyes caught Dani's over Kari's shoulder, and the way they skimmed right up and down her sent a spark of electricity down her spine. He was *definitely* more trouble than he was worth.

Or maybe not. Maybe he would be worth the trouble.

"*Izakaya!*" Kari said.

Jian grinned. "Definitely. Let's go. All the rounds on me." He slapped a hand on Slate's shoulder. "You up for it?"

"Hell yeah." Slate nodded. "Dani, *izakaya*?"

"Explain it to me like I'm four," she reminded him, laughing lightly.

"Drinking!" Kari hooked her arm. "Come on. The night is young, and we need to celebrate!"

CHAPTER THIRTEEN

IZAKAYA

... humans attribute the horrors of Marius'
bloodlust to the Black Plague, one that did exist
but was not as virulent as the humans believed.
It is often believed this coincidence played a part
in the acquittal, which was...

– Gherald Schmidt, Faerloch Historical Archives

As they walked, Dani found herself next to Slate, and she wasn't blind to the fact that
she was walking closer to him than was strictly necessary. Her arm continually brushed
his and each time, the heat of him seeped into her body deliciously.

"What'd ya think?" he asked her. "Not bad for your first fight?"

"You're very good at creating suspense in a match. It was pretty epic, I'll give you that."
She smiled impishly at him. "Seems like you have *quite* the female fan following. Bet you
have no shortage of offers to warm your bed."

"That's too many women to maintain." Slate waved a hand casually, but his eyes had an edge to them again, a wickedness that made her dream of bedsheets against skin.

"I'd help," Jian tossed in.

Kari laughed, the sound rich and full like a pleasant bell, and hooked her arm through Dani's once more. "Me too," she said gleefully, and Dani shook her head at her with laughter written in the lines of her face. "But Slate doesn't do it for the crowds. Or the money."

"It's fun," Slate replied. "Maybe eventually I'll get bored of fighting and move on. No good story ever started by sitting at home."

Jian grinned, linking his fingers together and draping them across the back of his neck. "Wait until you see the finals, Dani. Slate does way better under pressure."

Dani's fingers brushed against Slate's in a casual gesture. "Can't wait," she said, locking eyes with Slate for a brief moment. Whatever was between them, this heat, this intensity… it crawled under her skin and lived there, and the alarming part was she *wanted* it to.

"We're here!" Jian announced, his grin broad as he held back a swath of fabric hanging in the doorway for Kari and Dani to go through. The fabric was a dark midnight blue, with a large Japanese character on it in a deep ruby red. "*Ojii-san*, four cold cups of sake, please!" Jian called through the doorway as he and Slate followed after the girls.

They removed their shoes in the entryway, placed them in the cubby spaces provided, then made their way over to a corner table. The tatami was warm under Dani's feet, and she glanced around the room appreciatively. She'd never been to an *izakaya* before. Each table was low to the ground, with four sitting cushions arranged around them. The bar area was devoid of tatami and was the only hardwood floor section. Four stools lined up along the bar, on the other side of which was the owner of the bar, or the Master, as he was called, according to Jian. When Dani asked if he was a martial artist, Kari laughed and informed Dani that *Jii-san*, which meant Grandfather, was the Master of Food and Drink.

"You call Jian a name like that," Dani whispered to Kari.

Kari chuckled. "That's because he called me *baa-chan*, which means 'old lady'."

"You *are* older," Jian added lightly. "By one entire minute."

Dani followed Kari to the table, folding her legs under her to kneel on one of the cushions. Dani caught sight of Kari winking as she urged Slate to take the cushion next to Dani, before the tiny woman skipped around to the spot across from Dani.

Dani glanced at Slate, and he offered her a sharp grin before an older woman dressed in a pretty robe shuffled over to the table, knelt at the head of the table, and removed four wooden boxes from the tray in her left hand. Each box was about four inches by four inches, and roughly two inches deep. A clay jug, holding a little under half a liter of liquid, sat inside, overflowing with clear liquid that collected in a fifth small box that held it. After the woman had placed a box in front of each of them, she then placed a small clay cup next to each box, the cups not much bigger than shot glasses.

"*Domo, baa-chan*," Slate said with a warm smile, and the woman bowed her head a little.

The woman started to rise, paused, then turned her attention to Slate. "Another fight this evening, Slate-*kun*?"

Slate's grin widened, and he nodded.

The woman's smile made the wrinkles all over her face crease delicately. "I am glad. This round is on the house. You may have the next round, Jian-*kun*." The woman inclined her chin toward Jian, whose smile widened enthusiastically.

"Thanks, *Jii-san*!" Jian called over Kari's head to the old man standing behind the bar, a white band wrapped around his head with the same Japanese character on it as the fabric hanging in the door. The old man didn't smile, but there was a warmth to his face as he inclined his head towards their table.

As the older woman shuffled away, Kari picked up the small jug from her box, letting the sake drip off the bottom before filling her little cup. She replaced the jug carefully to ensure the liquid inside the box didn't slosh over the side. Dani watched Slate and Jian do the same, and mimicked their actions. She'd never had sake before.

"To Slate, and to his kicking ass *again* tonight!" Jian announced, his voice a deep bellow that filled the room. The other tables in the room, some obviously familiar with the trio Dani was with, raised their cups as well.

Dani lifted her cup, and they clinked them together as Kari, Jian, and Slate all yelled, "*Kampai!*" together.

Dani laughed and took a sip. Jian downed his sake in one gulp, as did Kari, but Slate took his time finishing his cup in a slow slide down his throat.

"This is pretty good," Dani said, staring at the clear liquid in her cup. She smiled and lifted the glass again, and did her best to gulp the rest of it down.

"That's the spirit!" Jian said with an easy grin, already pouring himself another cup.

This *izakaya* was a favorite of theirs. It was minutes from the studio, and its location made it a perfect gathering place for post-testings and events. Half the staff at the bar had gone through his studio at some point over the years. Even *Jii-san* had studied at the studio, but in the era of his father.

Their waitress—Suki—kept bringing them sake as Kari began sharing stories with Dani about their childhood.

"I kid you not, Dani, the other kid *shit his pants*, right there on the studio floor." Kari leaned across the table toward Dani. "Slate and Jian *scared the shit out of him* in their two-on-one sparring match."

Jian had his head on the table, crying from laughter, and Slate patted the top of his head to comfort him.

"The best part was my father..." Slate started, and Jian waved his hand weakly like he couldn't take it. "He's got a pretty epic poker face, and he's sitting on the testing board with a couple of guest masters, and he is covering his face, *shaking* with laughter."

"Was it one of his students?" Dani asked.

"*Kami* no," Kari said. "Sometimes, if testings are small, we will organize the event across the schools in the area. It was one of Kim's students," she whispered that last part, "from Kim's Karate on the other side of town."

The sake kept flowing. They ordered some food as well, and the place started to get loud—so loud they needed to raise their voices to be heard. Word got around real fast that Slate won his match tonight, and people kept buying them rounds and toasting his success and good fortune. Several current and former students came by to say hello. The men were polite, but Slate noticed how Dani caught their attention. She was exotic and breathtaking, no doubt, her hair all pulled over one shoulder as she twisted it in her hands casually, and the tee shirt she was wearing just wouldn't behave. He noticed that every single time she leaned forward or shifted a little too much, a slim edge of green lace bra would peek out.

"Oh shit, I've got the hourglass on my Snapchat with Aika. Dani, quick, selfie!" Kari said.

Dani leaned over the table and as Kari took a couple of seconds to pick a ridiculous filter—both of them dissolving into giggles with each new one—Slate couldn't help himself; her ass was right there...

He pinched the back of Dani's thigh playfully just as Kari took the picture. Dani jumped a foot in the air, whirling her face towards him, green eyes wide with surprise and a touch of delighted amusement.

"Slate!" Kari scolded. "You ruined it!"

He laughed. "I did no such thing."

"Dani, hold on, let's take another. Slate! Don't!" Kari added as she saw his hand shift.

He laughed again. "Okay, okay, I won't."

It was well past midnight by the time they called it a night. Jian was so drunk he fell off his cushion, and Kari made the executive decision that it was time to go home. They paid their tab—well, Jian paid. Kari took his card and swiped it and signed for him—and told Dani, "Hush, under no circumstances does a beautiful woman pay for her own drink at an *izakaya*. There are plenty of old men to pay for you."

"Listen, Slate, bro," Jian slurred, one arm slung over Kari's shoulders to keep him standing. She was tiny, but she was strong. "You were... you were awesome tonight. Top marks."

"Thanks," Slate chuckled, humoring him and patting his cheek affectionately, but a little too hard to be considered gently. "Go home, drunky-face."

"And Dani, you're cool. Let's be friends." He gave her a cheeky grin.

"Thanks, Jian." She grinned. "We can be friends."

"We're going home now." Kari jostled him. She kissed Slate's cheek and Dani's as well. "We'll see you both later, *ne*? Come, *ototo-kun*, time for bed."

"Do you want help?" Slate called after her, cocking a brow.

"Nah, I got it."

The twins started walking down the street towards their house.

"*Baa-chan!* The night is young!" He heard Jian slur.

"You stink like sake, and it's late," came Kari's reply.

"They're fun, your friends," Dani commented, lips still curled in a smile.

"That they are," Slate agreed with a laugh, shaking his head when Jian nearly pulled Kari to the ground in the distance, and her reprimanding voice could be heard all the way down to their end of the street. "Never a dull moment with those two, for sure."

For the rest of their walk, they discussed the fight circuit. He was still so amped from winning that when Dani asked him about the rules and regulations on their brief walk back to the studio, he was a little too animated as he explained it to her.

"It's so different than traditional martial arts, though," he added, as they approached the alleyway where she'd parked her bike. "You'll have to come by the studio during the daylight hours and see for yourself."

"Maybe I will. Are you going to ask me out again?"

His breath choked up his throat. "When do you wanna?" It came out a bit more rough than he'd anticipated.

She made a good show of thinking about it. His heart stuttered.

"This weekend," she settled on, giving him a cheeky grin. "You pick the place. I want to be *wowed*, Slate Melisande."

"My bedroom is right upstairs, love, if you're looking for wow-factor."

The air between them suddenly sharpened, tense and hot in the space between breaths. Their gazes locked, and Slate slipped a hand along her jaw, stepping in close enough that the heat of her body was a torturous caress. He was desperate for her in a way that made him ache with want.

"Can I kiss you again?" His mouth was already brushing hers.

Her eyes were already closed. She wasn't breathing. "Uh huh…"

He pressed his lips to hers, soft and easy. He truly did have every intention to take this chemistry between them slowly. Something about her simply fractured his self-control. He had the mad desire to strip her naked and run his hands over her skin until she was breathless. Just a taste of that fire came out in this kiss, his hand shifting until he had a palm curled around the side of her neck. Her lips parted, and his tongue was in her mouth, tasting her. She made the smallest little sound in the back of her throat, a catch of need. She braced her hands against his chest, the pressure feeding him in a physical way.

He'd never been so starved for female touch in his life, but when it came to Dani, he wanted *more* and he wanted it *fast* and he wanted it *now.*

Part of him wanted to fuck-all with the ten-dates shit. It would be nothing to take her upstairs and into his bed. Spend the rest of the night learning how she ticked…

"What date number is this?" he whispered. "Ten, right?"

"I don't know…" She grinned against his mouth. "Four, maybe."

Damn it. He truly wanted to take this slow and feel it out. Perhaps he was just cautious—afraid they'd burn so hot they'd end up burning out.

"This weekend," he said, pulling back and mustering a long, even breath to calm his pounding pulse. "Wow-factor."

"Text me," she added, finally dropping her hands from his chest, but not without trailing her fingertips. Goosebumps erupted over his neck and spine. She gave him a long look, eyes darting to his mouth before giving his whole body a once-over.

"Go home, Dani," he chuckled. "Before we end up in my bedroom for real."

She nodded, pacing backward down the alley to her bike. "Don't leave..." The words started out a little stuttered. She swallowed and tried again. "Don't leave the district by yourself, remember."

"Yes, ma'am," he replied. "No leaving the district without permission, got it." He grinned. "I'll be fine, love. I've lived this long, haven't I?"

Her brows pinched. She opened her mouth, but he interrupted her. "I won't leave! I promise," he added with a grin.

She swung her leg over her Vespa and revved the engine to life.

"This weekend," she said.

"This weekend," he replied. He didn't want her to leave. He wanted her to stay—to come upstairs with him, even just to watch a movie.

He could tell that she wanted him to ask her to stay. Both of them were torn against the idea—to stay would likely lead to *more*, since they couldn't seem to stop themselves when it came to the other.

But she didn't ask. And he didn't offer. Then she was gone. Out of the alley, onto the street. He stayed at the mouth of the alley until he couldn't hear the sound of her engine anymore.

He cursed himself all the way through the studio and up into his apartment. Stepping into his bedroom, he was suddenly and fiercely lonely. Aching hopelessly for a redheaded lorekissed woman.

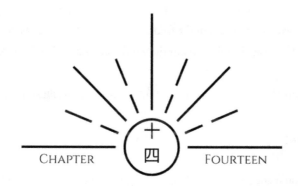

CHAPTER FOURTEEN

SECRETS BEHIND EBONY EYES

... Possessing the feather of one of these creatures allows for the individual to discern the truth of the world, from glamours to lies, and has led to a sharp decline in their numbers...

- Gherald Schmidt, Faerloch Historical Archives

Slate was on a high.

His father knew right away, of course. Slate didn't see him until the morning after the match, but the moment Ebisu came out of his bedroom and saw Slate making breakfast, he chuckled. "Someone had a nice evening."

"I won my match," Slate said, handing his father a bowl of rice with a fried egg on top and a bowl of miso soup, even though he knew his father would eat hardly any of it.

As much as Ebisu came off like he didn't enjoy Slate fighting in the pro fight circuit, he inquired after all the details, down to how he threw the spinning hook that ended the match via knockout. Slate wondered for years if his father had once been into a little pro fighting back in his youth; Ebisu would never say.

Slate toyed with the idea then and there to ask his father about seeing Dani's griffin in the garden. He wanted to ask about the faeries, about what his father *knew*. He'd wanted to ask for days, but he hadn't figured out the words yet, and he'd been preoccupied with the match...

"You have something on your mind, my boy," Ebisu said, stealing the idea right out of Slate's head.

Slate held his breath, choosing instead to focus on measuring tea leaves and refilling their mugs.

"Dani said you made a new friend in the garden the other day." He tested each word as they came out, slowly and haltingly, tasting each one.

He dared to flip his gaze to his father's. Ebisu was watching him, head tilted slightly, his weathered face unreadable. Slate's heart crawled up his throat.

"I have many visitors to the garden every day," his father finally said.

Slate waited, but his father said nothing else, merely sipping his tea.

"So..." Slate hedged. "Are you gonna tell me about your *visitors*? Especially about the rather large, *winged* variety?"

Ebisu's expression gave away nothing. "There is no need. They are your friends too, are they not?"

And with that, his father left the room, humming under his breath, leaving Slate standing in the kitchen, absolutely fucking *flabbergasted*.

What did his father *know*? He could tell from the set of his father's shoulders that Slate would get nothing more from him, not right now. Frustration, and a tiny bit of worry, vibrated down his spine.

Dani had said she wanted to be *wowed*, and Slate wasn't about to disappoint. She met him at the studio, and they started the evening walking through the open-air market in the center of the district. There was everything to be had there—from trinkets and bobbles to authentic kimono dealers, food vendors, farm stands, and flower shops. There were fast food and coffee shops, swanky restaurants, and shady basement sushi joints.

"So." She turned her attention to him and away from the almost hypnotizing rhythm of a rather impressive display of *maneki-neko*. "What's the plan for dinner?"

"We," he said with a little grin, "are going to *make* dinner."

Her brows lifted, mouth quirking into a smile. "You can cook?"

"I'm not bad at it, for sure."

They picked up fresh ingredients to make tempura and sushi, with an udon soup. Then, they wandered back to the studio, and he brought her upstairs to his apartment. Slate watched as she took in the open space—the living room, dining room, and kitchen were all an open floor plan with hardwood floors and tatami.

"What?" he pressed, noting the slight shock on her face.

"I... well. I'll be honest. When you said you lived with your father, I don't know what I was expecting, but it wasn't *this*."

He chuckled. "Listen, just because I'm a *boy*—"

She laughed and sat at a barstool at the kitchen counter while he busied himself getting everything together to make sushi. He handed her a small mug of fragrant green tea.

They talked about little nothings while Slate worked in the kitchen. At some point, his father came home.

"*Tadaima*," came his father's rough, aged voice.

"*Okaeri*," Slate drawled. "Where've you been, *ossan*?"

His father leveled him a look. Slate gave him a cheeky, wicked grin.

"Dani-*san*, wonderful to see you again," Ebisu said. She smiled at him.

"Notice how he doesn't answer me." Slate rolled his eyes. "And here I am, worried about his health and well-being."

"Shall I remind you who the parent is in this household?" Ebisu asked. "I am old, but I still remember an errant teenage boy who used to conveniently forget to tell his father when he left the house."

"Listen, I was a *teenager* then."

"You left your house without *permission*?" Dani quipped, a faux-gasp on her lips, even as her face crinkled playfully. Slate's heart flipped over in his chest. "How dare you be so irresponsible to your poor father? He worries about your health and well-being!"

Ebisu tapped her cheek affectionately, a deep chuckle pulling his face. "I like this one. I must tend to my night flowers. Enjoy your evening, children."

His father strolled down the hall. Dani hurriedly called after him, "My friend is in the garden!"

Ebisu simply waved over his shoulder and disappeared up the stairs that led to the roof.

"Anything?" Dani whispered.

Slate stared at the spot where his father had disappeared from view. He'd texted Dani immediately after he'd confronted his father about Sellie in the garden, and told her every detail—or lack thereof. "Not since that first chat, no. Cryptic as ever."

"I'm seriously convinced your mom was lorekissed... I mean, it's even possible your mom was a real witch, like Maddie." Dani sipped her tea. "How else would he know about faeries or have a Familiar or befriend a griffin?"

"I dunno," Slate said, chopping vegetables. "But... I'm also... I dunno. Never mind. It's crazy." He shook his head.

Zlaet, son of Aredhel...

All this talk about him being lorekissed had the gears turning in his head. Where did the magic come from? His father's side? Or...

His mom's name was Ari, that much he knew. Beyond that, he knew little else. Was it too much of a stretch to think that *Ari* was short for *Aredhel*? Assuming, of course, that Aredhel was a woman's name.

Ari... Aredhel...

"Tell me. I won't think it's crazy."

He eyed her sidelong. She watched him patiently, expectantly. Slate was quiet for a minute. Telling Dani everything that was going through his head didn't feel like a breach of intimacy. It felt normal. More normal than telling Jian or Kari, even. Which was odd. "My grandmother is a *miko*. Do you remember what Roger said that first night, something about a Mystic ward being maintained by *miko* and umm... *manyeo*, which are like, mythical witches or sorcerers or something, I think."

"I remember. Wait... *wait.* Do you suppose your *grandmother* is a... a *Mysticfolk*? Do you think your dad knows about the Eastern Mystics? Do you think..." She leaned forward on her barstool, hands white-knuckling her teacup, shamrock summer eyes imploring him. "Do you think you're not lorekissed but like... the *Mystic* version of that?"

"I don't know," Slate said quickly, shaking his head. "I also kinda wonder... I dunno. Remember I said my mom's name was Ari? Is it too much to think that maybe Ari and Aredhel are the same?"

Dani cocked her head, humming in thought. "Maybe. Could be a nickname..."

"I'm crazy, right?"

She bit her lip and sat back in her chair, her eyes wandering around his apartment, as though she could pluck the mysteries of his life out of the walls. "But... why would the fae—the High Fae Council—be interested in you? That doesn't make sense. Who is Aredhel to anyone?"

"My entire life doesn't make sense right now, love." It came out in a whip. He snapped his eyes to Dani. "Sorry, sorry, I didn't mean to come across like that."

"I understand." She beckoned him with one finger. He came closer to her and she touched his face, a stroke of her fingertips along his jaw. His entire nervous system stilled under her touch, then relaxed, as though he'd taken in a deep breath of sunshine. "You have a lot going on right now. Let's just have some fun, alright?" She smiled up at him, and it made him feel lighter just seeing it.

They had a spectacular dinner. It was relaxed and laid-back, comfortable and intimate. It was so effortless that Slate found himself periodically holding his breath just to watch her, not daring to even breathe lest he somehow break the spell over them. He was incredibly keyed into this slip of a woman. He was aware of her every moment. She both rattled his cage but also had this unerring way of soothing him. Slate knew he was a temperamental guy—pretty emotional during the best of times—and she made him feel more centered.

He was uncharacteristically comfortable with her. As if they'd orbited each other in this kitchen many times before. There was no awkward learning curve. She moved, he moved, like shadows woven from the same cloth.

And she was beautiful. Everything about her attracted him; he couldn't get enough of her. The way she talked with her hands when she was excited, how much she loved her animal friends, how smart and bright she was, how expressive her eyes were, like he could read every emotion through them. He wanted to hold her face and count all her freckles. He wanted to kiss her mouth and hear the sound of her. He wanted to breathe her into his lungs.

God, he was crushing *hard* on her, wasn't he?

After dinner, they rode into the city, and Slate took her to an arcade that doubled as a bar. It was somewhere he and the twins spent a lot of time while Jian and Kari attended the University of Faerloch. It was packed to the walls on a Saturday night, but Slate was comfortable around people and comfortable in how he could work a room. Dani stayed close to his side, but she was a magnet for the male gaze, and more than once, Slate found himself sizing up a guy or making eyeballs at someone to *back up a bit.*

They had fun—or at least, Dani seemed to be enjoying herself. That was all he truly cared about. This arcade allowed players to win tickets, and Slate combined all their tickets together and got Dani a stuffed animal from the prize rack. He didn't have many choices, but he chose a little stuffed fox.

"Oh, Dash will love this," she laughed when he presented it to her, her face crinkling with delight.

It was well past midnight by the time they made it back to the studio.

They shared another goodnight kiss that made his heart crawl right into his stomach and proceed to be digested.

He was still wide awake in bed when he got a text from her.

Dani: *I'm home.*

And a short video message of Dash and the little stuffed fox snuggled together in what Slate assumed had to be Dani's bed.

Slate: *He has a new best friend.*

Dani: *Haha, he has no shortage of friends here. I had a great time tonight. A+ wow-factor. Let's do it again.*

Slate grinned, his heart pounding in the pit of his stomach with nervous excitement.

Slate: *When?*

Dani: *You decide this time. Good night, Master Melisande.*

Slate: *Good night, Daniella.*

CHAPTER ⊕ FIFTEEN

ALMOST NORMAL

... after the disappearance of their prominent Matriarch, their House fell into obscurity from the fae of Faerloch and the Silver Valley alike, choosing instead to isolate themselves with House Taernach on the Isle of...

– Gherald Schmidt, Faerloch Historical Archives

As the days and weeks went by, Dani found that the days she spent with Slate stood out like beacons compared to the rest. It was also getting harder to remind herself that he was just a simple fling. Dani didn't *do* long-term relationships, but everything with Slate was *easy*.

It felt... almost normal. And if Dani had learned anything at all, it was that her life was rarely normal.

When they weren't on one of their dates, she found herself gravitating to her phone, and they shot messages back and forth near-constantly. So much so she teasingly questioned him as to whether he actually had a real job.

He gave her a snarky, sassy reply about making his own hours and being the *'master of his own domain.'*

Goddess above, she couldn't wait to see him again. She was absolutely nuts over him, to the point where her chest would physically ache every time she drove away from him. That made her nervous but didn't stop her from answering his messages with a silly grin on her face.

Casual and fun, she reminded herself.

"Yoohoo! Earth to Dani!"

Dani hurriedly stuffed her phone into the pocket of her scrubs, whipping her face up to find her coworker leaning against the exam table. She hadn't even heard Caroline come into the room; she'd been far too focused on her rapid-fire messaging with Slate.

How very... teenage-crush of her. Dani winced, offering her friend a sheepish grin. "Sorry, what? Did you need something?"

Caroline laughed, her baby blue eyes sparkling. "No, I was just wondering where you ran away to this time. Must be someone good, if you keep disappearing to text with him." She waggled her brows and plumped her blonde bob of hair suggestively.

Dani said nothing, feeling her cheeks heat a little. She didn't know how to explain what Slate was to her. They were hardly more than friends, with the extreme exception that he turned her bones to mush with a well-placed grin. And his *sass*.

Their relationship was light and fun, or at least, that's what she was telling herself. Despite the easy intimacy and explosive chemistry.

All she knew was that he occupied all of her waking thoughts and all of her nighttime ones too. And she was counting down the hours until she could see him again—tomorrow morning for breakfast and a drink: date number six. It was pathetic, because every night, she'd found herself sleeping with that stupid stuffed animal he'd won her at that hole-in-the-wall arcade joint.

Moments like that sometimes had her contemplating if she should break things off. Sleeping with a stuffed animal because of a guy? Yikes.

Yet no matter how nervous she was, she couldn't seem to make herself write that 'break-up' text to him. She simply didn't want to, nor did she feel compelled to seduce him before their ten dates were up. Now that they were more than a few dates in, it would feel... slimy. Like she'd be using him. Her stomach churned at the idea.

"So, what's his name?" Caroline drawled, sitting in one of the chairs pet parents usually occupied when their fur-baby was on the exam table.

"Slate," Dani replied. Caroline was a busy-body who loved gossip and drama, but Dani adored her. There were a few casual mortals Dani would hang out with regularly, and Caroline was one of them. She was always throwing excellent parties, especially around the holidays. "He's a martial arts instructor over in the Eastern District, across the river."

Caroline made a sound of approval. "Interesting. And how did you two meet?"

"We just... ran into each other one day," Dani said. It wasn't far from the truth.

"And what's he look like?"

Dani fiddled with the long cotton swab container lid. "Tall, super fit, dark hair—"

Caroline whistled.

"Blue eyes, Caroline. You've never seen eyes like his before. Deep and rich, like gemstones." Dani couldn't get them out of her head.

"My *god*, girl, so tell me you've slept with him already, jeez." Caroline fanned herself dramatically.

Dani laughed. "No, not yet. We're taking things kinda... slow, I guess."

Her coworker scoffed. "Why on earth would you do that?"

Good question... she thought, suppressing her nerves again. *Casual and slow*, she reminded herself. It was starting to sound like an excuse.

Her phone vibrated in her pocket. Her fingers twitched towards it like an impulse, and she flushed when Caroline laughed at her.

But it wasn't Slate. It was a different number.

Unknown: *Hey girl! It's Kari. Let's hang out this weekend. Yoga and tea?*

Dani blinked. She very much liked Kari, even if she had the feeling she had some crazy secrets going on.

Dani: *Yes! That sounds great.*

"So," Kari drawled, nudging her shoulder into Dani's playfully. "What date number are we at?"

Dani hoped her face wasn't as flushed as she suddenly felt. "Six."

It was another gorgeous spring day, May bleeding gracefully into June. She and Kari had caught an early yoga class in the city, and now Kari had insisted on a cup of tea and a stroll up the walking path that wound along the Loch River. In the distance, Dani could see the *torii* that marked the pedestrian bridge into the Eastern District.

"Six?" Kari whistled. "Wow. Getting serious."

"Nah, just... you know, fun," Dani said with a smile, hoping she came off as nonchalant even as her heart jammed into her throat. Date number six had been downright *magical*. It hadn't been as elaborate as the one before—it had only been breakfast—but it'd been so damned *easy* and comfortable.

It was unnerving, but she couldn't seem to stay away.

"And what's the magical number?"

Dani didn't try to pretend she didn't know what Kari was asking. She sipped her tea to unstick her throat. "We said ten."

"Ten? Ambitious. That's nine more than I'd give any man... or woman, for that matter." Kari waved a dismissing hand. "I don't have *time* for dates. Most of them aren't worth my time anyway. I get in, get my rocks off, and then tell them to buzz off. It's a rare soul who gets me for a second date. Or even a second fuck."

Dani laughed. "Honestly, same. Most of my dates don't make it past maybe a couple of weeks before they start getting too clingy for me. I'm all about the fun of dating."

Kari nodded easily. "Yeah, no, I totally get it. It's like... well, for me, I get bored."

"Bored isn't the nicest way to put it." Dani winced, shaking her head.

"Well, that's how I'd put it. I get bored. I like variety." She gave Dani a wink, her smile sly, and she fingered the lid of her coffee cup. "Slate doesn't bore you."

Dani's breath stuck in her ribs, her throat tight. "No," she finally said. "Um, no. He hasn't... he's not boring." She gave a little shrug, and added hurriedly, "I just don't like clingy, needy men, and that tends to happen after a few dates."

Shut your mouth, Daniella, she scolded herself, all too aware of Kari's curious gaze on her. What was she doing, talking to Kari like they were best friends? Kari was *Slate's* best friend and here Dani was, telling the other woman there was a good chance that she'd eventually dump Slate.

Dani liked easy relationships. Light. Noncommittal. Nothing deep. But eventually, all the men she dated became too clingy. When they did, she moved on. That's how it worked, and she was fine with that.

But Kari laughed and flicked her nose, wringing a surprised gasp from Dani. "Don't worry, lady," Kari said with a grin. "I asked you to hang out with me because I think you're interesting, not because you might potentially fuck my best friend. You're your own creature outside of him. If you dump him, then whatever. We can still have tea and do yoga together."

They stopped along a bridge. Kari placed her tea down and hopped up to sit on the wide railing, spinning her body so she was facing the river. Dani joined her.

"Tell me about him," Dani said.

"Who? Slate?"

"Yeah."

"What do you want to know?"

"Who you think he is." Dani didn't look too closely behind her question; she was just being curious.

Kari sighed. "Slate is... well." She paused, a little furrow between her brows. "He's trouble. Kami help us, he's so much trouble. You wouldn't know it at first, but he's so mischievous. In the best way. He's playful and confident, but not cocky. He can be kind of emotional sometimes? Little bursts of temper—"

"I've seen that." Dani nodded. "Almost like his emotions get ahead of him. He always backpedals though."

"Always," Kari agreed. "He'll be the first one to apologize. He really *cares* deep down. He feels a lot. He's impulsive as hell, though. But he's passionate, and he cares." Kari exhaled in a hard rush. "He's not perfect by any stretch of the imagination. He can be a total fuckhead. But he's a decent fuckhead. Anger is his first emotion, I will say that much." Kari nodded. "When he's scared, he's mad. When he's sad, he's mad, when he's mad, he's *freaking mad*. But he knows it, and he'll be the first one to walk away when someone pisses him off or hurts his feelings."

Dani got that impression too. Some men in the world were aggressive, and they *wanted* you to know how angry they were. They'd make lots of noise, but also take action and get physical with others when their emotions overwhelmed them.

That's not the vibe she got from Slate at all.

"He's pretty to look at, too," Kari added. "I mean, not as pretty as *me*, of course. But he's pretty enough."

Dani laughed, reminded all over again why she liked this woman.

A steady beat of silence fell between them. The sounds of the river, the people walking around them, the traffic in the distance. It was comfortable.

"I don't have many friends, you know, so this is nice," Kari said quietly, breaking the silence.

Dani gave her a look. "What do you mean, you don't have many friends?" Dani found that hard to believe. Kari was funny, spirited, and quick to smile. Everyone seemed drawn to her.

Kari shrugged. "Oh, I mean, I know *lots* of people. I'm friendly with loads of people. But I don't have many *friends*. Especially girlfriends. I have a couple that I hang out with from high school but... it's not the same. They're all getting married and having kids."

Dani crinkled her face. "I don't have many friends either, Kari. I don't like *people*—I like animals." She grinned at Kari. "Does that count?"

The other woman cut her a foxy grin. "That counts in my book."

"Well," Dani hedged. "I don't see why we can't continue being friends."

Kari gave her a smile—a genuine one, Dani realized, and it nearly stole her breath how stunning Kari was. No wonder she didn't have many female friends. A lot of women probably found Kari to be an intimidating person to be friends with. "I can count on one hand how many people in this world really *get* me." Her gaze shifted until she was staring out over the river again. "I'm a pretty good judge of character, and I knew the moment we shook hands you'd be on that short list."

Dani's heart skipped a beat. "Do Jian and Slate not... get you?"

She laughed. "Jian gets me, but he doesn't count. Jian is... Jian and I are the same person, split into two different bodies. He's my other half, literally."

Dani cocked her head, considering the twins. Jian hadn't given her the same bestial vibe that Kari exuded. Whatever Jian was—if he was anything at all—it wasn't the same as whatever Kari was. Because Dani was convinced Kari was *other*. She wasn't sure what, exactly. She had ideas, each wilder than the last. But there was no doubt in her mind that Kari wasn't mortal.

She was convinced Kari wasn't *Lorefolk*, either.

"And Slate..." Kari's voice trailed off, and something crossed her face. Anxiety? "Dani, you have to know, I'm the type of person who has a plan for everything. I view life like a giant chessboard, and I know all the pieces, all the moves, all the consequences of every action. I'm quite good at the game, if I do say so myself." A devilish grin, then it faded. "But, when it comes to Slate... I don't know the next best move."

Kari spun around and slid off the railing as gracefully as a cat jumps off a counter. "The game must go on, sweetcakes, and the next play is going to be *huge*. Just... fair warning."

Dani didn't dare breathe. "What are you, Kari?" she whispered.

Kari said nothing, only giving Dani a foxy grin.

That little grin jolted her. Dani blinked, then smiled back.

A little reminder that her life was most definitely not *normal*.

CHAPTER SIXTEEN

A FOX IN THE HENHOUSE

*... who could manipulate chi—the energy of life—
in others, were of great curiosity to the Covenant
of Witches...*

— Gherald Schmidt, Faerloch Historical Archives

Slate's days moved in a haze, his high continuing. Between the victory of his most recent match, and his new thing with Dani, he was in the clouds. His students could tell—not in such overt ways as knowing he was seeing someone new, but they absorbed his positive energy. His good mood overflowed into the studio.

One night after class, Slate, Jian, and Kari were loitering around the studio. It wasn't unusual for the twins to haunt the floor after-hours with him. Kari usually handled some business while Jian and Slate engaged in a little play-fighting.

Tonight was different. Kari wanted Slate to help her work through one of her higher belt patterns, and Jian was stretching, laying on his back with his legs along the wall.

"You're forcing that transition," Slate explained, popping to his feet and showing her what he was talking about. She watched him, nodding, then tried the movement again several times, cursing herself each time she failed. When she finally succeeded, Slate nodded. "Better."

She continued to practice, and Slate spoke up each time he saw room for improvement. With every passing moment, he became more and more aware of how uncharacteristically quiet the twins were. Kari kept flipping her ponytail over her shoulder, something Slate knew she did when she was worked up about something.

"Something bothering you, Kari-*baa*?" Slate asked.

He didn't miss the way her eyes flickered to Jian, the two of them having their weird twin-exclusive conversation. Slate's chest tickled with slight annoyance—he didn't like secrets or lies.

"Actually, yeah," Jian said. He flipped his body so he was sitting up criss-cross on the foam floor. "We need to talk."

Slate's eyebrows rose. "Sounds serious...."

"Kinda is."

Silence spread around the room, thick and uncomfortable and jittery. Slate bounced his eyes back and forth between the twins. "Well? Out with it. What's up? Did I do something?"

"*Kami*, no," Kari said. She stopped her pattern and flipped her hair again. "No, it's not you, it's..." Once more, her eyes slid to Jian.

"It's us," Jian said. "It's..." Jian floundered for words, huffing through his nose, "It's... well. Kari, I don't..."

"Slate," Kari said, hands on her hips. "We know what Dani is."

Slate froze, feeling like he'd inhaled ice. "And what, exactly, is that?"

"We know Dani is lorekissed," Jian said, "and we know that you know that."

Slate blinked. He hadn't heard that correctly, had he? He stared at Jian, then flipped his eyes to Kari—who had started on her pattern again—then back to Jian. "Okay..." he said. "That's... alright... well..." He floundered for something to say. "How do you know that?"

Part of him could guess the answer. And his heart raced over it.

Impossible.

"Because... because..." Another flickering look between the twins. "... we have magic too," Jian said softly, almost guiltily, a furrow between his brows.

Slate didn't breathe. Didn't move. Could hardly *think* past the thrumming of his own pulse in his ears.

"Explain." It came out hardly more than a tense plea, an echo of warning.

"Well," Jian hedged. "Dani is lorekissed; she belongs to the magical community called the Lore, or *Lorefolk*. Her magic is European-based—"

"Yours is Asian-based..." Slate finished.

More shared looks between the twins. "Yeah, basically." Jian nodded. "Europeans call it *Mystic* magic. Magic that hails from our pocket of the world—Japan, China, Korea, Thailand, Vietnam, India, you know."

"What are you?" It was a demand. He didn't want a magic lesson, didn't need another one. His head was spinning.

Jian gave him a long look. "Kari's a *kitsune*—"

"A *kitsune*?" Slate whipped his gaze to her. "A... *kitsune*? You—you're a... a fox *yokai*?" He knew what a *kitsune* was—Japanese mythic beings, fox spirits with shapeshifting magic. They were tricksters, often taking the shape of a beautiful woman to lure travelers.

Kari's mannerisms, her grace, her power, the shape of her face, the unique color of her hair—it made so much sense that Slate couldn't believe he'd never thought as much. He even described Kari as a *kitsune-gao*—a fox-faced woman, with her narrow face and high cheekbones.

She flashed him a grin. But it didn't quite come across as devilish as usual.

"Prove it," he whispered.

Kari glanced at Jian, and her gaze lingered for a moment. Slate looked between them, lungs tight. With a little sigh, she reached her fingertips under her hair at her nape. She produced a tiny rose-gold leaf, and Slate's stomach seized at the sudden *realness*. As real as the Lore had been when Dani had come over that fateful afternoon and blew his mind.

She touched the leaf to her forehead. The leaf disappeared... and there was a shimmering of light, like the way countless golden leaves ripple when falling from the ginkgo trees around the shrines, and suddenly Slate was looking at himself. A perfect replica.

"Holy... fucking... shit..." he breathed.

His other self touched his forehead and with another shimmer, Kari returned. Except she didn't return to her *Kari* self, but rather, some sort of fox in-between. Red lines marked her face, two on her forehead that blended into one down her nose. Red lined her eyes and her lips, nearly identical to the fox-faced masks at the shrines. Two large fox ears unfolded from her hair as though they'd always been there, and she shifted her cotton pants a little and three stunning, thick tails swept out from under her uniform top, flirting with the floor.

He was stuck somewhere between awe at the sheer impossibility of it, and also a shade of anger. Why was this kept *secret* from him? These two people... were his best friends. He had known them for nearly his entire life, and he'd had *no idea*.

"You're not saying anything..." Kari finally said, eyeing him. She smoothed her hands over her head and the ears disappeared, along with the markings and tails.

"I'm... processing my feelings," he said. He tore his eyes from Kari and back to Jian. "I'm gonna guess. You're a *kitsune-mochi*."

Jian chuckled awkwardly. "No, I'm not a fox witch. Though I guess in some circles, I could be? But I'm a *manyeo*. It's a type of witch."

"Dani has a friend who's a witch," Slate added absently, something that popped past his stunned mind.

Jian shook his head. "No, it's not the same. *Manyeo* have the ability to tap into the *chi* in living things and create enchantments, wards, and manipulate magical properties using it. It's how I brew potions for healing and how I create salves and medicines. I'm a witch-doctor, basically."

"He can do so much more than that, but he's being modest," Kari added. "He can even do magic other *manyeo* can't do."

"Why's that?"

"Because of our parents," Jian continued. "Mom's a *kitsune* like Kari and Dad's a *manyeo*. The combination gave us both some interesting magical quirks."

Slate rubbed his whole face, tapping into the rapidly draining well of self-control inside him to not lose his shit. "Okay..." He felt like he was going to burst out of his skin with emotions. Confusion, anger, a hint of sadness. He was steadily approaching *overwhelmed*. Slate didn't consider himself a guy who stressed out easily, but by the *kami*, the last few weeks of his life had been *stressful*.

"What..." He buried the heels of his hands into his eyes. "How did this all come about? Why tell me now, since you've both *clearly* been keeping this a secret for a long ass time." His tone was icy and acerbic.

"I knew Dani was lorekissed the second I met her," Kari answered. "I could smell her magic. And... something about it tickled my fox senses, if you want to call it that."

"Dani's magic is animal-based," Slate muttered, still covering his face with his palms. A headache started pounding right behind his eyes.

"Ah, I see," Kari said sagely. "And... she and I had a conversation in the shrine. She hinted at me that you know more than you let on. And the faeries are terrible gossipers."

"Faeries?" Slate peeled his hands away from his face.

"Yes, the ones in your father's garden. Said something about you and the fae having an altercation and Dani's pet griffin has been hanging around."

"What does my father know?" It burst out of him suddenly.

The twins shared a look. "*Jii-san* knows everything," Jian answered after a moment.

A stone settled in Slate's stomach.

"Slate, your grandmother is a *miko*, and I'm not talking like a regular one," Kari said slowly. "She has magic—*miko* commune with *chi*. They can't manipulate it, but they can see it, read it, and work with magical tools to maintain wards or enchantments. Ebisu-*jii-san* has some magic of his own, not pronounced or anything, but it's there. He can see *chi*, I think."

Breathing was difficult. "My father knows *everything*?" It came out slightly strained.

The twins nodded.

"But Ebisu-*jii-san* keeps many secrets," Jian added. "Some topics he doesn't talk about. He was the one who originally begged our family not to tell you anything—"

"It was his idea?" Slate interrupted, bursting to his feet. He felt jittery and almost ill. Shock, disbelief, anger... a touch of betrayal. He hated being lied to, and he could usually sense when someone was lying to him. But to have maintained this lie his whole life? Everyone knew about this dangerous and seedy underworld... and no one thought it was in his interest to know?

"He preached that you didn't need to know," Kari said, echoing his thoughts.

His mind was spinning, and the world didn't seem to follow the same set of fundamental rules anymore. Kari continued speaking, eyeing him. "And the magical community is pretty need-to-know."

"And you didn't think *I needed to know*?" His voice was escalating. "I have the High Fae Silver Valley Council hunting my ass *down*—"

The twins paled visibly.

"And I've *almost died twice* because they're trying to *kill me* or *kidnap me*, and now you're telling me if someone in my immediate family had thought to fucking *share* with me, it could've been avoided?"

"Why is the Silver Valley Council after you?" Jian whispered, visibly tense.

"I don't know!" Slate threw up his hands. "I don't know..." he said, his breath coming fast. "I need some air."

"Slate..."

He didn't stop, simply stormed off the training floor and down the long hallway. He punched out the access door, rattling the heavy steel on its hinges.

The alley was empty, dark, and cool. He took several deep breaths, pulling fresh air into his lungs, trying to level out his pulse. Angry, he was so *angry*. He knew he was only reaching for the anger first because he felt so *lied to*. So... *betrayed*.

His whole life, his two best friends had been magical beings...

... and his father. His *oto-san*... the one person in this world who was the rock in his life. He'd known too? Slate supposed it made sense that his father would know about the Eastern Mystics. Kari wasn't wrong; Slate's grandmother, Ebisu's mother, was a *miko*. He supposed it was fair that Ebisu at least knew that much.

Need-to-know basis. Why was Slate not on the list of *need-to-know*?

Slate pressed his forehead to the cool steel access door. His head pounded fast and rhythmic behind his eyes, and there was both a tightness in his chest and a jittery sensation in his hands. Bile ghosted the back of his throat. He swallowed hard. Once. Twice.

He heard the front door to the studio shut, then heard footsteps. He prayed Jian and Kari would leave him alone.

They did. They didn't come down the alley and soon, he lost the sound of them.

He wasn't sure how long he stood with his head pressed to the access door, trying to find his center, trying to calm down. He couldn't. He couldn't get a grip.

He needed to get out of there.

It took him half a dozen tries to punch in the door code correctly. He ripped the door open and stormed up the stairs, a hurricane given flesh.

Ebisu was in the living room, working on a Sudoku puzzle with a cup of tea when Slate came storming in. His father didn't even blink at Slate's barely-tempered aggression, didn't say anything as Slate slammed through the apartment and towards his bedroom. He could feel his father watching him, boring into the back of his head until Slate disappeared into his room.

Part of him was dimly aware that he wasn't exactly behaving like a grown-ass man, but you know what, he didn't care at the moment. It's not like anyone around him decided to treat him like an adult anyway, hiding shit from him his whole life and lying to him.

Ugh. He *hated* being lied to. *Despised* it.

He practically ripped his uniform off and changed into some cloth shorts and a tee shirt. Grabbing his gear bag, he dumped some extra clothes and shit into it. He didn't think; he just acted.

He was back in the living room in mere moments. His father's eyes tracked over his face, slid to his hands, to his bag, then back to his face. There was a calmness in the lines of his expression, but a wariness in his eyes. "Where are you going so late?"

"*Out,*" Slate snarled. "I don't wanna hear how dangerous the city is. No one here gets to tell me what's dangerous anymore. I'm over it."

Ebisu rose gingerly from his floor cushion by the *kotatsu*. "You seem aggravated. Why don't I make some tea and—"

"No. I'm leaving."

The calmness hardened a little. "Sit." The request changed to a demand. "I'll make some tea for your nerves."

"No." Slate stormed to the door. "I'm *leaving.*"

"Slate."

He floundered for a heartbeat, hand hovering over the door handle. For a moment, just a moment, he checked his impulsivity, the wild, erratic pulse in his throat. It wasn't the first time in his life where he'd felt out of control—and every time it happened, his father had been the steady hand.

Not today. Not tonight.

He left.

CHAPTER SEVENTEEN

DANI'S HOUSE

... had the ability to speak to the wild beasts of the Forest of L'el, to speak directly to their wild hearts...

- Gherald Schmidt, Faerloch Historical Archives

"Man, I still don't get it. How come they all love you so much? Even the freakin' lizards like you," Caroline complained, standing on her tip-toes as she reached deeper into the kennel she was washing. The wall of kennels, four tall and five wide, was mostly empty that night—prime time for a good scrub.

Dani, however, was sitting in one of the four large kennels that lined the wall perpendicular to the kennel wall. These kennels were designed for large dogs, floor to ceiling with thick glass walls and wire-mesh doors with slits along the bottom to slide food in for aggressive animals.

"I just have a thing with animals," Dani said with a shrug, watching a female dog hesitantly accepting kibble from her palm.

"Yes, I know," Caroline said with a sigh, pulling her head out of the deep kennel and eyeballing Dani and her charge. "She won't let anyone else near her."

The dog in question was a stray that had been brought to the hospital by a good samaritan. She'd been clipped by a car and broken her back leg, which was currently in a neon pink cast. The stray had a deep fear of people and had refused to take food from anyone, which became an even bigger problem when she'd gone into labor and birthed five tiny puppies.

Dani had spent the last hour in the kennel, sitting cross-legged with her back against the wall, coaxing Missy-Loo—the name they'd decided to give her—to take food from her. Her puppies were squirming about in a low, large plastic box filled with blankets. The dog had finally started taking food from her twenty minutes ago, but only one piece of kibble at a time.

See? You're safe, and so are your babies, Dani reassured the dog with a soothing voice, projecting safety and warmth to her with her mind. The dog had refused to respond until now, but finally, Dani got impressions of hesitant appreciation and images of her uncertainty.

I promise, Dani reinforced, reaching out with her other hand and tentatively petting the canine. The dog's tail gave a small jerk.

Her phone buzzed in her pocket. Dani set the bowl of food down in front of her, within reach of the dog, then she dug out her phone from her pocket. She had a message from Roger.

Roger: *Are you well?*

Dani smiled, and her thumbs flew across the digital keyboard as she responded.

Dani: *I'm good! :) I'm at work. What's up?*

Roger: *Have you been seeing that male? Slate Melisande?*

Dani's smile widened a bit, and she fought the urge to roll her eyes at Roger's overprotectiveness towards her.

Dani: *A bit, here and there.*

In fact, she was supposed to see him this weekend—they hadn't made any firm plans, but she was debating another trip to the Den, sans the fae attack this time.

Roger: *Indeed. And things are... well?*

Dani: *Swimmingly. Ask what you want to ask me, Roge.*

Roger: *No more signs of the fae?*

Dani: *None. We've kept pretty close to the Eastern District. I was thinking about bringing him to the Den again this weekend.*

Roger: *I see.*

A soft, small, wriggling ball was dropped into her lap. Surprised, Dani tucked her phone into her scrubs pocket to focus on Missy-Lou.

"Oh! She's showing you her puppies!" Caroline gushed, her voice pitched with envy.

Dani smiled, reaching out to gently rub Missy-Loo behind her ears as she nudged the puppy closer to Dani, as if insisting the woman inspect the baby she had produced. "Yes, she's beautiful," Dani crooned and picked up the still-blind puppy. Both mom and babies were an unknown mix of breeds that had resulted in a mottled brown coat with white coloring. She kissed the little wriggling bundle on the nose. The puppy squeaked, then yawned. Dani smiled, knowing the puppy trusted her because her mother trusted her.

For the next ten minutes, Missy-Loo brought each one of her puppies over to Dani to show them off. Dani took her time cuddling each one, impressing images of comfort and safety to each of them. By the time all five puppies were wiggling in her lap, the mom was greedily eating the food Dani had brought her.

The door to the kennel opened and Dani peered around the corner to see the secretary's dark head peek in. "Dani?" the secretary—Mia—called. "There's a man here, requesting to see you? Are you expecting someone?"

Dani blinked, taken-aback."No... there's a man here? For me?"

"Well, I didn't want to say whether you were here or not in case he's a creep," Mia explained. "Though, he is *quite* attractive..."

Dani's heart lodged into her throat. She glanced at the clock. 10:12pm. "What does he look like?"

"Delicious—dark hair, tall, the *bluest* eyes—"

Dani carefully dislodged all the puppies, putting them back into their plastic bin. She projected calm to the mother, keeping her movement light but efficient. She heard Caroline croon to Mia, "That's Dani's *boyfriend*..."

She skirted out the door, smoothing her scrubs and fixing her ponytail before she walked into the waiting room.

There he was, leaning against a bare wall, with a gear bag at his feet.

Slate flipped his eyes to hers. At once, she knew something was wrong. He looked... stressed somehow. There was a hardness to him, to his shoulders, to his face. His eyes were too vivid, too large for his face, a tightness around them, a smudge of red, a strain in the line of his jaw...

He reminded her of an animal caught in a cage. Unnerved, wary, one wrong slip of the hand could throw him over—either into tears or anger, she wasn't sure.

Anger is his first emotion, I will say that much.

"Slate." She offered him a smile, and she saw his shoulders ease just a fraction. "Come here." She beckoned him. "Mia! I'm popping into exam room three!"

"Take your time, doll."

Slate hiked his bag onto his shoulder and wordlessly followed after her. She opened the door for him, and once he was inside, she shut it. The door barely clicked and he was in her space. She sucked in a swift breath when she quite suddenly found his arms around her waist, his face in her neck. She gently looped her arms around his shoulders.

"You're shaking," she muttered.

"I've had a fucking *night*." His voice was muffled into her neck. His breathing was a little ragged, a little uneven. Despite the fact this was in no way sexual, a shiver raced down her spine as his breath warmed the side of her neck.

She waited him out for a minute, but he fell silent again. Heartbeats passed, and his breathing leveled out, his shaking dialing down.

"I don't know why I'm here," he rumbled. "I... I left and I walked and this is where I ended up." He finally pulled his face out of her neck and looked at her. He seemed less wild to her now. "I can leave. You're working."

"It's okay." She laid a hand on the side of his face with a smile. "It's slow here, anyway. What happened? Do you want to talk about it?"

He released her, and she leaned her shoulders against the door and watched him start to pace the small exam room.

"I uh... I had a little conversation with Kari and Jian tonight..." he said after a couple of minutes. "Did you—did you know Jian is a fucking *witch*?" He ran his hands through his hair, jostling the hair tie loose. "Like, like a real one. A magical one. A *manyeo*. And Kari! Kari? She's a *kitsune*!"

Dani's lungs seized at the confirmation of the vague impressions she's had of Kari, of that *tingle*... "She told you?"

"Yeah." Wild eyes landed on her again. "Did you know?"

Dani tilted her head to the side. "Well... I had an odd feeling about her, I guess you could say."

His eyes narrowed. "You knew too? And didn't tell me?"

"No." She gave a little laugh, shaking her head. "I had nothing more but a *feeling*. She never told me anything directly. And it's not my place to out your friends. They told you when they wanted to tell you." Despite the honesty of her words, and her firm belief that outing a magical person wasn't polite, it still made her chest tighten to see the shimmer of betrayal on his face.

"I feel like my whole life is falling apart," he whispered thickly.

Her heart punched through her chest at the sheer rawness in those words. Despite her misgivings about a relationship with this guy, she couldn't help but feel overwhelmed *for* him. She knew how it felt, had been there—that feeling like the rug was suddenly ripped out from underneath you and standing became a struggle.

"Your life is not falling apart," she said, some instinct tugging her forward, one step, two. She offered him a half-smile. "Things are a little weird right now, but that's okay. It will balance out. What is it they say—the hardest battles are saved for the toughest warriors, or something like that, right?"

He gave her a ghost of a smirk. Then his face fell and his mouth pinched into a hard line. "I hate being lied to. I can usually tell and... I had no idea and I just feel so... I'm so *angry* and I have this headache that won't quit and my father! My father *knows something* and he's keeping secrets too!"

He mirrored her steps like a string was being drawn taut between them, pulling them together until they were sharing space. Dani held her ground, and after a moment's hesitation, he reached out to cup her face and press his forehead to hers. His breathing instantly seemed to settle, and she marveled at how comfortable it was, to be this casually intimate, to be this close to him. So comfortable and so...

Right.

A little part of her whispered the word, that this was *right*. And that made her tense a little, a hint of anxiety rising, but not enough to pull back, not when he seemed so upset. It was like her own panic was overwhelmed by the need to soothe this man.

So fast. This was going so fast.

And yet...

"Why don't we go back to my house?" she offered. "Get a little space from home, process everything. You look like you're all packed for a sleepover anyway." She grinned, and he dropped her face and took a step back—but not too far back.

A little flush appeared high across his cheeks. "Sorry, I just... I don't know what I was thinking. I just needed to get out."

She laughed a little and nodded her understanding. "It's okay. And I won't forget our ten-date rule, mind you, just because we're having a sleepover," she teased him with a grin. It managed to pull a smile from him. She shifted towards the door. "Let me go talk to Mia. My shift is nearly over anyway, and it's slow."

Mia was fine with Dani cutting out early. The secretary kept eyeballing Slate in the waiting room while Dani spoke to her, and Dani couldn't blame her. Her expression said she was both intrigued and nervous about him. He still had some of that wild energy about him, and it was both frightening and alluring at the same time.

Dani wasn't frightened of him, though. Anxiety at their quickly-evolving relationship aside, he reminded her of a large predatory cat, and Dani had never been scared of an animal in her life. Well, except when she'd faced a pack of hellhounds when she'd rescued Sellie. They'd been so focused on their prey that nothing she'd said had gotten through to them.

No, Slate himself didn't scare her, even when he'd been so fierce in their scuffle with the fae. She trusted him, weirdly enough.

"I'm warning you now," she said to Slate, breezing into the waiting room with her regular clothes on instead of scrubs, "I have *quite* a few animals at home. All kinds."

He shrugged. "Whatever. Animals are fine. They don't bother me."

"I mean it—they're everywhere. But I'm pretty sure I can find a furry-friend-free area for you to sleep." She gave him a cheeky grin, and once more, a hint of a smile pulled at his lips.

The words made her think of her own bedroom, where only she and Dash slept, and the idea of Slate in her bed made her stomach pitch hotly. *I didn't say he could sleep in my bed*, she reminded herself. *Keep your head out of the gutter.* After all, it wasn't exactly time appropriate, given Slate's whole world was in limbo. It was likely the last thing on his mind.

The drive went quickly, even though Dani drove at a reasonable speed for once. The entire time, she had to split her attention between the road and the way his body felt pressed against her back, one hand on her hip, the other gripping the bar hold.

Twenty minutes later, Dani pulled into her quiet suburban neighborhood, going even slower and keeping her engine noise low as they went. Slate's grip slackened around her, sitting back to observe the various houses going by, some lavish, some modest. Finally, they pulled into the driveway of her modest yellow house. The garage door opened automatically at the touch of a button.

She killed the engine, waited for Slate to slide off, then followed suit. "Here she is!" Dani said with a smile, gesturing with her hand to take in the place. Sellie swooped down from the sky and into the garage in an impressive aerial feat, considering her size. The griffin had followed them home from the clinic and didn't seem impressed with the early departure as she eyed Slate haughtily.

Dani laughed. "As you can see, this is where Sellie makes her nest." She gestured to the back corner of the garage.

"A great nest indeed." He smirked, tipping his head at the griffin. Sellie clicked her beak at him in return, only slightly mollified.

A nightlight came to life near Sellie's nest, softly illuminating the room. Dani smiled and jerked her chin towards the door that led from the garage into the house as she wheeled her Vespa into its place inside. Slate nodded and followed after, and there was still a lingering tightness about him. The urge to take his hand suddenly had her palm itching, and she squelched the unfamiliar feeling.

So fast...

She flicked on a light and they both slipped off their shoes in the entry. The garage led directly into the back hallway where she had laundry and a half-bath, with the kitchen straight ahead. Dani led the way through the hall and past the galley-style kitchen and into the living room. A family of squirrels was curled up in a blanket on the couch, two raccoons were playing on the carpet in the living room, and a large and rather fat rabbit was asleep wedged between the couch and the side table, his long ears flopping over his eyes. Other critters scurried around, but the moment Slate stepped in behind her, everyone froze.

"It's okay, he's a friend," Dani said out loud. There was a beat of still silence, then movement resumed, albeit a little more cautiously. She dropped her backpack near the stairs.

"I have some nighttime chores to do," she said, tilting her head. "You can hang out here or—"

"I can help you, if you want," he offered. He gently dropped his bag on the floor next to hers. The much-heavier sound startled the animals into several beats of silence again. "Sorry..." he whispered.

Dani threw a smile toward the raccoons, who were already sniffing in Slate's direction. "They're okay. They acclimate to new people quickly."

"Do you have new people over often?" he asked with a teasing air as she walked around the house in her standard nighttime routine. Slate followed more slowly, and she felt his eyes acutely as he watched her move.

She paused, holding the fish food over her enormous salt-water tank, and glanced back at Slate. "Umm, no, not really. But the animals adapt well."

"They trust you, *ne*, not to bring someone scary home." He gave a slow nod of understanding as he glanced at the curious raccoons, who were now less than a foot from his feet, sniffing wildly.

"That they do," she grinned and finished feeding the fish.

He continued to follow her around. Dani sneaked several peeks at him, worried he'd be unsettled by her unusual home. Maddie didn't mind in the least, and Caroline had been alarmed at first but had come to adore being at her home. Roger tolerated the mess her friends could make because he was her friend, but she knew he was a clean-freak at heart, and not particularly fond of small furry animals. However, despite the fact she had *wild* animals in her home all the time, it was still pretty clean. The windows were always open at least a little, bringing in birds, bugs, and sometimes faeries, but also fresh air. She expressed to her friends the importance of doing their business outside, and thanks to her magic, they mostly listened. It was nice, like nature had crawled in to live with her.

"Suitable for the night?" she teased lightly, a bit hesitant.

"Of course," he said. He followed her back to the kitchen. "Did you think I'd be weirded out by all the animals or something?"

Dani hopped onto the counter and lifted her gaze to Slate's. "Some people are." She shrugged. He filled the small kitchen with his broad shoulders, making it seem even smaller. But most of the earlier strain had left his muscles and his jaw. Only the slightest tightness remained around his eyes.

"I'm not some people, then, I guess." Watching her, Slate took a step toward her, then another.

She eyed him carefully as he made his way over, but she didn't stop him when he stepped between her knees. The heat of him licked over her front as he planted his hands on either side of her hips and braced himself on the counter. A shiver raced down her spine, and she locked eyes with him as he drew nearer, caging her against the counter.

"Thanks for letting me stay here," he said, voice pitching lower, soft enough that little butterflies caressed the inside of her belly. "I'm sorry I crashed your night..."

"It's fine." He was so close to her. Her hands itched to touch him, and she decided not to deny herself. She lifted her right hand and slid her fingers over the soft gray cotton of his chest until her palm was flat over the strong beat of his heart. "You can make it up to me."

"Oh yeah? How's that?" A different kind of light started to simmer in his endless blue eyes.

Her eyes flickered to his lips before bouncing back to his eyes. "You could kiss me," she offered, her voice a low whisper that mingled their breaths together.

CHAPTER   EIGHTEEN

THE CHALLENGE

... considered the most dangerous, and potentially powerful, ability in the Lore. It has become a myth, even to the long-lived Lore, but the Historic Society of Gaea will not forget the horrors that transpired during the Wild...

- Gherald Schmidt, Faerloch Historical Archives

"You could kiss me."

Her words stroked fire through his blood, his heart rate spiking up. Slate leaned forward and brushed his mouth against hers, tasting the summertime warmth of her. A desperate need roiled through him, suffocating him until he could hardly draw a full breath. He wanted her with a desperation that made every other relationship in his life pale by comparison.

He didn't think he'd ever *want* someone else as much as he wanted her. It was visceral and startling.

One of her hands slid up his chest, tingling his skin until she looped her palm around his nape and pulled him towards her. He shifted his body forward, curling his fingers behind her knees and tugging her closer until they were flush. She gasped, a subtle but sharp inhale, and her mouth opened to him.

Heat flushed his head in a quiet roar. Slate slipped a hand along her face, tipping her head back a little bit more so he could kiss her harder, taste her mouth, slip his tongue inside. A sound escaped her that had every nerve ending in his body standing to attention.

She pulled back with a gasp. "Do you want to share my bed for the night?" she breathed.

"I thought you'd never ask."

"Just... sleeping... you know..." she said absently, and Slate wondered if she was trying to convince herself as much as him. He cracked a grin.

She pushed her hands against his chest, a silent demand to move. He didn't, not right away, reluctant to put any space between them. He relished the heat of her body, the softness of her curves pressed against him. Yet he relented and she slipped off the counter.

She led the way, her hand looped in his. He snatched his bag as he passed, a tension vibrating through his body. Every step felt ages long. It took an insane amount of self-control not to yank her to a stop right on the stairs and kiss her again, take her clothes off, touch every *inch* of her skin.

She barely had the bedroom door open before he dropped his bag on the floor and tugged her back in for a kiss, pressing her against the wall next to the door. A little noise in her throat was her only protest before she melted against him and looped her arms around his neck. Her palms traced his back, his shoulders, fueling the fire in his blood.

A distinctly irritated chattering sound from behind him made him pause. He felt her grin against his mouth.

"Dash," she whispered.

"Is he gonna bite me?" Slate asked, pausing long enough to glance over his shoulder to see the shadowy form of a small furry animal uncurling from her bed. He couldn't stop himself from returning his lips to her skin though, kissing the line of her jaw, caressing his mouth down the column of her throat.

"No..." she gasped. "He'll be a good boy and give us privacy."

There was a grumble and more annoyed chattering—a sound of protest—from the bed, but a moment later, Slate heard a light thump and felt a momentary brush of fur against his ankle as the little creature zipped past them and out the door.

Dani pushed against his chest, and rather than let her slip out, he stepped back and tugged her after him. It was dark, with barely a sliver of streetlight from the curtained window, but he'd always had great night vision, and it took only a glance to get an idea of where the bed was. He backed up, stealing a kiss here and there, until his legs hit the edge and he sat hard. She was straddling him in a second, kissing him again, tracing her hands over his shoulders, his hair, loosening the hair tie.

His hands scrambled for the edge of her shirt, and they stopped kissing each other long enough to tug it over her head. The shirt hadn't even hit the ground before Dani's lips returned to his, and Slate's palms smoothed over the newly exposed skin of her waist. He skimmed his hand up and over her bra, the dark textured material hinting at lace, making his blood heat.

He couldn't breathe, the heat swirling between them so intense, he thought he'd drown. He flipped them over, pressing her back against the mattress. He peeled his tee-shirt off and tossed it blindly before returning his lips to hers in a frenzy. Her hands slipped over his skin, tiny nails digging in, tugging him closer. It was a fire, a brand, his skin feeling starved for her touch in ways he couldn't even comprehend.

"What date number?" he asked roughly, kissing down her neck, tasting her skin.

"I... I don't... six, I think..." A pitched moan escaped her as he scratched his teeth gently along her left shoulder.

"Damn..." Why did he agree to ten dates again? Whose idea was this anyway?

Right. It was his. Because the way she kissed him that first night made his very skeleton melt. Had she *breathed* the right way that night, he'd have taken her right there on the floor.

He could push it—that much he knew. He was pretty confident he could seduce her right now. The intensity between them was a living, beating, pulsing energy that had his blood rushing to all the right places. He would do, say, *be* anything to get skin-to-skin with her and soothe the burn she left behind with each brush of her fingers. His body was alive for her.

But...

"If you—" the words slipped out of her mouth.

"Don't." He placed a finger against her lips. "We said ten dates, we'll stick to it. I kinda like a challenge."

He sensed she wanted to argue, wanted to say *fuck it*, so he parted her thighs with his knee and pressed his leg against her core, the heat of her permeating through her jeans. She was *scorching*.

Fuck him, this was *definitely* going to be a challenge. He wanted to pet every inch of her skin until she was boneless underneath him.

"*Slate.*"

"Good, Daniella?" He shifted his weight, stroking one hand up her torso and ribs, over the textured lace of her bra until he could crawl the tips of his fingers under the material and tease her nipple.

"Oh *god,* yes." She arched into his hand, undulating under him, pressing closer to his knee. Her breathing turned ragged, a personal symphony, and her hands gripped him, fingernails biting into his back.

"I want you so bad, I can't think straight," Slate rumbled, dragging his mouth down her collarbone, along the swell of her breast.

"Then let's just—"

"No," he laughed raggedly, lips brushing over her skin as he spoke. "It's a challenge." God, she was *not* making this easy.

Dani let out a little sound of frustration, and his resolve wavered for an instant. "I promise, it will be worth it," he said.

"I'll hold you to that," she retorted, her voice breathless.

Slate grinned at her. "I'd expect nothing less." He stroked a hand over her skin again. "Can I just... I just wanna touch you."

"You can touch me all you want," she moaned, and her hips rolled beneath him. Heat shot through him, right down to his cock.

Drawing in a breath for control, he pushed back and reached down to undo the buttons of her jeans. He surprised himself with the steadiness of his hands. "Lift your hips," he whispered to her, the sound a little more ragged than he'd anticipated.

She complied, lifting her hips and shimmying out of her jeans. He tossed them aside and pressed his mouth to her hip bone. She squirmed, gasping his name, the sound of it sending his heart into his skull. *More, more, more,* it pounded through him incessantly. The intensity of his need choked him, his lungs sticking to his ribs. He skimmed his hands over her skin, following his mouth, until he was kissing her again. She arched up, bringing them skin-to-skin and it was so good, a groan escaped him.

It was mouth-sex. Her hands were ceaseless across his back and shoulders, shaping every inch of him as though she couldn't get enough of him—just like he couldn't seem to stop touching her. He slipped his hand down her body once more until he could cup her sex through her underwear. She ripped her mouth away from his in a stuttered gasp.

She was absolutely *soaked,* right through the fabric. Heat flushed through his head, making his brain spin in his skull before it rushed right to his cock. "Oh shit, you are so fucking *wet,* fuck. You gonna come for me, love?"

"Probably..." A near-sob escaped her. She ground her hips into his hand, body tense. "*Slate...*"

Arousal choked up his throat in ragged, pulsing anticipation. "*Yes,* Dani, *louder...*"

She cried out, body thrashing under his as his hand worked her into an orgasm. Her fingernails bit into his back, and her hips bucked. He scratched his teeth along her shoulder again, sucking the skin, swirling his tongue. He could practically *taste* her ecstasy, lights and colors woven in the sound of it. The heat between them was a drum in his throat; he'd sell his soul to banish this stupid scrap of underwear.

But he didn't want to rush her, rush them. The sexual chemistry between them was heady—the whole purpose of the ten-date rule was to curb the intense spark between them.

Sexual intensity aside, Slate liked to date women, for the most part. And he was very much enjoying dating this one in particular.

She came down slowly, only her heaving chest moving as she went limp. All that was left was the echo of racing hearts and uneven breathing around them. Finally, her hands loosened their death grip, drifting down his spine.

"That..." she whispered, "was probably the best orgasm of my life. And my clothes are still on."

He grinned against her skin. "A+ wow factor?"

She laughed weakly. "Yeah, that definitely... yeah. A+ wow factor."

He shifted his body off hers, turning to lay beside her, head propped on his hand. She shifted too, until they were facing each other. His breath escaped him at what he saw. "Your eyes..."

She blinked. "What about them?"

He reached out his free hand and touched her face, leaning closer. "They're sorta... glowing..." It wasn't a trick of the light. The outermost edge of her eyes was rimmed iridescent green, like how a cat's eyes catch light in the dark, but not as intense. A memory assaulted him—the night after the Den when the High Fae found them. He remembered seeing something strange about her eyes then too. Was it magic?

"Are they?" She tilted her head a little, the gesture reminiscent of the animals she communed with. She popped off the bed to hurry over to the vanity on her dresser. She flipped the switch to the small lamp next to her bed as she went, and Slate's attention instantly snagged on her ass as she leaned forward to inspect herself in the mirror. His perusal was cut short when she twisted around to glance at him with raised brows.

The effect around her eyes was gone, and once more he saw only lovely gilded green. Slate shrugged. "It looked like the edges of your eyes were glowing, just a little."

She glanced back at herself, wrinkled her nose, and turned back to him. Seeing her front in the soft light, he noticed she had a small paw print above her panty-line, on her right hip, far smaller than the griffin feather down her spine. She noticed his glance, and her grin was impish as she plopped down on the side of the bed. "It's Dash's paw print. He's family, you know? Just like how I have Sellie's feather on my back," she added with a little jerk of her thumb over her shoulder.

He smiled. "I like that. I'd love to get some tattoos, but Japanese people are... *particular*."

"Oh?" She cocked a brow.

"Yeah. It's... not proper to get a tattoo. People might think you're part of the *Yakuza*... like, the Japanese mafia."

Dani's lips twitched into a smile. "Ah. I see. Bet your grandmother would love that."

He frowned in thought. "Shit, maybe I *should* get some then."

She laughed, then leaned over to switch off the light. The bed dipped as she shifted to lay down opposite him, mirroring his position. As his vision adjusted to the dark, he found her face in the shadows. Even then, she was so *beautiful*. He had to curl his fingers into the sheets to keep from reaching for her again.

"Why is it," he laid the words gently in the dark between them, "that I feel like I could burst out of my skin just being around you?"

"Because I'm an incredible woman who's complex and mysterious and oh-so-sexy?" Her grin was evident despite the dark, but he thought he heard a catch in her voice.

He chuckled softly. "All those things." A beat of silence, then, "It's not just me, right?"

She didn't respond right away, and his lungs caught.

"No," she whispered. "I feel it too."

Slate woke up early, the barest rays of sun sneaking in through the window. He wasn't sure what had awoken him. He lifted his head slowly to survey the room. He saw the flash of a copper tail disappear out the door. Ah, that must've been it. He'd felt the fox stir.

Sometime in the night, he and Dani had shifted. They weren't exactly spooning, but he had an arm thrown over her hip and their legs were tangled together slightly. He was still shirtless, and sometime in the night, she'd stolen his tee-shirt.

He dropped his head to settle back into sleep when a little nose peeked back into the room. Dash stared at Slate for almost a full minute, then stared at Dani, before he let out a soft yip and spun in a circle.

He recognized it as the universal sign of '*get up, I need something.*'

Dani shifted slightly and the fox got all excited, panting and tapping his little feet in a quick rhythm against the floor, and he gave another yip.

"I'll do it." Slate pressed his mouth to her shoulder.

"Don't..." she mumbled. "He can do it himself, he's just needy." He saw a ghost of a smile on her lips, but her eyes remained closed.

Slate chuckled. "Well, it's not often I get to play with a fox. You sleep, I'm awake anyway."

Dani mumbled something like 'good luck,' before snuggling deeper into her pillow. He almost wanted to stay just to watch her sleep, but that would have been creepy, so he slipped from the bed instead. She muttered something else unintelligible and rolled into the warm spot he'd vacated, tugging the covers up and over her head. He smiled and shook his head at her. Clearly, she wasn't a morning person.

Slate left the bedroom on silent feet. Everything was quiet in the house, the quietest it'd been yet. He glanced around carefully as he navigated his way to the kitchen, following Dash, who didn't seem at all pleased that Slate was the one who'd gotten out of bed. The raccoons were sleeping on the couch, and the little family of squirrels from the night before were gone, presumably outside to forage for food.

In the daylight, her house came alive with color. Subtle but tasteful, each room a different muted hue—cerulean, sage, and woody browns. It was earthy, calming; a space where nature blended seamlessly with a man-made structure in a way that tickled a sense of nostalgia in him.

The kitchen was small but well-organized. Slate felt a little awkward as he rustled through her cabinets, looking for a glass or a mug. He snagged one from the third cabinet he checked, rubbing at his temple with his other hand. He still had the ghost of a headache right behind his eyes. He had painkillers in his bag, but perhaps water or caffeine would cure it first.

Stress headache.

He found a bag of coffee and blanched at the smell of it. He hated coffee. So bitter. But in the same cabinet were a bunch of different teas, so he grabbed one and set the kettle on the stove.

The little fox was sitting right outside the demarcation between the living room and the kitchen, his red tail swept around him, watching Slate. Slate cocked his head and watched back, crossing his arms over his bare chest. Dash blinked—one eye, then the other.

"You are awfully cute," Slate settled on. "I bet you'd get along swimmingly with my friend Kari. She's a..." A little flash of hurt stuttered in his lungs. "She's a bit of a fox herself. Figuratively and literally, I guess."

Dash continued to watch him with that unwavering, predatory stare. Then, without a change in expression whatsoever, he turned tail and trotted off out of sight.

Alright. Slate had a sneaking suspicion he was being weighed and measured by the little fox, and all Dash's musings were probably being back-filtered to Dani.

Tea boiled, steeped, and the first blissful sip taken, Slate wandered through the house. The sliding door to the backyard was cracked open, with a little cut-out in the bottom of the screen located right at the slender gap, which was open just wide enough for a fox or a raccoon to sneak in.

The morning air was crisp, fresh, and quiet. Slate pulled it deep into his lungs as he stepped outside onto the back patio. Summer was coming fast—the cool nights would be little more than a refreshing memory in a handful of weeks. He stretched, careful not to spill his tea, his body tight. The memory of last night came into sharp focus. Dani's fingers digging into his skin, her body arching under his, the sound of his name...

He needed to stop thinking about it or he'd give himself a hard-on.

How she'd come off the bed as her body erupted...

He buried his face in his mug. *Stop thinking about it, Melisande, or you're gonna be in trouble.*

He couldn't though. She occupied all his thoughts. He felt so *charged* by her, like she awakened something in him. Every moment they spent together felt less like he was getting to know her and more like he'd always known her. Her spark, her soft kindness, her warmth—everything was easy and effortless. Even last night, from storming through the streets and suddenly finding himself at the doorstep of her work, to tangling together in her sheets. All of it had felt *right*.

He caught a flash of orange in his periphery, and looked down to spot Dash zipping past him. He had something in his mouth, which revealed itself to be a filthy green tennis ball when the little fox zipped back to drop it at Slate's feet.

"You wanna play fetch or something?" Slate asked, lips quirking as he crouched down to grab the ball. Dash snatched the ball back and ran around the yard, madly gnashing at it with his teeth. "Well, bring it here, you silly thing, and I'll throw it for you."

Dash ran a few more circles before he dropped the ball by Slate's feet again. No sooner did he reach for it than the little fox snatched it again and ran with it. He chuckled. "You're teasing me, aren't you?" he said. "Payback for kicking you out last night, huh? Come here, I bet I can throw it farther than your mama."

Finally, the fox came back and let Slate pick up the ball. Dash sat beautifully poised, waiting, his gaze fixed on the tennis ball. Slate threw it hard. That fox was fucking fast, darting off after the ball, bounding the last few steps to catch it. He came zipping back, but stopped a few feet in front of Slate. He dropped the ball and sat, watching him. Slate watched him back. A minute crawled by... two minutes... He wondered if the fox was thinking about whether or not Slate was worthy of another round of fetch.

Finally, Dash nosed the ball closer until Slate could reach it. He picked it up and zinged it again. He let out a startled laugh when Dash took off so fast that he tripped and tumbled a little. Regaining his footing, the little creature snatched the ball and trotted back towards Slate.

"Damn, are you alright?" Slate chuckled. "You just ate it so hard."

Dash yipped, spun in a circle, then once more sat and waited for Slate to throw the ball. They did a few more rounds of this before movement caught Slate's attention. His heart flinched into his throat before he realized it was only Sellie making her way into the backyard.

"Well, good morning," Slate said to her. "Are you well-rested?"

She clicked her beak at him, making her way to a sunny patch in the yard. He was startled when images impressed into his mind of lovely warmth and the sensation of flying, but later in the day. The images were crystal clear in his mind and he wondered if that was how Dani's magic worked for all of her animal friends. She'd told him that magical creatures as sentient as griffins could communicate with folk as they pleased.

Slate supposed it was an honor that Sellie deemed to speak to him.

The griffin ruffled her feathers in a regal fashion and settled herself in a nice sunny spot in the yard, bread-loafing like a cat with all her limbs tucked under her body. She watched lazily as Slate launched the ball again. Dash fetched it but deviated from Slate to go pounce on Sellie. He bounced around her, chattering, trying to bite her beak playfully.

Slate grinned at how cute it was, considering the fact that Sellie could eat Dash if she had a mind for it. But the griffin had no such fancies, it seemed, humoring the little fox and playing with him, tolerating his jumping and bounding and spirited little bursts of running.

A click came from somewhere above him. Slate glanced back and spotted Dani opening the upstairs window. His heart flipped in his chest at the sight of her, hair twisted over her shoulder, and still wearing his tee-shirt. It made his mind jump back once again to the night before, sending a hot shot through his blood.

"Winning the affection of my animal friends to try and seduce me into another date?" she called lazily.

"Is it working?"

She crinkled her face at him, smiling. "Maybe. Dash likes the way you play fetch, but he says he still doesn't like you."

Slate laughed, and her answering smile was genuine, real, and unguarded. It sent a shot through him in a different way, right to the center of his chest.

Shit.

Slate didn't want to dive too deeply into his own feelings. He was a little afraid it was all him. He liked to date, and he was always on the passive lookout for someone who clicked with him. No one had ever felt as effortless as Dani, and he partially wondered if the ease of them made him feel hyper-attached to her. As if his own emotions were getting ahead of him, whispering in the back of his brain something that sounded a little too close to *she's the one.*

I feel it too.

Something in the way she'd said it, like it hadn't exactly been a *good* thing...

Dani yawned and stretched. "Want to make some breakfast together?"

His smile widened. "Only if you stay in that outfit."

Another laugh rang out as her head disappeared from the window. Still smiling, Slate headed for the slider door.

They spent the rest of the day together. Slate grew quieter and quieter as the morning dragged into the afternoon. Dani had to work, so she offered to drop him off at home on her way.

He wasn't looking forward to going home.

He didn't know where to begin to pick up the pieces and patch his life back together. There was no going *back*, there was no returning to how things had been. No way to go back to normal.

He wasn't looking forward to settling into a new normal. And as the day marched on, he started to feel bitter and angry again over it. He wanted to teach his martial arts programs, work with his students, and live his goddamned life. He didn't want to keep looking over his shoulder for the High Fae, didn't want to think about the secrets that shrouded every corner of his life.

"You've grown quiet," Dani said softly. They were sitting in the living room, watching a movie. He was sitting on the floor in front of her, feeling too restless to sit idle on the couch.

"I don't wanna go home," he told her. "I don't wanna deal with Kari and Jian. I wanna be angry about it, but I'm not angry. I'm just..." He huffed out a breath and shot to his feet, anxious and restless. He paced the living room. "I'm just..."

"Your feelings are hurt," she offered, curling her legs underneath her and stroking Dash's luxurious tail.

"Yeah," he agreed. "My feelings are hurt. And that sounds stupid, doesn't it?"

"No," she assured him. "But nothing is going to get better if you don't go home and talk it out with the twins and your father." She offered him a smile, then cocked her head to the side. "Why don't we get out of here?" she suggested. "Go get something to eat, go for a walk. We can count it as another date."

His heart crawled into his throat. "Did this count?"

"Last night?" She paused, and something flashed across her face, but she slowly nodded her head. "Yes, I'm going to say it did."

"So what number would this next one be?"

"Date eight, I believe."

He grinned. "I'm game." And just like that, she made him feel calm and centered. She grounded him. Maybe that was why his feet had taken him to her work last night. Everything else swirled around him in a crazy cocktail of chaos, but she remained steady in the storm.

She made him feel like he had the world under his fingertips.

Maybe he did.

CHAPTER NINETEEN

THE SUBTLE ART OF SECRETS
PART ONE

... little more than myth itself among the mysticfolk, a hearth in the bowels of Mount Fuji in Japan is believed to be the final resting place of these creatures, glowing ever-blue...

— Gherald Schmidt, Faerloch Historical Archives

Eight dates.

Why had she agreed to this again?

For the millionth time, her mind kept circling around Slate and his ten-date rule as she sped her bike out of the Eastern District and towards work.

After last night, and how utterly gentlemanly he'd been in bed, she couldn't lie to herself; she'd panicked a bit. 'Casual and fun' was surely becoming more than casual, and that freaked her out.

But when he'd been pacing her living room, with that *look* on his face...

She'd been unable to stop herself from proposing another date. And not because she'd *wanted* to wipe the unhappiness from his expression, but because she'd *needed* to.

She should just sleep with him. He'd looked ready to cave last night; she bet she could get him to give in without too much trouble. Sleep with him and then kick him to the curb with the rest of the trouble.

Why was she even bothering with all this red tape? She should wash her hands of him—he was probably going to turn out to be more trouble than he was worth. His father was keeping secrets, his friends were keeping secrets, and he himself was a mystery, what with his wavering heartfire and the attention of the fae. So what if he had a body that made her mouth dry with sexual anticipation and a wicked grin that made her panties wet?

Goddess, the way he kissed her, touched her. It made her whole body come alive with so much *want*... and with such *intensity*.

More than that, she enjoyed him as a person. Trouble aside, he was charming and funny, well-rounded and playful, but responsible; he was just plain fun. She couldn't seem to stop herself from enjoying his company in general. They were slipping into a seamless intimacy that freaked her out more than a little bit.

Was he going to be the type that dropped an 'I love you' after they had sex? Every single man she'd dated and slept with had fallen instantly in love with her. They always wanted more. She simply didn't want anything to do with that. Bar none.

She wasn't ready for that sort of commitment. Maybe one day, she told herself, but certainly not now.

She liked the guy, but she wasn't interested in letting this become a *real* relationship. The kind where you can become deeply attached to someone, only for them to leave you.

Dani considered talking to Caroline about it, but she wouldn't understand, especially with all the magical baggage attached to Slate. Maddie would tell her to go for it, happily assuming Dani had finally found *the one*.

Roger...?

She doubted he would be able to see this from her point of view. To him, Slate was an unknown, a possible threat that could bring her to the attention of the High Fae. He wouldn't be able to give her the right advice, because his advice would be the opposite of Maddie's; drop him like a rock and walk away.

Startling steel-blue eyes and bead-tipped braids flashed in her mind, and her chest tightened with an old pain. Kat would have known what to do. Her eyes pricked with moisture, but Dani blinked the tears away and took a turn that had her Vespa wobbling a bit, shoving thoughts of her best friend away as she focused on righting the bike.

Stable once more, Dani shook her head to clear her mind. She was overthinking this and starting to get irritated at herself for it. She would... see through this ten-date rule thing, and when he started to get clingy after they had sex, she would walk away, regardless of how Slate felt. His feelings were not her responsibility.

It's just fun, nothing serious, she reminded herself. Then she could move on, and enjoy her life without the mess of mysterious martial artists and the High Fae.

Even if the thought of hurting him when she walked away made her heart twist.

Slate found himself standing in front of the Meho household, hand hovering over the door handle.

Was he ready to do this yet?

He and Dani had taken a walk through the park on the other side of the river. He thought he'd worked out most of his nervous energy, but it was coming back in full force now as he stood on the stoop. He was still pretty angry, and the idea of going home and having his father be the recipient of his lingering hurt made him want to puke, so this had to be it.

He couldn't avoid this.

He opened the door. Inhaled one steady, deep breath.

"*Tadaima...*" he called.

The response that came back wasn't Jian's rich tenor or Kari's equally rich but lighter tone, but something deeper and far more aged. More cheerful. Joon-*san.*

Joon was in the living room, sitting at the *kotatsu* with his laptop in front of him. "Slate-*kun,*" he said, smiling. "How are you?"

Slate swallowed. This man right here—someone he considered his second father, was... well. Not *mortal.* What did Joon-*san* know about his fight with the twins? "Uh, fine, thanks. Twins home?"

Joon tilted his head toward the stairs. Slate nodded and made his way there. Each step up the stairs made anxiety burst like bubbles in his chest. What was he supposed to say to these two? These two people who were his best friends, his family, as close as siblings...

His feelings were still hurt.

He felt like he'd missed something huge. Like watching a television show and missing the season finale and having to pick up with the next season. It was confusing and disjointed. His mind was constantly extrapolating information from what he knew to fill in the pieces he didn't have.

And he just felt so *stupid*. How could he have not known? Not seen? Some parts were so crystal clear within the context of *magic* that he felt unobservant and dumb.

Clueless. He felt like an idiot, big time.

It was embarrassing. Embarrassing and awkward.

He could hear their voices coming from Kari's room down the hall. Slate's steps stuttered slightly, and he debated turning around and simply leaving. But the moment he got to the door, he heard Kari say his name, beckoning him.

He slid open the door. Jian was at the desk, his laptop open in front of him. Kari was sprawled on the futon—Slate could see she was watching a show on her phone. Both twins glanced in his direction though, the moment he appeared in the threshold.

Jian tipped his chin. "Shut that behind you, *ne*? Dad's working in the living room."

Slate stepped inside and shut the door. The click of the slide sounded like a gunshot in the tense silence of the room. It spread between them, tight, anxious.

Kari broke it first. "Who's talking first?"

"I met Dani by accident in the street a few weeks ago." The words burst out of him. Everything he worked out in his head, everything he'd prepared to say, simply evaporated. "I was the last fight on the card that night, and I missed the bus. I was walking home, and a High Fae male caught me alone in the street. She and her pet griffin Sellie rescued me with a couple of well-placed iron bullets and some serious scare tactics."

"The burn marks on your hands..." Jian said. "Iron wires?"

Slate nodded, swallowing thickly. "I didn't really believe what had happened, then Dani just kept... appearing in my life, and so... she came over one day and dropped everything on me about magic and the Lore. I went with her to the Den—"

"The Den?" Kari interrupted, sitting up. "*The* Den? Like... with the really *big* female in the *dirndl* that runs the place? Loraine?"

"Yeah..." Slate stared at her. "You know it?"

"Know it? Jian and I were *regulars* in university. Haven't gone in a couple of years now..." Kari mused. "There was a guy there always... a vampire. Handsome in this plain kinda way but kind of scary."

Slate nearly choked. The description was vague, but Dani had told him how scarce vampires were, which meant... "Roger?"

"Yes!" Kari gasped. "Did you see him? He's famous or something in Faerloch; never got up the nerve to go up to him though. He's pretty aloof."

Slate nodded. "He's—he's Dani's best friend..."

"No *shit*. Wow!" Kari chuckled lightly. "Small freaking *world*."

"You know..." Jian tilted back a little in his computer chair. "I thought I recognized Dani... but I couldn't place where I knew her from. And it's been a while."

"So you went to the Den..." Kari prompted Slate. "And?"

"And..." he said, picking up where he left off. "And—and I met Roger and Dani's friend Maddie—"

"Maddie is *great*," Kari sighed, "and hot as fuck. Asked her out once, but apparently, she's married."

Slate stared, trying to get his head around the fact that his friends had known all of this—known these magical beings—and he'd been in the dark.

"Then?" Jian asked, and Slate could feel him studying his face.

Slate was quiet a moment, studying him back, before he continued. "And... and Dani and I were on our way home, and the High Fae found us again. They... they tried to kidnap us, or something? Tried pulling us into glowing circles on the ground. Dani calls them *portals*, says it's fae magic, how they get around from place to place swiftly. Roger and Maddie rescued us. Maddie said I have an allergy to iron." He held up his palms, still lightly textured and scarred. "Dani thinks I'm lorekissed, like her."

Silence greeted those last words, ringing through the room. Jian and Kari made eyeballs at each other. "That's what we think too," Jian finally said.

Slate's world narrowed down to his best friend's words. "What?"

Jian shifted slightly, tilting his chair back. He huffed a breath through his nose. "We've kinda thought maybe you were *something* a bit more *other* than just... mortal." Jian gestured to Slate. "I mean, look at you. Strong, sturdy, fast. You are a physical specimen. Your *chi* is powerful and healthy... and it's..."

"It's not uncommon," Kari picked up where Jian faltered. "We knew several lorekissed at uni similar to you. Some lorekissed have magic, some have physical characteristics. Not all lorekissed have *fae* in their lineage. Some have werefolk or witch... *lorekissed* is just a term for someone who has Lore magic somewhere in their lineage."

"We never really thought much about it," Jian added. "I mean, we knew your grandmother was a *miko*, so by the nature of how genetics work, you have *something*. But it's not uncommon around here. Everyone in this damned district has a drop of magic, especially the old families."

"But we did kind of assume you got a bit from your mom's side too." Kari shrugged. "A bit of diluted *mikoism* isn't gonna turn you into... well, what you are."

"We wondered if maybe your mom's side had something—was something—and it got passed on to you," Jian added. "Or not. Genetics are super arbitrary. But, if you were going to develop magic, you'd have known by puberty," Jian continued. "And you didn't, so it never mattered. We kept going with our lives, knowing that you were maybe a bit *other* and that *jii-san* didn't want you to know anything. A lot of families keep secrets."

"It didn't seem strange to you that my *father* was keeping secrets?" Slate demanded.

"No," Kari replied casually. "The magical community can be tedious and dangerous. It's need-to-know, Slate. There are loads of people in this city with a drop of magic in their blood who spend their entire *lives* knowing *nothing* about the magical world. You never showed anything weirder than a knack for taking more hits than the other guy and maybe a weird ability to influence a room and detect if someone lies to you. All common and innocent lorekissed tendencies. You didn't need to know."

He swallowed hard, swallowing that knowledge, the possibility that had the fae never approached him, had he never run into Dani in the street, had his entire life not flipped upside down, he'd know none of this. He didn't know if he was hurt and put-out by the idea, or angry that this all got dumped on him. "So... you weren't ever gonna tell me? Ever?"

Again, the twins shared a look.

"I wanted to," Kari said softly. "Because eventually... Slate, magic preserves the body. Jian and I... aging slows down. Dramatically. Our parents? Hundreds of years old."

His head spun. "Hundreds?" he breathed.

"Hundreds."

"They look... they look like parents to me," he continued, boggled. Joon and Anzu looked a touch older to him. Not *aged*, per se, but older.

Jian nodded. "Part of it is a glamour. Public perception of aging. Our parents don't actually look any older than we do. But eventually... eventually we will have to disappear from Faerloch. People start getting a bit suspicious when the neighbors don't seem to *age* as swiftly as everyone else."

"And you would've just... left?" Slate said, an arctic burn in his chest. "Just... left me?"

Kari pressed her lips together in a thin line. "Like I said," she whispered. "I wanted to tell you. Someday. Maybe after Ebisu-*jii-san*..."

"How old are you both?" Slate asked suddenly.

They both looked startled. "Same age as you," Jian responded.

"Really?" He eyed them both.

"Truly. We've been friends all our lives, dude. We *grew up* together." Jian's face was calm but serious, and the look in his eyes... a challenge. Jian was daring him to call him a liar.

"You've never—" The words choked in his throat. Slate swallowed hard. "Really? My age? It's not a *glamour* or some shit? You've never had to pack up and *abandon* your life before?"

"Never." Jian's stare was steady—gray to blue. "I was not looking forward to the experience. You are my *best* friend." The words sounded strained.

"*Kami*. I hate both of you sometimes," Kari said, voice thick. "Stop *feeling* so much, *ji-ji*. I'm gonna cry."

"Sorry," Jian laughed. "You feel the same way, *baa-chan*."

Slate slid his body to the floor, sitting crisscross, staring at nothing. So much rattled through his brain. The first thought that jumped into his head—this was the reason the twins didn't have many close friends. Because they would eventually outlive them. Jian and Kari had *friends*, certainly, but neither one of them was ever interested in branching out, and neither one of them had any interest in dating or settling down when that seemed to be the trend lately.

Why bother, when you'd have to pack up and leave it all behind someday? Vanish into the wind.

"We're sorry, Slate," Kari finally said. "You have to know—you have to *believe*—that it wasn't all just one big crafted *lie*. It wasn't about you. Magical families always keep secrets. It's how they survive rubbing shoulders with mortals."

He flipped his eyes to hers, then to Jian's, then back to Kari's. She was sincere; he could tell she wasn't lying to him.

Well, that wasn't entirely true anymore, was it? Apparently, there were two people who were better at lying than Slate was at sniffing out said lies.

God, he hoped they weren't lying to him anymore. He didn't know if he could handle it a second time.

"I understand." He nodded. "I didn't... I'm sorry I blew out on you guys last night. There's been so much *shit* happening—"

"Let's talk about that for a second," Jian interrupted, tilting back in his chair. "What the actual fuck is going on? The Silver Valley Council is after your ass, and you show up at my house with iron burns. When did you develop an allergy to iron? That's *very* fae lorekissed shit."

"I don't know!" Slate tossed his hands up, then ran his palms over his hair. "I dunno. It was new to me too. I've always been a little sensitive to certain metals. But this is like, a whole new bag of shit."

"Fae are after you..." Kari mused. "Why? What do they want with you?"

"You're asking the wrong person."

"Lorekissed are going missing..." Jian hedged.

"Yeah, the *female* ones," Kari retorted. "Last I knew, Slate's got the wrong hardware for that."

"They kept calling me a different name," Slate offered. "They called me Zlaet, son of Aredhel."

"Zlaet?" Jian leaned back and crossed his arms, mouthing the name silently a few times. "Well, it's kinda close." Jian shrugged and huffed out a laugh. "Wouldn't that be something, the great and mighty fae looking up the wrong name in the proverbial phone book?"

The idea pulled a startled laugh from him, which died off when he thought about that *second* name. "Okay, but listen... what if Ari and Aredhel are the same person?"

The twins sobered at that. "Heady thought," Jian mused, rubbing at the back of his neck. "We don't know shit about your mom..."

Kari angled her head to the side. "That's for sure a *jii-san* question."

"You know he won't talk about it," Slate sighed.

She shrugged. "It's worth asking again. The fae targeting you is problematic. Even if they have the wrong guy, you don't just tell the High Fae *'oh, sorry, not me!'* They won't just apologize *'sorry, chap, our mistake'* and leave you alone. Roger told you there's a *coup d'etat* happening in the Silver Valley? I've heard it's a political *nightmare* going on."

"Do you know anything, Kari-*baa*?" Slate watched her face.

She leaned back on her hands and exhaled sharply. "No, it's all rumors and hearsay. Stuff I've picked up here and there. Not my circus, not my monkeys."

"Might be your circus now." Jian gave her a pointed look. "I'd like for Slate not to be kidnapped by the Silver Valley Council."

"I'll second that motion," Slate added, raising his hand.

Kari rolled her eyes at them. "Well, I'll dig around. But until then? Slate, don't leave the district alone. There's—"

"I know, I know, there's a *ward* around the district, masking my *chi* or aura or whatever."

"It masks aura, which thankfully you don't have a big, magical presence, and fae can't sense *chi*," Jian said. "But more importantly, the ward keeps violence out of the district—it reads the *chi* of everyone who enters. Ill-intended people can't get in, for the most part. Hence why there's not much crime here. You're safer here... relatively."

"No shit. That's cool."

A beat of silence filled the room. Head spinning with too much information, Slate turned his attention to Kari. "So," he started, "is that what you *really* look like, or do you just embrace the idea that *kitsune* shapeshift into beautiful women and lure male travelers to their deaths?"

She laughed. "No, this is what I really look like. These are the *real* goods, Slate. But technically, I have three forms or... sometimes Lorefolk call them skins, especially werefolk." She winked, and just like that, the tense pressure eased out of the room. Kari disappeared to make tea, then came back and chatted his ear off about magic and *kitsune* and *manyeo*, backfilling years of knowledge.

"So, you have three tails." Slate frowned. He'd migrated from the floor to the futon with Kari, spread out on his back, staring at the ceiling. "But that's too many for someone your age?"

"Yep," she said, sipping her still-hot tea. "I have a *shit ton* of magic for someone my age. More tails, more magic."

"How many are you supposed to have?"

"Legends say like, one tail for every hundred years of life. *Ka-chan* has six, and she's hundreds of years old."

"*Damn*," Slate whistled. "Your mom does *not* look that old."

"Yep, so needless to say, I'm pretty freaking amazing." She tossed her hair over her shoulder.

It was getting late by the time Slate said goodbye. He felt so much better, the relief lending a feeling of lightness to him.

"Slate!" Kari called out from the door. He turned around in the middle of the street. "Let's go out soon—us, you, Dani too. Lunch somewhere!"

"Sure, I'm game."

"*Oyasuminasai!*" Kari called.

Slate waved over his shoulder. "Night."

CHAPTER TWENTY

THE SUBTLE ART OF SECRETS
PART TWO

... leading to an increase of changelings–fae children being raised as mortals by mortals. This trend tapered off around the mid-to-late 18th century, when...

– Gherald Schmidt, Faerloch Historical Archives

His apartment was quiet when Slate arrived. He dropped his keys and wallet in the basket on the table by the door. He peeked into his father's room. Empty. Perhaps Ebisu was up in the rooftop garden.

Nerves heightening again, Slate dumped his bag in his room and continued to the door at the end of the hall. Beyond was a set of stairs that led to the roof. He slipped on the extra pair of shoes at the door and jogged up the stairs.

He found his father in the back corner that overlooked the road and the district, tending to the strawberries. It was hands-down Slate's favorite spot in the garden. He not only had a great view of the Eastern District, but also the river and the skyscrapers of Faerloch in the distance.

"I saw you come home," Ebisu greeted him without looking up. "I was surprised, I did not expect you still for a day or two."

Slate perched on the edge of one of the boxes and snagged a ripe strawberry out of the basket next to his father. "I decided to come back."

Silence fell between them as Ebisu picked strawberries, and Slate ate them. Slate spotted his father's cat slinking through the plants a little ways away. Slate's breath caught in his lungs at the reminder that not everything was so innocent here, either.

"Have you spoken to the twins?" Ebisu asked.

"I have..." Slate hedged. He wasn't at all surprised that his father knew where his foul mood last night had spurred from, but he was now wondering what his father knew of the details. "That's where I was, actually, over at their house."

"Were you there last night as well?"

"No. I, uh... I stayed with Dani for the night."

"I see."

More silence fell between them. Slate debated how he wanted to approach the subject, if he wanted to at all. He chanced a sidelong peek at his father. His weathered face, his salt-and-pepper hair, a man who was once ageless in Slate's mind was now far frailer than he liked.

"If I ask you some questions," Slate started, "will you answer them truthfully?"

Ebisu's hands stilled on the strawberry plant. "That greatly depends on the question, my boy."

Slate's heartbeat heightened—as did a touch of anger. "Wait, does that mean you plan to *lie* to me if I ask something you don't wanna answer?"

"No. I've not lied to you before; I would not start now."

Slate rolled his memory around, searching for the truth in that statement. *Had* his father ever lied to him? Slate was sensitive enough to the tells of people lying that his immediate reaction was to think... he hadn't. He didn't have any distinct memories of Ebisu lying to him. Then again, look how well that worked with the damned twins.

"You knew what the twins were," Slate stated.

"Are you asking, or are you confirming my knowledge?" A calm question.

Slate pulled in a slow, steadying breath. "I'm confirming your knowledge."

"Then yes, I know what they are. Joon-*san* and I have been friends for an age, it seems. I met him when I traveled abroad to Japan for a semester in school. Our friendship rekindled when he and his wife moved to Faerloch and had their two children."

"And... and *obaa-san* is a *miko*? Like, with magic and everything?"

"Also correct. Which, by the nature of genetics, gives you potentially a drop of magic in your lineage."

"And you didn't want to tell me?"

"No."

"Why *not*?" Slate pressed.

"Does knowing of magic make you a better martial artist?" His father gave him a pointed look.

That question threw him for a moment. "Uh... no."

"Does it make you a better friend?"

"No!"

"Would it have somehow benefited your life up to this point?"

"*No!* In fact, it's completely fucked it up!"

Ebisu simply shrugged. "Then what does it matter if you knew? You do not possess magic, the knowledge of it does not benefit you, ergo, you did not need to know."

"But you kept this huge secret—"

"Slate." His father leveled him a look. Slate's insides pitched—a knee-jerk reaction to being on the receiving end of a look like that, usually under the context of 'training.' "Are you upset because you missed the benefit of knowledge, or are you upset because someone kept a secret from you?"

It was a loaded question, and it stifled the rise in his anger. He was certainly pissed off that the three most important people in his life were keeping secrets from him, perhaps not outwardly *lying*, but ghosting over the truth. "Perhaps if I'd *known*, I wouldn't have been surprised by the damned fae..." he muttered, knowing he sounded like a petulant teenager.

His father cut him another look, expression suddenly hard. "What about the fae?"

Slate gave him the same look measure for measure. "What do you know about them?"

A long, intense staring contest, but then the older man chuckled lightly. "You remind me—" He cut himself off, waving a hand. "It is near impossible to know about one and not have heard about the other," he said instead. "Magical communities often overlap."

Slate knew what his father had been about to say. He should push for more information, to find out more about the mysterious woman who'd birthed him, this woman his
father refused to tell him about.

He balked. Bringing up his mother historically never amounted to anything other than
a sense of painful heartache from his father. It was why Slate had never been curious
enough to know more, not if the price of knowledge was his father's pain.

"Tell me about these fae," his father said with a gesture of his hand, the hardness
returning to around his eyes.

"They've... been approaching me," Slate said carefully, choosing in that one moment
to not tell his father he'd been attacked. He wouldn't risk straining his father, not when
he was already too frail for Slate's liking. "They keep calling me a different name—Zlaet,
son of Aredhel."

He was *certain* he saw something ghost over his father's features, but it was there and
gone before Slate could pin it down. "Interesting," was all he said.

"Interesting? How is that interesting?" Frustration rose, but he forced it down.

"Is that your name? Zlaet?"

"No!" Slate exclaimed, even as the particular lilt of that name on his father's tongue
resonated in him, banging around in his head like a long-forgotten dream.

"Then it's simply interesting."

"Dani thinks... Dani thinks I'm lorekissed." The words clawed out of him, as though
they were desperate for air.

His father gave him another long, intense look, so Slate continued, "She thinks—and
the twins think it too—that perhaps I have a little drop of something from... from my
mother. Her name was Ari, right?" He watched his father closely, choosing to nudge a
little.

Ebisu turned his attention back to the strawberries. "You are not lorekissed," he said.
Slate didn't miss the tightness in those words. "And... Ari was not lorekissed either."

"You're certain?"

"Very certain."

Slate stared at his father for several heartbeats, processing. Processing what he heard,
what he'd learned, parsing through his memories from the last few weeks. His father
wasn't lying to him. He wanted to trust his father, but after the chaos that had defined
his life recently, he wasn't sure he trusted anything anymore.

Was it as Jian had said earlier? *Genetics can be arbitrary.* Dani had said her parents didn't have any magic or anything. Could his... whatever lorekissed magic he had, like telling truth from lies and being hardier than everyone else, have skipped generations?

"So... not lorekissed?" Slate pressed.

"Correct. You are not lorekissed. Neither was your mother."

"You're *sure, ossan*?" It was on the tip of his tongue to offer his palms as proof, but that would require explaining where the burns came from, and Slate wasn't ready to handle that conversation yet. He'd already had enough stressful conversations for one damned day.

"I'm sure," his father repeated calmly.

"So that's it?" Slate finally settled on. "I was kept out of the loop because magic is *need-to-know*?"

"The magical underworld is small, yet dangerous," Ebisu said. "All I ever wanted was to raise you in a safe place with friends and community. I suppose I still failed despite my efforts."

"Do you have any idea why the Silver Valley Council is... interested in me?"

Ebisu was silent for a moment, then shrugged his too-thin shoulders. "What those in the Silver Valley want is a mystery to most, my boy."

Slate sucked in another deep breath. He pulled his hair out of the tie and shuffled his fingers through it. "Does your sudden dip in health have anything to do with magic?"

This time, something most *definitely* crossed his father's features. A shade of pain, like longing and heartbreak rolled into one. But once more, it was gone before Slate could truly process what he saw. "Yes and no. It is a curse, you could say. I acquired it during my adventures in my youth. Only in the last few years have the effects begun to show their ugly tethers, I'm afraid."

Tendrils of panic crept up Slate's throat. "A curse? Can it be reversed?"

His father chuckled lightly, though Slate hardly thought this was a laughing matter. "No, my boy, nothing can reverse it. It's quite alright, I've known for a while now. Perhaps I aspired above my station, believing it wouldn't affect me. Joon-*san*'s magical herbs have certainly done wonders to keep the effects at bay, but my time in this place grows shorter."

There was something in Slate's throat and he swallowed it hard. "You aren't allowed to die on me, *ossan*," Slate tried to tease, but it sounded too thick.

His father laughed at him, though. "Death is abstract. I fully intend for my spirit to live on in this garden when the time does come." His father got to his feet slowly with the basket. "But! My time has not yet arrived, and this *ossan* can still show you a thing or two around the *dojang*. Up, up, now! I'll bet your patterns are garbage. I shall have a look at them now that the mood suits me."

Slate winced. He knew his patterns were trash right now. He'd been so focused on the fight circuit and distracted with his new and shiny relationship with Dani that he'd neglected some of his basic training and disciplines. "Can I practice first?" he asked, standing and following his father through the garden.

"No."

CHAPTER TWENTY-ONE

NO GAMES

Of the four branches of magic, the Great Goddess is believed to be the second youngest to her siblings, with the Great Spirit alone below her in Cosmic Age...

- Gherald Schmidt, Faerloch Historical Archives

"So, wait a sec," Slate drawled, tipping back in his chair. "Hold up a *minute*, here. Are you saying the two of you can *talk inside your brains*?"

"You got it," Kari said.

"All the time?"

Dani's face stretched wide into a smile as Slate slammed his chair back down on all four legs, eyes narrowed in resolute suspicion, flipping between each twin.

Kari leaned forward on the table, bracing her elbow against the surface and propping her chin in her hand. "All. The. Time." A sly smirk.

Slate's face mirrored Dani's thoughts exactly on the whole thing, and laughter erupted around the table.

Kari composed herself first. "Twin empathy plus magic. I told you," she turned to Dani, "that Jian and I are pretty much the same person across two different bodies."

"So you really do have telepathy?" Slate's amusement wound down to little more than a sharp grin.

Kari shrugged. "I guess, in layman's terms, that's what you'd call it. But it's more than that. It's... hard to describe." She glanced at Jian, and Dani knew exactly in that instance they were doing the exact thing they were discussing. "It's like a language made of images and feelings and yeah, words. Filtering through his mind is as natural to me as breathing. Jian and I have literally no secrets."

"That's so... intimate..." Dani muttered. She was torn between being fascinated and being alarmed by it. Having someone in your head all the time? There was fae magic that did that, magic that allowed someone to get inside your head and make you feel things you didn't want to feel...

"It's normal for us. We each have little mental shields, but it's like the mental equivalent of rice paper doors—it doesn't do much and you still get echoes."

"That's just not right," Slate groaned. "You each know about each other's *sex lives...*"

The day was a stunning start to the warmer months. Summer was in full swing now. The trees were green, the flowers bloomed, and the students were on summer break. The four of them were enjoying a late lunch on the boardwalk of the Riverside District, further north than the ritzy condominiums and restaurants. The food was excellent, the drinks were flowing, and the conversation was perfect.

Dani had to admit—it was a great way to spend date number nine.

She'd waffled for a few hours after Slate had texted her to see if she was interested in going out with them. It wasn't that she didn't think she'd enjoy herself, but part of her was still caught up in trying to keep things between her and Slate simple. Going out with his friends seemed to tread along the fine line between *casual* and *real relationship*.

But she was here, and it was date number nine, which meant she was one closer to getting Slate naked between her sheets. She could assess the situation from there.

Which likely would be dumping him. Which was fine.

Totally fine.

They finished their lunch and headed along the crowded boardwalk. Kari nabbed Dani's arm and tugged her along to window-shop, letting the boys get ahead of them a little. Dani humored Kari's envious sighing over the pretty trinkets in the windows, but her eyes kept drifting back to Slate. Watching as he laughed with Jian, the easy way they interacted, how Jian's collected but devious reserve somehow weirdly balanced Slate's somewhat emotional and manic temperament. It was magnetic to watch.

"That's what happens when you've been friends since the cradle," Kari commented idly.

Dani whipped her eyes to the *kitsune*, who was now shifting through a clothing rack outside the shop they'd paused at. "What?"

"Jian and Slate. How they play together. I can't even—" Kari paused, then sighed. "I can't even explain to you the depth of that friendship. The trust between them is second to mine and Jian's, and that's saying *a lot*."

"It's nice..." Dani's gaze drifted back to the boys. "It's nice to watch them. It's nice to watch two people so in sync together."

"Trouble, the two of them." Kari chuckled. "Men like them should come with warning labels."

Dani cracked a grin. "Oh? How so?"

The other woman shrugged, a subtle grace of movement that was at odds with her sly smile. "Fighters who are also lovers make for dangerous partners." She waggled her brow. "Dangerous for the heart, that is."

Wasn't that the truth, Dani thought wryly.

"Maybe not Jian as much—he's pretty collected. A little fiery underneath, a little simmer of heat and temper, but it's a shade to Slate's." Kari grinned, eyeing the boys. "I mean, when Slate was a kid, his 'otherness' made people wary of him... he got made fun of a *lot*, but as an adult? He's got this energy that's so magnetic. Maybe it has something to do with being lorekissed, but the older Slate gets, the more his energy draws people in like planets to a star."

Dani considered that for a moment, gaze once more drifting to the man in question. He caught her glance and grinned, a sharpness around his eyes once more, and she hurriedly looked away with a little flush. He had shaken her life to the core, hadn't he. She wasn't sure yet if it was a good thing.

Kari laughed softly, missing nothing. "You two are on a completely different playing field, though. And I don't say that to freak you out or anything." She held up a dress, examining it for a moment against her frame before she put it back. "I'm just telling you... I think the rules are different in whatever game you're playing."

"There's no game," Dani said emphatically. No game, other than this silly ten-date thing.

Kari made a little noise in the back of her throat but said nothing.

"There's no game, Kari," Dani repeated, a flutter in her throat that tasted a bit like panic. "It's just... he and I are just having a bit of fun, that's all."

"Oh sure, lady, I believe you. I'm *all* about that life, I've told you. I don't play games unless I set the rules." A flip of those too-smart thunderstorm eyes. "And I think you like to have rules, too. And I *also* think Slate has thrown away the playbook for both of you, and that freaks your ass right out. Because you *want* to play, but... you don't know how anymore."

Dani shook her head, feeling her throat constrict with something that tasted like shame. "There's no game, Kari. Like I said, Slate and I are just having fun." Her voice was firmer now, but she forced herself to smile a little. "I'm not looking for anything more than that, and Slate knows that."

At least, she hoped he knew that. She'd never hinted that she'd wanted anything more, at least.

"Sure, babe, I get it," Kari agreed easily enough, but Dani wondered if the budding friendship she was developing with this woman would survive when things with Slate went south.

It was only a matter of time with him. Her track record with men gave her no reason to believe Slate would be any different. Eventually, he'd start to press for more commitment than she was ready to give.

It tasted like a half-truth even as she thought about it, a little piece of her whispering that Slate was, in fact, different.

Not for the first time, she wavered about whether or not she was doing the right thing.

Slate's eyes were drawn to Dani when she and Kari returned, like a magnet drawn to its opposite charge. Her summer-green eyes caught his for a brief, heart-stopping moment, but Dani's gaze slid away from his, a little furrow between her brows. Raising a brow at Kari, he cleared his throat and asked, "Whatcha get?"

"Something sexy, of course," Kari replied breezily. "And I paid for it with the studio credit card as a belated birthday present to me, so thank you, Master Melisande, for my new dress!"

Slate rolled his eyes. "Didn't I already buy you something from Amazon?"

"Oh! Yes! You absolutely did!" Kari laughed. "But that was a *necessary* expenditure—"

"A black uniform top with pink piping is *hardly* necessary," Jian drawled.

"Listen, you chucklehead, I have a certain image to uphold when I teach."

They strolled down the sidewalk, bantering. Slate found himself watching Dani, watching the way she smiled, how her nose crinkled when she teased Jian, how her mouth popped into a wide 'O' when he pointed out an apothecary store— "I can whip up some basic remedies for you to have on hand for your animals if you want..."—and the two of them disappeared into the shop, with Slate and Kari trailing behind.

He felt Kari sidle up to him and slip a small hand around his elbow. "Picked a flighty one this time..." she mused softly.

Slate glanced at her, but she was watching Jian and Dani. Slate turned his attention back to them—Jian was whispering some conspiratorially to her as they perused the shop. Dani laughed, her face crinkling, and Slate's heart jammed into his throat.

"You think, *baa-chan*?" he said, a drop of sarcasm coloring his voice.

Kari laughed lightly. "Oh, I don't think. I *know*."

Slate said nothing. There was nothing to *be* said. He... already knew that, to a point.

It made his lungs tighten in his chest. He liked Dani. He liked her a lot. He was comfortable with her. She was one of those people that tempered him with hardly more than a soft touch and a look. He'd never met a woman who blended into his life as seamlessly as she did.

For certain, she flipped his entire world upside-down, and while a part of him still remained angry that the veil had been lifted around magic, he also felt like he was seeing the world clearly for the first time in his life. It was chaotic and complex and dangerous. But part of the magic included her, this sassy yet sweet redhead who played hero for one, single, life-altering moment.

And if he was given the choice to go back to his regular old life, and he had to trade knowing her for it?

He wouldn't.

They exited the shop with Jian ladened down with a few ingredients and a new book.

"You're such a *nerd*," Kari teased. "You are literally the only person I know who reads biology and botany books for *fun*—"

She tensed, the smile dropping from her face. A heartbeat later and a fine shimmer of tension blazed through Jian.

And Slate knew... because he could feel them too. *Fae.*

The feeling was there and gone, but for one heartbeat of time, he'd felt them as clear as he felt the air in his lungs.

The High Fae had found him again.

"Impossible," Jian whispered. "I suppressed your *chi*. Your presence should be invisible... they couldn't have—"

"We have to go," Kari said hurriedly. "Right now. The car is warded."

Jian swore. He dropped a hand on Slate's shoulder and pushed insistently. "Go. Go back to the car."

"I'll distract them," Kari said. Slate didn't miss the way she and Jian made quick eyeballs at each other, having a rapid-fire telepathic conversation over the twin mental plane.

Slate snatched Dani's hand. "Let's go." He tugged her close, linking his fingers between hers. He turned and pushed through the crowd. Her hand squeezed his hard; he could practically taste her panic in the back of his throat.

Despite the throng of people milling about, Slate met with no resistance as he barrelled through them; none of them were even glancing his way, but they all seemed to step out of his path at the exact moment he needed them to. It was odd, but he was too worried about the High *fucking* Fae on their heels to care right now.

Why did this keep *happening?*

"Oh shit," Jian swore from behind them.

Slate pulled up short. Not fifty feet away, a trio of High Fae wove carefully through the crowd towards them. Easily distinguishable from the rest of the people—Slate could see right through their glamour—pointed ears, platinum hair, and soft leather boots and cloaks as though they'd stepped right out of a high fantasy novel—

"Slate..." Dani whispered.

"Go, that way." Jian pushed them both towards a shop. "Through the shop. Go out the back, get to the car—"

"Wait, Jian!" Slate twisted around. He saw a hint of muted orange ghost through Jian's eyes, and he could've sworn a tendril of smoke curled around his best friend's fingers.

"I'm not afraid of the High Fae," Jian growled.

A thrum of icy panic beat against Slate's pulse, indecision warring. It was Dani's hand tightening like a vise over his fingers that spurred him. Get to the car. The car was warded, get Dani out of here.

"Don't die or get kidnapped," he snarled at Jian.

"Not gonna happen. Go. Now."

Slate turned and darted into the nearest shop, tugging Dani along behind him. She was breathing unevenly, her face so pale, her freckles stood out in harsh relief against her skin. He wove through the racks, dodging patrons. Not a single one paid them any extra mind.

A tingle pulsed behind his eyes, a shade of pain.

"Come on, this way." His body moved on autopilot. He pushed through the back of the shop, into the adjoining warehouse, and out the emergency exit. The alarm didn't even sound. They found themselves in a long, dim alley, narrow enough that Slate could probably stretch his arms and touch his palms to both buildings. Crates and boxes lined one side, making the space even tighter, separating them from the mouth of the alley.

His instincts shrieked at him, an icy flush rippling down his spine. This was a bad place to be.

He pinged his eyes around. Crates and boxes between them and freedom. Behind them... a ten-foot wrought iron fence, smack in the middle of the alley, a division between properties of the front and back buildings. Beyond it, the alleyway was a straight shot to an open street—freedom.

Shadows moved at the mouth of the alley. Dani gasped, pressing closer to his arm.

Three High Fae.

"We're trapped," Dani hissed, breath stuttering out of her lungs. "We're fucking trapped..." Her eyes were limned bright chartreuse again. Her gaze shot upwards, then pinched shut.

"Talk out loud," he said. "What are you thinking?"

"Sellie..." she said through gritted teeth. Her voice was pitched a little from fear, but stable enough despite the situation. "She's coming, but she's so far away." She took another shaky breath. "And of course, I don't have my *stupid gun*." Her eyes darted around them, and he was reminded of a trapped animal.

"How long?"

Her mouth pinched into a hard line. "Too long," she responded, and her voice cracked a little.

Slate took a few careful steps back, pushing her behind his shoulder. Without taking his eyes off the approaching fae in front of them, he tried the access door they just exited. Locked.

"Nothing is gonna happen to you," he rumbled at her.

"You..." her voice shook a little, "you don't know that."

"How 'bout this," he amended. "I won't *let* anything happen to you."

"*Zlaet.*" The High Fae called to him.

"That's not my *name!*" Slate growled. Another careful, calculated step back. He didn't have to look over his shoulder to know the wrought iron fence was uncomfortably close. They'd never make it over the top, not before the fae blazed the rest of the distance between them and grabbed them.

He had to buy them time. Time for Jian or Kari to find them. Or fight his way out.

"You are a difficult male to find at best, Zlaet," one of the High Fae said with that lilting accent. "Even now, you are heavily glamoured. But we have our ways."

"Listen," Slate began, herding Dani another step back. "What do you even want with me? I haven't done *anything* to offend the fae—"

"You are to appear before the Council." They stepped ever closer. Slate's palms tingled, a burning sensation pulsing at his temples. "Your presence has been kindly requested—"

"Yeah, by who?"

"The *Titania,* Lord Zeyphar."

"Zeyphar can fuck off."

The trio of fae stopped. One of them assessed the structure of wooden boxes and palettes stacked to one side, narrowing the already-thin alley. "If you wish to bring your female with you, that would be acceptable"—behind him, Dani silently gripped his arm, her fingers like claws of panic—"I am most certain Lord Zeyphar would like to meet your lorekissed... friend."

Slate clenched his fist so hard the bones in his knuckles cracked. Something burning yet frigid pressed into his lungs at the mere *idea* of subjecting Dani to whatever mysterious hell awaited him in the Silver Valley. They would take her—over his dead fucking body.

"You can all go to *hell,*" he snarled. The crates and boxes began trembling. "You can tell this *Zeyphar* guy he can drag my fucking *corpse* to your stupid Council—"

The one fae sighed and waved a casual, dismissive hand. "We will take you by force then, Zlaet. If he puts up a struggle," he added to his compatriots, "kill his female."

A choked sound of terror from over his shoulder burst whatever cold fury was pushing on his lungs. Slate let out a single breath.

The crates and palettes *exploded*.

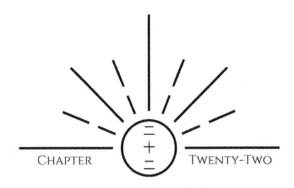

CHAPTER ⟨ ⟩ TWENTY-TWO

FOXES, FAE, AND FIRE

... of the four elements, it is often believed Fire is the most difficult to control and the least practical in the application of...

– Gherald Schmidt, Faerloch Historical Archives

Shards of wood scattered to the four winds. The fae shouted in alarm. Dani screamed, her fingers releasing their death-grip on his arm in surprise.

"Go, *go!*" Slate shouted, twisting and shoving her towards the wrought iron fence. She grabbed the metal. Slate linked his hands together for a foothold and shoved her up with everything he had. She jumped, scrambling, but she was clinging to the top of the tall gate in a heartbeat.

He followed on her heels, hissing in pain as the iron scorched his hands, but he didn't stop, launching himself up and over the top and free-falling the ten feet to the ground. He twisted his body, arms held up, and Dani launched herself from the top of the gate. He caught her and set her on her feet.

Her fingers dug into his arm again as she steadied herself. "Slate!"

"Go, go!" He pushed her towards the mouth of the alley. She gripped his hand, and he surged past her to tug her along.

"Slate, what just—"

"I don't know." He wasn't sure, he didn't want to think about it. He was focused single-mindedly on the mouth of the alley, on freedom, on her safety. His head beat to the rhythm of his heart, every step sending a bolt of pain up his spine.

He tripped. Dani's hand slipped out of his.

He hit the ground hard, breaking his fall on his forearms, jarring his shoulders.

"Slate!"

His feet were trapped in another glowing circle.

"Run!" he shouted at her, eyes trained on the fae who had simply portaled themselves from one side of the iron fence to the other. "Run, get Kari—"

Fire licked up the sides of the alley, suddenly and swiftly, blue and blazing hot.

Dani's scream bounced off the brick walls, and she ducked down next to him.

Kari materialized from nowhere in her *kitsune* form; large fox ears and three thick, elegant tails trailed her mostly human body. She flicked slender claw-tipped fingers, and a spout of flame roared overhead. Dani crouched closer to him, wincing at the heat that radiated from those ghostly blue flames.

Over his shoulder, he saw the three fae fall back a step at the assault, and the circle holding his feet weakened, before it vanished entirely.

"Go!" Kari shouted. "Jian has the car on the street! Go, go!"

Slate scrambled to his feet and booked it, snatching Dani's hand as they bolted for the mouth of the alley.

The sleek black Mercedes was waiting. Slate yanked open the back door, urging Dani inside. He looked up just as Kari slid across the hood, flipping around to slide smoothly into the front seat. Slate followed after Dani, slamming the door shut.

Jian floored it.

She couldn't stop shaking.

Dani fisted her hands together in her lap, sucking in a tight breath to try and quell the tremors. She couldn't even get words out of her throat; everything was locked tight.

What had just happened?

One minute, she'd been tucked behind Slate's shoulder, that gate at her back and his body the only thing between her and the High Fae. Then she'd felt this... surge of ice come out of him, flowing through him, like an arctic snow carried on a swift wind. A moment later, and all those crates...

Rubble. Everything in front of Slate, save for the High Fae, had been turned to rubble.

Next, she'd been over the fence, the wrought *iron* fence. She glanced at Slate's hands but looked quickly away from the damning evidence of the burns on his palms.

Then the fire. Blue fire, blazing hot and sinuous and ghostly. She wouldn't be surprised if the hair on the top of her head was a little singed.

And now she was sitting in this car, shaking like a leaf. Not a scratch on her. Sellie had just reached them, and she felt the imperious concern in her friend's thoughts as she followed the car from the sky. Dani could barely gather herself to soothe Sellie, but she couldn't have the griffin landing on the car if she got too worried.

I'm fine, I'm not hurt, she assured her friend.

She couldn't say the same for Slate, though. Aside from the scorches on his palms, his forearms were scraped raw from falling on the pavement. He had a couple of nicks on his face, too, maybe from the exploding crates.

Those *crates*.

She shook the image out of her head, squelched down the trembling fear in her gut, and glanced once more at Slate. He glanced back, but didn't smile; he seemed almost as shell-shocked as her. His nose was bleeding. His breathing was ragged and he shifted his palms to the seat in front of him, eyes closing. He was shaking too.

His chilled aura was gone once more. His heartfire was little more than embers again. It couldn't have all been her imagination...

Could it?

She'd never seen a magical being go from *zero* energy to... whatever *that* was.

Lorekissed, she reminded herself. He was just lorekissed.

And yet the feeling in her stomach didn't dissipate.

"What happened?" Kari asked gently, rotating around in her seat. She was back in her 'human' skin—no sign of tails or ears or red markings—and she scanned Slate first before turning to Dani.

Dani opened her mouth but closed it again when her throat stuck. She shook her head and tried again.

A hand rested on her knee. She flipped her eyes to see Jian reaching blindly between the seats toward her. A calming flow of magic slipped through her bones, settling her quaking and smoothing all her nerves down.

"Better?" the witch-doctor asked, glancing at her in the rearview mirror.

She hesitated a beat, then nodded. "Yes," she replied thickly. "Better." She turned her gaze back to Kari. "I don't know what happened. The High Fae... the High Fae cornered us and then... and then Slate just..."

"Jian..." Slate's voice rumbled from her left. "Brother... pull over... I'm gonna puke."

Dani glanced at Slate, and sucked in a sharp breath. He wasn't only bleeding from his nose; blood dripped from the corner of his eyes.

"What?" Jian slammed on the brakes and veered the car over. Slate barely waited for the car to come to a complete stop before he was out of the vehicle. Dani's eyes widened when Slate flew to the guard rail, bent double. By the time she'd scrambled out of the car herself, concern fueling her, he was already dry-heaving. The sound of his retching filled the air, and she placed a comforting palm on his spine.

She snatched her hand back, gasping. His skin was *blazing.* Beyond feverish. Jian appeared at her side, taking her place with an outstretched hand. He didn't make a sound when he encountered the heat coming off Slate. His face tightened, brows furrowing.

Shifting his grip to Slate's nape, Jian focused for a moment before muted orange magic, like a thin veil, rippled out from his hand. It was several breathless moments before the sounds of Slate's heaving eased, and the tremors in his body calmed, but they didn't cease entirely. He was still trembling. Something was off about his hands—the veins were too dark, tracking up his arms.

Dani couldn't stop the shiver that warred with the protective urge to put her arms around him. Warm fingers snapped her out of her stare, and she glanced down to see Kari's fingers wrapped around her arm in a gentle grip.

"What else happened?" Kari whispered to her softly, a gentle insistence.

Slate held his hands out, and Jian pressed his own palms to the scorched skin. More muted orange magic flared. Slate hissed out a painful breath.

"He..." she whispered, watching Slate intently as Jian's magic stitched his skin together, "he *exploded*. Well, not him, but the wooden boxes around him. It was..." she paused, pulling in a deep, wavering breath, "it had to be..."

"Magic," Kari finished for her with a hushed voice, looking grim as she glanced back at her twin and Slate.

Jian's gray eyes assessed Slate from head to toe and back again. Dani watched as the scorch marks faded, and the darkness in Slate's veins receded.

"What's... what's wrong with me?" Slate's voice was too gravelly, too thick.

Jian was silent for a minute. Dani finally tore her eyes away from Slate to watch Jian's tight face, her lungs stuttering in her chest.

"I don't know," the witch-doctor finally responded.

CHAPTER TWENTY-THREE

STIRRING

... telekinesis is often considered the fifth least common of the traditional fae magicks, but it is unusually prevalent—in far reduced strength—among lorekissed, leading some to cite the notorious Salaì, who cavorted with many mortals, most notably Leonardo Da Vinci. Salaì was brought up on charges of...

— Gherald Schmidt, Faerloch Historical Archives

Slate woke up in his own bed with no memory of how he got there.

Dawn resonated its soft glow through his window, illuminating his room. He lay in bed for a long, quiet moment, staring blankly out the glass, trying to pull his thoughts together.

Pieces of yesterday came back in clips and phrases. Bolting through the crowded board-walk. People moving out of his way like a choreographed dance. The feel of Dani's smaller hand in his. Kari disappearing. Jian disappearing. Running through the shop and out into the alley.

The trio of High Fae in the alley.

Zeyphar.

The explosion of wooden crates and palettes.

Slate lifted a hand and studied it. Tightened it into a fist, the knuckles standing out in sharp contrast.

He felt nothing now. Not a single tingle. Had that been magic? Had that even been *his* doing?

He couldn't deny that it had *felt* like he'd done it. Did he have some kind of latent abilities? Jian had said genetics could be strange—it was entirely plausible for him to have lorekissed tendencies, and also have it be exactly as his father said. His mother wasn't lorekissed. Dani had said as much as well; her parents didn't have any magic either. Entirely and fatally mortal, and the sadness in her voice when she spoke of them was proof of that mortality.

If you were going to develop magic, you'd have known by puberty.

Slate was further out of puberty now than he had been when he started it. He remembered hitting puberty—he'd been around 13, and the reason he remembered it so vividly was because his hair had started turning silver below his ears. A little premature graying, his father had mused.

But other than that, nothing odd had happened to him. He'd experienced puberty like every other adolescent boy—mood swings, flares of temper, a streak of aggression—all properly tempered by martial arts and his father's stern but level disposition. Textbook teenage boy. No magic.

He supposed he'd noticed a strangeness about himself in the last couple of years, but he only thought it strange now in hindsight and with the context of magic. His heightened sensitivity to metals, like iron. A restlessness inside him he could only quell inside a fighting arena. He thought perhaps he recovered from injuries more quickly than most.

He'd dismissed it as maturity, as hitting peak physical condition.

Slate flexed his hands again, but the sight of them scorched from the iron lingered in his head. He took a couple of even breaths, putting himself into a sort of meditative state he'd learned in the studio.

Waited.

Nothing. Not a stitch. Where had it come from? Was it even magic? It wasn't the exact *same* feeling, but what had come over him in the alley reminded him of the night the twins revealed their magical lineage to him. He'd felt out of control, mindless. Acting purely on instinct.

And when the High Fae had said they would kill Dani, that same mindless impulse had come over him. Times ten. Times a hundred. It had been so pure, this burning yet frigid fury. He would be *dead* before he would let the High Fae have her.

The feeling had been like a burning beacon in his chest.

Maybe he needed to ask his father again; he'd felt like Ebisu had been holding something back. And yet Slate was nearly certain Ebisu hadn't been lying when he'd said Slate wasn't lorekissed. Was his father as oblivious as he was in all this? Had genetics truly just... rolled the lottery with him, and hit a bingo?

He reached across to his bedside table and snatched his phone. There was a message from Dani, from last night. His heart did a little loop in his chest.

Dani: *I'm home safe. The twins escorted me. I hope you feel better.*

He barely remembered the drive home. His head had pounded so hard, his vision kept blacking out with every pulse. He maybe had a memory of laying somewhere with an ice pack over his burning eyes. Maybe felt someone run light fingers across his brow. After that... nothing. Blank.

He still had the shade of a headache. The same one that hadn't gone away in weeks. Always simmering behind his eyes, a distraction but manageable.

Maybe if the magic happened again, he'd talk to his father again. If it really was just wonky genetics, at the very least, his father deserved to know that Slate was more or less a ticking magical time bomb.

On the bedside table next to his phone was a tonic, and a little note from Jian—*Take this when you wake up. -J*

There was hardly more than a shot in the vial, so Slate popped the cork and downed it easily. He laid there in his bed again for a long time, drifting in and out of sleep, drifting in and out of dreams, all of them of tall, dense trees and hallways carved of stone.

When he woke up again, he didn't remember his dreams.

The next few days blended together like a fever dream. There was a qualifying match Thursday night, and Slate slipped deep into competition mode. When he wasn't teaching, he was training. He certainly didn't forget what had happened with the High Fae last weekend, and he certainly didn't forget about his minor burst of magic.

But those pieces became shades in his mind as he focused his attention forward, toward that qualifying match.

Toward what was going to be his and Dani's tenth fucking date.

He poured all his jitters into training. All his stress bled out through his running shoes or his heavy bag. Ten dates. He felt like a teenager gearing up for his first romp. His mind kept jumping back to the one night he'd slept over at her house; the sound of her, the way she'd felt under his body as he spiraled her to orgasm.

"Dude, you've got it *bad*." Jian whistled.

It was Thursday afternoon—hours stood between him and the qualifying match. Slate said nothing, letting the muffled thump from his gloved fists hitting the focus pad speak for him.

"I don't think I've ever seen you this fired up about a *woman*," Jian continued in a musing tone. "Damn, I might even be a little jealous."

A grin ghosted over his face at that. "Still my number one guy, Jian."

His best friend laughed. "I hope so! So, what? This is date number ten, right? Damn, I didn't ever make you out to be a *ten-date* kinda person. I still don't understand the point."

Slate considered that himself on several occasions. Why bother with all the red tape? He tried to think back to all the women he'd ever dated and slept with—not many, but enough—and ten dates was a long ass time to wait for sex, even for someone like him who enjoyed the process of dating women. He'd been seeing Dani now for... god, almost two months?

But the way she'd kissed him that first night right here in the studio. The intensity had rattled his bones and rattled them enough to make an impression.

"I dunno..." Slate growled. He paused, mind slipping as he focused on the combo he was doing, mind and muscles working together. "I dunno, Jian. Something's different about her, that's all."

"Something different how, you think?"

"Dunno. Maybe it's magic."

Jian chuckled. "One of the Divine Laws of magic, Slate, is you can't make people genuinely fall in love with you. Some fae have the power to manipulate emotions, but the mind is a terribly complex piece of meat between your ears. It always knows the difference. Deep down, it knows."

"Maybe she's manipulating my emotions then."

"I seriously doubt it." Jian chucked the focus pads away in favor of kicking paddles. He clapped them together hard, making a startlingly loud *thwap*. "Maybe she's your one and only." He waggled his brows. "Your umm... well, we call it *Tamashoko*."

"*Tama*—what?"

"*Tamashoko*," Jian repeated as Slate kicked the paddles light and fast. "Like, the one person tied to you by the red thread of fate and shit. Lore has the same concept, different species just call it different things. Werefolk call it *mates*, fae call it *mayts*... the one person who is your heart and soul in another body."

"That's not... no," Slate settled, feeling a little flush creep over the back of his neck.

"I'm just messing," Jian laughed. "I've just never seen you so wrapped up, that's all. Besides, I'm not sure if there is a term for whatever there is between lorekissed. Maybe they don't have fated people. Maybe there's too much mortal in them for it." He tipped his shoulders in a shrug.

Slate didn't reply. Dani was different, that was for sure. He liked her a lot. Like... *a lot*, a lot. It was more than the intense sexual chemistry between them. It was in the ease of their conversations, how effortlessly he orbited her, how it seemed like she wasn't invading his life but rather fulfilling her designated place within it.

And that *comfort* is what stopped him from pulling the trigger on canning the ten-date stipulation. Because—as amped as he was, certainly, for the sex—he didn't want it to simply *be* just sex. He wanted to *date* her, to *know* her.

He wanted to hang out with her. All the time.

"Alright," Jian said. He dumped the paddles and clapped Slate on the shoulder. "You ready for tonight?"

"Yep."

"How do you *feel*?" The pointed way Jian said it gave Slate pause.

"I don't feel strange or anything," he replied with a small shrug. He fisted his hands and studied them. "Nothing strange or weird. No random magical bursts."

Jian huffed out a breath through his nose and gave Slate a once-over. Slate knew his best friend was assessing his *chi*, seeing things Slate couldn't even fathom. "Alright. Well..." He tapped his fist against Slate's shoulder. "Eat, relax, stretch. You, my friend, have a match to win tonight."

Again.

She'd been unable to say 'no,' again.

After the encounter with the fae, Dani had been ready to wash her hands of Slate, to walk away from the phobia of fae he kept bringing into her life. Sure, when they'd managed to make it safely home in the Eastern District, it had been hard to leave him and go home, even though Jian had assured her he was safe. Sure, she kept thinking about him since then. But she'd also started having nightmares again, nightmares of the fae stealing into her room, leaving her upright and screaming in the dead of night.

But then he'd asked her to go to his qualifying match, and she'd answered before she could even process it.

Sure, I'd love to!

And it was true, even as her chest tightened at the memory of that magical explosion in the alley. Despite the terror he inspired because of the fae that kept coming into his life, she'd *wanted* to see him again.

And she wasn't ignorant of the fact that it would be date number *ten*.

Suffice to say, Dani was nervous.

It was a *good* nervous, she'd decided. Good nervous in that her heart wouldn't stop fluttering in her throat. Good nervous in that her mind kept drifting over finally, *blessedly*, getting that man naked.

Goddess above, it was going to be so good.

Good enough to banish the cold fear inside her at the memory of the exploding crates. Good enough that she hadn't brought herself to tell Roger about the incident with the fae.

She didn't want him to succeed in talking her out of this, knowing she was putting herself at risk every time she was with Slate outside of the Eastern District. And the match *was* outside the Eastern District.

Her heart fluttered right into the pit of her stomach—lower, even. Her body was absolutely amped. When was the last time she had a little action? Must've been at least a year ago now. She didn't exactly date a lot of people, in general. 'Date' being a generous term for it.

She'd known from the first minute she'd interacted with him that Slate Melisande was going to be a *wicked* soul in bed.

She met him and the twins at the studio, and just as they had the first time she'd come to a fight-night, they walked over the pedestrian bridge towards the arena. She could tell Slate was amped; she could feel the energy pouring off him. But it was a different energy than the one that had rippled off him in the alleyway, a heat rather than a burning cold. He kept sneaking little glances at her, and a small part of her was almost ready to tell him to take her in the locker room, right against the wall of some bathroom stall.

She refrained—barely—and thankfully found herself immersed in the matches preceding Slate's. Kari made for a lovely distraction too, constantly in Dani's ear, explaining the rules and the nuances. It was complicated enough that it gave her something to focus on, rather than imagining Slate's sweaty chest above her.

To which all her focus promptly gave up the ghost when Slate came prowling down the aisle for his cage fight. She was caught between marveling at his easy, graceful strength and the chilly aura that seeped off him. It was colder now than the heat from earlier, like he'd narrowed his focus with deadly intent since she'd last seen him.

Her mind flashed back to the alley, to when the boxes and palettes had exploded. To Slate leaning over the guardrail and dry heaving as magic choked his body for the first time. And a shade of fear closed over the pulse of arousal that raced through her blood.

Fae.

Slate wasn't fae. He was lorekissed, with some potentially latent magic now bubbling to the surface. He looked mortal. He felt mortal—for the most part. His father was *very* mortal. Lorekissed. Everyone thought so. And Dani assured herself that Roger would certainly know otherwise, and Jian and Kari would too.

Even if the taste of the cold energy that had come off him had been so much *like* the High Fae.

Those sapphire eyes flipped in her direction, catching her gaze. The barest ghost of a smile curled his mouth, his face softening a little bit. The fist around her stomach eased, and her entire body reacted to that look.

Dammit, how could he affect her this way? She couldn't stop watching him.

He took a mouth guard from Jian and entered the cage. The match began.

All of the other matches faded from memory as Slate's sinewy moves and grace lit up the ring. It was mesmerizing, far more exciting than the previous match. Round one was decided quickly, then during round two, Slate took a hard hit to the head. Gasping, Dani shot from her seat, pulled up as though tethers yanked at her as a protective urge swelled in her chest.

Gritting her teeth, she forced herself back into her seat, ignoring Kari's smirk. Slate was swaying on the spot, and her fingers curled in her lap. The ref separated the two fighters, and she knew the entire arena was watching with bated breath to see if Slate would hit the ground.

He braced one hand against the cage and shook his head a couple of times. His mouth was bleeding. She could hear Jian talking to Slate: *"Breathe, breathe, you good? Come on, brother, you got this, shake it off..."*

She could have sworn a light simmered deep in his eyes, like the glow coming through a thick, deep glacier. He focused that intensity on his opponent, and Dani tracked him as he paced back to the center of the ring, shaking out his hands. The ref asked if he was well enough to carry on, to which he nodded, and the match continued.

In a series of moves that was difficult for her to even follow, he won by a technical knock-out in the third round, just as he had before, securing himself a spot in the championship title fight that would take place in just over two weeks.

The crowd was insane, on their feet, cheering, screaming, stomping, and clapping. Slate pulled his mouth guard out and gave a sharp, wicked smirk for the crowd as the ref grabbed his arm and thrust it into the air in victory. And once more, his iridescent eyes caught hers, and Dani's throat dried out with sexual anticipation.

Goddess help her.

CHAPTER TWENTY-FOUR

WORTH IT

... is believed to be magic before magic, chosen at the inception of the Cosmos...

- Gherald Schmidt, Faerloch Historical Archives

The twins pushed for a celebration round at the izakaya again—"We're going to the *finals again!*" Kari squealed—and it was all Dani could do to nod and go along with it when all her body wanted was to tangle itself with Slate's.

Watching the way he'd fought had amped her sexual frustrations to a new height, and she was practically chomping at the bit.

But what was another hour? She'd waited ten whole dates, she could wait an hour.

That hour crawled by. She enjoyed herself, but couldn't stop watching the clock. She could feel the sexual anticipation pulsing off Slate like a wild, chaotic hum. A countdown was ticking between both of them.

Kari and Jian bade them goodnight with little knowing smirks on their faces, but Dani couldn't bring herself to care about it, not when she was nearing the finish line. Slate opened the side access door to the studio. He ushered her inside, and faster than she could process, the door was shut and her back was against that door.

They both simply detonated.

Kissing, devouring, burning alive.

She melted into him, looping her arms around his shoulders, a moan escaping her.

Finally, her body cried out at the feel of the hard lines of his body pressing into the soft ones of hers.

"I've literally not stopped thinking about this for *days*," Slate muttered, kissing down her neck, shoving his hands under her clothes, skating rough palms over her skin. She arched into the touch, so ready for it that it felt like her skin was alive with sensation at every brush of a callused finger.

"I almost asked you to take me in the locker room before your fight," she confessed, and her breathing stuttered when he pressed his lips to her left shoulder and sucked at the skin there. Heat speared between her thighs, and she squeezed them together with a whimper.

"Holy *fuck*, I would have." The heat of his breath was a brand on her flesh.

She let out a ragged laugh, fingers gripping at his shoulders. "I know."

He pulled his head back, but before she could complain, he was tugging at her shirt, pulling it up and over her head. She didn't see where he tossed it before he tugged her deeper into the studio. Halfway up the stairs, he lost his shirt too. She hadn't even recovered from the feel of his bare chest against her skin before her back was once more against a door, this time the one leading into the apartment proper. His lips found hers again, and he was *devouring* her. Her head spun. *Goddess*, how could anyone be this good of a kisser?

His hands roamed over her torso in a ceaseless caress, molding her lace-covered breasts in his palms, dipping down to squeeze at her jean-covered ass. He pressed his knee between hers, and the pressure of his thigh against her molten core tugged a gasp from her, head falling back against the door. "Slate..." she moaned, low and helplessly.

His hand twisted the door knob. The door gave way behind her. He guided her backward through the threshold and gently shut the door behind him. The snick of the lock snapped like a gunshot, the only other sound their frenzied breaths.

They both froze.

Slate covered her mouth with his hand. "My father's home," he whispered softly into her ear.

She peeled his fingers away from her mouth. "I'll be *extra* behaved then." At least, she'd try to. She was struggling not to snatch at him and rip the rest of his clothes off.

He grinned, that edge returning to his eyes, a hint at the wickedness he could promise between the sheets. Dani had to press her thighs together, her breath turning even more shallow.

They crept down the hall on silent feet, past Ebisu's room. Slate stopped and peered inside. A soft sound greeted her ears—some kind of gentle noise machine playing quiet sounds of nature. Slate nodded once as though he were satisfied with what he heard and slid the door shut, and they moved onto his room.

The door was opened, shut, and locked with a speed that made her dizzy. Slate pulled her against him once more, mouth going for her throat. She gripped at his shoulders, marveling at the way his muscles bunched beneath her fingers.

More. She wanted *more.* She arched into him, tilting her head back to give him better access. "Goddess, fuck me already," she moaned. "Right here, right now."

He slid a hand over her breasts and along her collarbone until his palm gently encircled her throat in the softest gesture that was more than a touch too possessive. She should've been alarmed by that touch, but she couldn't bring her passion-soaked mind to care about anything but the feel of his erection nudging at her bare abdomen, the heat of him muffled by the thin material of his shorts.

"Are you staying the night?" he asked, pressing a kiss to her jaw as he tilted her head the way he liked. His hand stayed on her throat, but his hold was oh-so gentle.

Tender, even.

Her breath seized in her lungs for a heartbeat.

"Are you going to make it worth my while?" she retorted, her heart hammering as *casual and fun* flashed desperately in her mind.

Slate nodded slowly, a hunger in his eyes that darkened them to cobalt, and his lips pulled back into a wicked grin that had liquid heat pooling in her core. Her knees went a little weak beneath her, but his other arm anchored her securely to his hard frame.

"Then... yes." She traced her hands over his heavily-muscled chest and up his shoulders—how could anyone be sculpted like him and not be a professional underwear model or something? "Don't disappoint me, Slate Melisande," she murmured, her own lips curling into a smile that clearly said *come hither*.

"Oh, I don't plan to, love." And he captured her lips. His tongue slid against hers, and a moan slipped free, her fingers tightening on his shoulders.

He guided her backward until the backs of her knees hit the edge of his bed. Her ribs tightened with anticipation.

She dropped back with a gentle shove from him, and let out a little squeak when she bounced and found him blanketing her in a flash, his heavier body settling over hers and pressing her deliciously into the mattress. His lips found hers again, devouring them as he anchored himself with his forearms planted on either side of her head.

She arched into him, craving even more of him as her bare stomach slid against the ridges of his abs. "More," she demanded in a whisper, a whimper escaping when he shifted enough to grind his heavy erection against her thigh. Then he was moving down. Down, down, *down*, his mouth forging a devilish path from her jaw, down her throat, between her breasts, along her belly, and past her navel. She couldn't draw an even breath.

He had her shorts off with an efficiency that would have won him an award, tugging them down her legs and tossing them over his shoulder without taking his eyes from her. His dark brows rose and he exhaled slowly in appreciation, gaze flitting between her dark green bra and her matching emerald thong. "All dressed up for the ball." He fingered the edge of the lace that hugged her hips.

She flipped her long mane out from under her shoulders, spreading it out along the mattress. She didn't miss the way his eyes snapped to the motion, lingering on the spread of red-gold locks against his dark sheets. "You like?"

He shrugged indifferently. She didn't have time to be properly offended before his mouth was over her skin again. His teeth scratched against her hip bone. "I like all of you," he rumbled with a wicked smirk, and liquid fire sizzled under the skin that he brushed with his lips. "But skin is better."

Dani's lungs stuttered as he hooked his fingers along the waistband and pulled the scrap of lace over her thighs, dragging the material deliciously against her heated skin. She was so wet, it was embarrassing, but she laughed breathlessly when he made a little show of throwing her panties over his shoulder with a whip-like gesture. And that laugh pittered out into a gasp when he looped his palms behind her knees and tugged her right to the edge of the mattress, spreading her wide for him. He settled down on the floor. Her cheeks flushed at such intimate exposure, but she was too aroused to try and cover herself, could do nothing but grip at the sheets beneath her hips.

He hooked her legs over his shoulders and the sight of him...

Like a man who didn't plan to get up for a while.

Her core clenched, and she knew he'd be able to see how much wetter he'd just made her, and he hadn't even touched her yet. "Oh Goddess..." she breathed, eyes locked on him as he slid his hands up her legs, skimming his fingertips towards the inside of her thighs. Her toes curled, mouth dry from raw anticipation. He was sin incarnate, wholly focused on his task. She couldn't stop herself from squirming, about to explode from want.

"Please," she found herself begging in a whisper, her hips rolling.

He flipped his eyes to her, a little grin quirking the side of his mouth. "Don't like the build-up, love?"

"I'm losing patience," she growled, about ready to touch herself and find some release from the fiery pleasure building in her body.

That grin widened a little and by the Goddess, could he possibly be sexier? Thoughts flew out of her head when he sucked a finger into his mouth, not breaking eye contact with her, and slowly, torturously slowly, ran that single finger along her sex. His eyes dilated with visible pleasure, and it intensified her own as sensation rippled through her from that small touch. She let out a ragged gasp, hips rolling helplessly, but he stilled her with his other hand, an effortless show of power as his finger moved back up through her folds.

She might die before this even started.

"Fuck me," he breathed. "Look how fucking wet you are right now..."

"*Slate.*"

He answered her by trading his finger for his mouth and she cried out, remembering belatedly to muffle her own voice with her palm. The pleasure was overwhelming, and she was immediately teetering on the edge of an orgasm. Her fingers gripped the sheets with desperation as her head fell back against the mattress.

He let out a sound that might have been a growl, and then buried his face against her, his tongue spearing inside of her with a strong thrust, and her entire body exploded. Her cry was muffled by her hand, and she nearly came off the bed. His hand on her hip tightened, pinning her as he ravaged her with his tongue and lips, licking her up until she thought she might die. Again. And again.

Dani's entire body was on fire, and she jerked, the pleasure bordering on pain, and she reached down to tug at his hair. "I can't..." she begged, wrung out, and he finally released her, a savage grin on his face as he surveyed her boneless body.

She was still trying to catch her breath when he stood and she watched—trying to even *think* straight—as he divested himself of the rest of his clothing. He moved in sure, confident motions, revealing a body sculpted to absolute perfection. Goddess help her, he was a *specimen*, wasn't he? Peak physical condition. Her eyes raked over him, from his broad shoulders down his chest, the planes of his stomach, then *lower*...

Her insides pitched, intense need swallowing her once more. Her skin flushed, and she couldn't focus on anything else but him. Right now. She needed him inside her this second.

Slate braced his hands against the mattress again and crawled over her. She slipped her hands over his shoulders, down his back, craving his skin, craving the feel of him. He kissed her at the same time as he pressed his hips into hers and they both moaned as the scalding heat of his erection slid against her drenched sex. She rolled her hips with desperation at the same time that he shifted his weight away, and she heard one hand reaching blindly for the bedside table.

"Don't bother," she gasped, undulating her hips against his. "I have a fertility enchantment. It's like... like magical birth control..." His mouth on her neck made stringing thoughts together entirely too difficult. "... and people with magic in their blood don't get human diseases, like STDs and stuff."

He pulled his face back, giving her a look, brows furrowed. "Wait, what? Really?"

She glared at him impatiently. "*Yes*, really. Can you imagine a vampire with a cold? Or herpes for eternity? Now shut up and kiss me."

He kissed her, but before her toes had finished curling, he pulled back again. "Even lorekissed?"

"*Magic in the blood*, so yes. Less talk. More sex." She wanted to feel *him*. Only him, sliding in and out of her, burning flesh against burning flesh. She *needed* it, and she let him know it as she arched her back.

He chuckled wickedly. "Alright. Good enough." His voice was deep, hoarse with his own driving arousal. It was a heady sight, the way he looked at her like he couldn't wait to be thrusting between her thighs. Her core clenched, and he leaned back slightly. He pushed her further up the bed until he could kneel between her legs. He braced one hand on the mattress by her head and fisted his cock with the other. Seeing his own hand wrapped around his erection made heat spiral through her, and she couldn't help but shift her hips eagerly. She nearly came off the bed when he rubbed the head of his cock against her aching flesh.

He flipped his eyes to her and shifted until he was pressed right against her entrance. He stopped, watching her, and Dani gave a quick jerk of her head, eagerly trying to move on him with her hips. A slow grin spread over his lips, breaking the intensity with which he'd been watching her, then he looked back to his cock as he slowly pushed it inside of her.

"Your self-control is *killing* me..." she complained, undone.

He gave a breathless laugh, just before he wedged the head of his cock inside her and both of them had to take a moment as pleasure overwhelmed them. Slate let out a harsh breath, and Dani whimpered, head falling back as the thickness of him sent her nerves haywire.

Then he was pushing inside her, a bead of sweat dotting his brow. "So *tight*," he hissed, shifting his grip from his cock to her hip, holding her down as he pulled out a little before thrusting back inside, planting himself deeper this time. Dani cried out, struggling to keep her voice quiet as she arched her back, offering her hips to him as she dug her nails into the muscles on his arm. He leaned down, and his mouth skittered over the skin of her neck, down to her shoulder, his hand shifting from her hip until he could slip a palm under her ass, angling her body until he was thrusting even *deeper* inside of her. She was convinced she'd combust at the easy pace he was setting.

"Faster," she begged. She arched up, thrusting her hips up and taking him in another fast inch.

He hissed through his teeth. "Easy, Daniella. You're so tight. I don't wanna hurt you." His face was a mask of tortured control as he gave another tiny thrust, that bead of sweat dripping down the side of his face.

"You won't," she begged, shifting her hips. "*Please.*"

His self-control snapped a little. With a final, powerful thrust, he seated himself to the hilt, stretching her until the pleasure became overwhelming. She thought her very bones would explode with it. This alone had been worth the wait—he turned her body into pure warmth and softness and delirium, ready to burst out of her skin with need. Slate pulled back his hips, and she moaned, spreading her legs for him as he thrust back inside. He bit back a curse, then widened his knees for better leverage as he started an easy rhythm of thrusts sure to destroy her. Pleasure licked up her spine. She wanted this, *needed* this, she wanted to drown in the feeling of him—

Tension vibrated through him. A responding heat flushed through her skull.

"Oh *fuck*..." he groaned. His hand on her hip tightened, pinning her, holding her in place as he plunged inside her. The rolling rhythm of his hips faltered a little, faster, slower... then faster again... she could feel his body swelling inside her...

"*Yes*..." she breathed, digging into his shoulders, sliding her fingers along his spine.

He growled her name as his thrust became frenzied, wild, enough to make her breasts bounce, and she forgot to be quiet as she cried out, clinging to him as he came undone above her, fucking her with a touch of crazed abandon.

She shattered, harder even than when he'd thrust his tongue inside of her. She shattered into a million pieces, and all she could do was cling to him to weather out the storm of pleasure that ripped through her.

Slate's thrusts ebbed, then he stilled, his face pressed into the side of her neck, his breath a rapid tattoo against her skin. She was liquid beneath him, melting right into the mattress. There was nothing between them but heartbeats and raw breathing. Slowly, Dani loosened her vise grip on his skin, letting her hands skim over the taut muscles in his back as she trembled a little from the sheer force of her orgasm. A shiver raced through him.

She squeaked when he moved, so suddenly she wasn't sure what had happened until she was over him, and he was flat on his back.

"You okay?" he asked, eyes flashing over her body in quick succession. "Did I hurt you?"

She couldn't help it—she laughed, shaking her head weakly. "That was the very opposite of hurt, if you couldn't tell."

He chuckled darkly.

She braced her hands against his chest and gingerly sat back, rolling her hips forward. She sucked in a deep breath, because he was still hard inside her, and he was hardening still more, filling her even deeper than when he'd been on top. He devoured her with his eyes, from her breasts—still wrapped in lace—and down, his hands resting comfortably on her thighs.

"You like a little show?" she asked him with a sensual smile. She'd never felt so sexy in her entire life, lips plumped from his kisses, skin flushed from sex. She felt *confident*. Powerful.

He stretched his body a little, tensing, then he sighed and tucked a single hand behind his head, grinning as he surveyed her. "What're you gonna show me?" Anticipation sparked across his face, and she felt him pulse inside of her.

She bit back a moan and laughed at the smugness in his expression. She rocked her hips a little, taking him impossibly deeper. He stilled, eyes darkening to midnight, and he inhaled sharply. He skated his palm over her body and with one expert hand, he undid the last piece of her clothing—her bra.

"Go on then," he said with a ragged breath. The garment slithered from his fingers to the floor. "Show me."

Completely naked now, she felt his eyes on her like a physical caress. A flush burned across her cheeks at the rawness of it, the potency of that stare.

It didn't last long, not when his hand cupped her breast, fingertips feathering over her nipple. She moaned his name, head tipping back. Her hips moved, rocking into his, riding him. He gasped out a string of curses, and his other hand flew to her hip.

It was deep and intense, and pleasure leached slowly through her blood, ratcheting up her body bit by bit. She was riding him much more leisurely than when he'd been riding her, but it was no less *intense.*

"*Slate...*" she moaned.

"Holy fuck, *yes...*" he growled. That hand on her breast migrated until his palm was encircling her throat again. Something about the gesture undid her, the possessive curl of fingers that were endlessly gentle on her skin. "Come on now, love. *Fuck*, I'm gonna come again..."

She cried out to the ceiling, and his other hand shifted until he could brush her clit with his thumb, circling it frantically as he began thrusting into her as much as she was riding him.

Dani's fingers curled around his wrist, clinging to him as bone-deep pleasure peaked, a slow cresting compared to the explosion from before. His body tensed beneath hers, and she heard him growl her name again. His hand shifted back to grip her hip, but his palm on her throat held her still and held her gently and it was a pleasure in itself.

She came hard.

He did too, his body bucking beneath her and his groan singing deep in her bones.

Slate's palm shifted to her nape and he tugged her to him to kiss her thoroughly, his hips thrusting upward in tiny, lazy movements that made her orgasm linger and her toes curl.

She was panting against his lips, trying to come down from the high, and she felt his mouth curve into a smile against her own. "Worth it?" he breathed against her.

She couldn't help herself; she smiled back. "Worth it."

CHAPTER ⚬ TWENTY-FIVE

A BIRD IN THE HAND

... the elusive Forest Dragon was thought to be extinct, until a nest was discovered in the Northeastern Ridge of L'el, and brought for study to the Silver Valley...

– Gherald Schmidt, Faerloch Historical Archives

Dani woke up with the sun bleeding in through the curtains. She blinked blearily, part of her still unwilling to open her eyes and be alert just yet. For a few moments, she lay there, comfortable and warm, her body heavy in a delicious way. In and out of consciousness, her mind flitting between the present and her memories of the night.

Hands down, it was the best sex of her life. Intense and hyper-sexual. She didn't know her body was even capable of producing such bone-deep pleasure.

Gently, Dani rolled over. She was still naked—Goddess, they'd literally had sex all night long. Dawn had been sneaking its inky gray fingers into the room before they'd finally fallen asleep. Slate was on his belly, blankets gathering deliciously around his hips, hair loose and in complete disarray around him. He was still very much asleep, the sharpness in his face softened by slumber.

Her heart choked up her throat, and it tasted like panic and running. There had been a moment last night—a couple of moments—where she thought she saw something about him that screamed *attachment*. That shouted *I want more.*

She couldn't be one hundred percent certain though. Was she making it up? Was she seeing something that wasn't there? Maybe she was crazy and this was literally all it was going to be between them; wild sex and fun and hanging out and having a drink and dinner sometimes...

No. It wasn't. It couldn't be. Men *always* wanted more than she was ready to give. Without fail. They'd sleep together two or three times, and then suddenly it was all, *Come to my parents' house for dinner* or *Why don't you sleep over this weekend?* The worst was when one of them flat-out asked her *to be his girlfriend.*

They always wanted more. Something deeper. Something that would demand unearthing hard truths she wasn't ready to unearth yet. Or ever, maybe.

She wasn't emotionally available for that kind of commitment. Goddess, to have to explain to someone that she could talk to animals? That her two best friends were a vampire and a griffin? Forget the drama about her parents. She didn't even know how she would get *into* explaining what happened to Kat and the fae...

You don't have to explain that stuff to Slate, a little piece of her whispered. *He already knows most of it. He gets it.*

No. It didn't matter. People came and went in her life. Kat. Her Mama. Her Papa. Even her neighbor, Mrs. Mulhern's husband... Dani had admittedly taken his recent passing a little too hard.

People left. It was just... worse if she opened up to them first.

Which, when looking at Slate, made the panic in her throat taste a little more like sadness. Because he walked into her life knowing these things. A small piece of her noticed that he fit into her life too seamlessly for it to be accidental, but that wasn't something she ruminated on too deeply.

He wouldn't leave. The echo in her wouldn't shut up. It drummed its devilish little fingers against her skull softly, but insistently. *He wouldn't leave you.*

Which was bullshit because he had the Silver Valley Council hunting his ass. Either he'd leave, or he'd be dead before summer was out. She didn't want to think about it.

Dani was spared her thoughts when his eyes slowly opened, and Slate sucked in a deep, sleepy breath. Her stomach flipped over as he blinked, bringing her into focus. So beautiful, his eyes, like the clearest oceans in the Mediterranean. Brighter than gemstones.

"Morning..." he drawled, his voice a delicious husk that awoke her body in more ways than one.

"Good morning," she replied. Despite her muddled thoughts, something about him pulled a smile from her.

He gave her one back, but it wasn't the wicked smile that always carried a sharpness to his eyes. This one was marginally softer—perhaps it was too early for wickedness, or perhaps it was something more.

"I can't stay for very long," she said, the words jumping out of her mouth.

He blinked at her. Did she see the smile slip a little?

"I have to get ready for work," she added, forcing herself to slow the words down, to not sound like a jittery teenager. Her skin tightened with nerves.

"Okay," he replied. Nope, the grin was back. She must be going crazy, seeing things that weren't there. "I forget that you work a big girl job with real hours."

"We can go out this weekend if you want. Tomorrow night." Again, the words jumped out of her mouth. As soon as they left her lips, she immediately wished she could pluck them out of the space between them. Why did she say that? Did she just offer a *date number eleven*?

What was she doing?

"Sure," he agreed, nodding. "Something fun, what do you think? Maybe go to the Den or something? Kari and Jian can come too?"

Stress she didn't realize she was holding onto bled out of her shoulders and stomach. Her throat loosened. "Yes," she said. "That sounds... that sounds fun."

Casual and fun.

He was ruined.

Ruined.

He couldn't stop thinking about it—the sex. Couldn't stop thinking about her. How she felt under his hands, under his mouth, how she tasted, how she sounded...

How she made him *feel*... alive. Alive and powerful and absolutely fucking weak all at the same time. Like he had the world under his fingertips and if she breathed the right way, he'd tear down kingdoms for her.

Therein lay the problem, of course, because he knew she had one foot out the door already, and should he breathe wrong, she would scatter like dry leaves on a summer breeze.

Why?

He wanted to hold her face and demand answers from her. *Why can't I keep you? Why are you afraid of the fae? Why do I sometimes catch panic in your eyes, like an animal caught in a trap?*

Obviously, he wouldn't, because that would make it worse. He just had to play this one carefully. Be patient.

But *why*? Slate didn't thrive well with bullshit and secrets and lies. Subtlety wasn't a specialty of his. But something about Dani was different. She made him *feel* different, he behaved differently around her, for her. She just... something about her just *clicked*.

He really liked her. The intensity of how he felt around her made him constantly question and backpedal in his own head, teetering this very fine, very dangerous line between *like* and *love*.

"Yoo-hoo, earth to Slate!"

"What?" He whipped his head to Jian in the driver's seat, blinking rapidly to clear his thoughts. "Wait, what?"

"Damn, he's got it *bad*," Jian laughed, making eyes with Kari through the rearview mirror. It was Saturday night, and they were driving to the Den to meet Dani, Roger, Maddie, and Maddie's husband Tony for a few drinks. Slate had a backpack in the backseat, and had said nothing to the twins as they eyed the backpack when he threw it in the car.

"Totally bad," Kari chuckled.

"I think she's ruined me," Slate said absently, twisting his hair, staring blankly out the windshield. He saw nothing of the city's nightlife. His vision was instead filled with soft curves and a flushed freckled face. "Best sex of my life. Bar none."

Kari made a sexy sound of appreciation from the backseat while Jian roared with laughter. Slate punched his shoulder—just hard enough to make his best friend flinch, but not enough to distract him from driving. "Shut up, I hate you both."

"He's in *love*," Jian teased, ducking his body slightly when Slate shoved his shoulder again. But Slate didn't answer right away and Jian gasped. "*No*. I was just kidding! You are! Are you?"

"No," Slate replied quickly. Too quickly.

"Liar," Kari hissed playfully from the backseat.

"Mind-blowing sex doesn't equate *love*, Kari-*baa*."

"Oh, I definitely know that, darling," she laughed richly. "I've had my lion's share of mind-blowing sex. Or... perhaps it's the fox's share? Either way." She shrugged. "I don't *love* any of my partners. Not like that. But I'm also *extremely* observant and I watch you with her."

"And what do you see?" Slate challenged, twisting around in his seat.

Her gray eyes assessed him with too much knowing. Slate was brutally reminded that his best girl-friend was a *kitsune*, and *kitsune* were renowned for knowing a great many things. "I see you ready to lay the world at her feet, and she's got one hand on the door, ready to bolt at a moment's notice."

Slate's lips thinned and he whirled back around. He ran a hand over his hair and twisted a stray strand again, staring back out his window, watching as the city rolled by in a casual blur. Kari's assessment was so accurate, it bordered on painful.

"She doesn't want a relationship," Kari continued.

"I know," Slate replied. And he did know. He just... it was a vibe. The same vibe that told him whenever someone lied to him. It vibrated every time something skittered across Dani's face, every time her body tensed, every time she spoke with a distinct wobble in her voice. Something about the commitment scared her. But he was also *confident* she liked him. Because the ease he felt around her definitely wasn't only him. She felt it too. He *knew* she was as charged to him as he was to her. He just knew. He was pretty sensitive to emotions and feelings. Always had been.

"I don't think she's emotionally ready for one."

"I *know*, Kari."

"... yet."

He pinged his gaze back behind him again, twisting in his seat.

"Dani reminds me of a little bird sometimes," Kari mused. "One of the little bold ones. She'll defend her nest and her friends fiercely, and she'll even feed from the palm of your hand fearlessly, but if you twitch wrong, she'll dart away."

He regarded Kari for a long moment. "And?" he pressed.

Kari smirked. "Keep your palm out."

The Den was absolutely packed when Slate and the twins pushed their way into the bar. Kari called out a loud and cheerful greeting to Loraine, and promptly disappeared to go greet the female were-bear. Slate barely contained an eye-roll. Kari was never in one place for too long at a watering hole—always making new friends and finding new lovers.

He pushed his way through the crowd, Jian tight to his back, but even his best friend nodded at a few patrons in greeting. Several lingering, lustful gazes followed the two of them.

"Been a long time since I've been here," the witch-doctor drawled, tipping his chin at some lovely male who flushed bright scarlet at his attention.

"Gonna find something to warm your bed tonight?" Slate teased him.

Jian shrugged indifferently. "Who knows. I'll wait and see what the night brings."

They came upon Roger's little table in the far corner near the bar. Slate's eyes zeroed in on Dani right away and his heart lodged right into his throat. She was summer personified in a blue tee-shirt dress with strappy sandals and her red hair french braided along her spine.

She was sitting on Roger's side, and had been leaning in to speak to the vampire when she noticed them. Slate had to stifle an uneasy feeling; her proximity to Roger had his fingers curling, and he didn't miss Dani's guarded expression when she first caught sight of him. It didn't last long, however, as a summer-bright smile wiped it away, and the knot in his chest eased a little.

He didn't fail to notice, either, the effects of that smile. Several people within Dani's vicinity all visibly brightened at her smile, like a ripple of happiness drifting through the Den with Dani as the origin point.

Slate had the feeling Roger wasn't as unaffected as he appeared. He also noted the way the vampire's shoulders tensed, just a fraction, when Dani slid out of the booth to greet them. "Hi!" she said cheerfully. She kissed Jian's cheek first, then Slate's.

He shifted his face just enough to catch her lips in a chaste kiss, rather than the one of the cheek she'd tried to plant on him. He grinned wickedly when her startled gaze flew up to meet his. A hint of wariness in her, there and gone, had him swallowing the flirtatious words that had been about to jump out of his throat.

"Hi, yourself." He was surprised with how smoothly it came out, like his heart wasn't jammed into his esophagus.

Over Dani's shoulder, having not bothered to get out of the booth for a greeting, Roger lifted a glass of wine to his lips. Slate didn't miss the way his eyes flashed towards some of the pub's denizens, the ones eyeing Dani. Had there been a hint of red in them...? The stares immediately ceased. The tiniest prick of ice threaded up his throat. He recognized it immediately as envy and swallowed it hard.

What did he have to be envious about? Roger's effortless show of power and authority... or the fact that Roger had more rights to Dani than Slate did?

Idiot. *Idiot*. Dani wasn't a *possession*. Just because they fucked didn't mean he had any right to her. They weren't dating...

Not really.

Where did he get off feeling so *possessive*?

His thoughts were interrupted by a melodious voice coming from the booth across from Roger. "*Oh, mon dieu!* It's Jian Meho!" Maddie gasped, hand flying to her mouth. She was sitting across from Roger with a large, olive-skinned gentleman who had to be her husband. "I haven't seen you in an age! Tell me Karisi's here?"

Jian laughed. "Oh yeah, she's running around somewhere."

Maddie bounded out of her seat and pulled Jian's face down to kiss both his cheeks, then turned and kissed Slate's. "Slate, *mon cher*, nice to see you again! When you said your best friends were twins... I didn't even *fathom* you meant the Meho twins!"

"I thought *trouble* was a decent enough description of them." He grinned with a shrug, and Jian's smile was savage.

The witch laughed. "By the Goddess, you weren't kidding. The amount of broken hearts they've left behind in my coven—Karisi!"

Kari appeared like a wraith at Slate's elbow and shrieked with glee at the sight of Maddie. They exchanged an enthusiastic greeting in rapid French, but Slate was hardly paying attention, his eyes drawn to Dani. She made a little shooing motion with her hand, and Roger raised a dark brow at her.

"Please?" she asked with the cutest pout. Why was it suddenly bothering him so *much* that she would look at someone like that, and not him? It was completely irrational, and he desperately tried not to watch her, but he couldn't *stop*. The slightest movement from her drew his attention like a bad tick.

Finally, Roger gave a haughty sigh before he shifted further into the booth with an eerie grace. Dani rewarded the vampire with another one of her vibrant smiles. Kari slid into the booth next to Maddie. There was room for three to a bench, and as Dani slid in next to Roger, she glanced back at Slate and *finally*, one of those smiles was for him.

She gave a little jerk of her chin, and he hoped he didn't look too eager as he slid in next to her. Immediately, Jian snagged a chair and planted it at the head of the table, facing backwards, and dropped himself into it before draping his arms across the top of the chair-back.

Roger's eyes briefly met his own over the top of Dani's red hair, but they were carefully blank, and Slate couldn't get a bead on him. The vampire's very presence was potent, but Slate held his nerve. He wasn't afraid of Roger, despite the fact that Roger could very likely separate his head from his shoulders without a stray breath.

"I wonder how many times we've been in here together and never knew it," Dani laughed in greeting to Kari, and leaned across the table, meeting Kari in the middle as they exchanged kisses on the cheek. The urge to stroke a hand down her back as she leaned forward, especially with the hint of a griffin feather showing above her neckline, was overwhelming, like his body *needed* to touch hers. Kari caught his eye just as his hand twitched, a warning in her expression.

Slow. Keep your palm out. Don't breathe wrong.

Slate shoved the disappointment down, knowing that Kari was doing him a favor. This was a light outing. Casual, easy. A date that wasn't a date. They'd slept together, but that didn't mean he should be putting his hands all over her all the time now.

"Hi, I'm Kari," the *kitsune* greeted Roger, offering a sensual smile. She stayed leaning against the table when Dani sat back, and held out a hand towards the vampire. She didn't seem the least bit intimidated by him. Roger had a quiet physical power to him, despite his lean appearance. "I know who you are, Roger Addington." A fox-like smirk.

"My reputation precedes me," Roger replied evenly, seeming completely unaffected by the sensuality that Kari wore like a cloak. He inclined his head, reaching out his hand to briefly shake Kari's. "Well met, Karisi Meho. You are well known to me as well. You and your twin are a great fascination to some of the Lore, especially those who aren't well acquainted with Mysticism."

Kari's smile was positively feline in its smugness. "Of course. Jian and I are quite popular."

"Indeed..." Roger's reply was accompanied by a slightly raised brow. He glanced at Jian then, and inclined his head. Jian returned the gesture, and only Slate's extreme familiarity with his best friend had him noticing the subtle tightness that vibrated across Jian's shoulders when the two made eye contact, but it was there and gone in a heartbeat.

A waitress, whom Maddie introduced as one of her covenmates Giselle, took their drink order, and Maddie introduced her husband. Slate didn't need Maddie to tell him Tony was retired military; it was evident in the way the man held himself, a quiet sense of power tempered by a sense of discipline. His dark hair was cut military short, and tattoos covered the olive-tone skin of his muscled arms. He didn't speak much, and was a quiet contrast to his much more bubbly wife. Tony was mortal, but he was Maddie's *tei enaid*—her soulmate. Slate learned that he would live longer than his normal mortal lifespan because Maddie had tied their life forces together with magic. It kept him young and healthy, at the cost of shortening Maddie's elongated witch's lifespan. Apparently, despite looking like he was in his late thirties, the man was well over 70, and passed his days as a stay-at-home father for their twins, Leo and Sara.

"You have powerful friends," Slate commented lightly, eyeing Roger before turning his attention to Maddie.

"Like calls to like," Maddie said with a little shrug. "Besides, Roger doesn't tolerate the weak for long. Your friends are no slouches either, mind you."

Kari grinned, waggling her brow. "As you said, power draws power. Are you sure you're married happily, Maddie?"

Tony slid dark eyes over to the *kitsune*, who winked back at him. "You can play too, tiger. We're all friends here."

Dani burst out laughing, and Slate couldn't help the grin that tugged at his lips.

The night continued, and Slate's worry over Dani's flightiness faded. He relaxed his stranglehold over himself, stopped worrying about making a wrong move. He found himself shifting closer, letting his eyes linger if they made eye contact, letting his fingers brush hers. Her smiles weren't always directed at him, but she seemed to be enjoying herself. The tight, icy knot inside him eased a little.

Kari vanished at one point and came back with a tabletop dice game. As she set the game up, Maddie asked Slate when his championship title fight was.

"Two weeks from tonight," he answered.

"*Merde*," Maddie cursed. "Sara has a dance recital that night, or I would come watch you fight. Are you nervous?"

"No," Slate drawled with a wave. "I'm pretty confident."

"Is he as good as he claims, *cherie*?" Maddie's nutmeg eyes twinkled in Dani's direction.

She shrugged casually. "He's alright, I guess." A flick of those green eyes in his direction. A half-smile.

It was the most flirtatious she'd been all night. Unable to resist, he slipped his fingers over her thigh under the table, playing with the hem of her dress as he let his fingertips caress the soft skin just above her knee.

Dani shifted slightly, and that caution returned to her face. He slid his hand away with a smile, and ignored the sharp gaze of the vampire next to her. Roger missed nothing, and Slate had to swallow the irrational urge to punch the guy in the face. That possessive feeling gripped his insides again.

Jian's knee nudged his, a silent reminder for calm at the same time as a gesture of solidarity. Jian, too, was observant. Slate forced himself to draw in a calm breath and focus on the game. He had to be patient. It irked him, playing games in subtlety and shadows. But then she laughed at something Kari said, smile crinkling her freckles, and his annoyance melted away.

He wanted this flighty bird of a woman to come to his hand. He knew she wanted to as well, so he would just have to wait her out.

Her gaze caught his own for the barest moment. His heart jammed into his throat. Then she dropped it, and Slate hardened his resolve. She'd come around. He had to be patient, that's all.

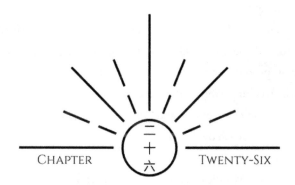

CHAPTER TWENTY-SIX

POSSESSION AND PANIC

...the shift in the common language for Faerloch to the neighboring human region, a Germanic dialect, was agreed upon by 2/3rds of the Gather, stating the mandate of the Secrecy of the Lore for their reasoning, and...

- Gherald Schmidt, Faerloch Historical Archives

It was after midnight, and the booze was starting to hit the table. Slate had refrained from drinking too much. He needed all his focus to play this careful game with Dani, but the rest of them, save for Roger and Tony, had become far more giggly.

Even Jian was laughing more, and Slate envied his ease.

He was far too aware of Dani to be at ease. Felt like he couldn't let his guard down for a moment.

And yet every time she laughed, he couldn't help himself. So when Jian told a ridiculous story from their childhood, and Dani laughed so hard he felt her press against his side as she gulped down air, Slate found himself sliding his hand over her nape.

A gentle squeeze, a tender brush of his thumb against the side of her neck, relishing in this hold that felt... right.

A tension immediately shivered through Dani, and Slate could have kicked himself. He dropped his hand, and couldn't avoid the pointed glance Roger threw him over Dani's head. Before he dropped his gaze away, a hint of amusement glinted in those mahogany eyes, and his desire to strangle the vampire returned.

"You know, it's getting kind of late, and Sellie wants to go home," Dani said, a touch too suddenly, and his stomach tightened into a frozen ball.

Fuck.

"So soon, *ma cherie?*" Maddie had a little frown on her face.

"You know Sellie. If I ignore her, she'll only try to get in here and the last time that happened, Loraine threatened to ban me from the Den," Dani laughed, but the hint of stiffness in it had Slate's heart wedging into his throat.

Double fuck.

"Shall I escort you to your bike, Daniella?" Roger asked, so smoothly that Slate had to grit his teeth a moment to quell his own aggravation.

Under the table, Jian's knee pressed into his own once more.

He sucked in an easy breath, willing his muscles to relax.

"No, I'll be fine." She leaned forward over the table once more to give a cheek kiss to both girls across from her, then leaned over to feather her lips by Roger's cheek. Twisting, she gave Slate a little smile that was that expectant '*Will you scoot out for me?*' look, but still with a *hint* of tension.

He hated it.

But he gave an easy nod and slid out of the booth for her, impossibly aware of Roger's stare. He gripped the back of the booth hard enough that his knuckles creaked, fighting to stop himself from touching her. The urge to soothe the faint panic he could feel in her with a caress was nearly overwhelming. It went completely against his nature to let her feel upset about something, and yet the means to soothe her were the source of said panic.

It was maddening.

"I had fun tonight," Dani said, and he wanted it to be only for him, but she said it more in a general way to everyone, but he smiled anyway.

"Me too," he told her, because despite this... thing... hanging between them, he simply enjoyed being around her.

Her smile wavered a moment, then widened as she leaned up to give him a chaste kiss on the cheek, but before he could even really enjoy it, she leaned down to do the same to Jian. She blew a friendly kiss to Tony, who actually cracked a small smile.

"Bye, everyone!" she waved, and she was once more the center of attention to several nearby patrons with her stunning smile. He wanted to growl.

Slate felt every step she took out of the bar, the distance pulling on him like she was the draw to his magnet. He rocked on his heels, and knew he couldn't stop himself, couldn't just *let this go.*

"Slate, don't—" Kari warned.

"I'll be right back," he said, bolting towards the door.

"Slate!"

But he was already gone, eating up the space between him and the exit in long strides. He punched out the front door, and there she was, straddling her bike, her dress riding up to reveal the spandex shorts she had on underneath. She was looking at her phone, but the moment the door swung shut behind him, she glanced up.

For a moment, he tasted a surge of anxiety crawling up her throat, there and gone. He saw her brows furrow with caution. But she smiled.

"What's the matter?" she asked, tucking her phone into the little pouch between the handlebars.

For a heartbeat, Slate faltered. What *was* he doing? What was he supposed to say?

Kari's voice echoed in his mind: *keep your palm out.*

"Just being a gentleman." He shrugged. "Making sure you found your bike okay."

He loped down the stairs slowly. She watched him, a smile still quirking the edges of her mouth. That same mouth he remembered being flushed from kissing less than 48 hours ago. A mouth that had wrapped around his cock and blissfully tortured him until he thought he'd burst out of his skin from sheer want.

"Well, as you can see," she patted the Vespa's front, "I found it just fine."

He left a calculated amount of distance between them. This was not at all how he pictured this night going. He'd imagined sitting next to her, running his fingers along her leg under the table, both of them finding some really terrible, transparent excuse to leave and go back to her house.

This whole interaction felt stilted and wrong. This was not how it was supposed to be.

She regarded him for a long moment. The air froze in his lungs, waiting. "You can't come home with me," she said finally.

"I know," he answered immediately. He crossed his arms, then remembered himself and dropped them, linking his fingers behind his back instead. He rocked a little on his heels. "I just..." He didn't have the words, not if he didn't want to scare his bird away.

He didn't know how to feel about it, but what bothered him was how could she *not* feel the same pull? She'd been just as into the sex, had claimed it had been the best she'd ever had. He'd seen the way she acted with him. What the hell was the problem? How could she go from having his head between her thighs one moment and barely able to endure his touch the next?

He wanted to be mad at her, but... he couldn't. Because he wasn't mad at *her*. There was something else. The same instinct in him that knew when someone lied to him was firing, but there wasn't a *lie*. It was... it was... something was wrong. Something about her nervousness... It sent red flags in his head that there was *more* to this.

She was resistant, and he didn't understand *why*.

He inhaled slowly, trying to relax his shoulders and his stance. "I... Can we..." he faltered for a second, backpedaling. *Can we talk? Can we hang out again? Can we date for real?* He shook his head. "Never mind." He forced a smile, but he knew it didn't quite make it to his eyes. "Text me when you get home."

He had to play patiently with this one. God, he hated the *games*. The subtleties of language and words. He didn't play it well. But Kari's assessment of them from earlier haunted him. Even now, perched on the seat of that bike, Dani looked like a little bird, head cocked, watching him, body tense as if she might simply take off with no notice.

She watched him carefully, then she gave a slow nod. "Sure."

It was like dragging his feet through thick mud, to make himself turn back towards the door to the Den. "Good night, Daniella."

"I don't want a relationship." The words jumped out of her mouth so fast, they slapped him. The sting they left wasn't on his face, though.

He paused at the top of the stairs, hand on the door handle. "I know," he replied quickly. "I... I already knew that." Slate glanced over his shoulder. There was something painfully tortured about how she looked at him. "Can I change your mind?" It came out far more strangled than he liked.

The sound of beating wings, and Sellie landed heavily on the stairs below him, her regal blue eyes snapping at him. Her feathers were fluffed in obvious irritation, her beak clicking with no small shade of threat. Behind the griffin, Dani's bike revved to life. Slate's heart crawled into his throat, and he shifted to look around the griffin. His eyes collided with meadow and sunshine.

"I'm sorry," she said, her face anxious, and it squeezed icy fingers around his throat. He wanted to say something, *anything*, to make her stay, but she revved her bike, and shot off into the night.

Sellie gave him one more haughty stare, before she launched herself into the air with enough force to make him fall back a step. He kept his focus on Dani's retreating form, frustration and confusion an icy cocktail over his skin.

Right before she turned the corner, though... she looked back.

His breath caught, a kernel of hope in the swamp of his frustration, but he couldn't get the sight of her panicked, wary eyes out of his head as he numbly walked back into the Den.

CHAPTER · TWENTY-SEVEN

SHADOWS OF WARNING

... led to a cease-fire to the strife between the Vampire Council and the High Fae of the Silver Valley. The Accord Talks lasted for...

- Gherald Schmidt, Faerloch Historical Archives

Slate was a scattered mess. He couldn't pull his own head together—forgetful, scrambled. He felt like he was drifting from one mundane task to another, then in a rush to recover himself, he ran around like a headless chicken, picking up the pieces of his life haphazardly.

His conversation with Dani on the steps of the Den haunted him. He'd blown it because he couldn't keep his fucking mouth shut. Couldn't *not* wear his goddamned heart on his sleeve. He must've crafted a dozen texts to her over the next two days. Typed them out and immediately deleted them. What was he supposed to say to her to recover this? He couldn't put this one back in the box, couldn't talk his way out of it, couldn't smooth this one over with charm and finesse.

And of course, she didn't message him.

He was so *irritated* by everything. It took him a long time of working through his own thoughts before he figured out what was agitating him so much.

He was missing something. That's what was bothering him. Somewhere across the ten dates, he'd missed some key warning signs. He'd been so distracted by the way she made him feel that he'd missed the shades of her voice, the strain across her shoulders, red flags and warning bells that left a trail of breadcrumbs to that one moment at the Den.

Slate knew she liked him too. He liked her... she liked him. It wasn't all *just* him. Sure, he was the one that was ready to dive right into something a little more serious than perhaps what she had in mind. But she still *liked* him.

Slate had been around enough trauma victims in his career as a martial artist to know the vibe those people gave off. Something had happened to her. And he'd bet his rank it had something to do with the fae.

But what did that have to do with him, other than the obvious fact that the Silver Valley Council was after his ass? Where was the connection between that and... them, Slate and Dani?

I don't want a relationship.

There was something *more*, and he was missing it.

Why was she so resistant?

He didn't want to push her, and that warred with this feeling of wanting to cocoon her in safety.

The routine of a work day helped clear his head a little. Distracted him from the near-constant drum of Dani in his mind, like icy fingers poking and prodding him to *talk to her, go to her, find her, fix it, be together.*

It was late Monday night. Slate was just ushering the last of his students out the door when the hairs on the back of his neck rose. A glance over his shoulder, and he saw shadows pulling and knitting together in the corner of the studio waiting room.

Slate said goodbye to his students. Shut the front door. Locked it.

"Can you *not* be a creep?" he said into the seemingly empty waiting room. "I'm trying to run a fucking business here."

From the shadows, Roger's lithe frame materialized. He was dressed rather casually today; navy slacks, a crisp light gray button-down with the cuffs folded once, and dark brown loafers that looked as if they'd come straight out of the box. He looked like a young entrepreneur looking to go play a round of golf rather than an ages-old bloodsucker. Like he belonged on the cover of GQ's 40-under-40.

"I did not realize you kept such late hours," Roger said with a careless shrug. "It is nearly sunset."

Slate braced his palms against one of the waiting room tables and leveled the vampire a bored look. "Can I help you with something?" Why on God's good green earth would Roger come see him?

"I want to see how dense you are," Roger answered with an equally bored tone, dry as leaves but offset by a sharp expression. Roger slipped his hands into the pockets of his slacks, and leaned back against the wall nearest to where he'd stepped from the shadows.

Slate's brows shot up as irritation sizzled under his skin. He was in no mood for this bullshit. "What the fuck do you want?"

"Do you plan on contacting Daniella?" Roger cocked his head to the side in a decidedly inhuman gesture. It was clear the vampire was a predator who wasn't used to being beneath anyone in the food chain.

"Why is that any of your business?" Slate nearly growled at him, fingers gripping at the table.

"As I said, my endless curiosity about your intelligence abounds," was the response, dry amusement heavy in Roger's silken voice. He regarded Slate like an insect, and Slate would've given anything to punch that look right off his face.

Instead, he didn't give the vampire the satisfaction of an answer. He simply leveled an even stare at him.

Roger let out a long sigh through his nose and straightened from the wall. He took slow, measured steps toward Slate as he spoke, hands remaining in the pockets of his slacks. "Because you'd have to be rather dense to not notice the way she reacted to that *possessive* touch of yours, Slate Melisande. And still more dense if you think you should be contacting her again after she made her discomfort clear." A smile that wasn't a smile, but a deliberate showing of teeth from one predator to another. The fact that those normally human-looking canines were longer than they should be wasn't lost on Slate.

He was almost mollified to think he might be considered a threat to the vampire.

Almost.

"I think she made it clear that you should leave her alone," Roger said quietly, and he stopped across the table from Slate, meeting him eye for eye.

Slate's temper was a raging blizzard inside him, but he strangled it as best he could. "As I said," he started through gritted teeth, "I don't think that's any of your business. Daniella can take care of herself."

"You are correct, she can," Roger agreed with a smooth nod, and his lips pulled into a thin smile. "But she doesn't have to. I am simply ensuring you understand the situation and she doesn't have to reiterate her feelings. If you are intelligent, you will back off."

A cool flush prickled across Slate's brow, sinking behind his eyes and pulsing a little. "And if I don't?"

Roger's eyes glittered like obsidian, and for a moment, they were no longer warm mahogany. They were red, a deep, blood red that had a faint glow. It was gone in an instant, and Slate blinked, a shiver trickling down his spine.

Dani had said Roger was old, but Slate had a feeling she was vastly understating that.

"I will not fight Daniella's battles for her; she is perfectly capable. This is simply a friendly... *reminder*." His tone was anything but friendly.

It took an impressive amount of self-control to not growl at this vampire when a possessive rage surged through his skin like a blast of icy wind. Possessive, and protective, and...

Reluctantly impressed by Roger, despite his rage. This vampire was clearly willing to kill for Dani, without hesitation. Slate idly wondered how difficult it was to get a vampire that old to be *that* protective of you.

Dani, Dani, Dani.

His lungs caught, and the thought rushed in and out that perhaps Roger wanted Dani for himself.

Because who wouldn't, right?

She was bright and kind and compassionate and smart. She was easy to like and easier to love.

But from what Dani had said, there was nothing sexual going on between the two.

That knowledge alone didn't fully satisfy him.

"If you upset her, Melisande, you are making it my business," Roger continued, eyes flashing with a hint of amusement, as if he could see just how hard Slate was trying to control himself.

"No, you are *choosing* to make it your business," Slate countered, growling. "Dani can't know you're here. She'd be so pissed. You *want* it to be your business because you haven't liked me from the start. Because you're fucking *jealous* someone *else* is sleeping with her."

Roger didn't even blink. He was so still that the hairs on the back of Slate's neck rose as some deep-seated hindbrain self-preservation instinct flared to life. "Excuse me?" Roger's voice was deadly quiet.

"You heard me," Slate growled, ice in his throat.

The vampire continued to watch him. Slate wondered if he was deciding how to best decapitate him and hide his body.

"A being of your youth cannot even begin to comprehend my feelings for Daniella," Roger said. A hard look, and more than ever before, Slate felt like the vampire was the closest he'd come to wanting to kill Slate; it was a palpable feeling that had his flight or fight instinct bristling. "The *only* thing that matters to me is that she is happy, and I will do whatever I deem necessary to ensure that. I will never tell her to stay away from you, but I do not like you," Roger hissed, but he stepped back, as if sucking a darkness back inside himself, and it felt like the knife at Slate's throat had been pulled away. "You are something that is not as it seems. Right now, you have an aura around you that is arctic with a hint of magic, yet the other night, you were decidedly mortal. You are dangerous, and you are inviting trouble to Daniella's doorstep, whether she knows it or not."

"Dani is not a *child*. She can handle her own shit—"

"I will deny her nothing, even you, if that's what she wants," Roger snapped, and it was the first time his words were colored with heat. "But you might be a danger to her, and you must acknowledge it if you care for her a drop of how much I care for that woman."

Slate froze.

Damn it, maybe Roger was right. Slate had the Silver Valley Council after him. Just him. Was he inadvertently putting a target on her back? He didn't know how fae culture worked. But in his experience with bad guys, they had no problem using partners as *leverage.*

"Whatever your feelings, and whatever mine," Roger said in a quiet murmur that sounded loud in the sudden silence around them, "whatever those are, they are less relevant than *hers,*" Roger spoke so calmly Slate wanted to launch himself across the room and shake him. "And regardless of my opinion of whether or not you are good for her, her body language clearly told *me* she did not enjoy your touch. Do not push her."

Roger turned on his heel, striding back towards the corner where he'd manifested, and words jumped out of Slate's mouth before he could stop them. "What if she needs to be pushed? What if she needs that to be... healed?" It was a leap out on a limb, but Roger watched Dani too closely to be ignorant, and as her best friend...

Maybe he knew what Slate didn't.

Roger froze, one hand held out towards the gathering shadows in the corner. He pivoted on one heel to regard Slate. He studied Slate for a long time, still with an expression that told Slate *nothing*. Not a single hint.

Finally, Roger cocked his head to the side, and his smooth voice was a menacing purr across the room. "Perhaps. However, Slate Melisande, if you hurt her? I will be back." Roger's eyes glinted, dark as obsidian. "Or should I say... *Zlaet?*"

Before Slate could even react, the shadows swallowed the vampire whole, until nothing remained but fading darkness.

Slate's breath left him in a violent exhale as a surge of anger rolled through him. He palmed the table and flipped it, fingertips tingling. The table soared across the floor. Farther than what Slate would have considered in the realm of normal.

He massaged his thumb into his palm, inhaling deep and steady. His hands tingled, and a shade of a headache suddenly speared him behind his eyes. It was the exact same feeling that had come over him the day in the alley with the fae. It was not lost on him that both times, Dani's wellbeing was involved in one shape or another.

The magic was awake.

But no sooner than it appeared, it started to fade, too quickly for him to grasp it and study it. Like holding water between cupped hands, until all he was left with was an impression of what had been for a heartbeat of time.

You are something that is not as it seems.

Perhaps it was something he needed to bring up to Jian at some point...

His latent magic bothered him too, among all the other garbage in his head. The wandering idea crossed his mind that he should talk to his father again, because something felt missing. But a part of him was reluctant to initiate that conversation. It felt like another added stress on top of everything else when Ebisu's health was already so fragile.

Slate stormed onto the mats, needing to lose himself in training. He couldn't focus on this anymore—he had a championship fight in less than two weeks. He needed to eat, sleep, breathe, and shit competition if he wanted a shot at winning again this year.

He didn't have time to think about overprotective vampires and flighty lorekissed women. Didn't have the energy to think about magic, or Roger's cryptic drawl of that fae name...

But Dani wasn't far from his mind, even if he wanted to focus on himself. She haunted him around the edges. So much so that as he drowned himself in a late night bath, he snatched his phone from the floor beside the tub and began crafting a message.

> **Slate:** *I want you to know I'm sorry if I came across as too pushy or over-bearing. You are hands-down one of the most incredible people I've ever met. And you are absolutely right in that I would 100% jump into a relationship with you. But that's not what you want, and I totally respect that. If you ever wanna hang out or something, you know where to find me. I'm always around. And you will always be welcome.*

He waffled for a minute with that draft. Did he sound like an asshole, like the prover-bial, cringey 'nice guy' that couldn't take 'no' for an answer? Was it genuine enough? Kami above, was he really sitting here, overthinking a text message?

He was.

He was because he wanted her to *know* what he was feeling. He didn't want to have to sit here and play word games with her. He wanted to put his feelings out there for her to know them.

That had blown up in his face at the Den though, so...

He wanted her to just... *talk* to him.

He pressed send.

Waited. *Delivered.*

Put his phone back on the floor. Waited. *Waited.*

Slate snatched his phone back up. His heart dropped into the pit of his stomach. *Read 11:32pm.*

Long minutes passed. Nothing. No three little dots. No response.

Slate draped his arm over the side of the tub and let his phone plunk to the floor. He heaved a deep breath out through his nose, the water around him no longer warm enough to thaw the prickle of ice that laid over his skin. The ball was in her court now.

Keep your palm out.

CHAPTER   TWENTY-EIGHT

GHOSTED

... Residing in the Sidhe—sometimes referred to as the Otherworld—it is believed these fae commune with mortals...

- Gherald Schmidt, Faerloch Historical Archives

The week crawled by in strange intervals of pacing. A sense of time blindness washed over Slate—some moments the clock sped by, and others, the minutes simply dragged.

Friday night found Slate and the twins in the studio. The boys had done a little training, then Kari had played with them a little, and now the three of them were cleaning and organizing the office and the stockroom. Kari was in the office, organizing paperwork, and Slate and Jian had dragged out loads of boxes from the back; they were sorting and doing inventory.

"Put *size 2 yellow belts* on that list," Slate said to Jian, "and... damn it, where did all the white belts go? We get one with every fucking uniform we order..."

"I cut up a few for a game of Flag Tag," Kari called from the office. "We didn't have enough actual flags."

Slate's mood was pretty sour, but he managed to bite his tongue. "Put white belts on that inventory list too," he said, chucking the empty box back down the hall. "All sizes."

"Slate, did you ever read the essays from the kids who applied to your Senior Internship Program?" Kari asked, holding up some manila folders.

"I did," he replied evenly, digging through another box and sorting its contents with Jian. "Did you?"

"I did. I thought Ronin's essay was well-articulated."

Slate said nothing, half his attention on what he was doing, the other part split between the fifteen other things he had on his mind. Mainly Dani. And why she continued to ghost him. Four days. Four days of no contact. They'd gone from *constant, daily communication* to nothing.

Ten dates to nothing.

Mind-blowing, earth-shattering sex to *nothing*.

He didn't want to sit here and dwell on how badly his feelings were hurt, but god-damned, his feelings were *fucking hurt*. But his feelings were his responsibility and he wasn't about to push them onto her. He fucking missed her, and he was torn between his determination to wait her out and his desire to go hunt her down and grab her face and—

A part of him wondered too, if this wasn't all just better anyway. Until all the heat came off him from the Silver Valley High Fae, maybe it was all just better.

God, that actually *hurt* to think about though, so he compartmentalized it away for now.

"Though, Isla Mei did have a nice essay too..." Kari mused, shuffling through the folders thoughtfully. "And she would be less trouble than Ronin."

"Kari, I don't really care right now," Slate snapped, deconstructing an empty box with abrupt, aggressive motions. "I'm probably just gonna pick Ronin."

"Jeez, alright. Don't jump down my throat," Kari retorted, unbothered by his icy attitude. "The Senior Internship Program is important to the health and function of this school. It deserves your full attention and not arbitrary selections—"

"I'm well aware of the *health* and *function* of this school, Kari. My fucking name is on the window."

"And we all know who the power behind the throne really is here."

Slate opened his mouth, his temper flaring. A whack on the top of his head had his head whirling around. Jian was frowning at him, a plastic-wrapped belt in one hand. "Easy, man. What's wrong with you?"

Slate threw a belt at Jian, who deflected it. "Nothing."

Jian continued to study him.

"Stop reading my *chi*," Slate snapped in a growl, chucking the organized and cataloged belts back into a sturdy box.

"I can't help it. It's all fucking haywire right now. What's *wrong* with you? You've been temperamental all week." He paused, and Slate had a feeling he was communicating with Kari. "Ah. Dani's ghosting you."

Slate said nothing, seething inside. His palms were doing that tingling shit again and his pulse was in his eyes. He wasn't even angry at either twin. He was just *emotional*.

He was just being stupid.

"Listen, bro, just... drop her." Jian began folding spare uniforms, eyes focused on the task. "She's dramatic and flighty. You deserve someone with a little more *stability*..."

"Shut up, Jian."

Jian froze. A frown appeared between his russet brows. He snapped thundercloud eyes up to Slate's. "Excuse you?"

"You don't know *shit*, okay? Shut up about Dani."

"What does that mean, I don't know shit? *You* don't know shit. Slate, you hardly know this woman—"

"You don't know *shit*," Slate repeated, voice escalating. "I *know* her. She's not some fucking *slut* to bang and leave high and dry." The words were a pointed jab, dripping venom. "She fucking *matters* to me. She's *mine*, and just because you're a jealous prick, Jian—"

"Slate," Kari interrupted, voice a whip, and it was the sight of ghostly blue flames in her irises that made him snap his mouth shut. She stood in the doorway of the office, her gaze bouncing between them.

Jian waved a hand at her, not taking his narrowed gray stare off Slate. "No, it's fine." He gestured with his fingertips. "Come on, lay it on me. Tell me how you really feel."

"How I really feel?" Slate snarled. "I feel fucking *mad* and *confused*." Things around him twitched. Trembled. Jian's eyes zipped between Slate and the items, then back to Slate, his frown deepening. "I can't stop thinking about her, and I'm pissed at myself because I missed something, some warning sign or something. But there's something *more* about her and..." His breathing was erratic and wild. "And you've got *no right* to say *shit* about Dani being flighty. Calling the kettle black, Jian. Something happened to her, there is a *reason* behind her drama, and you've got no fucking right to drag her for it."

Jian didn't move. Didn't even blink. All he said was, "You need to take a breath and *calm down*."

Slate hadn't realized he was breathing so shallowly, hands flexing in his lap. The tingling had traveled up past his wrists, nearing his elbows. The pulse was sharpening behind his eyes. He held up his hands—they were trembling, and the veins were too dark again.

"It's back..." he mused.

Jian lurched towards him and gripped his hands. A muted orange glow flared from Jian's hands, then seemed to sink and seep into Slate's skin. Slowly, the darkness in the veins retreated. The shaking slowed. The tingling dissipated. He still had a pulse in his temples, though.

Jian was silent. After another minute, the magic faded. He placed a hand on Slate's forehead, and Jian's magic flowed through him like a delicious, thick warmth, easing the pressure from his head.

Kari appeared, kneeling softly next to them as Jian said, "Getting pretty worked up over this woman, *ne*?"

"Sorry," Slate replied mulishly.

"No, I'm sorry," Jian said. He removed his hand from Slate's head and pressed it to Slate's chest. "You've been saying all along she's different. And you're right, maybe I'm a little jealous. You're my best friend, and it's turning into a full-time job to make sure nothing happens to you. I don't particularly like the idea of you throwing yourself away for some girl who doesn't seem like she gives two shits about you..."

"It's not like that..." Slate said. "She's just... she's nervous and flighty. Something happened to her in the past, I just know it. It's like Kari said. She's a little bird. A nervous bird, like she's been stung by her own shadow too many times before. And I don't like playing waiting games."

"You've never been one for subtlety, that's for sure." Jian frowned, studying Slate's body. "Why the *fuck* is your body doing that shit?"

"What shit?"

Jian was silent for a moment. "It's like…" he hemmed for a second, "it's like one second, your *chi* is screaming, swelling like you're about to detonate, and then the next… nothing. Sometimes it just thrums, like it's restless… it's like… it's like…" Slate's body began to emit a bright, clean white glow. His *chi*.

"Does it look different? What do you mean?" Slate looked down at himself, studying the glow.

Jian made a face. "It's like you have two different *chi* signatures, but they both have the same flavor. It's weird. It's… I dunno, I've noticed it for the last few years, maybe. Some erratic patterns, but nothing alarming. Not like *this*."

"I've never smelled anything like it either," Kari mused.

"I thought I'd be able to figure it out if I could feel it while it's active, but I'm not finding squat." Jian looked frustrated. The glow dissipated.

"Maybe it's genetics?" Kari offered. "Mixing *miko* and lore somehow? A little… magic developmental delay?"

Jian hummed. "Maybe," he said with a sigh. "I don't know enough about it. I'll have to do some research." He gave Slate another once-over. "You feel okay now?"

Slate nodded, flexing his hands. Everything was smoothed back down, sans the shade of a headache.

Jian regarded him for a long, steady moment. "You said 'it's back'… what'd you mean?"

Slate shifted his attention from his hands to his best friend. "It happened earlier this week. I, uh… I threw the table across the room." A little heat raced up the back of his neck. "I had a little visit from Roger, and he and I had some *words* about Dani."

"The vampire?" A shade of distaste flashed over Jian's face. "Well…" he mused. "I wonder… You know, some fae have empathy magic that allows them to manipulate emotions. Not super common, but… I mean, I certainly noticed the way Dani magnetizes a room. You're certain your feelings are your own?" It was a lightly asked question, but his eyes were serious. "She has some form of empathy magic with animals… it's not a far stretch of the imagination to think she might be bewitching you a little. Or even Roger."

A protective surge had a growl slipping loose, and Jian's brows shot up. Slate pulled in a hard inhale to force that urge down. "You make it sound like she's some conniving bitch."

"Nope, I'm just asking what's going on inside your head, bro, that's all."

"The inside of my head is *fine*, minus the fact that I have a headache that won't go away. Listen, if you don't like her—"

"I like her fine. But that doesn't matter if she is using magic on you." Jian frowned. "Right now, I'm more concerned about the erratic behavior of your *chi* and the magical poisoning you keep giving yourself every time someone talks shit about her. And I don't like the idea of anyone playing you along."

Slate snapped his mouth closed, swallowing the hint of nausea that worked its way up his throat. "She's not using magic on me. I *know* that. You said so yourself; the brain always knows the difference." Though, he did remember the way her eyes rim verdant green on occasion, but he didn't think that had anything to do with it. Somehow, that had felt like... something else. Something he couldn't explain because he didn't know enough about magic. "It's like... I dunno. I told you, she's different. It's like I'm a moth and she's a flame, but it's not magic, it's... all of me toward all of her." Slate shook his head, rubbing at the back of his neck.

"I see..." Jian was studying him.

"Besides, Roger is fucking *old*. Dani'd have to be super powerful to influence him, don't you think?" Slate added.

The twins made eyeballs at each other. "I'm with Slate on that one." Kari shrugged.

Jian chuckled. "For sure, vampires are... well. They're *vampires*. She'd have to be full-fae and even then..." He sucked a tooth. "Nah, you're right. Not possible."

"So stop calling her a bitch," Slate snapped once more.

"Not once did I call her a bitch—"

"It was *implied*—"

"Knock it off, both of you," Kari interrupted them. "Like children, kami. Stop it. Listen, Slate obviously likes Dani, and I'm pretty confident she'll come around—"

"You think so?" God, did he have to be so fucking *hopeful*? He pulled in a breath and nodded, trying again with a little more smoothness and charm. "You're right, she'll come around when she wants to."

Kari gave him a little look Slate didn't know how to interpret. Sneaky and sly. Talk about conniving. "—and because the Silver Valley Council fae aren't just gonna *go away*, we gotta watch out for Dani too."

"Do fae do that?" The words jumped out of his mouth. "Like, do they take people for bait?"

Jian gave him a look, cocking a russet brow. "Is she bait? If the fae go after her, what are you gonna do?"

"Kill some folk, that's what," Slate growled. "They hurt her over my *dead fucking body*."

Jian nodded slowly. Slate was certain he saw some lingering suspicion on his face. The twins glanced at each other before Jian's gaze swiveled back to Slate's. "If that's how you feel…"

"… then we'll watch her back too." Kari winked. "We'll make sure she's not bait."

Slate swung his gaze between both of them, back and forth like a round of tennis. "So, wait…" he said, frowning. "We just went from 'Dani's a queen bitch who might be enchanting you' to 'she's now our best friend'? The fuck is wrong with you guys?" He was getting whiplash from this sudden change.

Kari laughed, rich and delighted. "I like Dani a lot! I want to still be friends with her. If you like her, we do too. She's clearly important to you."

Slate cocked a brow, then glanced at Jian. Jian shrugged, giving Slate a little devilish smirk.

Slate pinched the bridge of his nose with a sigh; he would ask if Jian agreed, but it was clear Kari spoke for both of them. Damned twin empathy link.

"Okay then," he said. This felt right too. To have his two best friends at his back in all of this mess.

"Why don't we go out for a bit?" Kari suggested, standing and brushing off her knees. "Let's go grab a drink, some dinner. Get the heck out of the studio. Get take-out from Toharu's." Slate could tell she was trying to lighten the mood, to clear the air of this heated conversation.

Jian stood and held out his hand to help Slate. He grasped it, allowing Jian to tug him to his feet. "Alright," Slate agreed, feeling… perhaps not better, but it didn't quite feel so hopeless now.

Deciding that he had to cling to that hope if he wanted any hope of focusing on his championship, he sighed and rolled his shoulders.

"You've got the tab, *ne*, Master Melisande?" Kari teased with a smirk, and something in his mind eased a bit. He cracked a smile, and followed after them as they headed out of the studio.

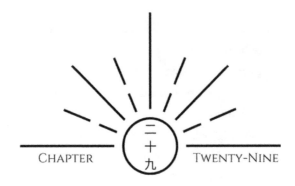

CHAPTER · TWENTY-NINE

THE GIFT OF INSIGHT

When the Vampire Council moved from Byzantium up into Siberia after the 9th century, there was an outcry over the vacuum of power that led to the human Sacking of Thessalonica not long after, where key...

- Gherald Schmidt, Faerloch Historical Archives

"Daniella."

Dani's head jerked up to find Roger studying her with gentle eyes and a little furrow between his brows. She realized he must have asked a question. "Oh, sorry. What were you saying?" She blinked twice, shoving her thoughts away. Thoughts about that *text* from ten days ago.

The lack of any since.

"I inquired after your plans for the weekend," Roger repeated, and his frown deepened and his eyes shuttered a moment. He reached for his bloodwine but kept his focus on her face as he took a small sip.

It was Thursday night, or rather, Friday morning, considering it was a little past one. She usually met him on Thursday nights, after her shift ended at midnight. A normal routine for them for, well... years now.

She dredged up a smile for her friend. "Oh." She shook her head, letting out a little laugh. "Umm, Maddie invited me to join her and some of the witches for a Sip and Paint Saturday afternoon. Otherwise, I think I'm just going to relax at home and have a quiet weekend with my friends." And by friends, Roger knew she meant her *animal* friends.

Saturday. The day she'd originally planned to watch Slate's championship fight.

She banished that thought.

"Two weekends in a row?" Roger asked with a half smile, but that smile didn't reach his eyes. "Your friends will be delighted."

Dani's laugh fell a little flat, but she gave a little shrug and said, "Well, I'm sure the witches will show me a good time Saturday. They're bound to use up my whole weekend's worth of energy in one night."

"Indeed..." Roger murmured, and took another long sip from his drink. He continued to watch her, and it was hard to read his expression. She thought she saw his eyes flicker, but she dismissed it as a trick of the light as a fresh stein replaced her near-empty one.

"Thanks," she scrambled to say, and saw the deer-shifter raise a hand and wink at her over his broad shoulders. Handsome, probably sweet as a button, like most weredeer were, and yet...

She had absolutely no interest.

"Yeah, I mean..." She shifted her grip to the base of her new stein, savoring the distracting cold against her palms. She didn't feel like drinking it, but the stein gave her something to hold onto, rather than holding her phone, which she'd been doing all week. "Iliana and Carrow are fun. I don't mind hanging out with them, and if Maddie shows up after her daughter's recital, it's bound to get a little crazy."

Hanging out with a bunch of women was perhaps something she needed anyway; a nice distraction. She'd considered inviting Kari.

Kari, who hadn't ghosted *her* when Dani had ghosted Slate. No, the fox-faced woman had appeared on her lawn one morning with two mugs of tea and a sassy sway to her hips as she informed Dani they were hanging out, whether she liked it or not.

She liked Kari. In fact, she'd talked to Kari a lot this week. Had truly been shocked the woman didn't seem to hate her for the way she'd turned tail on Slate. Yesterday morning, Kari had stopped by and Dani hadn't been able to help herself. She'd casually asked how the boys were. Kari had just sort've half-shrugged.

"Good. Jian's working long hours at the hospital this week, and Slate's in training mode. He doesn't talk much when he's like that—usually one hundred percent dialed in. Training by day, teaching by night." The *kitsune* had given her a sly look. "Why don't you call him? You clearly miss each other."

Dani had flushed and buried her face in her tea mug, sipping the hot beverage to unstick her suddenly dry throat. "No, no, I'm... I'm not interested in a relationship."

"So I hear," the *kitsune* had mused, but then she'd changed the subject. Kari's insight bothered her, but that went too far into thoughts she wasn't ready for, so she'd let it go, too.

But she hadn't been able to let go of Slate. The man who *seemed* to be making all the right moves and saying the right words. The one who *seemed* to want something casual, and yet... Her heart told her something different.

Her mind flashed to those words...

If you ever wanna hang out or something, you know where to find me.

The words seemed so tempting. Too tempting. Because her heart hadn't been touched like this since Kat, since her parents.

Roger was different, she realized with a start, sitting straighter in her chair. Roger was a millennia old vampire, with enough power that even Loraine respected him. For some reason, she truly believed he'd always be around, even long after she died. Perhaps that was why she'd felt so safe bonding with him, becoming best friends with him. It had always been safe to let him touch her heart.

As for Maddie... Maddie had done what Maddie does when she adopts someone, and after a few years, Dani had stopped resisting.

But Slate...?

Holy cow, this was a whole other level. If she let this thing between them grow stronger, it would obliterate her when he left. He wasn't immortal like Roger, like Maddie. He could die.

And the Silver Valley Council...

The idea made her sweat, so she took a small gulp of her drink.

Roger was still watching her, and the words jumped out of her mouth before she could stop them. "What are you staring at?"

She immediately regretted it, especially the way she'd snapped at him, and she crinkled her nose with a sharp exhale. "Sorry, sorry... I'm just... I guess I'm off tonight. What are your plans this weekend?" She forced a smile and waggled a brow. "The ones you can tell me about, you mysterious vampire, you."

A startled smile cracked the vampire's lips, and he chuckled with a shake of his head. "I am always surprised at how easily you can do that."

"Do what?" She cocked her head to the side, suitably distracted from her thoughts by his candid behavior—for the moment.

His smile widened. "Nothing, Daniella." That smile faded, and he took a sip of his wine. "Now tell me, does your preoccupation have something to do with a certain blue-eyed male?"

Her eyes darted away. "I... no, of course not."

It had absolutely nothing to do with the fact that Slate had thrown the ball back in her court, the way she'd always wanted one of her ex's to do, and now... she didn't know what to do with the ball.

Was, frankly, quite terrified of it.

Especially because after everything else, his very presence kept bringing her greatest fear back into her life; the High Fae.

A fear of relationships, and a fear of the fae, all balled into one male.

No, she reminded herself firmly. She wasn't *afraid* of relationships. She simply had no use for them.

So... naturally, she'd told him flatly that she didn't want a relationship. And he'd said...
I know.

I know.

Even after his face, his words... they had all screamed he'd wanted more with her, that night she'd driven away from him at the Den, he'd still acted like that was absolutely fine.

And since then, she'd been in this general state of... constant distraction.

Which had only gotten worse when she'd received his text, of course. She could still remember the way it had felt, when her heart had plunged into her gut, then slowly churned as she re-read the message over and over.

And a little piece of her was absolutely devastated over that text. A little piece she tried to ignore. A little piece that kept reminding her that while this was exactly what she wanted, it had somehow felt like he'd been breaking up with her. He'd agreed with her, and said they could just be friends. Friends with benefits, even. The type of relationship she'd always wanted.

... Right?

It shouldn't feel like a break up.

"Daniella." A calm, steady voice pulled her back together. She glanced up and took a deep breath, letting it calm her racing mind as much as his voice. "Have you seen Slate at all?" His question was even, completely non-judgmental.

And still, Dani tensed, a tremor zipping along her spine. Her fingers strangled the ceramic mug. "Nope. Not at all, actually. It's over, you know? It was bound to happen. We were just having fun. And as usual, that ship has sailed. Moving on, you know, just another day. I've told him I'm not interested in a relationship." She gave a smile she hoped looked cheerful, and gave a shrug she hoped looked unconcerned.

After all, he wasn't the first male she'd complained about.

"I see," Roger answered carefully. He sat up and steepled his long fingers together. "Daniella, you must know. I took it upon myself to visit with Slate last Monday evening." He spoke the words calmly, almost matter of factly, and her heart skipped a beat.

She stopped breathing. "What?"

"You seemed troubled by his possessive pestering, so I made sure he was aware of that. Some people are too dense to read the signs, after all." Roger's shrug seemed careless, but there was a tightness around his mouth.

"Why did you do that?" she demanded, feeling hurt and a little annoyed he'd go behind her back like that. She sat back in the booth, her fingers falling loosely from the stein to the table.

Roger straightened as his expression sobered immediately, and he reached out a hand to touch a single finger to the back of her one limp hand. "Daniella, I know you can handle yourself, and it's *your* business." He pulled his hand back, but he stayed leaning forward, holding her gaze intently. "I was merely concerned for you. I won't apologize for that concern, nor the actions I took. Your happiness is important to me." He finally sat back, and his lashes shaded his eyes as he focused on his near-empty wine glass. "You know I'd do the same for Madeline, or anyone else who I care for."

Roger rarely said anything so starkly... emotional. The sincerity of his statement melted away her hurt and annoyance, because she absolutely believed him. If something upset

Maddie, or his current lover Peter, or any of those close to him, Dani absolutely believed he'd step in. That was the kind of male he was.

She sighed, and reached across the table to brush at his hand, offering him a small smile. She still wasn't happy about it, but she couldn't be upset with him, couldn't fault him for being who he was.

Sitting back, she slowly curled her fingers around her stein once again, and the words just popped out. "What did he say?"

Did she want to know?

Probably not, but she couldn't have kept herself from asking if she wanted to.

"He essentially told me it was none of my business, but with a far more colorful vocabulary." His expression told her nothing beyond that, nothing a small, tiny, insignificant part of her had been listening for.

"He's right, you know," Dani finally said, not looking up from her beer. "But I... understand." She gave her head a little shake, and took a long drink of her beer. "You don't need to worry, though," she told Roger, licking the foam off her lips. Roger's eyes dipped from hers a moment before his focus shifted away, towards the bar. He needed only to incline his head a moment before that deer shifter was back, replacing his glass with a fresh one filled with deep ruby bloodwine.

Dani continued, "You don't have to worry at all. Slate's not... anything to worry about. He and I had our fun, and I can handle it from here."

A pause. Then, in a voice that was almost reluctant, Roger asked, "Why is it over?"

Dani shifted in her seat, shrugging a little. "It's better this way."

Roger studied her for a long moment, then cocked his head to the side. "You say you have not seen Slate. Has he been messaging you? Bothering you?"

"No! No, it's not like that." Dani shook her head. "He's not a bad guy, Roge, it's just... I mean, I don't want a relationship."

"And this mood you're in, it's not because he's been hounding you all this time for a real relationship?" Roger was watching her closely.

"What? No! Of course not! He hasn't said anything to me since that *one* text!" Dani hissed, annoyed at herself for not masking her own feelings better.

"So... where is the problem?"

Dani stilled, and her gaze flashed up to find Roger watching her with one brow raised, a hint of a smile on his lips. For a heartbeat, she thought she saw something else, something... sad? But it was gone, replaced with amusement as he studied her.

"The... problem?" she repeated dumbly, feeling a hint of anxiety fluttering in her chest.

Roger let out a slow sigh, and took a long pull from his wine glass. Long enough that it distracted her from some of her panic as she blinked at the now-half empty glass of wine. She'd never seen him drink so much in one go.

"Daniella, you are telling me you do not want a relationship with someone, and yet I can see you are plainly bothered that he has been respecting your wishes and leaving you be. That seems to me like a conundrum, and likely indicates what's truly bothering you has nothing to do with either of those two things." He wasn't looking at her as he spoke, his focus lingering on the glass in his hand.

Her heart stumbled in her ribs, and she pulled in a breath. She tucked her fingers in her lap so Roger wouldn't see them trembling.

She should have known better. His focus zeroed in on her, and his entire body stilled. "Daniella," he spoke in a soothing, smooth voice. A vampire's voice, as silky as a lullaby. "Take a breath."

She let that voice lull her, let it blunt the razored edge of fear, and pulled in another long breath. Her chest loosened.

"Listen to me. You can go home, you can forget about him. You can move on and everything can return to normal. Is that what you want?" He held her gaze as he spoke. "*If* that's what you want, I will do everything in my power to make it a reality. If it is what you *truly* want."

Slowly, he reached out a hand, and left it palm up on the table between them.

She reached out a now-steady hand to slide into his. His skin was cool against hers, and he squeezed gently, then loosened his grip until she could break the hold with ease. It settled her enough to really imagine the future he painted for her.

Going back to a life before Slate.

Before the fae, before the twins. Before the flirty texts, before ten dates.

A life *without* Slate. Without his rough hands and his wicked grin and his wild emotions.

Her stomach clenched with a roil of instinctual panic that was far different from the anxiety she felt when considering letting someone into her heart. It was more raw, less defined, and far more powerful.

Her eyes flared, and Roger lips curled into a small, almost sad, smile. "I don't think that's what you want, is it?"

No.

No, it wasn't. The idea of forgetting Slate, of going back to her life like he never existed? She'd not thought of it that way, and it was so instinctually *wrong* it obliterated her other fears for a moment. Obliterated the fact that compounding her trepidation about a relationship with him was his mysterious attachment to the fae.

Words lodged in a throat that was suddenly too tight. Breath lodged in ribs that were suddenly too constricting.

"Daniella, I think you know what you want to do. It's okay. No matter what, you won't be alone." Roger's words were spoken so gently, so softly, even in a pub full of beings with superhuman hearing, she knew these words were meant only for her.

Dani met his gaze, and found, in the eyes of a vampire that made most beings in the Lore shudder in fear at the simple mention of his name, a sense of strength she'd never experienced before. A sense of reassurance.

No matter what, she wouldn't be alone.

Dani inhaled sharply as a sizzling energy filled her. It was wild and chaotic, neither good nor bad, but she knew... she couldn't sit still.

"I have to go."

Roger blinked, eyes darkening. He gave a nod of his head, pulling his hands back from hers and under the table. "Never alone, Daniella, remember that."

She nodded, but she was already scrambling for the edge of the booth. She tugged her jacket up and slid it on, and a cool hand snapped around her wrist, gentle despite the suddenness. She froze, and found Roger had moved too fast for her to see, standing next to her and towering above her.

"Daniella, it's raining, let me—"

"I have to do this, Roger. I... if I stop to think, I'm going to chicken out," she confessed in a rush, speaking low in a vain effort to keep from being overheard. "Please. Trust me." She locked eyes with him, hoping he could see in her the things she couldn't put into words.

Roger hesitated, his gaze flipping to the windows across the room before returning to search her face. He released her wrist, and reached out his other hand to brush the back of two fingers over her cheek, before dropping both hands to slip into his pockets, taking a step back. "I do trust you, Daniella. Always. Please, be safe."

Unsaid was the fact that Slate might have already made her a target to the High Fae. A fact she should be taking care with, but right now...

Right now, she couldn't stop thinking about sapphire eyes that had this glow from within she'd seen on no other person. And Roger was still going to let her go out into this storm, to do something that was a thrum in her blood.

Because he trusted her as much as she trusted him, she realized.

"Thank you, Roger," she breathed, because she realized now everything her friend was doing for her. The clever way he'd guided her in this conversation. He'd given her the gift of her own insight.

He inclined his head with a small smile. "You have no need to thank me, Daniella. Ever."

She lurched towards the vampire, saw his brows raise slightly before she caught herself on his arm and leaned on her tiptoes to place a soft kiss against his jaw. "You're a good friend, Roger. I mean it."

Roger didn't seem to breathe until she'd taken a step back, but he offered her a wry smile. "Of course, Daniella. Anything for... a friend."

"I'll text you tomorrow, I promise," she told him, trying to quell her insides from attempting to wrap around her heart. She gave him a little wave and popped her hand up in the air towards the bar. Out of the corner of her eye, she saw Loraine dip her head before Dani shot for the exit.

She couldn't stop. Couldn't second guess herself.

She slammed into the door, and burst out into the rainy night, oblivious of the way a vampire stood vigil by his table, hands in his pockets, watching her leave.

CHAPTER ☩ THIRTY

FOR A REASON

... universal agreement of the Divine Laws of Magic. For the fae, mayts and the mayt-mark cannot be manipulated or replicated by any magic, which is consistent with the werefolk scent marker believed by many to be...

– Gherald Schmidt, Faerloch Historical Archives

It was dark as pitch, with sheets of rain pounding over her, but the street lights were her guide. The warmth of summer was her cloak against the chill of the wet. Her jacket was mostly water resistant, but her hair was plastered to her skull by the time she made it to her bike she'd left in the shelter of the alley.

The hammering of her heart in her ears was almost enough to drown out the sound of the engine as the bike started up. Sellie sent her a curious poke, roused from her dozing in her protected nest on the roof.

Go home, she urged her friend.

Sellie's mind became sharp, alert, and her question became more imperious.

I need to do this, she pressed upon the griffin, and sent an impression of feelings she couldn't put into words.

The griffin didn't respond right away, likely sifting through such feelings that were far more complicated than could be sent to a normal animal. Dani was two blocks over when Sellie's response came. It was heavily skeptical, and tainted with disgruntled disapproval, but she insisted she'd stay with Dani until she reached her destination.

Thank you, my friend. She glanced towards the sky, but her sight, even with the visor of her helmet, was distorted by rain. Dani took another turn, trying to breathe past her racing heart and tight throat.

Was she really doing this?

Holy cow, she was.

She reached the end of Birkenweg Street, and her heart flipped when she veered her bike left, instead of right.

To the Eastern District, instead of towards the suburbs.

Her emotions became a jumble, because she realized...

She'd ignored him for almost two weeks. She'd ignored him, and essentially told him off, the last time he'd seen her.

What if he didn't want to talk to her anymore?

What if he hadn't kept pestering her because he had no interest anymore?

The thought that he'd not want to see her again had her Vespa swerving wildly, and a piercing sound from above and a mental warning from Sellie flashed in her mind. She straightened the bike, but her mind was already tumbling over possibilities.

What if she was too late?

Her throat tightened. She swallowed hard, swallowed the sock in her throat.

She was stuck. She was a mess, stuck between being afraid of letting someone into her heart, and afraid he'd already walked out of it.

Anger pricked beneath her skin when tears leaked from her eyes. *Why am I so messed up? Why is this so hard?*

She blinked, and the Melisande Martial Arts building was in front of her, with her brain urging her to *notice.*

But her mind was scattered, and it was all she could do to guide her bike to the edge of the road across from the studio, still trying to pull herself together. She felt a firm impression from Sellie: *I'll wait for you in the garden.*

She was too jumbled to argue, to tell her friend to go home, so she focused on the bike beneath her as she yanked out her key. Her fingertips were trembling, but her body was mostly stable as she tossed her leg over, and stepped back.

Rain slipped down her shirt as she tugged the helmet off, and left it hanging from the handle of her bike—the witch magic would protect it from water damage, and she didn't have the brain capacity to focus on anything else but the monumental task she was about to do.

She turned toward the studio, and she finally noticed what her brain had been urging her to at first—the lights in the training room were on.

She almost tripped, halfway across the road toward the building, when her eyes snagged on movement inside the illuminated space. A figure spun, beating the ever-living snot out of a standing heavy bag, the base rocking from the force. He whirled, and the bag slammed to the floor with a back-kick. It was when he was reaching down to stand the bag back up that his eyes collided with hers through the glass.

Her entire body froze, and her mind blanked as Slate Melisande straightened to his full height, his shoulders heaving, brows lifting, eyes widening.

For one long, tense moment, neither one of them moved.

Then he was scrambling for the lobby, disappearing from view a moment before the studio door was shoved open.

The sound of bare feet slapping on wet concrete, and a voice that haunted her dreams. "Dani!"

His tone, that rumble that still sent shivers of carnal memories down her spine, was laced with surprise, concern, and a relief so profound she couldn't even process it. He reached out, like he wanted to snatch her up and bring her out of the rain, but froze with his hand an inch from her arm. His fingers curled into a fist and he dropped it back to his side.

"Are you okay? What's wrong?" He scanned her body, then searched the street.

Dani could only stare at him, could only swallow as her throat dried up at the sight of him.

His hair had come loose a bit, and dark strands quickly plastered to his face in the rain as he stared at her, a little furrow between his brows and a curve to his shoulders like he was ready to shield her from the rain at any moment.

"Hey, let's go inside, *ne*. It's fucking pouring—"

"Wait!" It came out like a squeak. She tried again, "I..."

The urge to run paralyzed her for a moment, and Slate's eyes darkened to a midnight blue at the same moment his handsome features sharpened.

He was concerned. For her.

After she'd ghosted him for nearly two weeks.

"I... don't know what to do," she confessed, the words rushing out with a fresh wave of tears, so much so that she had to squeeze her eyes shut again, mortified. She pulled in a trembling breath. "I... don't even know why I'm here, but I... I just..."

She had no words. Panic squeezed her throat, and still, her feet wouldn't take her away from him, as if her very instincts were overriding her flight response.

You're here for a reason, her mind reminded her, and her eyes flashed open. She looked up at him, and the words exploded from her. "I'm sorry."

CHAPTER ◯ THIRTY-ONE

CHARADES AND LIES, OH MY

... with each generation, the population of lorekissed has correlated directly with Lore–Human relations. The percentage of lorekissed within the human population has reached new heights since the 1960s AD, and scholars believe that trend will continue if Angeni Kennedy is successful in her...

— Gherald Schmidt, Faerloch Historical Archives

Slate had imagined a thousand different scenarios of Dani coming back to him, each one more wildly creative than the last.

But when he'd closed his hand over the smooth leather of the heavy bag, thrusting it back to its feet, his eyes had been drawn to the window. He had *not* been expecting to see Dani there, in the middle of the night, out in the pouring rain.

His heart had been a wild drumbeat in his ears as he'd bolted for the exit.

Rain-soaked, sobbing, apologies spilling from her mouth like the rain spilled from the sky. His first instinct was a protective surge that rose sharply inside him; what was wrong? Was she in trouble? What else would bring her to his doorstep at just after one in the morning, in the pouring rain?

But she was here for... *him*?

"Sorry for what?" His heart hammered in his throat. She was here and she was real, and it was taking every ounce of self-control he possessed to not smooth his hands all over her. He was still reeling from the shock of seeing her—still trying to force his heart back into an even rhythm. He didn't know he could *need* someone as much as he needed oxygen.

God-fucking-*damn it*, was he in love with her?

He was. Really bad. Heart pounding, throat dry, skin alive, *bad in love*.

Fuck.

"I..." she faltered again, flashing her eyes open and searching his face. She rocked on her heels, as though she were a bird about to take flight.

Slate held his breath.

"I know this is crazy, and it's late, but... I'm sorry for ghosting you. I just... I don't *do* relationships, you know? I don't. But—but I can't stop thinking about you." Her words faltered, and she reached out a tentative hand toward him before she whipped it back and curled her fingers into a fist. "I don't know what you've done to me, but I can't get you *out* of my head."

She fell back a step. Then another. It was a colossal effort to keep his hands to himself. To not reach out and halt her backward flight. Something like an icy panic crawled up his throat at the idea of her leaving. He would do anything, *anything*, to keep her right there.

"I don't want a relationship." She shook her head, water trailing and twisting through her hair, turning the fiery strands a red wine. "I don't... I don't want *that*," she continued. "I don't *want* what you want, but I also... the idea of walking away from whatever we have, for it to be over?" Her gaze skittered from his, and she gave a little helpless shrug.

Slate didn't move, didn't react, didn't dare twitch. An instinct inside him fluttered, telling him that this moment, right now, was absolutely pivotal. One wrong move, and she'd leave and he'd *never* see her again.

"I just want..." she paused, "can we just do something *easy*?" Her eyes were gilded again, a soft suffuse of a brighter green than the natural emerald. "Something casual. And fun."

That feeling when someone lied to him flared to life, by myth or by magic, he wasn't sure. She was telling him half-truths, things she only partially believed. He could see it—the stark emotion in her face. She was scared and alarmed and nervous and it was so deep, it shadowed everything else she was feeling.

Saying she didn't *want* a relationship was easier than saying she was scared of one. Easier than admitting and embracing whatever confused, complicated emotions skittered across her face. It was easier than saying she didn't want to trust him or perhaps that she didn't want to trust her own feelings. It was easier to say she didn't want any of it.

She was lying to herself as much as she was to him right now, a stark desperation in her eyes as though she were holding onto the lies like a lifeline. Maybe she wasn't ready to face those truths, but she was *here*, which meant she wasn't ready to walk away from him either.

Because there was something *more* between them. They both knew it, but neither one of them could quite put a finger on the pulse of what that *more* was.

A tiny bubble of hope inside him flared, but he sucked in a slow breath, feeling like one wrong move would send her scattering. "Okay." He nodded carefully, chewing every letter as it came out of his mouth. She was *here*, and he would agree to anything right now.

So long as it meant he could have more of her, spend more time with this woman who'd crashed into his life by mere accident, even though nothing about them ever felt *accidental*.

He wanted her, and he was ready and willing to take whatever scraps of her he could get. Whatever she wanted to offer, he'd take. Part of Dani was better than none of her. He was willing to be a part-time, some-time, fun-time boy toy, if that's what it took. Anything to get her to *stay*, even if it meant settling for something *casual*.

Even though they both knew it was a lie. They both knew he wanted more. But Slate was willing to do, say, *be* anything to keep the illusion alive and beating between them. He would do whatever she wanted. Whatever pace she set, he'd follow.

Without hesitation. Without conditions.

He nodded, eyes roaming over her face, her freckles, her trembling mouth... He swallowed past the tightness in his throat. "Okay, we can do that."

She blinked. "Just... like that?"

"Yes. Just like that." He offered her a small smile.

She blinked again, searching his face, and he hoped he wasn't giving away how desperate he was for her to agree, for her to *stay*. For several agonizing heartbeats, nothing but the rain fell between them. Her breath came in little puffs, water dripping down her face, wicking off her jacket, spiraling toward her limp fingertips, and he thought she'd never looked more beautiful.

"You..." she stuttered. She pushed her hair out of her face, a visible shiver wracking her shoulders. "You're okay with... casual and fun?"

"Yeah." He nodded again, swallowing his heart. "Whatever you want. I want what you want."

God help him, but he could see it in her eyes. It was plain this entire conversation was little more than a charade—an illusion. She knew it. He knew it. But right now, both of them were grasping for this lie, for anything that would give her a reason to stay. She opened her mouth, and he could hear the words she was about to say, hear the words that would call him on his bullshit.

He didn't think; he just acted. He closed the distance between them, bringing them nearly chest-to-chest, and placed a single finger against her lips. She inhaled quickly.

"I want whatever you want," he said again, injecting insistence and reassurance into every syllable. Her gaze dropped away from his. He shifted his hand until he could tip her chin up, encouraging her to look at him again. "I don't want it to be over either. If you want... if you want something light and easy, then you can have it. I..." It was his turn to flounder a little for words, torn between choosing carefully and just giving her everything he was feeling. "I will give you whatever you want, and I'm *okay* with that. Trust me. I'm a big boy; I can look after myself."

That was, for certain, a truth. He felt it in every fiber of his being; he'd deny her nothing, and he'd take whatever emotional stress came along with it.

Her eyes flickered back and forth between his, and he found he could read her like a book. Saw something in her shift to sadness, even as the tightness in her shoulders eased. The knot of frost eased off its stranglehold around his throat, and he pulled in an even breath.

"I'm sorry," she whispered, low enough that he had to strain to hear it past the pounding rain, and she lifted her hands to lightly press her fingertips to his chest. Each little flutter of contact was a lightning bolt through his body, like he was starved for her touch. He shifted his hand along her jaw, until he could slowly curl his palm around her neck in a gentle hold, caressing his thumb over the frantic pulse he found there. She tensed, he tensed, ready to whip his hand back, afraid she'd bolt.

"I'm a mess, you know?" she continued, her eyes skittering away. She didn't push his hand away, though, allowing him the contact. "I... I don't think I knew it until you came around. You..." her voice cracked around the edges, "you deserve something better than—"

"I don't want anything else."

Her lower lip trembled again, and she finally lifted her eyes back to his. She stared at him, searching his face, and he offered up a smirk. "I promise," he told her, voice low and firm.

She fell silent, watching him. The anguish on her face slid away like the rain dripping off her chin. Tentatively, she took a step closer to him, angling her head back to stare up at him. His eyes dropped when she nibbled on her lower lip, and his lungs stuttered.

"You know... I've really missed your kisses," she murmured, and he felt it like a physical touch when her own gaze dropped to his lips.

The corners of his lips tugged upward, and he stroked a thumb over her damp skin again. "Have you now?"

Her own lips curved upward, and the sight of it eased the knot in his chest. She licked her lips, and tilted her head to the side. "Are you going to make me ask?"

His answer was a flash of a crooked grin, shifting his grip from her nape to angle her chin up, heart pounding out a marathon behind his sternum. He watched her eyes flutter closed, and he thought he was going to burst out of his skin. He brushed his lips over hers.

The contact was feather light, but it sent sparks shooting through his blood. She let out a little sound—a feminine sigh—and he pushed just a little more, kissed her just a little deeper, bringing up his other hand to cup her face as he eased his lips over hers, running the tip of his tongue along the seam of her lips.

She tasted like rain, sunshine, and pure addiction.

Her fingers on his chest clawed into the drenched fabric of his shirt, and a small moan slipped from between her lips as he angled his head to delve deeper. He was a starved man and she, the forbidden fruit. Her lips parted under his kiss, and he slid his tongue along hers, crowding his body closer until they were pressed chest to breast, tangling his fingertips in her wet hair. His whole world fell apart and stitched back together with each taste of her, his heart a drum beat up his throat.

"Do you wanna come in?" he breathed, unable to keep his mouth shut, not when he could taste her need, her desperation. It was a twin to his own, a thrumming instinct that made everything around them fade away.

"Yes."

"All the way in?"

"Yes."

"To my bedroom?"

"*Yes.*"

CHAPTER · THIRTY-TWO

RUNNING DEFENSE

Touch is considered a key aspect of the mating process in many races, particularly for fae and werefolk. Interestingly, the notoriously sexual nymph and dryad races place a higher importance on...

— Gherald Schmidt, Faerloch Historical Archives

Heat pitched through Slate, a pure, physical reaction to the sound of her voice. Why was everything so fucking intense between them? Intense emotions, intense sex... He breathed deep, trying to calm his racing heart, and smoothed his fingers up and over her face, brushing her hair back in a caress that felt as natural as breathing. A flicker of emotion darted across her face, but she didn't run.

"You're soaked," he murmured, willing himself to step back.

"So are you," she said, and finally, he saw her lips quirk into a true smile.

Slate chuckled, and glanced down between them. "You can borrow some of my clothes, if you want."

"Are we going to need those?" she whispered, and heat seared through him.

Fuck him, she was going to be the death of him.

"Not if you don't want them," he answered, a desperate bid to sound *smooth* when she fired all his fucking switches. Her eyes darkened to a rich pine, and her breath hitched.

"Come on," he murmured, and willed himself to drop his hands from her face. He made like he was going to simply take her hand but stopped himself, faltering for a moment. Instead, he held out his hand like an offer, and prayed to the gods she wouldn't refuse him.

Her eyes flipped between his face and his hand, something haunted flashing across her face. He held his breath, his body stiller than stone, watching her. A moment's hesitation... she reached out and slipped her fingers through his.

His lungs loosened in a silent rush of air. He closed his fingers around hers. A spark zipped through him and for the briefest, faintest moment, he sensed her churning panic and this bone-deep quaking inside her, held back by the thinnest ribbon of resilience and determination.

It was gone faster than it was there, but he was certain he'd felt something.

He gave a little tug of his hand, guiding her back to the studio. She was trembling, just a little, and he didn't think it was only coming from the intensity of whatever emotions were bouncing between them. It might be summer, but she was soaked to the bone. By the time he was opening the apartment door, her trembling had evolved into full-out shivering, and she was clenching her jaw to keep her teeth from chattering.

A change of plans, then, maybe. The idea formed in his mind even as she slipped off her shoes and let him lead her down the hallway. He didn't go to his bedroom; instead, he pulled her to the door across from it. He opened the heavy door and urged her inside, and watched her face as she took everything in.

Her lips parted and a delighted surprise lit up her eyes. He couldn't look away from her, watching raptly as she spun in place to study the entirety of the little room.

Fuck, it was as though her very presence was awakening everything inside him after nearly two weeks of being asleep.

"This... is amazing. I've never seen a bathroom like this," she murmured, stepping toward the deep Japanese bathtub, much deeper than a western tub and featuring a flexible handheld showerhead outside the tub, where one washed before soaking in clean hot water. The entire room itself was the shower, fully waterproof and separate from the toilet room.

It was one of his favorite places in his house; nothing beat soaking off the soreness of a good workout. She ran a finger over the edge of the tub, which came up past her knees.

The room suddenly felt different with her inside it. It was small, and the floor of the shower portion of the room was covered with beautiful teakwood planks, cleverly concealing the drain. A slender window at the far end was the only view to the outside world, and during the day, it illuminated the hand-crafted wooden tub. An overturned wooden bucket, where he sat to wash, rested against the wall under the showerhead, beneath the slender window.

"No toilet?" she asked, turning back to him with a raised brow.

"Uh, no. It's in the room next to this one. Traditionally, your bathing area was always separate from where you do your business." He grinned with a shrug. "The entire room is basically a shower with a soaking tub."

She slid her toes along the teak floors. "Incredible..." she breathed. She was still shivering, though it had eased slightly.

Resisting the urge to rub his hands over her body to warm her, he reached for the faucet of the tub and turned it on hot. "Get naked." He tipped his chin toward the tub with what he hoped was a casual—if not a little wicked—grin.

Dani's brow creased in confusion, gaze flicking towards the bedroom. "I thought..."

He knew her hesitancy had little to do with his request and more to do with the fact that this wasn't his bedroom and they weren't about to just go fuck in his bed.

But they were both soaked to the bone, and he could see her lips and fingernails were tinged blue. He supposed sex would warm her up pretty fucking quick, but it was... this was so much more for him than that.

Casual and fun, Melisande.

Slate swallowed his insecurity and hid it behind another grin. "Are you opposed to a hot and wet bath, love?"

She blinked before a cheeky smile wrinkled her nose. "Well... when you put it like that.... can't really pass up a chance to take a bath in this cool room, anyway."

Slate smiled, and glanced down at the rising water, testing the temperature with his fingertips. He reached for one of the little bottles on a small shelf next to the tub, and selected one of Jian's herbal concoctions. He busied himself with pouring some in the water, but all of his attention was dialed into her even as he watched what he was doing.

The water turned a milky blue color, and in his periphery, he saw Dani reach for the soaked hem of her shirt.

His heart stuttered a little, and he had to regulate his breathing as she peeled off her clothes to reveal creamy skin sprinkled with the freckles he'd become so obsessed with. Slate went a little weak at the knees at the sight of her; slender, shapely legs, the tuck in her waist, the expanse of skin. Her hair was a heavy curtain down her back. His palms itched to touch her. Instead, he grabbed the flexible shower head as she hung her sopping wet clothes on one of the pegs by the door.

He twisted the settings around, watching her out of the corner of his eye as she turned to survey the almost-full tub.

He sprayed her.

She let out a squeak and darted back, whirling around to peg him with a wild look. His lips pulled back into a wicked grin that was a touch cheeky.

"You—" she started, but he sprayed her again. She threw her hands up to ward off the water, and laughter slipped from her lips as she spun away to avoid the water. Grinning, he snagged his arm around her waist and tugged her closer to him, laughing with her as he doused them both with warm water from the showerhead.

Her laughter escalated, and she shoved her hands against his chest in a vain attempt to escape. He laughed and tugged her flush with him, her naked form against his still-clothed one as he mercilessly sprayed her with water.

She let out a delighted shriek, trying to twist away. "Slate!"

It was a damn good thing he'd kept his clothes on so far, or it would be impossible to conceal his erection as her body squirmed against his. Chuckling, he angled the water away from her. "Shh, love, you'll wake up my father."

Dani smiled, breathless and gasping as her laughter petered out. Slate's damned heart jumped into his throat again at that *smile*. No wariness in her eyes now, just amusement and a mischievous glee that tugged at his heart. He tried not to analyze too deeply how it made him feel, and focused on the fact that he'd made her laugh. If even for a moment, he'd banished whatever demons haunted her about relationships.

About them.

And she was no longer shivering—mission accomplished.

"My turn." She crooked her fingers for the showerhead. "Get naked."

He handed her the showerhead and stripped. She sprayed him this time, laughing as he opened his mouth like a dog to catch the water. When she'd hosed him off to her satisfaction, she handed him the showerhead and turned to the tub. Once more, she ran a finger along the edge, before she stepped over the tall lip and into the steaming water inside.

She sank against the edge of the tub, a hum of pleasure escaping her lips. "This smells nice," she commented, watching her hands as she cupped the hazy blue water in her palms. He watched her draw in a deep breath, the steam wafting from the water in sensual ribbons.

Slate grasped the bottle from the lip of the tub. "Jian made it... he gives me idiot-proof labels." He studied the fine, minute handwriting. "This one is scented... 'tired, pissed off, had a weird day'."

Which was a pretty succinct summary of his life for the last two weeks. The last two *months*, really.

She let out a half-hearted chuckle. "Snarky, just like Jian."

Silence fell between them as Slate affixed the shower head back to the wall. He could feel Dani's eyes on him as he lathered soap over his hair and body to wash the sweat off from training. He turned his head and offered her a teasing smile. "Enjoying the show, love?"

"You don't need me to tell you how good you look," she said with a laugh, and Slate grinned as he rinsed off the soap then turned off the showerhead, running his fingers through his hair. In the bath, Dani was sunk so low only her nose and eyes were showing above the water, knees drawn up to her chest. Strands of her long hair floated like red-gold seaweed.

Some of the cautious skepticism returned to her face as he approached the edge of the tub. He braced his hands against the edge.

"I'll wait in the bedroom for you?" he asked, trying to sound nonchalant. His original, true intention had been for her to have a hot bath and be warm. Offer her a little slice of peace after whatever fucking shit they'd just unearthed out on the street.

But since he was in the business of deluding himself tonight, sure, he could pretend he wasn't dying to be in that bath with her.

He could pretend his desire to touch her didn't go so far beyond casual and fun that it bordered on *love*.

Sure.

He could be patient. He understood how to play a waiting game. The delusion and lies between them only went so far—it wasn't so much as he was looking to change her mind about her resistance to relationships but rather he wanted her to *trust* him. To *want* him. To *choose* him. If he was smart enough, if he played this right...

God, he sounded like a selfish prick, even inside his own head. But he was just... it thrummed inside him, this insistent, nagging feeling that there was more. More than fear and trauma and unsaid words. More between them than casual relationships, delusions, and sex. And he held onto that nagging like it was a fucking *lifeline*.

He pushed off the tub and made like he was headed for the door.

Because despite, well, everything, right now, this was all supposed to be *casual*.

"No."

The word jumped from her lips and shot right to his thrumming heart. Tremulous relief vibrated through him as he looked back at her with a raised brow. "No?"

She was watching him, nibbling on her lower lip.

He wanted to be nibbling on that lip.

"You can join me... if you want," she offered, and he had the distinct impression she was just as surprised by her words as he was.

His blood pressure jacked up, but he offered her a wicked smile with a sharpness around his eyes. "I'll keep my hands to myself... unless you don't want me to."

That earned him a smile, and he shifted trajectories to ease himself into the tub, settling his back against the edge opposite from her. Water sloshed over the edge to accommodate his much larger frame, and it lapped against the creamy skin of her shoulders. She watched him settle into the hot water across from her.

He should have just taken her to his bed, should have given her the casual sex she'd wanted, rather than the far more intimate act of bathing together. That would have been the safer move, but...

He hadn't been able to ignore her shivering, because he *cared* about her and wanted to wrap her in safety and security when they were both walking on eggshells in an earthquake.

He had to be mindful of every move and every word.

He felt like he was in a sparring match, watching for every twitch and every tell. And running defense like crazy. Slate didn't play defense well.

Silence settled around them. Neither of them was touching; the tub was easily big enough for two. He settled his legs criss-cross, not wanting to initiate contact before she was ready—she still had her arms wrapped around her raised knees, looking vulnerable and small against the wall of the tub.

Slate breathed through his racing heart. She was here. The hard part was over. He just had to play carefully so he could keep her.

"Do you wanna... spend the night?" The question was out, but he paired it with a smile, trying to look like her answer didn't matter to him.

She regarded him for a moment, then lifted her face from the water. "Are we going to have sex in your bed?"

He inhaled sharply, heat shooting through his head. "That was the plan..."

She nodded once, a little smile curving her lips, and Slate's throat stuck a little. "Then, yes, I'd like to."

Fuck him, the memory of her, tangled in his sheets, mouth tasting every inch of her, set fire to his blood. She made him feel things he didn't know he was capable of feeling. But... he suffocated the little piece of him that was frustrated and annoyed and *insecure* at the idea that she was in this for sex.

All she wants right now is casual, Melisande, he scolded himself mentally. *That's the agreement. We have to just be patient. Whatever she wants. Let her come to you.*

She returned to watching him. He felt like he was under surveillance, like how her little animal friends watched him, weighing and measuring him, assessing his worth. He took the scrutiny with grace.

"A bath together doesn't seem entirely... casual," she mused carefully, trailing her fingertips through the water, making patterns in the milky blue surface.

"Hey, I offered to wait for you in my bed." He grinned, trying to unknot his stomach from the sight of her guard coming up again. "I could have been waiting in there, sprawled out and naked, for you to use as you please."

Every word out of his mouth tasted like poison and dirt.

She laughed, but it was forced. She glanced at him but averted her eyes quickly, lashes fluttering down. "I don't want you to think... It's not..." She huffed out a breath. Her gaze flipped to his once, then back down again. She skimmed her fingertips over the surface of the water. "I don't want it to be like I'm *using* you, but... I kind of am, aren't I?" She glanced at him again, daring him to spill his truth, to break the delusion.

He wouldn't, but he also wasn't going to sit here and let guilt eat her alive that she was using him. They both knew he wanted more, they both knew she didn't. It was his choice to follow her pace, to play along with the *casual and fun* she wanted.

What she didn't realize was that her self-awareness gave her away. It meant she *cared* enough that she didn't want to hurt him—she didn't want to use him. She was showing her hand, and she didn't even know it.

Still wasn't gonna get him to break the spell of the lie they were carefully weaving though. Not part of his game plan to keep her.

"Daniella, look at me." She dragged her eyes to his. "I want whatever you want. I can look after myself. If I couldn't, I would've told you to go home."

She didn't answer right away, and his heart thundered into his head at the way she searched his face. He tried to project as much relaxed confidence into his features as he could. She probably saw right through him—of course she did.

But he was trying like hell to give her what she wanted.

"Besides," he scrambled to add, giving a little shrug, "around here, baths aren't really that intimate. We have bathhouses, where everyone gets naked and bathes together, separated by gender. I'm surprised Kari hasn't taken you to one yet; there's a nice one near her house."

She blinked with alarmed surprise. He grinned. "What? Did you think I didn't know you were hanging out with Kari for the last two weeks?"

She didn't look at him, choosing instead to play with the water. "I didn't want to hurt your feelings."

His feelings *were* hurt, of course, that she'd spent all this time with one of his best friends rather than him, but he wasn't going to *tell* her that. "Kari needs more friends. Poor thing spends all her time around me and Jian. Can't be good for her health." That earned him a chuckle from Dani, and he grinned. "Have her take you to the bathhouse. It's nice."

Her gaze slid away again as she nodded. "Taking a bath in a bathhouse sounds casual," she murmured slowly. "This one isn't." She flipped her gaze towards him again, something unreadable on her face.

His skin tightened. He answered carefully. "Uh... no. No, this one's a bit more... personal."

The silence swelled with tension this time. Her eyes started to rim vibrant green again and he lost all sense of propriety. Lost his patience.

"Holy shit, just come over here," he growled, opening up his arms for her.

She hesitated for a moment before she shot forward to slip her arms around his neck and straddle his lap. He tugged her to his chest at the same moment that her lips collided with his. His skin burst with sensation, with the feel of her breasts pressed into his chest, her hands threading through his hair, her hips hovering *dangerously* close to his suddenly rock-hard erection. He traced his palms over her spine, one sliding around and up along her ribs until he could cup a breast. She gasped into his mouth when he stroked his thumb over her nipple.

Just like the first time they had sex, it was as if they simply detonated. Took right off—from zero to downright intense in the space between heartbeats. He was trying to remind himself, trying to keep things *casual* and *light* and *easy*, but it was like all his good intentions crumbled to dust when they were kissing. His feelings, her fears, all of it was washed away by the chemistry exploding between them.

Whatever her fears, whatever his feelings, it was suddenly about sex and nothing *but* sex. He had to be touching all of her right now. Starving. He was starving for her.

She made him feel so *charged*.

She gasped his name as he chased water droplets down her neck, her fingers digging into his shoulders. She lowered her hips over his, rocking herself against his aching erection. He groaned against her shoulder, scratching his teeth along the sensitive muscle between her left shoulder and neck. She moaned to the ceiling, pressing a little harder against him.

He plunged a hand between them, teasing his fingers along her folds. His head spun; even through the water, he could tell she was *so wet*.

"Slate…" she begged. "Right now. Right now before I explode, *please*."

He fisted his cock beneath the bathwater, rubbing the head against her. She made a little sound—like a cross between a moan and a sob—and she slowly worked herself over him. Taking him inside her inch by breathless inch as the water in the tub sloshed.

The pleasure was searing. Slate tugged her face back to his, kissing her feverishly, thoroughly, tongue sliding along hers as she rocked her hips, creating a shallow but intense rhythm. She was so tight, the pleasure bordered on pain.

She took him to the hilt, tipping her head back and moaning his name. The column of her throat, her damp breasts, the angle of her chin, the sheet of fiery hair that was tumbling down her back… all of it was his undoing. Her hair painted the water with shades of copper and gold, and a single drop of water dangled precariously from one nipple as she rolled her hips and clung to his shoulders, her fingers digging in hard.

He gripped her hip with one hand, keeping her tight and deep as she slowly started to fuck him, and curled his other around her throat in a possessive hold, careful not to hurt her as his head fell back to watch her riding him.

Kami above, what he wouldn't give to just *keep* her. To have her like this whenever he wanted. To wake up next to her and see that warm smile, the crinkle of her nose, the freckles dusting her cheeks, every morning... He wanted her fiercely, like he'd never wanted anything in his entire life. All of her. It was uncanny and intense and he thought sometimes he might drown and die from the way she made him feel.

Most of all, he wanted her to *want him like that too*—

"I..." she gasped. "Slate... I'm..." her voice pitched with each syllable.

An inferno of pleasure rushed right to his skull, pulsing behind his eyes. He could practically taste her impending orgasm, and it was a pleasure itself. "*Fuck*, yes, come on, Daniella..." He shifted his grip from her hip to circle a thumb over the little bundle of nerves above where he was buried inside her.

A slow, tumultuous wave of pleasure crested over them both as she cried out, hips jerking over his pulsing cock. As she tightened and spasmed around him, he couldn't stop his own orgasm from exploding. He slipped his hand from her throat to her back of her neck and tugged her to him. Like a magnet, his mouth found that sensitive spot on her left shoulder, just at the curve of her neck.

She clung to him, making little sounds at the back of her throat as she writhed against him, her body clenching around his erection as he came undone. All thoughts fled from his mind. He moved on pure instinct as he thrust his cock inside her. He wasn't sure what possessed him to do it. He didn't stop and question the insanity of it. He bit her, right where her shoulder curved up to her throat. Hard. Hard enough to draw blood. Hard enough to leave a mark.

She cried out his name, nearly sobbing, and her core spasmed with a fresh orgasm. Instead of pushing him away from her neck, she clung to him, her hips moving in a frenzy as her body shook above his.

He might be able to come again too, overwhelmed by the power of the pleasure that rolled through him. His hips were still thrusting when she went limp against him, breasts crushed against his chest as her fingers loosened on his shoulders.

She shivered, and an answering tremor raced along his own skin.

They didn't move for several long moments, his heart a thunderous roar in his ears. He pulled his mouth away from her neck, trying to focus and right the world that had suddenly gone upside down.

He opened his eyes, the sound of their panting breaths loud in the small room. He sucked in a sharp breath, horror flooding his skull.

"Oh *God*," he hissed, hands on her shoulders as he yanked her back from his chest to study her neck. At the bloody bite mark where her neck flowed into her shoulder. "Oh, *fuck*, Dani, are you okay? I'm... oh shit, I'm sorry. You... you're bleeding." A thin ribbon of crimson trickled from where he'd bit her, trailing between her breasts to stain the water.

She blinked slowly, eyes once more outlined a glowing green, then looked down to where her blood was mingling with the bath water. "Hmm? How bad?" Her voice was languid and sultry, a bit dazed.

Slate hissed in a slow exhale, feathering a gentle finger against the wound, a shimmer of horror tightening his ribs.

He'd *bit her*.

What the fuck was wrong with him?

The bite mark was bloody, but when he smoothed gentle fingers over it, he could see it had already stopped bleeding. He frowned.

"Get up, love, let me get you something..." His insides were in knots, guilt washing away the last bit of pleasure that lingered from the sex.

Dani reached up a hand to touch the bite mark, and his eyes snapped up to see confusion on her face. "It didn't hurt... When you... I don't think I've ever come that hard before," she confessed.

He gave her an incredulous look. How could that *not* hurt?

"We should get you—" Slate started, but she lifted her hips and his voice cut off at the feel of her sliding off his cock. She shifted back, still fingering that mark, and he rallied himself to surge from the tub. He snagged one of the two towels hanging by the door, then twisted back to kneel next to the tub and bring the material to her shoulder. She was inspecting her red-coated fingertips.

"It doesn't hurt at all," she mused again.

"Well, that's good, I guess," he muttered darkly, fury at himself throbbing through his skin. He dampened the corner of the towel and gently dabbed at the wound. What had possessed him to fucking *bite* her? He didn't even remember having a conscious thought about it. Instinct had just... taken over.

"I'm sorry..." he said softly, peeling back the towel gently and inspecting the bite mark. He frowned. It was colorful and bruising quickly. "You're probably gonna have a little scar or something..."

His ribs tightened in a sting of guilt. Which wasn't a strange feeling to have in the context of *biting* someone.

What was strange was the little nugget of possessive satisfaction in there too. That was *his* mark. *His.*

He stuffed the feeling down, and dropped the towel to the floor. Dani's hand fell away from her shoulder, and she pulled in a deep, satisfied breath. "The orgasm was worth it. Should I worry about this becoming a regular thing when we have sex?" Her eyes were laughing, teasing, and it eased some of the tightness in his lungs.

He smiled. "No. I promise. I don't know what came over me."

He better not get in the habit of getting dental; he wasn't sure he could handle the feeling again, that he'd physically *hurt* her. He couldn't help himself; he slipped his palm along her jaw, cradling her face in his hand. She nearly sighed at the touch, and it was a shot of openness, of vulnerability—she didn't seem to have the energy left to feel wary of him. Of them. Of whatever this was between them.

Or perhaps this all lived within that superficial realm of *casual* to her.

"Wanna go fuck in my bed now?" he asked, desperate to keep panic from tightening her face. He injected wicked delight in his voice, curling his lips into a grin.

Of course, he was also desperate to get her under him, to feel her body writhing against his...

He was already hard for her again. Arousal edged into her expression, focusing on him. "I think I can handle that," she answered, her own lips curling into a smile that had his heart flipping.

He grinned. "Let's go."

CHAPTER · THIRTY-THREE

TWO SECONDS

The ability to tie one's life force to another's is believed to have originated by the Kushim Coven, whose prowess in the water element, and blood in particular, was well known by their neighbors in...

— Gherald Schmidt, Faerloch Historical Archives

Slate woke up just after dawn, watery light bleeding through the window, casting the room in dim shades of gray.

He wasn't sure what woke him until he felt the bed shift, heard Dani slide out and tiptoe over to the dresser, where he knew her clothes from last night were resting. He heard the shift and slip of clothing against skin.

And he just knew she was about to make a sneaky exit, and everything inside him tightened up. Lungs froze, heart stopped, stomach churned. He could vomit right then and there from how much he hated this.

But he was a big boy, as he'd kept telling her last night, a big boy who was more than capable of handling his own feelings, so he stretched his body and opened his eyes, mustering a lazy half-smirk in her direction. "Places to go?" he rumbled, voice gravelly from sleep.

She froze, and he could practically taste her guard coming up. But she flashed him a little smile and crinkled her face. "I have some errands to run before work. I didn't mean to wake you..."

He gave a half-shrug. "It's all fine, love, I haven't been sleeping much lately anyway."

A confused frown. "Why?"

He gave her a pointed look with a cocked brow. "I have a title fight tomorrow night."

Her eyes widened, lips forming a little adorable 'o.' "Right. I... well... I didn't forget!" she added quickly, flushing across her freckles. "But I didn't... I thought..."

"You can still come, if you want," he said, saving her the trouble of trying to phrase her thoughts and feelings around it. God only knew he hadn't been expecting her to show up. Certainly a little part of him *hoped* she would, but he had been trying to be realistic with himself. "Open invitation."

She pulled on her shirt, but said nothing at first. A fine tension cut lines across her shoulders, her face, framing her eyes. Long heartbeats went by. Slate counted his own breathing in order to keep his lungs from bursting out of his chest from sheer angst over this woman. "Will Kari and Jian be there?"

"Of course. And feel free to invite anyone else. We'll probably go out after, win or lose."

She nodded slowly. Some of the tension bled out of her. "Maddie can't, and Roger's not *that* interested. But..." she hesitated for a second, then nodded once, almost resolutely, "alright... I'll come."

He grinned, and he hoped it didn't betray the spark of unadulterated happiness that flushed through his system, coupled with the shot of nerves at the idea of her coming to watch him. He shouldn't be *nervous*. She'd come to a couple of his matches now. It shouldn't affect him at all to have her there.

But she tripped all his switches.

"Only if you want." He stretched, then tumbled out of the bed. He slid by her to reach into his closet, and he couldn't stop himself—he brushed his fingers over the bruise on her neck. Every time he'd been on the cusp of orgasm, buried deep inside her last night, he'd been invariably drawn to that *spot*. It freaked him out a little; every time he let his mind slip, he found his mouth drifting over it, teeth scratching it gently, tongue lavishing the hurt. Or curling his palm round her throat and running his fingertips over it.

She assured him it didn't hurt. But it was colorful and bruised and the sting of the guilt at marring her skin was potent inside him, even at the same time as a little piece of him was smug with satisfaction over it. Which was weird. Confusing. He didn't like the feeling. But it was hard to overcome at the same time because whenever he touched it, she moaned *really* loud.

He caught himself belatedly and zipped his hand back, a rush of anxiety flushing him, expecting caution to jump into her eyes, expecting her body to tense.

It didn't. In fact, goosebumps erupted all over her collarbone and throat and a little shiver trembled through her.

"Sorry..." he mumbled quickly.

"It's alright. I told you, it doesn't hurt." She gave his naked body a once-over he pointedly decided to ignore lest he dump her back in his bed. "Maybe you're not lorekissed, but a *vampire*," she mused, a hint of teasing delight in her voice.

"Ugh, no." Slate rolled his eyes. He opened his closet and started rifling around for some clothes. "Drink blood and sleep in a coffin during the daylight? No *thanks*."

She laughed lightly, and his whole body came alive at the sound of it. "Roger doesn't sleep in a coffin—"

"You don't know that."

"I've been to his apartment. He lives a very normal, urban lifestyle."

"That you know of. It's probably all just a carefully crafted facade." Slate did not forget the little *chit-chat* he'd had with Roger last week. He wondered if Dani had ever found out her best friend came lurking around, trying to push Slate off her.

He still was undecided about whether or not he *liked* the vampire. Slate mused that perhaps under different circumstances, maybe he and Roger would have been good friends.

Might be a pinch hard to be friends with someone who was in love with the same woman he was in love with.

Hindsight was always 20/20, and now that Slate had Dani in the palm of his hand for the moment, he could almost—*almost*—appreciate what Roger was trying to do.

Looking out for her, as best friends do, best intentions at the forefront of his mind. Still, Slate was annoyed and aggravated over it.

He also hadn't forgotten Roger's warning; that Slate had likely already made Dani a target herself to the Silver Valley Council by pure association with him.

His attention snagged back to Dani, jerking him from the depths of his own thoughts as she studied the bruise in the mirror on his closet door. "Still doesn't hurt," she said idly. "Though it looks like it should *kill*."

Slate shrugged easily. "Magic," he tossed the word out offhandedly.

She chuckled. "*Vampire* magic, maybe." Another teasing smile, and he rolled his eyes.

His father was still in his bedroom when Slate and Dani crept down the hall past the bedroom and through the living room. She paused to put her shoes on at the door, and Slate didn't miss her guarded expression, the tense lines of her body. Slate mustered a deep, even breath. Casual, this was all supposed to be *casual*.

He hated that word now.

"I'll see you tomorrow night?" she said quietly, hand on the doorknob.

He nodded, giving her a nonchalant shrug. "Sure. Like I said, totally up to you. Text me if you think you're coming. Or text Kari, either way." He tried to sound like he didn't care.

He did care, damn it.

"Okay. Well... see ya!" She gave Slate one last smile and she was out the door. He heard her skip lightly down the stairs, then heard the heavy access door at the bottom open and shut.

Slate stood rooted to the spot for several long moments, hands flexing at his sides. He bolted to the door and pressed his palms to the wood, peering out the peephole. She was gone. Something inside him tapped insistently against his skull. *Go after her, follow her, find her, go, go, go...*

He literally had his hands on the doorknob before he chomped down on that urge. "Idiot, idiot, idiot." He tapped his forehead against the wood.

"I thought you and Dani-*san* had broken up?"

Slate whirled around to see his father come ambling down the hall and into the kitchen. Slate heaved a sigh and dragged his feet to the breakfast counter. "I thought so too..." He flopped himself into a barstool and rested his chin in one hand. "She came over last night."

"Ah." Ebisu turned the kettle on.

"She just... she just wants something *casual*," Slate spit the word out, hating everything about it. He kept no secrets from his father. They talked about everything, or rather, Slate talked about everything. Ebisu had always been his sounding board.

For most things, usually.

Once again, he considered confronting his father about the weird magic he'd exhibited, but tossed it out again.

Perhaps a little part of him didn't want to find out how many secrets his father had kept from *him*. And yet here he was, spilling his. He couldn't help it. For certain, Slate had never kept secrets about his dating life. Every awkward teenage boy question had been handled with truth and grace, and Slate was forever thankful his father had never made it weird.

Ebisu hummed thoughtfully. "You do not want something like that, *ne*?" He poured a cup of tea and slid it across the counter.

Slate poked a stray tea leaf. "No." He huffed out a hard breath and twisted a strand of hair mindlessly. "But... I dunno. I'm just an idiot, I guess. I can't fucking say *no* to her, so here I am." He darted his eyes all over the kitchen, as though the appliances and cupboard held the answers to everything he wanted. "There's something different about her. But she's just so *nervous* and guarded and... and..." He growled. "But she also *wants* more too? Am I making sense?"

Ebisu nodded sagely. "I understand completely."

Slate fell silent, staring blankly into the kitchen, mind whirling, picking apart the pieces of her he saw last night. Shades of anxiety and fear, yet there was something in her that was determined to *try* and see it through, something in both of them that wanted it more than words could properly describe.

Something inside him that thrummed and vibrated and beat against his skull: *Go, go, go, go find her. She's yours, she's yours...*

"I think I'd marry her in two seconds," Slate mused softly. "I'm crazy, right?"

Ebisu chuckled, shaking his head, but he said nothing.

"What, *to-san*?" Slate's mouth pulled into a smile, a little flush dusting his cheekbones at his father's obvious humor over such an outlandish statement.

"Nothing," Ebisu chuckled. "The heart wants what the heart wants, Slate. Sometimes you have a choice, sometimes it's fate." He reached across the counter and rested a weathered hand against Slate's cheek. "You will forge your own path."

Slate frowned, laughing. "Why are you so cryptic, *ossan*?"

His father smirked, some sharpness around his eyes that was twin to Slate's own. "I am old, my boy. Cryptic is part of my job description."

CHAPTER THIRTY-FOUR

THE FINAL FIGHT

It is estimated that the percentage of true witches burned at the stake was actually quite small and that the majority of those persecuted were lorekissed. A good amount of those burned were ordinary humans, but their numbers are more difficult to track. Kreugal Bindestop spoke hotly for the intervention of...

- Gherald Schmidt, Faerloch Historical Archives

Why did she feel like she could throw up?

This was perfect. This was *fine*. This was everything she could ever ask for in a casual and fun relationship. A little bit of sex, a little bit of hanging out. Casual, casual, *casual*.

Goddess, she was starting to hate that word.

Dani pulled her bike into the alley next to the studio and killed the engine. It was Saturday night—the night of the title fight. Above her, she heard the soft sweep of wings, and a distinct impression of faeries and gardens as Sellie settled into her customary spot in Ebisu's garden. The griffin impressed feelings of comfort and serenity, utterly at home on the rooftop. She even had a little nest up there, crafted out of bits of tree branches and stolen laundry.

Comfortable. Peaceful. The griffin planned on staying in the garden while they were at the championship match.

Her fingers tightened on the handlebars, knuckles white. She didn't want anything serious, and she didn't want things to be *over* with Slate either. She... really liked him. Just liked him, generally, as a person. This was how it had to be. This was the best of both worlds. She could have her cake and eat it too.

Right?

Right. And he'd said it was fine. He said he was totally okay with it. And she believed him. She totally believed him. He hadn't said or done anything alarming or weird, nothing untoward or pushy or clingy. He made her laugh, he made her body feel amazing...

So why did this entire situation make her feel gross and dirty?

This was exactly what she'd asked for. He was giving her exactly what she wanted.

Even though a little part of her knew it wasn't what he wanted.

But it didn't matter. He'd said so! He said it was okay!

She didn't want to break it off with him, which would be the logical conclusion to feeling guilty and terrible about what they were doing. Because she just... couldn't.

The knot in her gut over never seeing him again was more powerful than the idea of letting her shields down with him in a real relationship. It was a mind-melting conundrum that was sure to leave her in an early grave.

The access door opened and Dani's heart jumped into her throat. She whipped her eyes up.

"Hey, lady!" Kari greeted. "You coming in or what?"

Dani swallowed her pulse and smiled. "Yeah. Yeah, I'm coming." She unstuck her hands from the handlebars and climbed off her bike.

"Kami *above*," Kari breathed as Dani came through the door. "What *happened* here?" The *kitsune* reached out and brushed her fingers over the bruise on Dani's left shoulder, exposed by Dani's pine-green tank top.

"Oh." Dani reached out and covered the mark. "Umm, nothing." She'd considered putting make-up over the mark but hadn't been able to make herself. The memory of that *orgasm*, when he'd sunk his teeth into her flesh and her entire world had exploded on a new level, had left her frequently stroking the bite mark over the last day and a half.

She'd never have guessed that something like a bite could set her off that way, and Slate had seemed drawn to that spot on her neck for each bout of sex the rest of the night. In an odd way, she'd wanted him to bite her again, to reach that peak of pleasure once more.

Which was definitely strange. So naturally, she'd put it out of her mind. For the most part.

"It looks like someone bit you—" Kari cut off her words and a foxy grin slowly spread over her face. "Ah, I see. Someone *did* bite you."

"It's nothing," Dani dismissed with a wave, purposefully walking down the hallway toward the main training floor. "Just things getting carried away, but in a good way." She gave an easy shrug, fighting the urge to touch her shoulder again, to run her fingertips over the little scabs that were already healing it.

"I'd say," Kari said with a laugh, but her eyes lingered on the mark as she kept pace with Dani, making Dani hyper-aware of it. She shoved down her annoyance, because sometimes the insight in the *kitsune's* gunmetal eyes was *unnervingly* observant. "Well, everyone's got their kinks, right?" Kari winked, and Dani couldn't help the smile that tugged at her lips.

"I don't know about kinks, Kari. I'm pretty sure that's your department, maybe even your brother's," she teased back.

It was so *easy* to be friends with Kari. It was almost as unsettling as the way Slate made her react. And yet Kari didn't seem bothered in the least by the way Dani was treating Slate. She had no doubts that Slate shared details with the twins about what was between them, and yet the fox-woman never seemed to judge Dani for it.

The little ball of guilt at the bottom of her stomach pulsed, and she pushed the thoughts from her mind. She was determined to enjoy herself tonight; she would try to untangle her emotions later.

She rounded the corner and there were the boys, on the training floor, playing a little hamstring sparring game. Kari had explained it to her once as a game of timing and strategy. The object of the game was to tap your foot against the other person's hamstring. Lightly.

Dani was surprised when she spotted Slate's father standing off to the side on the blue mats. She'd never seen him in the studio other than that *one* time when he'd walked in on her and Slate making out in the chair. He fit into the environment effortlessly, and she could almost imagine him as a younger man, critically assessing his students for mistakes with those sharp eyes. He was tossing out a firm direction here and there, Jian was laughing, and Slate's temper was showing as he growled at them both.

Slate's eyes cut in her direction for the briefest moment as Kari and Dani stepped onto the mats, long enough that Jian snapped his instep against Slate's hamstring.

"Focus, Slate," Ebisu said as Slate growled at Jian.

"I *know*."

Ebisu's dark eyes flickered over Dani, then did a double-take as his attention zeroed in on the bruise on her neck, a little frown creasing his aged face. She flushed and immediately wished once again she'd covered the mark with something, maybe a sweater.

Jian noticed it too, and unlike Ebisu, the witch-doctor didn't keep his mouth shut. "Damn girl, what happened there?" The words popped out of his mouth and that fast, he sucked in a quick gasp, a devilish grin spreading on his lips. Color dusted Slate's cheekbones and he lashed out, kicking Jian hard enough that the other man's knee buckled, but he was laughing too much to care.

Kari was grinning too, and Dani wondered what she was telling her twin. Probably something outlandish. Dani flushed, and Kari cocked out a hip. "Hush *ji-ji*, Slate needs to focus, and Dani's already as red as a tomato." Kari winked at her, and Dank resisted the urge to cover her face with her hands.

Jian's grin widened as he straightened. "Hey, I don't judge, after all, I—"

"Focus." Ebisu's voice cut through their laughter with a firm command, no louder than a normal volume, yet the twins and Slate all muttered a very hurried "yes, sir."

It wasn't long after her arrival until it was time to go, but she enjoyed watching as the twins and Ebisu warmed Slate up for his fight. The man was a ball of energy, shaking his hands out, pacing. He didn't stay still for anything. Dani could taste that chilly aura bleeding out of him, like the first breath of winter. She wasn't the only one who noticed; Jian followed Slate's movements with a keen eye and interestingly, so did his father.

Just as they were walking out the door, Ebisu held Slate back in the studio for a moment, waiting for the three of them to go outside ahead of Slate. Dani looked through the window and saw the older man had both hands on either side of Slate's face, forcing Slate to look right at his father. And Slate was nodding, frowning a little, but nodding. It pulled a little at her heartstrings—that's where Slate's habit of touching everyone's faces came from.

Slate joined them, that restless energy humming off him, and they began the walk across the pedestrian bridge toward the arena.

"What'd *jii-san* want?" Kari asked, brows raised as she glanced at Slate from where she was arm-in-arm with Dani.

Slate shrugged. He was walking along the top railing of the bridge like a balance beam, flawlessly. The grace he had was uncanny, and Dani couldn't watch him for long. *Lorekissed.*

Just lorekissed with some great athletic abilities.

Even as the way he moved reminded her entirely too much of the way the High Fae moved; graceful, flowing, but with power. Her stomach tightened, reminded anew of the challenges she was facing if she wanted this... thing... between them to work out.

"He wants to talk tomorrow," Slate answered. "Probably wants me to stop fighting in the circuit."

"He doesn't like that you fight professionally?" Dani asked.

Those blue eyes caught hers and her breath stuck in her throat. "Nah. He tries to talk me out of it all the time. 'Martial arts is about avoiding the fight. You need to set a good example for your students.' Stuff like that." His voice was pitched exactly like his father's, slight lilting accent and everything. "I dunno. Maybe I'll retire. I haven't decided yet."

As the arena came into view, Slate grew quieter and quieter, going into a fight-mode. More predator than man. He gave all of them a chaste goodbye before he headed into the locker rooms.

"Slate's fight will be last tonight," Jian said as the three of them walked down the aisle toward the front rows. "He's the main event."

"How many fights before Slate's?" Dani asked. Kari led them toward the center of the arena to where three seats had 'reserved' papers taped to them, right in the front row. She offered them a sensual grin before snatching the papers up and planting her ass in one. Dani followed suit, and Jian sat on her other side, sandwiching her between the twins.

"A few; they are all title fights. They'll be good ones, though," Kari picked up where Jian left off.

The twins weren't wrong. Each match was riveting and intense. The crowd was visibly charging around them at the conclusion of each fight, bringing them closer and closer to the main event. To Slate's final fight.

Jian disappeared eventually, heading off so he could be ring-side with Slate again. Halfway through the fight just before Slate's, Dani noticed Kari's distraction. Her eyes kept bouncing around the arena, watching the crowd.

"What's wrong?" Dani asked, leaning in to speak to her over the din.

Kari frowned. Something sparkly shimmered between her fingers—a delicate leaf of rose gold, the exact shade as her hair. "I don't know," she muttered, flicking her eyes around restlessly. "Something feels... off."

"Off?" Dani's heart skipped, a sour feeling spreading through her.

"Yeah..." Kari mused. "Jian feels it too."

The fight finished, the winner and title champ of that weight division declared. The lights dimmed, the strobe effect intensifying. The crowd went absolutely crazy as the commentator announced the final fight of the night—Slate Melisande against Gustav Montague.

Kari tensed ramrod in her seat. "Something... is *very* wrong..." she growled as Slate came prowling down the aisle.

Dani's eyes followed him, swallowing hard at the strange, almost-magical aura that came off him. He skipped lightly up the stairs, entering the cage. Kari's hand suddenly latched onto Dani's wrist.

"We have to go," the *kitsune* hissed at her. "Right now."

"Wait... what?" Dani whirled her eyes back to Kari, tearing them away from Slate. "Kari... the match is about to—"

An explosion rocked the building.

The screaming in the crowd shifted from excitement to terror in a heartbeat. Another explosion rumbled the foundation, and suddenly, everyone was on their feet, scrambling for the exits. Bodies were suddenly rushing past them, jostling Dani as she wrestled down her own fright.

What was happening?

"Kari!" Dani shouted, reaching for the *kitsune* as the crowd forced her apart from the woman.

Kari dove between two people to snag Dani's wrist once more. "We have to leave," Kari hissed at her and tugged Dani toward the nearest exit. Dani's eyes flew to Slate, who was looking around with wide eyes in the center of the cage. Jian was shouting something at him from the cage door. "We've been followed," Kari growled, tugging Dani through two people who were pushing at everyone in their scramble for the exit. "The High Fae are here."

"What?" Kari's small hand was impossibly tight around her wrist, tugging Dani along, but Dani looked over her shoulder, toward where Slate was now rushing toward a frantically beckoning Jian. The High Fae? The Silver Valley Fae? "Kari! Kari! The *boys*..."

"The boys can take care of themselves," Kari called back to her, pushing and shoving through people. "Jian's got—"

A heavy hand fell on Dani's shoulder, yanking her backward. She shrieked, and Kari's fingers slipped from her wrist as she was propelled back into a hard chest.

"Kari!" She reached for the female, eyes wide and horror choking her throat. The *kitsune* whirled around, ghostly blue flames dancing around her eyes, and bared her teeth as she zeroed in on the figure behind Dani.

Dani tried to twist around, to see who had grabbed her, but the edge of a knife appeared at her throat, the edge razor sharp, and she froze. Fear flooded her system with adrenaline, making her hyper-aware as she looked down at the knife.

It was slender and gleamed silver, wielded by graceful, long fingers. A fae blade. A fae hand.

Her breath stuttered out of her. Around them, the crowd shoved on, oblivious to what was happening in the middle of the aisle, a mere dozen feet from the exit.

Kari snarled. In her hand were five rose gold leaves, held like a hand of cards, but poised to be thrown like knives.

"Do not move, fox monster," a lilting voice said from over Dani's head. "Steady now, or I *will* kill her."

Dani's heart plunged into her stomach, and she tried to quell the shaking migrating up her body—any little movement, and that knife would split her flesh like butter. She didn't dare breathe. Over Kari's shoulder, she saw two other forms emerge from the receding crowd like wraiths, all tall and slender and gliding with that immortal *grace*.

So much like the way Slate had moved on the bridge railing.

Kari growled, baring her teeth, eyes shifting slightly, head tilting as though she knew exactly what was stalking behind her.

"Hurt her, and it won't be me you have to worry about," Kari hissed, the sound coming out feral, canine, and ferociously at odds with her pretty face. Blue flames danced over her hair like little wisps of visible temper. Despite her words, her hands came up in a decidedly submissive gesture, eyes darting around, taking in her surroundings.

"Kari..." Dani whispered, fear eating her from the inside. A High Fae had her at knifepoint. Flashes of Kat's face, her placid smile with the horror in her eyes, had Dani trying to swallow past a throat suddenly as dry as a desert.

"It's okay, babe. Nothing's going to happen to you." Absolute conviction in Kari's voice, locking her eyes with Dani's. But Dani's eyes were lost in the distance, lost in herself.

Instead of herself and that knife, when Dani looked down, she saw the back of long legs, except they were upside down. Or rather, *she* was upside down. She felt slender strong fingers clutching at her as she bounced on a fae male's shoulder, spirited through a portal in her bedroom in the dead of night a few weeks after her parents' death, not yet seventeen. Remembering the acrid taste of terror, of the chemicals from the cloth they'd held over her lips, her muscles locked as echoes of the past mingled with the present.

This can't be happening. Her heart pounded in her ribs.

"Walk, fox demon."

Kari growled when a hand shoved her between her shoulders, pushing her back toward the ring. Dani was turned around and marched back down the aisle too, through a now-empty arena, toward the cage ring. She barely processed her own feet underneath her as she walked, terror lining her very bones as all too familiar slender fingers gripped her shoulder.

Inside the cage was a different scene. Three more High Fae stood in the ring, looking decidedly martial. Slate stood shock-still, still in his shorts and shin guards, breathing deep and erratically. His eyes were near-glowing with icy, burning *fury* as they locked on the sight of her being marched to the edge of the ring after Kari.

Jian was also being held at knife-point by one of the soldiers, the High Fae taking a far more aggressive approach with him—the very point of the knife was held right against the flesh over his jugular, a hand gripping his hair, tipping his head back. He, too, had his hands up in a submissive gesture, but smoke curled around his fingertips.

Dani and Kari were herded up the stairs and into the cage itself. Kari was forced down to her knees, and her eyes flitted to Jian, then to Slate, then to Dani. Their fae escorts stood vigil near her. One stood directly at Kari's back, a steady hand on one shoulder, a knife point pressed against her nape, ready to plunge it into her spine at the first sign of resistance. It was clear who they thought was the biggest threat. And it was clear they'd picked her most vulnerable targets to keep her in line.

The knife relaxed ever-so-slightly away from Dani's skin. She sucked in air, her head spinning, body tense and shivering. She made eye contact with Slate, and she saw the fury in his blue eyes shift to something closer to fear. Footsteps sounded down the aisle beyond the cage; slow and deliberate. Dani's eyes pulled away from Slate's. A male, cloaked much like the other High Fae, approached the cage.

"Well, well, well," the figure said with a savage grin. "There he is. The man, the myth, the legend. *Zlaet, son of Aredhel.*"

CHAPTER THIRTY-FIVE

ZLAET, SON OF AREDHEL

... the most powerful of fae glamours. It is even capable of masking and delaying the development of magic enough that the individual's aura mimics...

— Gherald Schmidt, Faerloch Historical Archives

Slate eyed the new male through the fencing of the cage. Tall, lithe—a High Fae, unmistakably. His long silver hair was pulled back away from his face while the rest fell to the middle of his back. His eyes were a bright, menacing blue that struck a cord of familiarity in him. The male was devastatingly handsome, enough that even Slate noticed—too lovely to look at, the planes of his face were too sharp, too angled, almost primal. He was dressed simply in cotton breeches, soft leather boots, a tunic, and a dark traveling cloak over his shoulders. He walked with a saunter that dripped with arrogance and power.

In a lazy, almost bored gesture, the High Fae raised both hands as if to pull back an invisible curtain in front of him. Each section of the octagonal cage rattled and screeched, twisting apart like a mangled flower opening its warped metal petals, tearing the cage away from the ring. Fencing flew into the surrounding seats, clattering into the chairs. In front of Slate, a piece of the cage fell forming a perfect ramp up to the octagonal floor of the fight ring.

"Oh yes, you are most definitely him," the male continued as he moved towards the ring, stepping onto the newly formed ramp. "You are an *exceedingly* difficult male to find, *Zlaet*. Difficult, indeed." The chain-linked fence of the cage wall hardly rattled under his graceful fae steps. "I do apologize. It's such a shame to have to resort to such... aggressive measures to ensure our meeting. So primitive, so mortal, but it was necessary, based on how you reacted to our other approaches. Can't have you running off before I've had a chance to speak with you." A pleasant smile, one that seemed to say *thank you for your understanding in this matter.*

"Who are you?" Slate growled, fists in balls at his sides. His bones cracked under the pressure. The color of those eyes... so familiar.

He realized it was like looking in a mirror. A blue so startling, he recognized them as his own.

"Me? Yes, I suppose introductions are polite." The male nodded again. He began to circle Slate in slow, easy steps, studying him with unnerving intensity. Slate didn't move, even when the male shifted out of his line of sight. He didn't dare twitch wrong, not with a knife at his best friends' necks.

At Dani's.

"I go by many names these days," the male said with a sigh. "My given name is Zeyphar, but more commonly I am called *Titania*... the king of the fae."

Slate's throat tightened. So this was the notorious Zeyphar. The king of the fae who had been hunting him for months.

Relief prickled in with the fear. Finally, they could settle this.

"But you, Zlaet, you can call me 'uncle'."

His breath froze in his lungs, utter stillness deep into his soul at that word.

Uncle?

Uncle? This High Fae was his *uncle*? The *king of the fae*... was related to him?

"No way..." Kari breathed.

Zeyphar nodded. "Yes, indeed. I have been seeking you for quite some time now, Zlaet." The male smiled, but it was a cold smile as he paced the ring. "It took me longer than I care to admit to narrow down your location. The Mystic ward over the Eastern District has proven to be mighty troublesome. However, you've taken to leaving the district more recently, yes? To participate in mortal fighting sports?" He gestured to the empty arena around them. "The Faerie Dust Glamour placed over you is starting to fade. Your aura is becoming more pronounced. Erratic, even."

"Oh *fuck,*" Jian breathed, eyes shifting from Zeyphar to Slate.

Slate met his gaze, and his stomach flipped at how pale his best friend was. Too pale. What the fuck was going on?

"What's Faerie Dust?" Slate snapped, his voice edged with anger. Everything was moving quickly, information pouring into him, his mind trying to grasp at pieces and put the implication together. The *Titania* was his uncle... a blood relative? Making Slate...

Zeyphar grinned, a malicious baring of teeth. "You." He pointed to Jian. "You explain. As a witch-doctor, surely you have heard tell of such a thing?"

The knife slowly pulled a pinch away from Jian's throat, giving him room to speak but not much else. Jian swallowed hard, then said, "A... a Faerie Dust Glamour is a very rare and very *powerful* fae glamour. It's... it's undetectable and suppresses aura and magical development."

Zeyphar rolled his hand at him. "And? Do not deviate from the details, good doctor."

Jian hesitated, eyes raking over Slate's form, no doubt reading his *chi*.

"It... they," Jian slowly continued, "they require a blood signature, which is how they meld seamlessly into the cloaked individual. And they can only be removed by someone with both the same magic and the same blood relation."

Slate's skin tightened over his body, and his eyes shot toward his supposed uncle.

"Indeed." A pleased smile from Zeyphar, like Jian had performed a good trick and deserved a treat. Zeyphar's eyes slid back to Slate. "It is how I was able to find you, Zlaet, despite the Mystic glamours your friend added to you. Blood calls to blood, you see." Zeyphar lips curved even further, cold and cruel. "A Faerie Dust Glamour is a tricky magic. It's not meant to be long-term. You see, magical energy continues to grow and develop under the glamour, but it festers like an untreated wound. It has no outlet; it can cause magical poisoning, erratic, uncontrollable bursts of magic, sickness, even death."

Slate pinged his gaze from Zeyphar back to Jian. He'd never seen Jian look more terrified in his entire life; pale, a touch green, like he could faint at any moment.

"I had *no idea...*" Jian whispered, and he was talking to Slate, something haunted and devastated in his expression. "I didn't... I can't *see* it..."

"Of course not." Zeyphar waved a hand at him dismissively. "Such glamours are rare and dangerously tricky, unorthodox, and as the good doctor said, they require a blood signature. My sister—your mother—was a thorn in my side, but I cannot deny she was an incredibly powerful empath. It was well within her magical capabilities to produce a powerful Faerie Dust. She cloaked you so well you do not even know who and what you are, Zlaet."

Nothing was making sense inside him. Trying to process this information was like sorting through a thousand-piece puzzle without a picture to guide him. He was picking up bits and pieces here and there, trying to construct something that made *sense.* A glamour? This *king* was his *uncle*? What about his mother?

"I'm not *anything*," Slate growled. "Just me."

Zeyphar laughed, the sound rich and smooth. "You, my dear nephew, are half-fae. Half *High* Fae, to be precise. You are *Zlaet Titania*, crown prince to the fae."

There was a ringing silence after that statement. Not a single person moved. No one breathed. Across from him, Dani's eyes widened, and Slate saw a wisp of alarm drift through them.

"What?" Slate whispered. The world pressed in on his ears.

"Your mother," Zeyphar continued, "was Aredhel Titania, princess of the fae and heir apparent. She took a mortal consort and had you. Making you the heir to the fae throne, as it stands now."

"Not true." The words came out as a knee-jerk reaction, a way to buy him time to think, to process. He'd wondered if *Ari* and *Aredhel* were the same person. Had said as much to his friends. His father explained that his mother had an important job that kept her away from them, but Ebisu had never elaborated. And Slate had never asked.

But... royalty?

He hadn't even considered the option.

Zlaet, son of Aredhel...

Zlaet Titania, son of Aredhel Titania, princess of the fae.

Zeyphar chuckled. "Have you not noticed how *other* you truly are, Zlaet? The Faerie Dust Glamour can only mask so much, of course. You would have noticed you are stronger, faster, more durable... you are a mortal warrior, are you not? A talented one, I should think. The best, even? The best in your academia as well, I would assume. Fae are naturally clever and intelligent beings." His smile widened, perhaps reading the shock in Slate's expression. "The silver in your hair is perhaps a dead clue. I would wager you are charismatic as well, able to read a crowd easily, yes?"

The more the High Fae spoke, the more images flooded through Slate's mind. Picking apart his own past and finding Zeyphar's words ringing true.

"I should even wager," Zeyphar continued in a light, musing tone, as though they were simply talking about the weather, "that perhaps you have some of your mother's ability, no? Have you any strange sensitivities? Able to feel intense emotions in others, able to persuade people, perhaps even project your own emotions onto others by pure accident, maybe even sense when people lie to you?"

That last one hit him hard.

"It's not..." Slate muttered, but some of his fury and fear were being replaced with numb shock. "I... I have Mystic magic in my blood, I know that. I'm lorekissed—"

Zeyphar threw his head back and laughed. "It is certainly an excellent combination to your mother's bloodline, but this is not the reason you are as you are. You are a fae, Zlaet. Tell me, am I lying to you?"

The silence in the ring was tense, like a collective breath was being held. Slate couldn't bring himself to look at Dani, to see her fear again. His heart began to race, and his hands flexed at his sides. He felt like he was breathing through pond water. "No..." he muttered. "But there are fae who can manipulate emotions—"

The High Fae male stopped laughing so instantly, it was alarming. "*You* would certainly be able to tell the difference, Zlaet, I assure you." He grinned. "After all, your talents must have become more pronounced lately. The Faerie Dust is fading from you. It was tied to your mother's life force and she is dead."

"Dead?" It came out clipped. "When?" The word popped out of his mouth, the only thing he could think to grasp at in the sea of unbridled chaos rioting inside him.

Zeyphar lifted one shoulder in an elegant half-shrug. "A few years now." He cut a sharp look toward Slate. "Surely you felt it? As a powerful empath, she would have had an emotional bond with you, similar to the one she would have shared with your mortal father."

The realization hit him in a crash so sudden, his breath stuttered.

The day his father had collapsed from 'sickness.'

Slate himself had felt *wrong* for a few days.

He'd felt his own mother's death. Suppressed by this... glamour.

"Aredhel and I never saw eye to eye," Zeyphar continued, pacing the ring leisurely. "Fae favor female leadership, so naturally, she was to inherit the throne, which she did not, unfortunately." He strolled closer to Slate and grabbed his chin with one hand, turning Slate's face side to side. "Perhaps she left her dear elder brother a final, parting gift... you."

Slate said nothing. He wrenched his face out of Zeyphar's hold with a growl, hand coming up to swat the fae away. But Zeyphar was unerringly quick, as quick and graceful as Roger, and neatly dodged Slate's assault as though Slate were no more than an annoying fly.

"I now sit upon the fae throne," Zeyphar intoned, bored arrogance heavy in his lilting voice. "And I have no heir of my own. Even with the Faerie Dust Glamour cloaking you, I can sense a great force swirling in you. You and I, Zlaet, the feats we could accomplish together..."

"What?" Slate growled, actively working to calm himself down, but the intensity of his feelings pulsed through him in a burning rage. Every part of him was on vibrate, right down to the blood pumping into his racing heart.

Zeyphar turned a placating expression toward him. "You will accompany me back to the Silver Valley, Zlaet. It is your birthright."

"Wait... *what*? You want... you want me to *join you*?" He found his voice, fury unsticking his words. "You tried to kill me *three times*."

"Kill you? No, no." Zeyphar waved a hand. "I merely instructed my attendants to come to collect you. It is not my fault you chose to fight them instead of coming quietly as they requested of you."

"You expected me to just *come quietly?*" Slate said.

"Yes."

So simple. A single word. Slate stared at him, a shaking starting in his bones. This man—male, fae, uncle, king, whatever the fuck he was—just expected him to... expected him to skip along after some strange fae *blindly*?

Happily, even. As if he couldn't possibly understand why Slate *wouldn't* want to come happily to the king.

"I expect obedience, nephew," Zeyphar added softly. "It is the only way we can make our people *stronger*."

"I'm not the obedient type," Slate growled.

"Are you not?" Zeyphar gestured around to the arena, the scenery of a fight cage, indicative of the discipline of martial arts. "Does this... *activity* not require you to obediently follow the advice of your trainers? Your... masters at arms?"

It wasn't the same... but Slate knew Zeyphar didn't see it that way. He seemed like the type that only saw what he wanted to see, and what he wanted was obedience and compliance.

Slate glanced around. Jian was still being held at knife-point, Kari was glaring at Zeyphar, a knife still poised at the back of her neck, and next to her Dani... Dani was shaking so hard he could visibly see it, eyes huge in her pallid face. The knife was close enough to her skin that he worried a stray breath might slice her.

She was terrified.

High Fae terrified her.

He was... *he* was High Fae.

He wanted to rush over there and grab her face and tell her that everything was going to be *fine*. Wanted to chase the terror out of her eyes. But he wouldn't lie to her. Nothing was fine. Everything was a mess. This was a nightmare. He couldn't even promise her that any of them would live through this.

He was so scared.

He was *so angry*.

"Since I could not know the situation of your life, and considering I wished to explain such a... delicate... situation myself, my soldiers were simply instructed to bring you to me. But you've chosen to be rather... stubborn, and far more adept at eluding them that I imagined you could be. Therefore, I made the necessary arrangements to attend to you myself," Zeyphar continued. "I am a busy male, Zlaet, but matters of blood are of higher importance." His tone was lofty, as though his presence was a great honor.

"Put down the knives," Slate demanded, an icy fury building in him.

"Of course." Zeyphar made a small gesture with his hand. "Such measures were simply to ensure I had the chance to properly explain the situation before you ran off again."

The knives held against Jian and Dani were removed, but not the one behind Kari. Dani's knees gave out from under her and she dropped like a stone. Kari reached out without shifting her upper body, carefully snagging Dani's wrist and tugging her close, even while eyeing the fae over her shoulder who held the knife. The fae allowed it, but never took his eyes off the knife at Kari's spine. The *kitsune* tucked Dani against her, and her thundercloud eyes made contact with Slate. She gave the smallest jerk of her head, just once.

Just one moment between them. And Slate knew that should shit hit the fan—which it was likely going to—Kari would get her out of here.

Relief was a balm in his chest.

Slate's mind raced. He flipped his eyes to Zeyphar. "Kari too."

The High Fae male glanced over at Kari. "I cannot honor your request, nephew. Fox children are devious. I do not trust her."

Kari growled in response.

"Alright... you have my attention," Slate said. "Now what? You want me to join you? And be what? A prince or some shit?"

"You are wasted here, Zlaet, in this mortal, iron-clad city." Zeyphar waved a casual hand around him. "You do not comprehend the *potential* you have. You must come back. You *will* come back. It is your birthright. You are a fae prince, the only one, and you *belong* in the Silver Valley." Zeyphar glanced around, alighting his cold blue eyes on the twins and Dani. "If it makes you feel more comfortable, you may bring your friends."

"I'm not interested in fae politics or titles or anything," Slate continued. "Besides, I hear the Silver Valley is in the *shit* right now."

Another casual wave. "Aredhel's death took a toll on the population. She was dearly beloved." Something about the way he said it stung Slate. It wasn't a lie... but it wasn't the full truth either.

Red flags burst through his mind. Despite all the questions and the mysteries, Slate knew without a shadow of doubt he wanted *absolutely nothing* to do with this male. Nothing. This entire conversation felt like a loosely veiled threat, a proverbial knife at his own throat.

"Come back with me," Zeyphar urged. The depths of his eyes glimmered maniacally. Alarm shivered through Slate, especially when it was *his own* eyes looking back at him.

Slate flipped his gaze around to his friends again. Kari, Dani, Jian. He tipped his chin up.

"No."

The king's eyes went flat. Emotionless. Then, they shifted rapidly to a probing, predatory curiosity. "Now, now, nephew. Think clearly. You, and myself—we can achieve *greatness*. An empire unto ourselves. A legacy to rewrite legacies. Together."

"I don't want that. Any of it."

Zeyphar's eyes narrowed. "You refuse me, then?"

A knowing pounded inside Slate. Instinctual. Primal. A red flag.

Death.

Death was the answer to that question. Slate dared to shift his attention around to each of his friends. The twins were afraid, but resolute. And Dani...

The High Fae male closed his eyes and steepled his fingers together, touching them to his chin in thought. "Here is the problem, Zlaet," he started. "If you do not come with me, I'm afraid you will force my hand."

"Force it how?"

"Either I drag you by might and magic with me, which will be unfortunate, but perhaps necessary." Zeyphar paused. "Or I will have to kill you. And your friends."

Slate's veins turned to ice.

"You see," Zeyphar said, once more pacing around Slate. "Aredhel was crown princess, heir to the throne, making *you*, dearest nephew, the next in line. I merely ascended the fae throne because, well, truth be told, you were your mother's best kept secret. And there are faerfolk who... do not approve of my reign. These rebels are a menace upon our people, a disease that weakens *all* fae." Zeyphar offered a pained smile and a helpless little shrug. Slate didn't think *anything* about this male was helpless. "I will not condone such instability among our great people. You must come back with me and stand at my side as my heir, to unite our people and suppress these *distasteful* and *selfish* rebels. I cannot risk civil war. Either you are by my side... or you are dead."

"I don't want it," Slate spat. "None of it. I don't want titles or royalty or politics. I just want to live my normal, very boring, mortal existence."

Zeyphar tsked. "That is not a risk I'm willing to negotiate." A deep, patient sigh. "Truth be told, nephew, these rebels will seek to find you, and if they manage to do so before you are safely behind the walls of our great city, there is no telling what harm will befall you and what the repercussions would be amongst our people."

"Rebel fae...? They would come after me?" Slate asked, barely breathing.

Zeyphar shrugged. "It would be kinder to kill you than see you in their hands, and safer for our people as a whole." He splayed out both hands in a decidedly magnanimous gesture. "But... you see, I would prefer a more *diplomatic* solution. News of your death could lead to a rise in dissonance among our people and breed a whole slew of uncivilized behaviors and riots and outrage, not to mention a whole host of missed opportunities..." he trailed off with an almost regretful sigh. "No, no. We must think these things through carefully now. It is advantageous to both of us for you to join me. I would see our people thrive again. United by your triumphant return at my side."

"That's it? Those are my two choices? Go with you, or... or *die*?"

"You make it seem as though the two choices are equal and opposite. They are not. One offers you a life grander than you could ever imagine, with stability for our people, securing the throne to the Titania line. The other is simply... messy." His expression was carefully blank. "I do not enjoy getting my hands dirty, Zlaet, but I'm not above it, should the need arise. I will do *anything* to protect our people, and as prince, you should be similarly inclined."

A shaking started in Slate's hands, that tingling sensation returning. How was this happening? How was this his life? How was he suddenly faced with this ultimatum? Where had everything gone so horrifically *wrong*?

Either he went with this... this High Fae king, who was supposedly his uncle with no proof, or he... or he *died*?

He'd never been so afraid, so furious, in all his life.

He made eyes at Kari again, where she was kneeling on the floor, hugging Dani. Dani looked shell-shocked, her eyes bouncing around at all the High Fae that surrounded them. Kari shook her head, gray eyes furious, a ghostly blue sneaking through them.

Slate swallowed, his mind fumbling furiously for a way to get out of this situation. "Do I have to decide now?"

The other male regarded him carefully for a long moment. "I understand this is a great deal for you to process, but time is of the essence. You must choose. Now, please."

Slate bounced his eyes back around to his friends.

"Your friends can come as well," Zeyphar said again. "You will want people in your court you can trust."

Slate's eyes snagged on Dani. She had a hand pressed to her mouth, like she could stuff her own emotions back inside her, and the decision was easy.

Never.

He'd *never* let her be taken anywhere near the Silver Valley. He wanted her out of here. He would say and do whatever he had to in order to make sure she got to sleep in her own bed tonight. If that meant... if it meant going with this fae, or even dying right here, right now, he would.

"If I come with you, will you let them go?" He tipped his chin to Jian, Kari, and Dani. "Unharmed?" he added.

Zeyphar cocked his head as though he were thinking. "You do not want them in your court with you? You can, of course, change your mind later, if you'd like to have some time to consider their merit to you."

"Yes," Slate agreed readily. "They walk out, right now."

"Slate!" Jian snarled. "Don't *even*."

"Fine," Slate quickly amended, thinking on the fly. He made eyes at Kari across the ring. "Jian comes with me. But the girls leave. The girls get to walk out. Unharmed and unharassed by fae." Kari would understand. Kari would do it—she'd take Dani, and she would do whatever it was Kari could do in her power to come find Jian and Slate. He knew Kari would take on the task, and with her connection to Jian, she might even stand a chance of finding them.

Zeyphar nodded slowly. "Interesting. Choosing the witch-doctor over the fox child."

He took his time turning in a slow circle, carefully eyeing each and every one of his companions, before looking beyond them to the ruined arena and stands.

The smoke from the explosions had cleared, offering the full view of the arena. Chairs and tables had been knocked about in the chaos of the stampeding crowd. Trash cans overturned, bags and purses abandoned, even some of the arena lights and cameras had been jostled loose and now laid shattered and broken on the concrete floor.

"It really is a shame," he mused aloud. "The fox child is dangerously powerful, and having both siblings would be beneficial... and..." Zeyphar's eyes sharpened as he took a longer look over Dani, as if noticing her for the first time. "And she..."

A wild possessiveness surged through Slate as Zeyphar cocked his head, regarding Dani like a cat with a mouse pinned underfoot. Zeyphar took a delicate sniff of the air and interest gleamed in his sapphire eyes.

"We can go right now," Slate hurried to say, something inside him demanding he pull Zeyphar's attention away from Dani.

"Why so impatient all of a sudden, nephew? Well, well, well, what do we have here?" Zeyphar waved a hand toward Dani and Kari. "A little lorekissed?"

Dani was snatched once more by the High Fae who was previously guarding her. Kari snarled, surging to her feet to grab her back, but the fae were quick to grapple Kari, forcing her back down, that silver blade at the back of her neck. Dani was hauled into the center of the ring, toward Zeyphar's outstretched palm. "You have Zlaet's scent all over you, *faeling*. Are you his latest female pet? Perhaps... are you the little creature who shot my attendant in the shoulder a few months ago? Iron bullets, very clever. Come closer, little one. Let me have a look at you. I, myself, have a personal weakness for those kissed by the Lore. Fascinating, your kind."

He grabbed her chin and turned her face back and forth. She was shaking, a mixture of terror and fury limning her eyes. Zeyphar inhaled swiftly. "What is *this*?" His gaze zeroed in on the bite mark on Dani's neck. Zeyphar turned delighted eyes back to Slate. "Did you...? By the Goddess—"

Slate lurched forward. He snagged Dani by the wrist and tore her away from Zeyphar, shifting to put himself between Dani and his uncle. Eyes huge in her too-pale face, a whimper escaped Dani at the flurry of movement, but she didn't flinch from him. Slate tucked her behind him to face Zeyphar, one hand lingering on her arm as he shielded her. "*Don't* touch her," he snarled.

Zeyphar chuckled darkly. "*Fascinating*. Exquisite. What a gift. The Goddess herself must be smiling upon me. She is unique, Zlaet, your instincts have chosen well. Green eyes like that in a *faeling*? I would hedge to say she's one of a kind—"

"She's going home," Slate growled. The one hand he had on Dani, keeping her behind his shoulder, tightened on her. "Right now. She and Kari are going *home*."

Zeyphar's eyes sharpened. "No. She *must* come with us."

Dani's fingers pressed against his bare back, hands curling into little fists. He could *feel* her shaking so hard it was vibrating his own bones.

"No," she whispered from behind him. "I'm going home."

"I'm afraid not, child." Zeyphar's softened voice was almost kind, if not for the delighted smile still pulling at his lips. "Zlaet *needs* you."

"No," Slate pressed. "That was the deal. I said I would go if—"

"No deal was struck, dearest nephew."

"You agreed—"

Slate sucked in a sharp breath as he suddenly found Zeyphar's face mere inches from his own. "Mind your place, young prince," he said softly, coolly. "Do not for a moment forget who you speak with. I am *Titania*. I do not dabble in promises and bargains casually. I have offered you exceedingly generous terms. Because you are kin, and blood takes care of blood."

Slate could feel the threat behind the words. Call it a sense. Call it magic. Call it whatever. But it was there, and he felt it. He gripped Dani's arm tighter, willing himself to have the mind and the words to play what was turning into a deadly game of cat-and-mouse.

"You demand I sacrifice my entire life for you... and you give me nothing in compensation," Slate hedged carefully. "How is that fair?"

Zeyphar waved a hand above his head, not breaking eye contact with Slate. Dani screamed as she was snatched from behind by another fae, and a knife returned to her throat. Slate whirled, but Zeyphar caught him under the jaw with one hand, forcing his face to turn back toward the king of the fae.

A golden circle appeared under Slate, trapping his feet to the floor. Zeyphar moved to speak directly into Slate's ear. "I offer you title, status, and luxury. Tell me again I am not fair," he whispered in a barely audible voice. Shivers laced along Slate's spine, goosebumps rising on his neck. "She *must* come with us."

The world was silent. In the space between heartbeats, Zeyphar had become sheer ice. Arctic. Black ice so dark even a light shone in would do nothing except accentuate how complete the darkness was. Zeyphar pulled back with a generous smile that didn't match the frost behind his eyes. He forced Slate's chin up to look at him. "You cannot be without her. She *belongs* to you. You're coming with me, and she's coming with you."

The tingling feeling in his hands migrated up his arms, pulsing behind his eyes.

"Let her go..." was all Slate managed, words nearly impossible to get out through the erratic beating of his pulse. "Let her go. I... anything. I'll do anything. I will come willingly. Just... let her go."

"I know. But this is not a debate. This is beyond you. Beyond me. She comes with us."

A rustling came from behind Slate. Instinct had him trying to glance behind him, but Zeyphar's hand was strong and tight on his face.

"Let me *go*!" Dani shouted somewhere behind him.

He saw her appear out of his periphery. Restrained by two hands on either bicep, marshaling her forward. She twisted her shoulders, wrenching them in a fruitless effort to be free.

The soldier looked to Zeyphar, obediently awaiting instructions as he stopped next to the fae king.

Zeyphar inclined his head in regal manner toward the fae, and a glowing portal appeared behind him, mere steps from Dani. All color leached from her face, and Slate's heart slammed against his ribs, lungs freezing.

"Oh Goddess..." she whispered in horror. She pinged wild eyes back to Slate. "*Slate!*"

Fury spiked so hard in him, he nearly blacked out. The magic trembled inside him, flooding him. He could feel it pulsing under his skin as his heart dropped into the pit of his stomach and turned to ice at the sight of Dani's terror.

The magic pressed outward, tumbling out of him with a single exhale.

Everyone except Zeyphar staggered back a step as though pushed. Forcefully.

Zeyphar's eyes gleamed with interest, and his smile widened as he regarded Slate with the curiosity of someone observing a fascinating insect under a magnifying glass.

The fae recovered swiftly, too swiftly for Jian or Kari to break free. Dani's eyes were pinging between him and Zeyphar, wide as saucers.

"I will, however, send your friends home, if it pleases you," Zeyphar said slowly, gaze lingering on Slate's face before he cast a glance in the direction of the twins. He then shifted his attention to Dani, his smile widening. "But not the female. The witch-doctor isn't nearly as valuable an asset as *she* is..." Zeyphar jerked his chin towards the fae soldier holding Dani. She dug her heels in, breath ripping from her as her eyes bounced wildly between the portal and Slate, but it did nothing to stop the fae from dragging her toward it.

"Your power. Your destiny. You have no idea what you hold, no idea what you have with *her*." Zeyphar's words were piercing tendrils of ice. He continued in his frozen whisper, "With her at your side, and my guidance, you will have a future grander than you could possibly *dream*."

Slate's eyes were glued to the portal, watching with a rising, fluttering panic as she was dragged ever closer.

This was happening.

Holy fuck, this was happening, and there was nothing to be said. Nothing to be done. It was either go to the fae capital with Dani held as leverage over him... or... or he didn't even know. He didn't know what waited for them after this moment, after this next breath. What waited for them beyond the faerie circle.

He had no more choices to make. None.

He swallowed his raging pulse. "No. I don't want this. Any of it." He tried to shift, wrenching against the hold of the golden trap, feeling bone and muscle pull to near snapping from the effort.

"With time, you will see the beauty of—"

"I don't care," Slate snarled. "This is insanity." To hell with caution, there was nothing left now. No deals to strike. No defense to play. He'd lost this one. Slate glanced at Dani. She met his eyes, and he saw there was nothing left but pure panic in her too-pale face.

He bounced his eyes back to Zeyphar. "I don't want your fucking 'grand future'. Or your fucking politics or any of it. Might as well wrap us in iron shackles now, because you are fucking *insane* if you think I'm not planning to fight you every step of the way."

Zeyphar showed no reaction except to hold up a swift hand. The fae holding Dani froze, and Zeyphar tilted his head as he stared at Slate. "Insane, you say."

No eye movement, no tenseness, not even a curve of the lips. He simply released his grip on Slate and turned to walk toward the edge of the ring. He waited there for a long moment without making a sound, staring out into the distance at nothing in particular. Then, he waved a hand, and the portal at Dani's feet disappeared. With a slow inhale, he turned back toward Slate.

Another casual wave, and Slate felt a colossal pull on his very skeleton, dragging him down to the ground to his knees. As soon as his palms touched the ground, his hands were trapped by the glowing circle surrounding him.

The king of the fae spoke in a plain voice with no intonation. "It is your mortal side that has made you irrational. I can fix that."

He took three steps back toward Slate and cupped his chin again. "Let's remove that Glamour now, shall we?"

CHAPTER THIRTY-SIX

FAERIE DUST

... distinctive coloring in their bloodline. Historians debate if the word 'sapphire' was attributed first to the gem or for their eyes, leading some...

— Gherald Schmidt, Faerloch Historical Archives

"No!" Jian barked. Chaos bloomed as Jian threw arms and elbows, skillfully dodging the knife. "Do *not* take that glamour off!"

"Control him," Zeyphar snarled. Instantly, another fae leapt into the ring and subdued Jian with few well-placed hits. The witch-doctor stumbled, and the knife returned to his throat, this time with two fae holding him in place. He was breathing hard.

Dani managed to dislodge herself, darting toward Slate, but she didn't make it three steps before she was seized again. Slate yanked at his body, ready to launch himself at the fae soldier who held her hostage, but he couldn't *move*. "Dani. *Dani.*" He tried to sound calm, tried to hold her gaze, but her eyes were darting around wildly, like a caged animal. "Everything's gonna be okay."

Dani shook her head, terror sketched in every plane of her face. He was sure she was about to pass out. He tugged even harder against the circle that held him fast, muscles and tendons pulling taut.

"Bring her closer," Zeyphar commanded, and the fae muscled Dani closer to Slate, a long blade of silver forcing her head up. Her eyes locked with Slate's, and this time, they held.

"I want you to see this, child. Zlaet will be a sight to behold. You should be the first to witness his rebirth." Zeyphar's eyes twinkled with manic delight. He moved toward Slate.

Jian yanked forward once more, his face a mask of rage and concern, but the knife brought him up short. Blood trickled down his neck from where the blade bit into flesh.

"Even without my intervention, your days as a mortal are over," Zeyphar said, crouching and tipping Slate's chin to the side as he studied him. "Sooner or later, the glamour would fade from you, and you would be a hurricane wrapped in skin. You are a powerful cocktail of Eastern and Western magic, and even your witch can do nothing to contain you."

"Don't," Jian gasped.

Slate's eyes darted over Zeyphar's shoulder to his best friend as Jian yanked at the firm hold he was in—one fae had Jian's arms twisted up behind him, the other had a fistful of his copper hair and the knife. More blood slipped down over his collarbone. "You can't take it off! You can't! You could kill him!"

"Jian!" Slate hissed, watching that blood, his lungs seizing with pure fury at the sight of it. Jian was gonna get himself killed...

Zeyphar smirked at Jian. "I'm the only one who *can* take it off, witch, isn't that right? The glamour can only be removed by a *blood relation* because of its signature."

"Let it come off naturally!" Jian pleaded. "You have to... you have to let it come off on its own, or... or take it off in small doses. Or else the influx of magic... the influx of magic on his system could kill him. It'll be too much too fast. His body needs *time* to adjust to the magic!"

"He would have received the highest care in the Silver Valley," Zeyphar commented airily. "But seeing as my nephew has spat in the face of my gracious offer and would rather be a prisoner than a prince, I will see it done here and now. Whether he lives or dies is up to him."

"No." Jian fought against the hold. More blood on that blade. "Don't. *Please.*" A little flame sparked to life, interlaced his fingers, weaving between the digits. Both fae holding him widened their eyes at the sight, but maintained their firm hold of him.

Slate's eyes jumped from the fire in Jian's hands to his eyes and saw them flicker toward his twin. Slate followed the stare. The High Fae holding the blade to Kari's neck raised a brow at Jian in a silent dare, angling that knife threateningly.

Kari let out a growl, defiance in her eyes, and Slate could tell the twins were talking mind to mind.

A taut, breathless second passed.

The fire around Jian's fingers fluttered, then extinguished, and he gave a tight shake of his head at his sister. He dragged his gaze back to Slate, and there was something stark and guilty etched into the lines of his face.

"I'm sorry..." Jian's voice was hardly a whisper.

He couldn't blame Jian, not when it was Kari, but coherent thoughts were slipping away like water through a sieve as Zeyphar's eyes glinted at him. Eyes full of malice. Anger but also something deeper. Curiosity. Slate was stuck like a fly to a sticky bug trap, tingling magic pulsing behind his eyes, up his arms. His veins burned darker, turning nearly black under his skin. His body was shaking—from magic or fear or rage, he wasn't sure—and he thought he might collapse right there from the riot wrecking his body from the inside out. It was like Zeyphar's presence, coupled with his panic for Dani, was accelerating something under his skin, something that writhed to be free.

Dani was hyperventilating, held firmly in place by the soldier.

Jian was breathing hard, eyes limned silver, on the cusp of absolute panic.

Kari was shaking, but he couldn't tell if it was from anger or fear. Slate knew Kari could blast her way out of here herself. But she wouldn't leave Jian. Slate was aware their twin empathy was deep-seated; they were one energy across two bodies. Kari might have explosive power and magic ten times over what Jian had, but should something happen to Jian, Kari would feel it too. They were linked.

Would she die if he did?

The thought was horrifying.

No, he knew Kari. She wouldn't leave Jian. Not unless she had a plan to guarantee his safety too.

Which she likely did. At least, Slate hoped she did.

Slate watched her eyes flip from Jian back to Slate, and he saw real horror there. Whatever was happening inside Jian's mind, whatever he was thinking about the glamour, Kari was thinking it too.

A shot of fear slithered through Slate—he recognized it as self-preservation. Amplified by the panic of the twins, feeding off them.

Zeyphar laid his palms on Slate's temples. "I cannot promise this won't hurt," he said with a growing smile.

Zeyphar's eyes flashed solid blue, the whites of his eyes and his pupils washed away from the intensity of that cerulean glow.

A massive pressure built behind Slate's eyes, then before he could even suck in a breath, it burst. It was as though someone was fishing around inside his head, uncorking his mind, his veins, his bones, and his blood. Every pop, every pulse shot pain through him, a horrid, terrible cocktail of ice and fire, burning and searing his insides. It filled every space inside him, every molecule. His blood was boiling, his bones scorching. He was coming undone, and yet being remade, his insides melting, then stitching back together in a fiery mess.

His vision blacked out, but it didn't negate the feeling. Magic—that's what it had to be—flashed over his skin, rippling in waves, crackling, searing the flesh from his bones. It was blazing, wild... he couldn't take anymore, he was going to burn up into nothingness...

Someone was screaming.

This was a nightmare.

It was as if every horrible fever dream Dani had ever experienced in her lifetime had culminated into this one moment as Zeyphar announced he would be removing the glamour. Slate was looking at Jian, and the panic on the doctor's face had Dani's insides clenching painfully. She knew nothing about glamours, but it was clear from Jian's protests that it would be bad to remove it, which only served to excite Zeyphar more, the fae's lips pulling back in a smile.

Dani was shaking so hard the fae who gripped her arm was likely the only thing keeping her from collapsing. She could smell him, musky with a hint of damp moss, and her skin crawled with every brush of his heated breath against the back of her head. Kat's 12 year old face kept flashing in her mind, flanked by two inhumanly beautiful fae, who'd led her away from Dani forever.

The horror in her crystalline eyes, even as a pleasant smile graced her best friend's full lips.

Dani broke out into a cold sweat, and the edges of her vision tunneled. She was next... she was going to be dragged away by the fae. Gone forever, lost through a glowing portal to who-even-knew where. She was having trouble hearing what Zeyphar was saying over the roaring in her ears.

Zeyphar. His *uncle*.

Slate was *half*-fae. Not lorekissed.

A fae *prince*.

The fear that came from that knowledge was enhanced further by the cruel portrayal of who Slate could be with that power, that lineage. Twin eyes of the deepest sapphires, a family resemblance that was undeniable. Would Slate be like that one day? She knew the fear was unreasonable, not even logical, but she couldn't shove it away, couldn't look at Slate anymore and *not* see Zeyphar in him when terror was already making her thoughts scramble in her head.

Zeyphar reached out and put his hands on either side of Slate's face, and Jian went deathly pale, watching his best friend.

Dani's breathing rushed out of her as Slate's eyes flashed wide enough to see the whites all around his sapphire irises, and his body bowed as his hands flew to his face to cover Zeyphar's, gripping hard. The golden circle beneath him vanished, either from Zeyphar's will or through whatever was happening to Slate. The roaring in her ears intensified, and Dani choked back a sob.

Jian was shouting.

Slate was screaming.

He was screaming like he was dying. Every orifice on his face was bleeding—eyes, nose, ears—as though his brain had turned into a bloody mess and was leaking out of him. Dark, *dark* veins crisscrossed his entire body. Up his arms, his torso, his legs, his face. His skin cracked open like hairline fractures across a delicate piece of china; white energy bled out of the cracks, skipping over his skin.

The entire building trembled under the force of the magic coming out of him. Cold aura like a fresh breath of winter rippled out from Slate's convulsing form; cold, but not nearly as terrifying as the deep-freeze that came off the High Fae male in front of him.

Seeing Slate in agony, his face twisted and bloody, snapped her into the present. A spike of a very different kind of panic shot through her. Heat burned bright in her chest, fury rising, higher than her own fear, until her body had room for nothing else but that protective fury.

"Stop it!" Dani shrieked, lunging forward, heedless of the knife at her throat or the fae hands gripping her tight. The edge sliced a shallow line into her skin, and a trickle of warm blood slithered down her neck, but she ignored it as she struggled against the High Fae holding her. "Stop it! You're *killing him.*"

He was going to die. He was going to fly apart at the seams and burst into nothing.

For this one moment, as anger and desperation swelled inside of her, it didn't matter what Slate's lineage was. It didn't matter that he was fae. Nothing else mattered but keeping this charming man who had made her laugh and moan in equal measures from dying right before her eyes.

To keep him from disappearing from her life... like everyone else had.

"Stop it!" She lunged again, struggling against the hold. She couldn't let him *die.*

Dani twisted around to look back at the fae holding her, teeth bared like she would bite if that's what it took, and screamed, "Let me go right now!" The blue-gray eyes of the fae widened and something like alarm crossed his face a moment before his fingers snapped open on her arm, releasing her. The knife fell away.

Her head was throbbing, her neck burning, as she hurtled herself out of his hands and down to the floor near Slate.

He was screaming. Goddess, it was heart-breaking and terrifying. Watching him writhe in pain, forehead pressed into the ring floor now, hands like talons, clawing into the surface. Skin cracking apart like china—

"Slate!" she cried. She crawled the remaining distance to him, reaching out a hand to him. Her fingers brushed his arm, and she snatched her hand back almost immediately—his skin was blazing hot.

He was sucking in air and blowing it back out in quick succession, and the white glow continued to flicker over his body. "Slate, *Slate.* It's okay... It's okay..." she sobbed, reaching for him again.

She noticed the dust around him taking form, swirling and dancing. She watched it gather slow momentum, twisting around him, with him—no, *them*, she and him—at the epicenter.

"Slate, hey..." She touched him again, more tentatively this time, touched his shoulders, his spine. "Slate—"

He flinched away from her touch. "Don't..." The word was barely audible. The swirling intensified.

Her breath jammed in her throat, watching raptly with no small amount of alarm as his heartfire suddenly swelled. Swelled so hot, she nearly scrambled back, the heat of it singing her senses. So much magic... so *fae*—

Slate's head jerked back and he gave a brutal yell to the ceiling that made her ears ring. His entire body slumped forward. He hit the ground, and went still.

Deafening silence fell.

The swirling dust settled.

The heat of his heartfire snuffed out.

No one moved.

No one breathed.

Every bone in her body stilled, down to the molecules in her cells. He was... he was...

No, no, no...

"Slate?"

Dani scrambled closer, heedless of Zeyphar as he crouched to peer at Slate across from her. She pushed at Slate's dark hair, trying to get a look at his face. He was absolutely still, pale as a ghost, dark veins twisting under his skin, the contrast alarming and horrifying and she couldn't breathe—

Tears burned down her cheeks as a hole opened in her chest. He was dead. This man who wasn't supposed to mean anything to her was dead, and it felt like her heart was being eaten alive by a black hole behind her ribs.

"He is alive, little *faeling*."

Zeyphar reached out to tip her chin up with long fingers, and Dani jerked back from the touch, terror shoving its way back under her skin. That *touch*, like the cool hands of the fae who'd smuggled her out of her bed, a cloth over her face, the subtle scents of flowers and burning alcohol scorching her nose.

"*Don't touch me!*" Her voice was nearly feral, her breath erratic in her lungs. "You are a *monster.*" But despite the panic and the terror, she was already grappling for Slate, trying to ease his head into her lap, moving them as far from Zeyphar as she could.

She looked away from the king of the fae, who was smiling at her like a predator eyeing a tasty morsel, and looked down at Slate, brushing his hair back from his too-pale face.

She was vaguely aware of a small scuffle behind her, and Jian's voice growling the words, "*Let me go to him.*" There was a grunt, and Dani tore her gaze from Slate to see one of the fae had sucker punched Jian. His voice came out strained as he rasped, "Dani?" It looked like he was trying to stay calm, but desperation colored his voice an octave higher than usual. "Dani... check for a pulse."

Dani fumbled for Slate's pulse, her fingers trembling so hard she nearly couldn't find it. She wasn't breathing, couldn't pull in enough oxygen.

Nothing... but then, barely discernible, she felt the flutter of a pulse.

Relief crashed through her so abruptly her vision wavered and the floor seemed to tilt sideways. She sagged, smoothing her fingers over Slate's dark hair. "He's alive," she rasped, hearing her heart pounding in her ears.

"You are a fierce creature," Zeyphar mused, then chuckled. She could *feel* his eyes on her, and her skin pebbled with goosebumps. "I cannot wait to see what your future holds." Her eyes flashed up, and his eyes—the same shade as Slate's—regarded her with such intense curiosity she swallowed hard. *High Fae.* "You could be a *queen*—"

The pulse of power that came from Zeyphar was a familiar pressure on her skin—familiar because she felt it every time she had a nightmare.

Under her hands, Slate inhaled a deep, sharp breath. She whipped her attention back to him. "Hey... Slate, Slate, come back to me." Her fingers shook as she smoothed his hair back from his face.

She saw one hand move, fist against the floor. She gasped as his heartfire suddenly burst into existence; hot and intense. The entire ring trembled. An aura pulsed off him, much like the one that pulsed off his uncle. The pressure, the *feel* of it, had bile building in her throat, and her fingers convulsed as terror shot through her. She whipped her hand back from his face.

The pulse intensified, like a heartbeat. Two beats... then nothing. Two beats... then nothing. Faster and faster, the time between the beats lessening and lessening.

"Dani!" Kari called sharply. "Dani, come here."

She wanted to. She didn't want to be anywhere near that magic. Her palms were clammy, her head light, but the sight of his face, the pain that furrowed his brow...

She remembered that face, kissing her, whispering sweetness in her ear. She remembered the feel of his palm, gentle against her throat, a wickedness creeping into his smile...

Rain-soaked skin, hands on her face. *"I want what you want..."*

She couldn't leave him. "Slate..." She reached out a tentative hand, pressing past the panic rising in her chest at the feel of that magic.

Half of her mind was screaming at her. He was *fae*. And he had *magic*. Powerful magic, from the way it felt to her. He was dangerous, just like Roger said.

But the other half of her mind... That new, budding instinct inside her that had only started speaking to her since she'd met Slate. It said: *Fae or not fae, he's still yours...*

"Dani!" Kari called again. "It's dangerous!"

"Dani, get out of there," Jian growled, and Dani's eyes flew up to see the urgency in the witch-doctor's face. Kari looked just as frantic.

A particularly powerful pulse nearly pushed her back from Slate, and her stomach wedged tight in her ribs. Both sides of her mind were screaming the same message now: *Run.*

As she shot to her feet, her heart twisted in her chest, yanking downward, like she'd left it with Slate. Fighting the need to go back to him, Dani shot toward Kari, wiping tears from her eyes. She twisted at the last moment, skidding to a stop to look back at Slate as Kari's small fingers clutched at Dani's wrist.

She had to go back. She couldn't leave him...

She would have gone back, too, if Kari hadn't yanked her down with a force that belied her tiny frame. Zeyphar, too, had backed away from Slate, though not nearly as far, eyes gleaming with a manic interest as he watched his nephew writhe.

A ripple of heat washed over them, but Dani was too distraught to be able to tell from where it was coming from. Dani's head was pulled down, and Kari wrapped both arms around her in a tight hug. She felt the brush lips against her ear, Kari's normally sensual voice terse as she whispered, "When I tell you, you are going to *run*. Don't hesitate."

Dani's insides pitched. She glanced at the fae behind Kari, and noticed they were all watching Slate with rapt attention. The knife at Kari's neck had slackened. She bit her lip, her stomach engulfed with so much fear she might puke, but she pulled in a breath and gave the tiniest nod of her head.

Across the ring, Jian had gone still as stone, eyes watching everything closely. The fae holding him was also watching Slate, and the knife at Jian's throat had dropped a little.

Zeyphar shifted around to crouch in front of Slate, leaving two feet of distance between them. Dani held her breath as Slate pushed one arm underneath himself, shaking hard. Blood dripped from his face, peppering the floor beneath him. The other arm made it under him. He pushed himself back until he could crouch, breathing ragged with bloodshot eyes.

Eyes that were *glowing*.

"Can you feel it, Zlaet?" Zeyphar's eyes were pinned wide and his face was lit up like a child's on Christmas morning. "This is the power that has been denied to you, hidden from you. Your birthright. Seize it, embrace it. You can shed the irrational mortal part of you. You have been lied to all your life, and *I* have set you free. This is what your mother did not understand. Her failure does not have to be your legacy."

The king of the fae rose to his full height and held out his hand. "Come, Zlaet. Let us take our leave now, for the Silver Valley."

Slate stared at the hand, shoulders heaving.

He grasped that extended hand. Dani's heart stopped beating.

No.

No. He... *no*. He wouldn't.

Was the power already twisting him into a cold, cruel High Fae?

She could see his heartfire, a raging bonfire that flickered and pulsed erratically. It was pulsing even faster now, so fast it was almost one big thrum of energy. Zeyphar grinned and yanked Slate swiftly to his feet. Slate swayed slightly, stumbling, stepping toward Zeyphar, gripping that hand tighter, with both hands now.

Slate's eyes tracked over to Jian, then Kari... then finally to Dani. Her lungs stuttered at the raw look he gave her.

Slate's hands tightened on Zeyphar's, his knuckles white as he dragged his eyes back to stare at his uncle. "I will write my own legacy," he growled, voice raw but strong. "I will forge my own path."

And all that twisting, magical energy *exploded*.

CHAPTER ✦ THIRTY-SEVEN

NIGHTMARES AND ILLUSIONS

Under Hylsdyr's influence, House Titania rose to prominence above the other 12, and that tradition continues to this day. House Titania historically avoided the term 'royalty' until the mid-sixth century BCE, when...

- Gherald Schmidt, Faerloch Historical Archives

The pressure of the magic pressed against Dani's ear drums, threatening to burst the sensitive membrane. She cried out, hands flying up to cover her ears as Kari's arms tightened around her, curving her body protectively around Dani. Only the *kitsune's* strong embrace kept her from skidding back from the force of the magical surge, which hit her like a sonic shockwave. Behind them, there came the screech of metal folding chairs scraping against the floor, the rattle of the downed cage vibrating from the force.

She felt the whisper of fur, saw a plump white tail with flickering blue fire skating over the strands of silken hair. Dani jerked her head up, and saw two pert fox ears unfold from Kari's hair, and her three long tails flowing behind her. The already distracted guards fell back a step in surprise.

Kari surged to her feet, shoving Dani toward the edge of the ring and down to the main floor.

"Run!"

"But Slate—"

"*Trust* me, Dani, we need to run right now," Kari urged, and the sharpness of her tone triggered Dani's self-preservation instincts. Her mind, her instincts, they thrummed with the need to run, even as her heart stuttered *no, no, no* in her chest.

Looking back toward Slate, hands still covering her smarting ears, Dani ran. The thrum of magic was a pressure on her skin, in her ears, like being deep underwater. Sounds and movement, it all felt muffled and dampened by the overwhelming force radiating from the epicenter of the fighting ring.

A deep *boom*, and the very floor trembled under her feet. She stumbled as another shaking rumbled the arena. Cracking, snapping, the strange cacophony of various structural components groaning and screeching. Fear and self-preservation were powerful motivators urging her to *run, run, RUN.* She kept *moving,* diving down the aisle and scrambling up the steps. She could see the double doors to the exit—

A hand grabbed hers. She screamed and whirled around, ready to claw someone's face off.

"Keep *running.*" It was Kari. The *kitsune* pushed her, twisting her around toward the exit. "Go, go, go."

Another guttural explosion, following by a more forceful racket and dissonance. It sounded as though the building was about to come down around them.

Dani dared a glimpse over her shoulder toward the octagonal ring.

Like trying to see through muddy water, she could barely discern the outline of the ring anymore. Dust, debris, and magic swirled and pulsed around a single standing figure.

"The boys—" Dani choked on the words.

"Jian's got it. Don't worry," Kari hissed as she pushed Dani further, keeping her body between Dani and the fae shouting behind them.

They slammed out of the double doors and into the front lobby to the backdrop of another forceful shove of an explosion. She lost her footing, keeping her feet under her only with the help of Kari's quick and firm grip under her arm.

They pulled up short. A gasp tore from Dani's mouth as three High Fae appeared, moving so fast her eyes couldn't track them. Kari didn't even hesitate. She hurled six shimmering leaves like throwing stars, and they vanished into puffs of smoke that obscured the space around them. Within the smoke, each leaf materialized into three identical copies of Kari and Dani each, all running in different directions.

She didn't have a moment to be impressed; Kari snagged her wrist and tugged, tugging them toward one of the exits as the smoke cleared.

The fae hesitated, eyes flying between the four copies of Kari and Dani, each now running in identical ways but to four different exits.

The middle fae barked a terse order, and they split up, each darting after a different pair. One of them got lucky, and Dani's blood froze as he began to close the distance between them.

They burst out into the night air, and Kari shoved Dani forward before whirling around and striking out with in a blur of motion. Kari twisted her body in an aggressive 360 jump and slammed her right foot into the fae's ribs. He staggered back with a grunt, but Kari was all over him. Dani gasped, hands flying to her mouth as the *kitsune* smashed the heel of her hand into the fae's face in two quick jabs followed by a swift elbow to his temple, then spun once more and slammed the heel of her foot straight into his chest.

He actually flew backward a dozen paces.

Dani was frozen; she'd never seen Kari fight like that before.

A flick of her fingers, and Kari dashed back after Dani. A wall of blue fire bloomed in her wake, blocking off pursuit as she gripped Dani's wrist and ran.

"Keep *going*, girl," Kari hissed when Dani twisted to look behind them. She swallowed hard against the irrational urge to dive back into the arena and find Slate, and put her focus into getting one foot in front of the other as they ran. Kari led the way. The further they got from the arena, further away from danger, the more Dani's adrenaline started to wane. Crash. Her knees wobbled underneath her with each step, her teeth chattering.

Slate. Slate was *fae*. He had magic. He was a fae *prince*...

And he was in trouble.

The emotions twisting in her chest left her gasping for air almost as much as the running was. She clenched her free hand, fighting back tears. "Kari... Kari..." she gasped, her energy spiraling.

Something in her voice must've alerted the other woman. She whirled around and her arms caught Dani as she collapsed.

"It's okay," Kari said, a firm but compassionate quality to her tone. "I got you. Come on. We aren't safe here."

Kari supported Dani with an arm around her shoulders as she urged them on a few more blocks, pace slowed to a fast walk. They turned a corner and hit a busy street. Traffic was lighter this time of night, but Kari managed to hail a taxi. She pushed Dani into the back seat first, then scrambled inside after her.

"Pub District," Kari said. She leaned forward and handed the cabbie a fistful of money, though Dani had no idea where she'd pulled it from. "Step on it."

The cab tore off through the streets. Dani hardly paid attention, her mind whirling. She was aware of Kari talking on the phone at one point—clipped and short—but she didn't know who she was talking to. She didn't care. The entire world was pressing in on her, panic like a noose around her neck, her world narrowing.

The cab stopped. Kari climbed out first before reaching in and dragging Dani out after her.

They were at the Den.

Kari took her hand, but instead of going through the front door, Kari took her down the side alley adjacent to the establishment. Dani stumbled after her numbly, seeing nothing. Her mind was *reeling*.

Kari pounded her fist three times against the side access door, but a voice came from the shadows behind them.

"What is going on?" It was a cold whip of words, and Dani felt familiar, slender fingers close over her upper arms. Roger was seething, his anger palpable as swirling shadows curled around Dani from behind. The vampire tugged her closer to him and twirled her around to inspect her.

Dani caught a glimpse of red in his eyes and found her gaze glued to the sharp lines of his face. A familiar face, something to focus on and hope the world would stop spinning.

Cool hands pushed her hair back from her face, tilting her chin up. Roger inhaled swiftly, and she winced when a gentle fingertip brushed at the nick on her throat. "Who did this?" His voice was calm but held such quiet fury that the hairs on the back of Dani's neck stood up straight.

"The High Fae. Zeyphar came for Slate. I have to go. Roger, please, take her." Kari was speaking rapid-fire, backing toward the entrance to the alleyway.

Roger's eye flipped to Kari, then did a double-take back to Dani, zeroing in on her neck—the bite mark. His eyes widened and his nostrils flared as his shoulders ratcheted with visible tension. His eyes snapped to hers, and he looked ready to speak, but then his lips pressed into a thin line, and he straightened to his full height without a word.

"I'll be in touch when I can," Kari called, and she was nearly at the exit of the alleyway.

Dani's head whipped to the side, and she shot out a hand toward the retreating woman. Roger snagged her around her shoulders with an arm, tugging her back against his chest firmly but gently, even as she cried out, "Kari, wait... don't leave me." The words popped out as fear became a vise around her heart.

Kari would be in danger if she left. Kari, who had come to mean something to her.

She would leave, too; disappear like Slate had disappeared in the dust and debris of the exploded arena. Like her parents. Like Kat.

"I have to, doll," Kari insisted, pausing on the sidewalk just outside the alleyway. "I have to go... I have to help Jian and Slate. They need... they need help." Kari's eyes were hard, glowing a faint, ethereal blue.

The words filtered through Dani's brain sluggishly, catching in the turbulent swirl inside her mind, but she realized Kari wasn't saying everything. Fear tightened her belly—had something happened to the boys?

"Daniella, you are *not* alone," Roger's voice was soft, a gentle reminder, even as he restrained her from going after Kari with his hands on her shoulders. "Karisi will be fine."

Dani wanted to make sure for herself, but it was like her body wasn't listening as she sagged and her knees buckled. Before she hit the ground, Roger scooped her up and cradled her against his chest. Her world continued to spin, and she squeezed her eyes shut, breathing through her nose.

"She's going into shock." Dani could barely hear Kari's voice past the roaring building in her ears.

"Her body and mind have endured too much," Roger murmured, voice tight with withheld anger. "Go. She will be safe with me."

The sounds of feet pounding against pavement came, and Dani reached up to grab her head, willing the world to *stop* spinning.

"Daniella?" Roger's voice, close to her ear. "Daniella, breathe. I need you to breathe."

The last thing she saw was the pained concern on Roger's face before everything faded to black.

CHAPTER THIRTY-EIGHT

A BAD CASE OF MAGIC

... the bloodlines capable of that level of control and power are lost to the general population, and have survived solely in the bloodline of House Titania...

- Gherald Schmidt, Faerloch Historical Archives

The world pressed in on his ears.

He could hear his own rapid, ragged breathing. Feel the beat of his heart drumming against his skull. The world took turns blurring around him, then coming into sharp focus—so sharp he could make out the individual dust particles in the air. Could hear the distant sounds of cars as if they were in the room with him. His eyes tracked over the scene. Smoke and debris painted his reality.

It was a mindless, chaotic blur around him. Where was he? *Who* was he? What was happening? Slate couldn't discern his own body from the rest of the wreckage around him. He was little more than a pulsing heartbeat.

His eyes latched onto one person, some instinct inside him zeroing in on her like a homing beacon. He followed the track of her fleeing the scene, her hair a red ribbon behind her.

Dani.

The sight of her had him sucking in a breath, digging deep into whatever reserves he had as he pushed his feet underneath him. The world tilted, swayed, as though he were walking across the deck of a ship on a stormy sea. Shouting. Someone was shouting. The sound kept switching volume like a badly tuned radio, one moment raging loud and the next like hearing a voice through a thick pane of glass. Some sort of deep survival mechanism kicked into gear. He wasn't safe here. He had to leave.

Someone grabbed his arm. A flash of copper hair.

Jian. Two Jians. Three. Back to one. Wavering in and out of focus. He was talking. Half his face was covered in little knicks from the debris. His eyes were clear, but two clear tracks lined down over each cheek, swathing a path through the dust and dirt on his face. Blood stained the skin of his neck.

"What?" Slate muttered, eyes locked on the blood, on the memory of fury.

More talking, gray eyes wide with desperation. Hands on his shoulders, anchoring him, turning him around, pushing him.

His feet were moving. Stumbling forward, dancing over the rubble that was once the fighting ring. At times, it was like he could navigate the wreckage with a graceful ease, and then he was stumbling, bloodying his knees with a clumsiness that had Jian's strong fingers gripping at his shoulders.

Each step brought his senses back to life. And the first thing he felt was pain. God, the *pain*. His whole body ached—rippling and collapsing with each agonizing step, like his cells were on fire. His vision tunneled alarmingly, the world swaying. Hands gripped him once more, pushing him along, catching him each time he stumbled.

Something was crawling under his skin, like static electricity pulsing into his organs and bones, sucking him inside himself. Like a great swirling vortex of magic and madness, threatening to swallow him whole. His head was hot and loud, the sounds and scents of the world overwhelming him like a *tsunami* threatening to take him under and drown him in the swirling void inside him.

He was gonna vomit.

"Jian..." Slate mumbled thickly.

"Just go, brother. Go, go!"

Jian's voice was an anchor against the wave. His fingers were wrapped firmly around Slate's wrist, tugging him along, guiding him god-only knew where. He could feel Jian's magic snaking through his body, like a thread, a net cast out over him, pushing the void of magic away and tugging whatever was left of Slate himself forward out of the nothingness. It was a lifeline, that's all Slate understood. A lifeline, and he focused on it.

Something else came along with that thread, though.

Fear, determination, guilt, and a crippling sense of loyalty wrapped in the flavor of sterile herbs and fire—

The slap of mild summer air hit Slate like a freight train. They were outside. The urge to puke up his guts escalated tenfold.

"Jian... the girls..."

Where was Dani?

"Kari's got it. Keep moving. Stay with me, stay focused."

He stumbled after Jian, towed along by his best friend, focusing on keeping his feet under him, tuning his attention into the thread of Jian's magic inside him. The thread that was the last stand between Slate's own consciousness and the awning pit of icy nothingness inside him.

Too much magic too fast.

It was pulling him under.

A whisper of a scent, one he *knew*. It plowed through his dazed senses to punch him right in his chest. "Dani..." Slate gasped. The moment he thought her name, panic squeezed his throat shut, clawing up into his skull like skeletal claws, flushing his entire body.

Was she here? Where was she? Was she alright?

His hands slipped from Jian's and he hit the ground. The tether to reality was gone, and all that was left was the void, sucking him closer to the black hole inside himself. He couldn't think. He couldn't breathe. He felt foreign inside his own skin, jittery and sensitive, like his nerve endings were rubbed raw from a wool sweater.

Only one thing kept him from imploding. The scent of sunshine and warm meadows. He gasped, his body trembling hard enough his bones jostled. He vomited right there in the middle of the street.

Hands grabbed him again, and the magic returned, tugging him out from the black hole almost as strongly as that *scent* was. Something intensely cool trickled along his spine, and Slate shuddered as his eyes shot open. His world tilted, and he was being hauled to his feet again. Forced to run. His body... he couldn't coordinate his limbs.

The feel of the pavement changed under his bare feet. The pedestrian bridge. His mind scattered as the void inside him heaved. Jian's hand tightened on his.

They barely made it across to the other side before Slate hit the ground again, another round of violent heaving racked his body. This time, though, Jian crouched and laid his hands on Slate's nape.

"What's wrong with me?" he whispered to Jian, teeth chattering.

The witch-doctor shifted his hand to Slate's forehead. It was ice compared to the intense heat over his skin. "You're releasing magic faster than your body can absorb it," Jian said. "Magical poisoning. Your magical aura is trying to consume you alive. Come on, we can't stop," Jian urged, trying to tug him to his feet once more.

"Can... can you..." stringing words together felt monumental, "... can you fix me?"

Slate caught a flash of deeply furrowed brows. Not a positive expression, that one. His stomach churned, and Jian slid an arm under his shoulders as he tugged him forward. "No..." he said after a beat. "It's not something to be fixed, brother. Either you settle... or you burn alive." He swallowed hard. "Come on. My dad... he can help."

Jian hefted Slate when he would have slid to the ground, and Slate had the feeling he wasn't doing much to keep himself upright at this point. Jian's voice broke through the fuzziness in his head, and his attention shifted from his feet to his best friend when he heard a distinct crack in Jian's voice, a heaviness.

"I'm... Slate, I'm sorry, man. I couldn't stop that bastard... If I did, Kari would've died..." His voice wobbled, and he shook his head. Slate heard him pull in a breath and felt the solid body supporting his own shudder an instant and stumble. Slate tried to get his feet under him.

"S'okay, Jian."

"Come on, brother. My house is close. You don't die on my watch." Jian hefted him up, and Slate managed to put some pressure on his own two feet.

But that *void*. It was pulling on him, sucking away who he was. It was icy yet burning, digging into his mind like long, gnarled fingers, gripping him and threatening to tip him over into frigid nothingness.

Their pace was reduced to a walk now, and Slate could feel Jian trembling. Slate's vision slipped in and out again, body overcome with moments of trembling weakness. His head fell forward, and he caught the sight of his hands out of the corner of his vision. His veins tracked dark and deadly under his skin.

They barely made it into Jian's house before Slate's knees gave out. Jian caught him, but Slate could feel Jian was on the brink of collapsing himself. Slate opened his mouth, tried to say something, but Jian's voice barked out a shout.

Lights flipped on, and Slate winced from the brightness of it. He started to slip from Jian's grip, but he never hit the ground.

New hands gathered him up. He grimaced, trying to struggle, barely aware of the familiar sights as he was hauled deeper into the Meho Residence.

Sensation pressed into him... sensation? That was the wrong word. Emotions?—paternal concern, confusion, a fiery temper fraught with worry.

Slate's mind scrambled, and he gasped for air like a fish. "Don't... don't... Please, stop it..." Slate tried to put words together, to tell them to stop touching his skin, to stop overloading him.

His vision blacked out. Brightness blared. Talking. Voices. Clipped, clinical.

"Jian, *stop.*" The whip of a familiar voice, one that was normally jovial. "I have him."

"I tried... I tried to keep his body from flying apart... but I can't anymore—" So much *guilt*, such heavy, bone-deep exhaustion in Jian's voice.

Slate tried to blink his eyes open, but he squeezed them shut again when the light burned his corneas.

More talking, the words blending together incoherently.

Slate felt Jian leave, that heaviness following him like a long cloak being pulled off Slate's trembling body. New hands pressed into his skin, and a new magic pulsed through him, more potent than Jian's.

He was going to burn alive. The magic in that pit was going to kill him—

There was a firm yank away from the void that still raged inside him. Someone else was pulling him out of the spiraling nothingness. *Joon-san.*

Hands cupped his face, rough, yet soft. Slate's focus snapped to the front, almost like it wasn't even his own focus. He blinked, the blinding light receding to reveal a weathered face. He gulped down air, felt it stick in his windpipe.

He realized he was looking at his father's dark eyes.

"Breathe, Slate." The voice was calm, the vocal equivalent of that relief, a sanctuary from the pain.

He tried to count his breathing, but his lungs stuttered with effort. "I'm dying... right?" he gasped in a ragged whisper. Joon's palms still pressed into skin, a firm touch along his spine.

"No," Ebisu said, and Slate's nerves went haywire at even the smallest tensing of those familiar hands on his face. "You will not die. Look at me." Slate's eyes snapped to dark eyes that burned with conviction, with calm focus and determination.

Slate pulled in another life-saving breath. "Everything hurts..."

A cloth was pushed against his nose and mouth. "Breathe," Jian said. When had he come back?

It smelled like herbs and lavender and magic. The pulsing behind Slate's eyes dulled. The pain in his skull lessened. "I feel terrible..." Slate muttered between breaths.

Joon's hands shifted towards his nape, and the *sucking* inside him eased a little.

"It's a side effect of the glamour," Ebisu said. "Your magical well has been filling since you were a child, and the Faerie Dust acted like a dam, keeping the energy from flowing to the rest of your body and mind, keeping your aura from being sensed. It was not meant to be a long-term solution. Now, that magic is poisoning you..."

He didn't finish, but Slate didn't need him to. He could *feel* that power trying to wash him away, trying to destroy a body that wasn't ready for it.

Slate didn't understand how or why. The questions faded from his mind, scattering like sand on a wind. He simply counted his breathing with his father, his calmness an anchor, a weight against the storm inside him.

Kari arrived, bursting into being from the fireplace. Slate's focus shifted away from his father, distracted instantly. "Kari... Dani?"

"She's safe," she replied. "I took her to Roger."

"To Roger?"

"Yes."

"She's safe?"

"Yes, I promise."

Minutes past. Or lifetimes. Slate couldn't know. Slowly, the tidal wave of magic ebbed off. Joon's magic pulled Slate away from the edge of the pit of frost inside him. Slate's breathing eased as the riot inside him slowly tapered off. The silence inside the house was tense. The pain faded to something at least manageable, and Slate opened his eyes.

"How do you feel?" Ebisu asked gently.

"I feel like... like... I can feel the entire world." He swallowed hard, swallowing bile. "It's..." His breathing stuttered. "It's overwhelming."

"Your mother's gift, I'm afraid," Ebisu said with a wry smile. "She was an empath, a powerful one." His father let out a sigh, but kept his fingers over Slate's jaw. "And you have nascent mental shields." His father *tsk*ed, but his cross expression seemed aimed at himself. When he looked back at Slate, his face was smooth once more. "Narrow your focus to just yourself. Your own breathing. My breathing."

Slate drew in a breath. The shadows at the edge of his vision retreated.

"He's got telekinesis too..." Jian said softly from somewhere behind him.

Ebisu's eyes didn't deviate from Slate, but his words were directed at Jian. "Telekinesis?"

"He blew up the arena. And he's had a couple of really erratic magical outbursts in the last couple of months."

His father nodded. "Interesting. Not a rare fae magic, but certainly not a common one." Slate was trying to follow the words, but it was a struggle to do much more than breathe with his father.

"It's... true... then?" Slate forced words together carefully, tasting them, listening to his own gravelly voice to make sure he was making sense. "I'm... a fae."

"Half," Ebisu replied softly, and Slate nearly choked at the wash of sadness, guilt, and fierce protective love that bled from his father over to him. "Your mother was fae. Full fae. She was to be the fae queen. *Titania.*"

Slate counted his breathing, even as his fingers spasmed. "That man... Zeyphar. He said..."

His father's face paled, skin tightening around his eyes. "Zeyphar?"

"Yeah. Zeyphar. Fae king... or... or whatever." Joon's fingers shifted along his back, and he felt the witch-doctor's magic continue to spread, continuing to tug him, an inch at a time, from the yawning void.

"Zeyphar is a false king. He speaks in half-truths, lost to the Malady that poisons his mind and his magic..." Ebisu shook his head. "It is not a conversation for right now. You, Slate, need *rest*."

His father's face slid from view, to be replaced by Joon-*san's*. He looked younger than Slate's father, even if he knew it was a lie, and Joon offered him a cheerful smile. He finally pulled his hands away from Slate's skin, and for a moment, Slate tensed, waiting for the magic to suck at his mind and soul.

His insides trembled… but held. Joon-*san* gave a nod of approval and reached for something out of Slate's view. Slate's eyes drooped, his body going limp. Magic and medicine was thrown at him. *Drink this, breathe that.* Jian hovered over his father's shoulder, watching with a sort of worried sharpness. He looked somehow haunted—gaunt, even.

His thoughts scattered at a pitched voice, but the tone was steady. Kari, off in the corner with his father. She was speaking softly, from the way Ebisu was leaning in, yet Slate could hear every word with perfect clarity.

He shuddered, and Joon-*san*'s face reappeared. Time seemed to slip away from him. One minute, he was drinking some potion, then he blinked, and he was somewhere else. A bedroom. Before he could ask, he blinked again, and different people were in the room, having a different conversation than a minute earlier.

He needed to call Dani. He needed to talk to her, find out for himself if she was okay. He needed to…to…

He drifted, eyes closing as if weights pulled them shut.

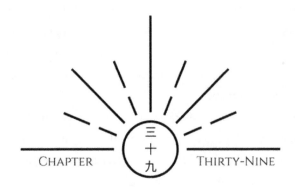

CHAPTER ☰十九 THIRTY-NINE

THE LIGHT IN THE DARK

... deep in Siberia, mirroring the one that encircles the Silver Valley. Many argue that the difficulty to reach Thule makes the exchange favorable to the vampires, but...

– Gherald Schmidt, Faerloch Historical Archives

Daniella's freckles stood out starkly on skin that was sickly pale, like a splattering of blood on white snow. Roger had to draw in another deep breath to keep the darkness roiling inside him from surging up and painting the world black.

Or red, depending on how messy it was.

The bundle in his arms weighed far too little, he decided, as he stalked towards the back entrance to Loraine's pub. Inevitably, his eyes dropped back to that mark. The one so close to where someone had nicked her with a knife against her throat.

If, and when, he found whoever had held Daniella by knifepoint, they were going to be... the darkness inside him surged with glee, and he grit his teeth to force it back down. That aside, he knew precisely who had left the *other* mark.

Red tinged his vision, but he reigned it back, drawing in Daniella's warm scent and letting it soothe the beast of rage inside him. Complicated... things had become *complicated*.

Before him, the door swung open without a touch, shadows slithering along the enchanted metal and along the ground beneath his feet as he stepped inside. Three gnomes Loraine employed froze in the middle of various tasks in the small kitchen, eyes flicking from his face to the woman in his arms, then back to his face, color leaching from their skin.

It was instinct to pull shadows around Daniella, to conceal her vulnerability from any and all who might pose even the smallest threat to her. He had merely to bare his teeth—canines elongated into sharp points—and all three of them fled from the kitchen.

"I knew she was going to cause trouble," growled a voice from the doorway the gnomes had just escaped through.

"You say that, yet you can deny her no better than I can," Roger said wryly, and it was a struggle to release the shadows, to allow the werebear to glimpse the female in his arms. Her burnished gold eyes darkened, and she sneered, but Roger didn't miss the way her expression softened a bit.

"I can certainly deny her more than *you*," Loraine drawled, crossing her arms to lean one muscled shoulder against the doorframe. "The great Roger Addington, or should I say—" A glint of warning in Roger's eyes, a hint of blood red that had Loraine rolling her eyes. "So touchy today, leech. Come on, let's get her upstairs." She jerked her chin toward the far door, the one that led upstairs to her personal den, and more.

"I don't know why you talked me into letting that girl frequent my establishment. So much trouble for such a small female, and with hardly a drop of magic in her veins," Loraine grumbled as she led the way up the narrow staircase.

"From what *I* recall, it didn't take much for me to convince you," Roger replied with a smirk, holding Daniella close to his chest as he ascended the stairs. It took concerted effort to keep his eyes off the bite mark on her neck, to focus on the stairs instead.

Loraine grunted, hit the second floor landing, and turned to continue to the third story. "Yes, well, my obvious weakness for the chit is the same reason we regularly have to threaten my patrons to stay away from her," Loraine muttered darkly. Roger caught a glimpse of Loraine peeking back, eyeing Daniella with a hint of protective anger that so frequently hung around alpha werefolk—and one didn't get much more alpha than Loraine.

To those outside of werefolk culture, the term 'alpha' was usually reserved for the head of each pack, but Roger knew better—knew it wasn't a title, but a term to describe werefolk with the dominance and sheer power necessary to lead others, whether they choose to or not. No, Loraine had no pack of her own, but her status as alpha was unmistakable to the point where even other alphas were wary of her.

"She is a beacon of light to many in the dark," Roger murmured, dropping his gaze to the woman in his arms.

"So *poetic*, vampire," Loraine snorted, but didn't dispute the fact. Roger knew Daniella helped calm her beast as much as the redhead soothed the writhing darkness inside Roger's black soul. Such a large effect from such a small package. Small, breakable. He could snap her in half with one hand... with no hands, in fact. The idea terrified him, and haunted him each time he let her walk out of his sight.

Until now, she'd always returned to him in good condition, more or less.

He ruthlessly shoved his protective urges back into the pit of roiling rage and darkness that lived inside him. He would not cage her, would not shadow her like a wraith and steal from her the independence that was part of what made her such a beacon of light. "It is an apt description."

"It is for that very reason you should keep your distance from her." Loraine rounded the stairs once more, to climb towards the fourth and final floor of her building. He caught a glimpse of a curled lip and furrowed brows. "Something about her... I don't trust anyone who makes me feel that way. She is a weakness."

Roger's lips curved slowly into a smile, one that would have made anyone but Loraine spit out their drinks in surprise—it was a tender smile, one that currently belonged to this very woman. "I have learned, over a millennia of existing in this bleak world, that a weakness is worth having if it also brings you happiness. Otherwise... it does not feel much like you are living at all."

Loraine paused on the steps, swinging her head around to pin him with a look. He did not allow many to see the real him, but he did not hide from Loraine. It was a rather useless endeavor anyway. "Such pretty words for someone with your... origin." Roger shot her a warning glance, and Loraine merely smiled. "You know if I didn't like the girl-child, I wouldn't have allowed her in my bar. Especially with all of the problems she brings along. Why do you not tell her of all the beings you have had to have special *talks* with?"

Roger raised a brow and started after Loraine once more as she continued to climb. "You think I should tell her I've had to claim her as my ward to those who frequent the Den in order to keep her from being pestered relentlessly by fae, werefolk, and who knows what else, who want to touch her, smell her, hear her voice?"

Daniella was indeed coveted... perhaps by *him* most of all.

Loraine snorted and paused at the top of the steps before a door that had faint glowing runes on it, invisible to any who didn't know what to look for. She brushed a large hand over them, and they faded from the dark wood. "I would pay good money to see how she reacts to finding out about your *claim*." She glanced behind her with a savage grin that made her look so much like her animal form—a ferocious and enormous polar bear—and Roger grimaced, glancing at Daniella's pale face.

She might hate him, if she knew how much he shielded her from the world of the Lore. From the world in general. Daniella was an independent spirit, despite her phobias, and fought tooth and nail for it. She'd told him, once, about the fierce fight she'd put up in court after her parents' deaths to be allowed her independence, rather than be subjected to the foster system.

No, he couldn't tell her about his claim, not if he wanted to stay in the light of her smile. He would bear the weight of her hatred if she ever found out, but he would continue to protect her from those who saw her smile and wanted to reach for it.

The nightmares haunting her already are more than enough as it is, Roger thought darkly.

Loraine stepped into the apartment that topped her building, and Roger felt the wards slide over his skin like oil as he stepped through them. He resisted baring his teeth at the feel of so much magic, and followed the werebear through the sparse living room and into one of three bedrooms lining the hallway to the right.

"She can stay as long as she likes, but she'll only be warded when she's in this apartment," Loraine said gruffly, gesturing toward the bed. There was a distinct *thump* above them, followed by an earsplitting whistle and an imperious hiss that filtered through the thick walls. Loraine released an answering roar that made even Roger's hackles stand straight up.

However, Selene was nothing if not a queen unto herself, for her answering rumble was displeased and not in the least cowed by Loraine.

"That stupid fucking bird," Loraine growled, stalking from the room. "If she wrecks my roof again, I'm gonna wring her feathery neck." Her voice faded from hearing, and Roger detected the click of a latch as Loraine took the rooftop access exit, slamming the door shut behind her.

Roger sighed and moved to place Daniella on the bed. She looked small amongst the covers of a bed meant for the oftentimes-larger bodies of immortals, and his fingers curled at his sides at the urge to touch her, to assure himself she was alive and well.

His eyes slid down her chin, to where the blood was drying on her neck. It was a rich, red color, a splash against ivory skin pale from trauma. His insides tensed, and his eyes dilated as his fangs slid down from his gums, throbbing with a hunger that was a siren's song in his blood.

One that was never quite silent, deep inside him.

Swiftly, he cut off oxygen to his lungs, blocking her rich scent from feeding said hunger. He blinked fiercely, and bared his fangs.

Not at her, but at the darkness inside, always waiting to *pounce*.

It was several slow, immortal heartbeats before the slide of power ebbed away from the cusp of his flesh, sinking back inside himself to coil like the viper it was.

He forced his eyes away from Daniella, and strode from the room in quick, long strides. He didn't even allow himself to glance at that *other* mark on her neck, knowing his own limits of self control.

She's lost to you, Marius...

In his mind's eye, he could see the light that staved off the worst of the darkness becoming dimmer, and suddenly, his oxygen-deprived lungs tightened with anxiety.

He shoved it deeper, *deeper*.

His body was tense, muscles twitchy, as he returned moments later with a glass of water and a sleeve of saltine crackers. He set both on the night stand beside the bed, still denying his lungs any of the sunshine-and-meadows-soaked oxygen. His fingers made quick work of tugging a blanket over her small form, and the darkness inside him bucked as his fingers itched to brush back her hair.

Burning Tartarus...

He was out of the room before his heart could manage another sluggish, old beat.

He smelled Karisi before he heard her delicate voice. He lifted his head from the tumbler of whiskey in front of him, and spied the *kitsune* as she wove her way through the patrons who mingled in the Den, even at this late hour.

He spied Loraine shifting from her position by the taps, straightening to her full height as she stared the small female down. Karisi paused a moment, wariness flashing in those vixen eyes of hers, but she smiled a moment later, a sensual one that had more than a few heads turning in her direction, and winked at Loraine.

The werebear revealed her teeth in a silent snarl, but a hint of amusement brightened her brown-gold eyes.

The *kitsune's* unusual rose-gold hair smelled freshly showered as she plopped herself into the booth across from Roger, all without a moment's hesitation from the weight of his stare. Her remarkable eyes, colored like the dark roll of thunder clouds and far too clever for a being of her age, dropped to the whiskey in front of him, and her slender brows shot up.

"I wouldn't comment, if I were you," he said with a curl of his lips, a hint of fang showing.

"I was going to ask where's mine." She threw her hair over her shoulder and popped her chin on the back of her hand. "And back off with the alpha-hole bullshit. It doesn't work on me, cupcake."

A low rumble came from his chest before he could stop it, and he pressed his lips into a thin line. He steepled his hands in front of him, and lowered his face until he could pin her with a look over the tips of dark claws that didn't normally make an appearance.

"Explain." His voice was smooth as syrup, but heavy with the weight of the darkness that continued to twist inside him, refusing to settle when Daniella's blood had been spilled.

Karisi's face shifted from slyly amused to serious in the blink of an eye. She, too, had power, and it glided over her skin in little licks of ghostly blue flame. An audible squeak came from a nearby dryad when three silken tails and fox ears erupted from Karisi's curvy body. Her canines, too, had lengthened as she cocked her head in a decidedly animalistic manner.

"I have fangs and claws too," she hissed, fire now smoldering in her eyes. "If you're done measuring your dick, can we talk like civilized beings?"

They held each other's stare for another moment, and Roger briefly wondered if this creature before him would actually put up a good fight before that darkness inside of him crushed her.

Daniella's smile, cheerful and easy, flashed in his mind, and he chastised himself for letting his control slip. He sat back in the booth, and lifted the whiskey to drain the tumbler in a single slide. The glass made an audible thump when he dropped it back to the table, and a wordless fawn with an apron around her hips switched it out for another whiskey.

And plopped a fresh one in front of Karisi.

Her massive tails settled around her, no longer weaving and bristling with fire. Karisi reached for her whiskey, took a healthy swallow, and mirrored his position as she slid back against the booth's cushions. "How is she?"

"Sleeping."

Karisi's eyes narrowed. "Can I see her?"

"Not right now, no." Roger's answer was neutral but firm. He saw Karisi's eyes flicker over to Loraine, who continued to stare at the *kitsune* with the unblinking eyes of a predator.

"You and Mama Bear are quite riled up," she commented lightly.

"We have a soft spot for the woman you brought to us injured and shaken. We don't take lightly to our friends being hurt, regardless of who is truly at fault," Roger answered darkly, sipping his fresh whiskey.

Karisi's chin bobbed in a slow nod. "Neither do I." She eyed the whiskey in front of her. "She'll want to know about Slate."

It was a miracle he kept the sneer from his face. He took a deeper pull from the crystal in his hands. "Yes, she will. And I'm going to want to know every detail of what transpired tonight."

Karisi eyed him, one of her ears twitching. "Even though you won't let me see Dani?"

"And why, pray tell, would I have any reason to mislead you about her condition? Trust me, Karisi, with her wellbeing. It would be best for you not to test my goodwill." It was spoken softly, because he was already teetering on the fine edge of his control.

So worked up for a woman? Viktor would be in stitches over it.

The thought of his friend helped to ease some of the tension from him, and Karisi wisely gave a small nod of her head. She proceeded to fill him in about the events that had transpired that evening, speaking concisely and with an attention to detail astonishing for one so young. Roger's eyes sharpened as he watched her speak, and a new hint of interest whispered through him.

Karisi could be a valuable asset.

She had great potential for dealing in what he liked best. Information. And information was Roger's greatest weapon. What else did this cunning woman know, regarding affairs she may not even know about?

But now was not the time to interrogate her. He digested her news in silence, slender fingers wrapped around the base of the crystal tumbler in his hand.

Zeyphar.

That little sniveling runt of a fae?

"What do *you* know, Roger?" Karisi's voice was frank, and her eyes were keen. He met them, and angled his head much in the way she had, one predator to another.

"Quid pro quo, as the fae say," he finally mused. Roger took another sip of the whiskey. "The last time I saw Zeyphar was at his sister's birth. I was part of the Vampire Delegation sent by our council, to offer gifts at the birth of the princess and reaffirm our neutral ties with the fae. Aredhel was a tiny babe, but Zeyphar seemed to regard her as an enormous threat. He did not bother to disguise his displeasure," Roger said dryly.

Karisi leaned forward, eyes gleaming with interest. "Can you get to him?" Unspoken was the fact that Roger might be one of the few who stood a chance of taking down the '*Titania*' of the fae.

Roger tipped his head back, swallowing the last of his whiskey. "No."

Karisi's brow cocked. "No? He's going to be gunning for Dani now, you know. Not just Slate."

A fact he knew well. That *mark* flashed in his mind, and he ground his teeth together. "My dear Karisi, are you not well-versed in the history of the Lorefolk?" Roger leaned forward, eyes gleaming. "The vampires and the fae went to war once. It is one of the varied reasons there are so *few* of my kind. The truce that exists now lies heavily on the ward reinforced with the blood of those aged vampires who sit on the seat of our council deep in Siberia." He ran a finger along the rim of his empty glass. "It keeps all vampires from entering the Silver Valley without express permissions, and it is a twin to the one that surrounds our sacred domain in the deep cold far north, to keep the fae from entering our lands."

Karisi's brows shot up, and a calculated expression flashed through her eyes. "So, you would only be able to take him out if he left the Valley."

"I have ears everywhere, my dear, but even a vampire can only move so fast. The shadows do not travel quite as fast as the fae teleporters can, though we can travel farther." Roger gave a little shrug. "Besides... are you entirely sure Slate will want his uncle killed?" An elegant arch of a dark brow.

Not to mention the potentially disastrous political fallout that it would cause, and not just for the fae. Rage simmered in his veins at the thought of the Council bone-bags who sat in Thule.

"Slate isn't aligned with Zeyphar and never will be," Karisi stated firmly. "And he will do anything to keep Dani safe."

"As will I."

Karisi watched him closely for a heartbeat. Then a sensuous smile graced her features, thinly veiling the threat of the fierce predator underneath. Her beauty did not move him, but he would be a fool to deny its existence. She was a beautiful oleander flower; lovely but deadly.

"Shall we agree to keep each other in the loop?" She arched a brow.

Roger gave a dip to his head, because that course of action was best for Daniella. The more information he had, the better he could protect her. "Agreed."

"And if Slate shows up to see Dani?" Karisi tilted her head to the side, and finished off her whiskey with a dainty flick of her wrist.

Roger stilled, the darkness inside him uncoiling, but he gave a small tip of his shoulders. "It will be up to Daniella, when she is awake."

"That's fair," Karisi said slowly.

"I will relay Slate's condition to her," Roger promised in a low voice. Because he couldn't keep something like that from her, no matter how dangerous the male had suddenly become to her wellbeing.

The *kitsune* slid from the booth with a graceful swirl of tails that shimmered with fire before dissolving away, along with her ears, as she straightened. She fished her phone out of her pocket and offered him a smirk. "Thank you. Now, what's your number?"

She had guts, at least. He eyed her coolly as he recited the digits, then felt the buzz in his pocket from his own device as she sent him her number. The fawn was back with another whiskey, holding one up for Karisi with a perk of her brown brows.

"No, thanks, gorgeous. I'll be heading out." She jerked a thumb over her shoulder, but gave the fawn an appreciative grin that had the female's brown cheeks turning red with pleasure. "But I'll be back." Karisi winked, and the fawn stifled a giggle as she hurried away.

Roger tried not to roll his eyes as he took a sip from his whiskey. "Be well, Karisi."

"Same, vampire. I'll be in touch." She took two steps away from the table, but paused, glancing over her shoulder. "Take care of her, *ne*?" She gave a pointed glance upward, and Roger tipped his chin.

The *kitsune* was out the door like a sleek wind.

Roger glanced at Loraine, who was eyeing the door like it had Karisi's face painted on it, and she wasn't sure what she wanted to do about it. Every sign of Loraine's protectiveness was a balm to the darkness inside him. Indeed, he doubted even Zeyphar could get through *her*.

A vampire and a werebear made for good bouncers, to say the least. Daniella was the safest she could be right here above the Den. It calmed the roiling darkness inside him, and he sipped at his whiskey.

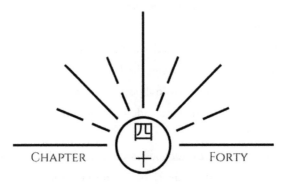

CHAPTER — FORTY

BROTHERS-IN-ARMS

... while magic seems to thrive predominantly in female progeny of witches, there are rare cases of males inheriting the magic. Kitsune, however, seem unable to produce male progeny at all, even human ones, which may be a contributing factor to the shrinking population...

- Gherald Schmidt, Faerloch Historical Archives

The morning sun was creeping in through the window. Slate inhaled deeply, blinking blearily at an unfamiliar setting. That wasn't his ceiling...

He waited a beat, and everything became sharper.

He was lying on a soft futon. In a bedroom. Jian's bedroom, actually. Plants draped and dripped from every available surface and wall, the room suffused with a comfortable, tropical humidity.

Slate stared at a plant for far too long, pulling his brain together from the thick fog of unconsciousness. His gaze shifted, taking in more of the familiar space. Unlike Kari's room—which was neat and organized—Jian's space was always a bit more chaotic, reflecting the inside of Jian's brain, constantly thinking about projects and theories and magic and medicine. A bookshelf stuffed to bursting with tomes and plants and little boxes of who even knew what stood vigil next to the window. A desk in the corner overflowed with bottles and vials and half-dissected plants and pestles and mortars and other tools of the trade. The sliding rice paper door that separated Jian's room from Kari's was open.

Jian himself was sitting at the foot of the futon, crossed legged and with his back against the wall, a book open across his lap. Slate blinked, focusing. His best friend looked *wrecked*. Smudges under his eyes, cheekbones sharp, like he'd lost weight rapidly. *Gaunt*. Thinner, his normally-thick muscles closer to Roger's leaner, slender build.

His lungs tightened at the sight, and his eyes tracked to Jian's calm face. Despite the fact that he looked like he'd lost ten—maybe twenty pounds—his best friend's eyes were alert and bright. They whipped immediately to Slate's the moment Slate shifted.

"Morning, sunshine." Jian gave him a little half-grin, snapping the book shut and dropping it to the floor. He shifted onto his knees, leaning forward to press the back of his hand to Slate's forehead with a clinical gleam in his thundercloud eyes. "Feel better?"

Slate swallowed, his throat dry and tight. Emotion flooded through him—anxiety, nerves, guilt. "I feel okay... I think..." His eyes widened, gaze shooting to Jian. "Dani?"

Jian held up a hand. "She's fine." He sat back from Slate, and Slate wanted to ask for details, but then those *feelings* ebbed from his mind, leaving him raw and empty. Jian assessed him with a critical eye. "You certainly look better. Your veins aren't dark anymore..." A penlight appeared in his hand and Jian swept the light back and forth between Slate's eyes. "Normal... Not gonna lie, you were touch-and-go for a minute there..."

He did a couple more checks. Every time Jian's skin touched Slate's, emotion speared through him. It took him a couple of times to realize it wasn't *his* emotion he was feeling.

He was feeling Jian's.

"Jian... I can... *feel you*," Slate breathed, lacking the right words to express what he meant. His mind was still sluggishly trying to pull itself from the mud. His vision kept wavering, but nothing drastic, like it had before.

Jian's gaze skittered over his face, assessment and concern furrowing his brow. "I'm...
not surprised. Your dad says you've got fae empathy magic. Pretty rare, as far as fae magicks
go." Jian shook his head, like he was overwhelmed but amused at the same time.

"Empathy?"

Jian gave a shrug, rubbing at his temple. Slate's eyes focused enough to notice the
gauntness again, and he struggled to bring up words, but Jian was already speaking. "From
what I know, you're supposed to be able to feel other people's emotions. I'm not sure
if anyone can block you, but you can even *manipulate* them. Make them feel shit. I've
heard, if you're powerful enough, practiced enough, you can even make people do shit
you want if you're clever enough about how you manipulate their emotions." He blew
out a breath and shook his head with a wry smile. "I don't know much about it, but it's
a very powerful, very *subtle* branch of magic." He rolled his eyes. "Naturally, you can't do
anything straightforward, *ne*?"

Slate swallowed hard, feeling bile rise up, despite the lighthearted amusement Jian was
trying to interject into the moment. He squeezed his eyes shut again. He didn't... he didn't
want that. He didn't want that kind of power over other people. He didn't want *magic*.

But that wasn't how this worked anymore. He opened his eyes and was once again
assaulted by the vision of Jian's haggard, drawn face. He grit his teeth. Nope, there was
no going back now. Just because he didn't want it didn't negate the fact that he *had* it.

"You cannot return to your boring, mortal existence."

Despite the way Jian looked, it wasn't fatigue or exhaustion Slate felt rolling off him.
Instead, he felt guilt churning off of Jian, boiling over like water on a stove. Slate tried to
clear a throat as dry as sandpaper. "Something's bothering you..."

Jian's eyes flitted between his before he slid off from the futon. He crossed the room,
snagged a cup from his desk, then returned to offer Slate the end of a straw. With a grateful
look, he sucked down the water, feeling it slither life back into him.

Jian returned to the desk, and set the cup on the corner. He lingered, and Slate watched
the tense line of his back. Jian's nimble fingers started messing around with things on his
desk—mindlessly organizing. Long heartbeats passed. Slate waited, knowing how Jian
operated when he was upset. If he didn't want to talk, he'd deflect with smooth charm
and a firm hand. If he did... you had to wait him out while he organized his thinking.

A far cry from Kari or even Slate. They tended to burst and ramble.

"There's something you need to understand," Jian said softly, and Slate dragged his gaze up from Jian's jittery fingers. "Kari and I..." He let out a hoarse chuckle, and shook his head. "I don't know how to explain it to you, but she and I share magic and energy."

"I know..." Slate reminded him slowly. "You've told me. You both draw from the same well of magic." Jian and Kari were magical twins; they were two different people, but they also *weren't*. They were the same energy across two bodies. Magic, and *chi*—life energy.

Jian nodded, back still to Slate, hands ceaselessly moving things around. It was something he did when he was distraught, and it made Slate's heart squeeze. "Between Kari and I being tied together... and our unique lineage, it... it gives me some neat magical quirks. Like, I'm immune to fire and I can manipulate it—"

Slate had seen that. He'd seen smoke curl from Jian's fingers. Had seen ribbons of fire thread between Jian's fingers.

"—but it's not *my* fire," Jian continued. "My father can't manipulate fire. He's not immune to it." He half-turned, pegging Slate with a look. There was something pleading in his expression. "It's Kari's. I steal it from her. My magic isn't... it's not *offensive* like hers. I'm a doctor. I *fix* things." A tingle in Slate's chest, a small, brief red flag, but he chose to focus on the grave look on Jian's face.

Jian looked away, fingers tensing against the desk. "That's what I do. That's what I *like* to do..." Jian reached out with one hand, running the pads of his fingers over bottles and vials that lined the back of it. "And I... if I could've saved you from having the glamour ripped off you, I would have. I could've burned them, you know? But... I couldn't." He blanched, and Slate's vision sharpened on the stark expression on his best friend's face. Jian swallowed and glanced over his shoulder. "Because if I'd used it last night to beat back the fae and stop that bastard from ripping the glamour off you... I would've killed Kari."

Slate felt his skin tighten over his skull, horror blooming along his blood.

"I would've sucked the energy right out of her and... and I can't..." Jian's voice was thick, but Slate couldn't quite see his face. He didn't need to. He could *feel* the emotion pouring out of his best friend; terror, guilt, this cocktail of swirling angst that stabbed Slate right through the chest. "You have to understand I can't *choose* that, man, I can't... Kari is... Kari is my other *half*. I know that sounds weird to you, and I can't explain it. There is no Jian without Kari, and I couldn't..."

"Jian, Jian, man, you know I'd never make you choose," Slate interrupted him, and his energy rallied as he pushed himself onto his elbows. He swallowed hard, trying to talk around the sock lodged in his throat. "Kari is your *twin*. Even without magical empathy or whatever twin shit you have going on, I'd never—"

"I thought you were gonna die last night," Jian blurted out. Orange flickered over the stormcloud gray of his eyes, and Slate stilled, breath catching in his throat. Jian pressed his palms flat to the surface of his desk, twisting away from Slate. "And I could do *nothing* but *watch* it happen. *Nothing*." His voice broke and he pulled in a stuttering breath. "And—and, I mean, Slate, man, you're my *brother*."

"Fuck, Jian, stop being so emotional," Slate said thickly, feeling overwhelmed. "I can *feel* you. Fuck. Don't even think—I'd never make you choose between me and Kari. Ever."

Jian didn't turn around, didn't look at him, but that copper head jerked in a nod, and he saw the way Jian swallowed hard.

The emotions pulled back, leaving Slate more room to think, to breathe.

"Jian..." Something clicked together in Slate's mind. "Last night... you pulled me out of the arena... what did you do to me? Is that why you look—" He managed a weak wave of one hand in Jian's direction, and Jian finally turned his head to glance at him. The way Jian looked... Slate didn't *quite* understand the entire scope of what Jian could do with magic, but this was more than simple healing magic. It looked like he'd somehow... traded his very *essence* to keep Slate's from being torn apart by the magical implosion inside him.

He'd traded his own body for Slate's, using his... *chi*. Using *life*.

Guilt that was entirely his own licked the sides of his stomach.

Jian froze a moment, then he eased out a breath and straightened from the desk. He closed the distance back to the futon, and folded his too-thin legs under him to resume his post at the end of the bedding. He glanced at Slate, and his eyes hardened. "Don't. My choice, man. Shut that down right now. I'll bounce back faster than you anyway." A wry grin that faded far too fast.

Slate wanted to argue, wanted to prod at the guilt he knew still swirled inside Jian, like a small, slow whirlpool. But he clamped his mouth shut, because Jian's expression could cut glass. When Slate eased back down onto the futon, Jian's eyes slid away.

"Your magic was eating you from the inside out. I needed to keep your body whole until I could get you... get you here, to my father." That guilt, that shame, it surged until Slate chest tightened.

Jian's eyes glanced towards him, then skittered away. "My magic is powered by *chi* and my branch of spells and enchantments are maintained by the *chi* of something living. Since I couldn't use your life energy to keep the magical poisoning at bay—"

"You used your own," Slate finished for him, hating that he'd been right. Jian *had* traded some of his own life energy for Slate's.

"Dad held you together. I knew he could. I did what I had to to keep you from flying apart at the seams. Don't be sorry, because you would've done the same fucking thing for me." Another hard slash of those eyes.

Silence swirled around them. Slate finally looked away, and nodded. It was true—he'd not hesitate to fall on the sword for Jian. Or Kari.

"I dunno what fate has planned for you," Jian finally said, his voice soft in the quiet room. "But I want in. Whatever that means."

Slate frowned. "What? There's no plan. Nothing's happening."

Dani's face flashed through his mind, with her sunshine smile.

He didn't *want* any part of whatever politics or complicated shit that was happening in the Silver Valley. He didn't *want* to be fae or have magic or anything. He just wanted to be *Slate*. He wanted that for *himself*, and... well, he also wanted it for her...

He cut off his own thoughts, draping an arm over his eyes as he set his jaw.

"*Something's* gonna happen." A soft rustling sounded as Jian scooted up to sit next to him. "You're a fucking *fae prince*. And I want a part in that. Don't leave me out. I don't like being kept in the dark."

Slate shifted his arm to peer at Jian as a little flash of hurt echoed from his best friend. He spied Jian dashing a quick hand over his eyes. Slate let his eyes drift back closed, anxiety flushing through him. This was a disaster.

Jian continued, his voice a little thick, "I was one-hundred percent prepared to march into the Silver Valley with you. I wasn't about to let you go alone."

"I know," Slate said. He stuffed the heel of his hand into one eye, feeling a pulsing headache starting again. "I had faith Kari would come find us—"

"Come find you where?" a voice quipped, more sensual, warmer than Jian's low cadence—warm like liquid fire.

Kari was standing in the threshold between the two bedrooms, one hand casually braced against the sliding door. She was freshly bathed; her wet hair braided down her spine, dressed in cloth shorts and a loose tee-shirt.

"In the Silver Valley," Slate groaned, breaking eye contact with the female twin and tilting his head back to rub at his temples. He speared his fingers through his hair.

"For sure," Kari answered, a hint of forced amusement that didn't quite hide the tension beneath it. He heard the soft swish of bare feet over tatami, before her carnal, spicy scent wafted over him as a warm body settled on the edge of the futon.

His nostrils flared again, and his mind stumbled at the sensory input.

Since when did he notice how these two *smelled?*

Jian was full of herbs, a sterile clean to him, with a hint of fire. Kari was fire with spice, and a hint of sex, as if it bled from her pores.

Kari let out a little sigh, and Slate cracked his lids to eye her as she smirked at him. "That was the plan. We—" she tipped her head in Jian's direction, "—were having a frantic argument last night while everything was going down, making contingency plans, deciding what to do about you and Dani—"

"Where is she?" Slate blurted out. The sound of her name uncorked him, a sudden, driving anxiety thrumming in his head. Ice prickled along his forehead, behind his eyes.

Kari gave him a long look, eyes narrowed. "I told you last night. She's with Roger. She's safe..." A flicker of her eyes. "You feel that, right?" She turned her question to Jian, elegant brows raised.

Jian matched her expression. "Yep. It's *way* more pronounced now though."

Slate ignored them, single-minded in his pervasive need to know more about Dani. "She's safe? She's with Roger? You're sure?" His eyes bounced between them.

Kari nodded, shifting her gaze back to him. "I'm dead sure, Slate. I dropped her off to Roger myself. When I went back to check in on her, after you were... out," she smirked, but the mirth died from her eyes, "well, Roger said she was sleeping." Kari twirled the end of her braid around her finger in a nervous gesture—fidgety like Jian. "They've... well, Roger wouldn't even let me see her. Loraine too. Both of them have closed ranks." She shrugged, glancing at Jian. "They're protecting her. I think Zeyphar is still hot in the city, and Loraine and Roger aren't taking any chances." Her tone implied she understood the need for the protection, even if she didn't entirely *agree* with being denied access to Dani.

In a way, Kari reminded Slate of a fox with its fur prickled in offense, eyes sharp and sly for retribution.

Slate pushed himself back up onto his elbows, conflicted emotions whirling in his mind. Were they his emotions? They *felt* like his, but how could he know for sure?

Frustration made him suck in a breath. "I have to see her," he said. He shoved his body to the edge of the futon and heaved himself into a standing position.

And promptly swayed, knees buckling underneath him. He collapsed back on the bed. Jian was right in his face, pressing a hand to his forehead, flooding him with fresh magic that leveled his world and receded the headache once again.

Slate tried to swat him away, unwilling to take even another ounce of magic from his best friend. But Jian was stronger, insistent, and his voice was firm. "No, brother. You aren't going *anywhere*." Jian braced a firm hand on Slate's shoulder. "Except home," he amended with a half smile.

Kari shifted toward Slate's other side. "When you're feeling better, Slate, maybe we can take you—"

"No," Jian said firmly, whipping his gaze to Kari.

"If Dani were chomping at the bit to see Slate right now, would you deny her?" Kari demanded, incredulous eyes focused on her twin.

"Without question," Jian fired back. "Zeyphar wants *Slate*. And he will do anything to get him. Dani's little more than *bait*."

A silent stare-down formed between the twins, and Slate tried to pull his thoughts together to state his own opinion, since they were clearly having an argument across the mental twin arena. But he couldn't, not when they were both right. Not when he couldn't even figure out how he felt about it.

He sagged, falling onto his back, and his voice sounded tired, even to his own ears. "It's fine," he conceded. He stared at the ceiling and suppressed the clawing, icy fingers that incessantly whispered at him to go find her, go find her, *go find her.*

He had a thousand other things to think about. He didn't have time to obsess over Dani, even if she somehow felt far more important than all the other revelations from last night. She was with Roger. Roger was a vampire, and they were supposed to be strong. Really strong.

Slate had no doubt the male could keep Dani safe from the Silver Valley Council and Zeyphar. If Roger wasn't up to task, then perhaps they all deserved to be pinned under Zeyphar's thumb.

Zeyphar. His uncle. His maternal *uncle*.

Slate was fae.

"Kari-*baa*..." Slate hedged. "Did you talk to my dad last night?"

She nodded slowly. "I did. I filled him in on everything."

"He was here all night," Jian said. "Sat right there." He pointed to the chair in the corner. "He stepped out maybe an hour ago."

"I need to go home," Slate said. He held his arms out toward the ceiling, studying his hands. He could feel the magic under his skin—this living, vibrating entity. He couldn't hold onto it; it was like trying to catch water. It felt different, and yet somehow he still felt like... himself. "I need to sort out my life."

He was a fucking *fae*. High Fae, he supposed. Him. Yesterday, he was Slate, master martial artist, teacher, school owner. Maybe lorekissed.

Who was he now? Slate... Slate what? Melisande? Titania? High Fae? That Zeyphar bastard was his *uncle*. The king of the fae was his *uncle*. Which made Slate... a prince? A fae prince.

He had magic? *Magic*?

Fucking ridiculous, but he could feel it pulsing through him, just under the surface.

It was too much. Everything around him had been a well-constructed lie, a facade to cover up who and what he was.

Why?

His father had *lied* to him.

No, a little voice reminded him. *He said you weren't lorekissed. Said your mother wasn't either. It wasn't a lie. But it wasn't the truth, either.*

Slate sat up and once more, he pushed himself to the edge of the futon. The twins let him stand on his own this time, but both were ready to grip him by the shoulder should he waver. Slate steadied his breathing, and the world didn't wobble. He flashed his eyes to Jian. "Take me home," he said. "We're going to find my father, and we're finding out what the *actual fuck* is going on."

Jian's eyes flickered to Kari's only once, then back to Slate. He nodded.

"Let's go."

CHAPTER FORTY-ONE

NOT ALONE

... believed to be the last of the Great Creator's four children to arrive in Faerloch, the first encounter with Shamanistic Magic came in the form of a skinwalker called Akecheta, who crossed the oceans from the Americas in...

- Gherald Schmidt, Faerloch Historical Archives

There was a dull ache behind her eyes when Dani's senses came back online. Her throat was dry and sore.

Because she'd been screaming.

Her memories came back to her in a rush, and she bolted upright in the bed.

Her world instantly teetered sideways, and she gripped at her suddenly pounding head before slumping back against unfamiliar pillows. She breathed through her nose, and the world stopped spinning. She eased her eyes open, and peered cautiously around her. The room was small, sparse, but it smelled clean. Next to the bed, a glass of water and some saltine crackers had been laid out with care. Sunlight filtered in through the blinds that covered the one window, illuminating the space.

Her stomach pitched, and she remembered the last face she'd seen—Roger.

Was this his home? Or one of the many apartment buildings he owned?

She reached for the water, and her thoughts slid sideways. *Slate.*

Slate, who was a *fae prince*. Nephew to... Zeyphar. *Titania.*

A flash of cold eyes, identical in color to Slate's, but empty of the warmth that filled them when Slate looked at her. A slashing smile, and a gleam of interest that sent ice curling through her blood.

Slate was a fae, and now the glamour keeping him mortal was *gone.*

Would he turn into someone like Zeyphar? The similarities in their faces, their *eyes...* it lingered in her mind as she sipped at the water. Her parched throat cried out with relief, and she drained more of the water from the glass, trying to quell the trembling in her hands.

The distant sound of a door opening drifted in through the mostly-closed bedroom door, and Dani froze, eyes flashing over to the slit in the doorway. A moment later, slender pale fingers appeared in the crack, and the door was gently pushed open to admit Roger.

His eyes flew over her in quick, assessing sweeps, the chocolate color of them darkening closer to ebony when they skirted past her neck. Without thought, the hand not gripping the glass of water drifted up to brush at the scabbing cut on her throat.

She swallowed, the memory of it making her palms break out in a cold sweat, and she swallowed another compulsive gulp of water.

Roger disappeared, only wisps of shadow remaining. Then he was back, at a speed that had her heart racing with primal reaction at the effortless show of power. He held a wet cloth in his hand.

"Daniella," Roger spoke softly, carefully, and approached the bed at a calm, slow pace. "You're safe, in Loraine's safehouse. This place is warded better than anywhere in Faerloch." He stopped with a healthy foot between him and the edge of the enormous bed.

"Safehouse?" she asked, her mind still numb from the memories of Slate, of Zeyphar, of the explosion that had rocked the arena.

Above them, there was a distinct sound of a very large beak pecking at the roof, and a thrill of sound. Sellie's thoughts slid against hers in a shiver of concern, imperious anger, and outrage. It was clear from the images that Sellie was beyond displeased that Dani managed to get herself in trouble again.

She winced, and Roger's eyes flicked upwards, before settling back on her face. "She has been most unruly. Loraine has threatened to strangle her."

That got Dani's lips to quirk towards a smile, but the amusement died far too quickly in a chest that felt far too tight.

"Slate—"

"Karisi told me what happened. She wanted you to know that Slate has stabilized, and he will recover from the effects of breaking the glamour. He is safe in the Eastern District." The words jumped from Roger's mouth, but he seemed less than pleased by them. His shoulders were unusually tense.

"I see..." Dani muttered. Relief slithered through her, but it wasn't enough to banish the weight of panic in her gut at the thought of the fae.

Her fingers curled around the cup in her hands.

Roger was watching her, and she saw his eyes flicker. Down to her neck.

She fingered the cut there, trying to calm her suddenly riotous stomach. "Eat some crackers, please," Roger murmured, and shifted until he could sit on the edge of the bed. He reached out and handed her the wet towel. He kept his distance though, and jerked his chin towards the towel, then murmured, "And maybe... you might want to wipe the blood off your neck."

His throat bobbed a moment, and she absently brought the towel to her neck, jerking her head in a nod. With her other hand, she reached for the crackers and slid the sleeve into her lap. Numbly, she opened the sleeve, and slid out a cracker.

It tasted like ash in her mouth. She forced one down, then another, and gulped down the last of the water. Roger wordlessly held out a hand, and took the glass when she offered it. His steps were absolutely silent as he retreated from the room, and Dani finished wiping at her neck. She didn't look at the crimson stain before she set the cloth, bloody side down, on the edge of the nightstand. Roger returned a moment later with fresh water in the glass. He set the glass next to her on the bedside table, then sank down to sit on the edge of the bed.

"What do you need right now, Daniella?" Roger's words were endlessly gentle, and gratitude welled inside her. What would she do without this male in her life? This familiar rock in a savage ocean that she could cling to.

But then the image of Zeyphar popped into her mind as he effortlessly used his magic to rip the metal fencing from the fight ring, and her stomach tightened into a cold knot. Would even Roger fall to that kind of power?

Would even Roger disappear from her life?

She forced down another cracker as a roiling panic churned in her gut.

"I need to think," Dani mumbled, her mind trying to slowly pick apart the pieces from last night, turning them over like shards of glass that might cut her if she wasn't careful.

Roger gave a slow nod. His eyes dropped back to her neck, and she had the distinct impression he wasn't looking at the cut this time. She resisted the urge to touch the bitemark, to bring up the memories of the pleasure that had boiled her blood.

She shut off the thought, and tried not to gag as she forced another cracker down. Roger's eyes lingered on her face, and they stayed that way a moment as she chewed silently. Finally, he tipped his chin and flowed smoothly to his feet. He brushed off his slacks and slid his graceful hands into his pockets. "Do you want something else to eat? Drink?" He phrased each word carefully, and her heart turned over once more at the simple care in his words, in his stance. Even now, his shoulders were curved towards her, like he wanted to shelter her from the world.

She looked away, and swallowed the ash in her mouth that was supposed to be a cracker. "Not yet. I just... I want some time to process and be alone."

She reached for Sellie, stroking her friend's mind with assurance. Even if her world was crumbling, she couldn't stop caring for this being who was as dear to her as anyone. Sellie gave a responding mental coo, trying to soothe her as best she could. Dani's skin tightened.

Could Zeyphar hurt Sellie?

Irrational terror clawed its way up through her, and her stomach clenched around the ashes in her belly. It was a struggle to keep it from showing on her face, but she felt marginally successful.

She took a sip of her water, let the liquid try to ease the desert in her throat.

In a swift, fluid motion, Roger planted a hand on the mattress by her hip. His face was right in front of hers, and her scent—musky cloves and cinnamon, with a hint of pure male, washed over her, derailing her thoughts as his eyes locked with hers.

"Daniella," he murmured, and the word was a command, locking her attention as if he'd used some of the seductive power native to vampire magic. Her entire body froze, even the churning inside her. "You are not alone. You will *never* be alone. Even when I leave this room, you won't be alone."

Dani swallowed hard, compelled to nod, compelled to believe him, maybe...

Black bled into the whites of Roger's eyes like a creeping shadow, a shimmer of red visible beneath the brown, and Roger's eyes dipped down. A different kind of stillness came over the vampire, one that made the hairs on the back of her neck stand up. The spell of his gaze was broken, and her heart thudded against her ribs. Not another heartbeat had crashed against her ribs before Roger was shifting. The black leached from his eyes, the red fading from the irises. He moved with uncanny smoothness, brushing his lips against the top of her head, barely a touch. "Call me if you require anything. Loraine can ask the gnomes to cook you some lunch."

And then he was gone, like the shadows had tugged him from the room on a midnight wind, so quickly she didn't even get another glimpse of his face. Her heart tightened as a swirl of confusion rippled down her spine.

Had Roger wanted to...?

Absently, her fingertips brushed her lips, which made her think of the last person to kiss them. Slate's face replaced Roger's in her mind, and the confusion in her mind mixed with a painful longing and a hint of panic.

So many emotions, all of them overwhelming. She buried them, shoved them deep like they were poison and she had to keep her distance, gulping down a gasp of air. She tipped the cup to her lips, letting the water slide down her throat, abandoning the crackers. Slate's face, with his charming smile and wicked glint in his eyes, stubbornly flickered through her mind.

She shoved her feelings deeper, blowing out a breath.

But those words....

You are not alone.

She held them to her chest as she curled up against the pillows, and closed her eyes.

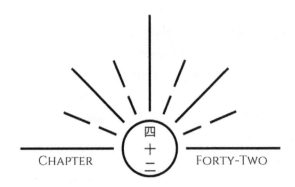

CHAPTER FORTY-TWO

THE STORY OF EBISU AND ARI

... rightful heir to the Throne disappeared into L'el, her fate one that did not reach Faerloch until many years later, when...

— Gherald Schmidt, Faerloch Historical Archives

The short walk from the Meho house to his apartment had been unsteady; Slate's vision spotted a little, his body felt achy, and a slight headache pulsed behind his eyes. Kari had looped her arm through his and her strength had leveled him. He caught his stride once they were at the door to the studio, though Jian had said the aches and pains might not go away for a while, despite the best efforts of magic and medicine.

"You've had a *powerful* glamour on you for your *entire* life," he said with a helpless shrug. "Your body is adjusting, becoming different, adding magic, settling. Shit like that needs time." He shook his head. "If the glamour had come off *slowly*—"

"I lived, Jian," Slate assured him, tasting a sour bit of guilt radiating off his best friend. "Heart's still beating."

Ebisu was in the kitchen when Slate opened the door to his apartment, twins in tow. His father paused when the three of them came through the door, dark eyes widening a little. Tendrils of paternal concern ghosted off him like curls of steam.

"I'm surprised you are awake," he said. He pulled out four tea mugs.

"We need to talk," Slate replied. He palmed the back of the couch to stabilize himself when his knees wobbled slightly. Kari's small hand immediately grabbed his elbow, but he gently shook her off. He needed to be able to get his own feet underneath him sooner rather than later.

Ebisu simply nodded. Kari and Slate settled on the couches while Jian darted into the kitchen to help, spiking a tea mug with magical remedies for Slate.

"Should I ask how you are this morning?" his father asked, moving carefully into the living area.

Jian carefully laid a tray on the *kotatsu* and distributed mugs. Slate strangled his, watching the steam rise in gentle swirls. He could *feel* his father... could feel his calm, his concern. He wasn't nervous, wasn't afraid. It was so much clearer than it'd ever been before; Slate had always been pretty sensitive and perceptive, but it was so crisp now, so clean. As if he were simply looking at his father and seeing his emotional grid.

"I feel okay..." Slate answered honestly. "I'm not good, but I'm okay. Better than last night."

Ebisu was quiet, and Slate knew he was waiting for more, so Slate continued, "I'm so overwhelmed. I don't... I don't understand. And I want you to be absolutely fucking *candid* with me. Please. Full transparency."

"What would you like to know?"

"*Everything.*"

His father nodded thoughtfully, studying Slate with a critical eye. Slate met his dark gaze steadily, feeling that calm, that concern, and now, now just the smallest *touch* of something that hurt. An ache like an old wound.

"I was a young man when I was kidnapped by the fae," Ebisu said. He sipped his tea. "I was returning home from a pit fight—"

"You did *pit fighting?*" Kari's mouth popped open in surprise.

A shade of a smirk twitched into life on his father's face. "Slate's love for fighting is not a fae trait, I'm afraid." That smirk disappeared. "I was walking home with a friend of mine—a lorekissed friend—and we were approached and kidnapped by the fae. We were dumped in the fae's court. I didn't see my friend again after that night.

"The political structure of the fae court was... tumultuous at the time. Zeyphar was not a king then, but a fae prince with too much power. His mother Rywin was *Titania*, and she appeared to turn a blind eye to what her oldest child was doing. It was not uncommon for Zeyphar to send his soldiers out, find lorekissed, and bring them back for a spot of entertainment.

"I was a solid fighter, and Zeyphar enjoyed throwing me into a pit fight with other fae to see what I was made of. Most fights I lost—desperately. Some I won, which I believe is why he chose to keep me around as long as he did. I was... something of a curiosity, I suppose.

"After one of the fights I lost, when I was being patched up by fae healers, a female came in, and she ordered everyone to leave."

"Let me guess. My mother," Slate said breathlessly.

"Precisely. She'd come to visit her brother for one reason or another, and he thought it prudent to show her his favorite toy."

"What was she like?"

Ebisu smiled. "Stunning, even by fae standards. Hair nearly white, with a sheen of gold. You share her eyes, but she was far more delicate. She carried herself very much like the princess. She was; regal, articulate. She could be spoiled at times, bossy always, with a clever head and a sharp tongue." There was such an *ache* around the edges of his father's voice that Slate felt his own throat close up tight. "She bossed me right out of Zeyphar's court and into her own. I traded a prison cell for a gilded cage."

"She didn't just... release you?" Slate frowned.

Ebisu shook his head. "No. She was endlessly curious about me as well. She didn't want to send me back, and I didn't ask to go. Fae who do not live in the city proper *rarely* see mortals. So, I went from being Zeyphar's prized fighting pet to Aredhel's prized show pet."

"This story better have a happy ending or I might throw up..." Slate said.

His father smiled. "She and I were friends, I suppose. I was certainly treated better—well-fed, well-rested, more freedom to move around her wing of the castle." Ebisu paused, eyes drifting down to the cup in his hands.

"Then Zeyphar launched his *coup d'etat*. He strategically set fires around the city, burning out key members of the fae political structure who'd opposed him. He killed his mother and her court—nearly all of Ari's court... burning them from their wings of the castle like one might smoke out vermin, before slaughtering them. He tried to kill your mother too. She and I barely escaped. We wandered the Forest together for five days, hoping for someone to rescue us.

"Ari was a princess, you must know. Soft and loved her whole life. Those five days in the Forest changed her. Changed us. She had nothing but her magic and her silk night dress. I had a stolen knife and fighting wit. I'm not entirely sure how we survived, but we did. And we were thankfully rescued by some surviving members of her court and taken to a village called Titan's Fen. It was a summer retreat for the royal family—small, secluded, tricky to locate.

"Because I had saved Ari, her court offered me my freedom. Said they would portal me back here to Faerloch, and I could be free." A little smirk that perhaps was a touch sly. "I obviously chose to take my freedom in Titan's Fen.

"Ari was never properly crowned Queen, but her court referred to her as that anyway, because her mother was dead and she was the heir apparent." A shrug. "And I was her consort."

"Gross," Slate whispered, a touch cheekily.

"We were in Titan's Fen two years or so... and you came along. Ari named you *Zlaet*. And fae are maternal, so fae children take their mother's name. So..."

"So I'm not Slate Melisande... but *Zlaet Titania*." A little part of him was devastated by the notion. As if his whole identity was being uprooted and torn away from him. He didn't even have a *name* to stand on. He didn't know who he was anymore. "How did we end up here?" He changed the subject.

Something deeper than sadness emanated from his father, even as outwardly, his face remained calm. He sipped his tea. "Zeyphar's people found the village. Ari shoved you and I through a portal, taking us back here, to Faerloch. You were not yet three years old."

"I don't remember any of that..."

"And I do not know if you ever will. She placed the glamour on you to hide you in plain sight. I believe it altered your memories as well. She was terrified Zeyphar would find you and kill you, kill his competition. She made the best decision she could with the information she had at the time."

A long silence circulated through the room. Slate nearly forgot Jian and Kari were there. Neither one of them had said anything, just listening, eyes bouncing between Slate and his father. He wondered what they were thinking, what conversations were happening along the twin mental field.

"Zeyphar said she's dead," Slate said into the silence, throttling his tea mug. "Said that my mother—"

"I know." Ebisu swallowed hard. "I..." he paused, pulling in a deep breath. "He did it himself. That much I know."

"*What*?" Slate's heart slammed against his sternum.

But his father only nodded and sipped his tea.

Slate sat back into the couch cushions, mind reeling. So, Zeyphar *himself* had killed his entire family. Killed his own *sister*. And yet he wanted to work with his *nephew*?

Groom him, more likely...

Anger pulsed in Slate's head, as ridiculous as it was for him to be angry over a woman he didn't remember. Angry because he suddenly felt as though that male had stolen an entire life not from him, no, but from his *father*.

Slate bounced his eyes around the living room, twisting a strand of dark hair mindlessly, his brain whirling. "One last thing," he said quietly after several long moments. "Why? Why this whole secret charade?" The idea that his father had kept this great secret his whole life, that everything he ever knew about who he was just... within a matter of hours, it all crumbled to his feet.

He could follow the logic—Zeyphar was a threat, so Slate needed to be hidden away, especially when he was a little baby. But why the secrets? Wouldn't it have been easier for everyone if Slate had been raised fae? Considering Kari and Jian were all magical and shit too, it wouldn't have been hard.

His father watched him for a long, painful moment. Slate could *feel* it, the emotion pouring out of his father—the fear, the hesitancy, the longing, the *love*.

"I—we—were thrust back into this mortal life with nothing but the clothes on our backs and each other," Ebisu finally said. "You are all I have left of Ari. I look at you, and I see her." Those dark eyes blinked rapidly and Slate swallowed the sock in his throat. "... and as your father, it was my job to protect you from forces that wanted to *kill* you. All that stood between you and Zeyphar was a powerful glamour... and me. I did the best I could with what I had. I taught you how to fight, how to self-regulate your fae temperament, instilled *morals* in you..."

He sighed. "I knew your glamour was fading. It was tied to Ari's life force and I—" Ebisu paused, and Slate could literally *feel* the horror of the memory of that day crawling through his father's mind. "I thought if I could keep the charade going, keep you 'mortal' for a little longer, keep you alive and fighting a little longer, then I could keep you. And I could keep Ari too. For just a little longer."

"*Shit*, Dad," Slate swiped his face briskly with the heel of his hand. "Shit, I'm not going anywhere."

"We wanted to keep you safe," Ebisu continued. "Zeyphar is a *terrible* male. He wouldn't have had any qualms with killing you as an infant, get rid of his competition. Had we been able to stay in the Titan's Fen, you would've been raised fae. But here in the city... it wasn't meant to be long-term. We were supposed to go back..."

"Why didn't we?"

Ebisu shook his head. "Time moves differently for fae. When one lives for centuries, your own sense of time slips differently."

"Were you and Aredhel *tamashoko*?" Kari asked. Her voice was thick and heavy with emotion.

His father nodded. "The fae call it *mayts*, but yes, it is a similar concept."

The silence stretched between them, thick and sad and heartbroken for a life that was stolen from them.

"So what now?" Slate asked. He held out his mug when Kari gestured and she refilled it for him.

His father stood gingerly with a little groan. "There is a new plan. We will be having some guests this evening, so you might want to get some rest, my boy."

Slate swallowed his tea hard. "Wait... guests?"

"Yes. I have been in touch with old friends in the Titan's Fen."

"*Fae guests?*"

"Indeed. So get some rest." Ebisu picked up the tea tray and headed into the kitchen.

Fucking what?

"Wait, wait, what? What does that mean? Why are fae coming *here*?" Slate asked, twisting around on the couch to follow his father with his eyes. "Dad? Dad. Why are fae coming here? What plan? Wait... the plan like... to *go back*?" Slate's eyes were huge. "Are you serious?"

"Very serious." A sharp cut of dark eyes.

He blinked, then twisted around and made eyes at the twins. Both of them just shrugged helplessly. "Wait. We... I can't just *leave*." Slate frowned. "We have a life here... a school, a business, a community who counts on us. We have responsibilities here!"

Ebisu sighed, and Slate tensed a little. "We must act quickly. Zeyphar and his entourage will likely scour the city to find you. Your aura is strong, and it will only be a matter of time before he finds a way around the Mystic Ward. Your magic is uncontrolled, wild. You need training, the kind that I cannot provide for you here. You are no longer *mortal*, Slate."

Slate ran his hands over his hair. "This is madness. *Madness*."

There was a heaviness in the next words Ebisu spoke that had Slate tensing even more. "You also need to assume your rightful role as *Titania*."

Slate froze, blinked at his father. "I'm sorry, what now?"

Ebisu held his stare. "It is your birthright."

Slate's eyebrows rose, even as his stomach bottomed out. "Yeah, no, you can't be serious. Me? *Titania*? Please."

"Zeyphar is not meant to be the *Titania*. He stole that title, keeps it through violence and scare tactics. It is your job to lead the fae, as it was your mother's before you." Calm words, spoken with a calm expression.

Slate stared at him incredulously. "No fucking way."

"Slate." Ebisu's eyes glittered with paternal exasperation.

"No. Absolutely not. Are you kidding me right now? I'm a *martial artist*." He shot to his feet, unable to stay still. His world tilted a second, but he maintained his footing as he started to pace.

"A martial artist who will make a fine *Titania*. You know how to be a leader—you are a master instructor with assistants under you, a student body you lead and manage. The same rules apply, just on a larger scale." A simple shrug. Like it was *that* easy.

"No. No, no, no," Slate spun on his heel, his pace increasing. His mind was reeling. His head was throbbing. "No. Tell your friends no."

"Slate."

He flipped his eyes up to his father, who remained calm and steady. "You cannot change the direction of the wind." Ebisu gave him a once-over. "You are still a bit pale. Get some rest."

CHAPTER · FORTY-THREE

CHOICES AND FATE

... the magical output of a lore being, or aura, is often believed to be interchangeable with life energy. However, scholars from Mysticism would argue that aura and life energy, known as chi, differ vastly....

— Gherald Schmidt, Faerloch Historical Archives

The sun was setting low over the city when Slate found himself in the studio waiting room with his father and the twins. He refused to sit, and instead found himself leaning against the heavy glass that separated the training floor from the waiting area. He'd slept off most of the day, and after some food and a bath, he was feeling leaps and bounds better than he'd been just that morning.

However, a restlessness beat inside him. A jittery, electric feeling pulsed through his blood. Like he was riding an incredible adrenaline rush, but without the physical symptoms. His heart was steady, his hands didn't shake. In fact, he was unnervingly steady, physically.

Every now and then, the memory of Dani from the night before flashed through his mind, making his heart squeeze painfully as an icy flush slid down his spine. The way she'd screamed his name when that portal had opened at her toes. The stark horror in her eyes.

The image of it was burned into his retinas, sketched into his memory.

A clawing, painful need to contact her contributed to the restlessness inside him. But he couldn't. First, he'd lost his phone. And second... Dani was afraid of the fae. And *he* was now fae. Frighteningly more involved than either of them had imagined.

Things hadn't been perfect between them, but now... he wondered if they could ever go back to what they'd been. Would her fear of the fae be directed at him now?

He almost didn't want to know.

He realized he was being a bit cowardly, but he also felt justified, considering all the fuckery happening in his life. He glanced back at his hands, flexing them. What he was having a hard time swallowing most was the constant swell of emotion that flooded him. Like an ocean, ebbing and flowing, closing in on him with a pressure that left a lingering ache behind his eyes.

Even with only his father and the twins in the room with him, he could *feel* them. Kari's breezy confidence, Jian's solid self-assurance, his father's endless calm, but flavored with such a heavy sadness that it left a cloying taste in his mouth. All these *knowings* just came to him. He didn't dare try to touch the swirling, living entity of magic vibrating in his bones.

He didn't want to blow someone's brains out, or something equally horrible, by accident.

Kari tensed first, a wave of alertness flowing off her. Slate felt it then—a presence. He cocked his head, listening. He could hear people approaching the studio door, the soft scuff of boots against pavement.

His father rose from his chair with a soft exhale of strain, and headed to the door. Slate straightened, watching, ready to launch himself across the waiting room and rescue his father.

The door opened.

A burst of delight and joy slammed into him. Slate winced and rubbed the heel of his hand into his eye. The pulse of emotion was not necessarily *painful*, but uncomfortable and unfamiliar.

Jian's eyes snapped to him. "Breathe. Pull your focus inward," he murmured, gaze sharp. Slate focused on him, drawing in a breath. Already, Jian's face was less gaunt, just as he'd promised. It eased him, to see Jian bouncing back so quickly. His face was fuller, and his skin had a healthy color to it once more. His muscles, too, seemed to be filling back out. "You won't feel everything so much. Breathe through your nose." Jian tipped his chair back on two legs, hands going behind his head, body the picture of easy and relaxed.

Slate exhaled with a little growl. First lesson he needed in magic: how to create mental shields so he could stop feeling the world.

His father returned, guiding three people behind him.

Correction. Three *fae*.

The three fae glanced his way, and froze predator-still. A trembling sense of joy, of aching familiarity, bled from them. Slate swallowed the sensation and met their gazes steadily. Two males and one female. A whisper of unease crept across Slate's heart, and he recognized it as his own emotion. There was no reason to be afraid. These were not fae out to hunt him down and kidnap him. He knew that. His father had prepared him. These were old friends, members of his mother's court. They were rebels, but not in the way Zeyphar had painted them to be.

"*Ty mai Matkha*," whispered one of the males. He was distinctly older, tall and thin, with silver hair pushed back from his brow, and soft, dove gray eyes. Eyes that gave Slate a very pointed assessment. "He is your spitting image, old friend." The words were directed at Slate's father.

"With Ari's tart temper and wit, I'm afraid," Ebisu chuckled softly. "Slate, this is Galyn Alva. He was your mother's political advisor."

"And now yours, my lord." Galyn gave him a gracious smile, but there was sincerity in there. Loyalty.

Slate resisted the urge to roll his eyes. Tendrils of amusement tickled him. He whipped his gaze to Jian. "Shut up, Jian," he snarled.

Jian laughed out loud. "Listen, bro, I didn't say anything."

"You were thinking it."

"Creep. Get out of my head." More rich laughter. It eased the knot of nerves in his chest a little.

Ebisu gave them both a stern look. Both boys shut up. Ebisu gestured to the other two fae. "This is Saida." The female gave Slate a single short nod. She was slight, but built like a fighter, with hard, flinty eyes and a heavy brow. Her golden hair was tied back in a tight plait down her spine, pointed ears peeking out. "She is the Guard Captain of Titan's Fen."

Slate's brow furrowed. "Your village has an army?"

"It has a *Guard*," Saida answered, her voice as hard as her eyes. "A damned good one. We try not to start fights, but we will finish them."

"And this male right here is Kallen Ewyt." The last fae was dark-haired with stunning heathered purple eyes and a strong, wiry build. Ebisu studied Kallen. "My friend, I'm not certain—"

Kallen crossed his arms, giving Slate a curious, assessing glance. "I was the captain of your mother's personal guard, and served as her eyes and ears in court."

"Spywork?" Kari purred.

His purple eyes shifted from Slate to Kari. "Of a certain sort. My expertise lies in shadow work and ward creation."

"You will be hard-pressed to find someone more skilled in barrier creation, wards, and portal magic," Galyn offered. "His magic is the cornerstone to the wards that protect Titan's Fen. One of Saida's best lieutenants."

Slate tipped his chin in acknowledgement, but his stomach was still churning.

"You used to play at the gatehouse with me." Kallen's lips half twitched into a smile, still studying Slate.

A tightness seized hold of him, the realness of his situation crashing over him again in a wave. "You—what?" He forced the words out.

"When you were a small child." Kallen shrugged. "You liked to portal-skip. Jump into one portal and instantly appear somewhere else. Made Aredhel crazy, but you'd laugh and laugh. You thought it was funny."

An amused ache punched through Slate, and his eyes flashed to his father, who had a fist pressed to his lips, a smirk behind his hand.

Ebisu caught his gaze. "It's true," Ebisu chuckled. "I'd nearly forgotten. Wild thing." He cleared his throat. "Let me introduce everyone," he continued. "These are Slate's closest friends. This is Kari—"

"Pleasure." Kari smirked, sensuality once more oozing from her pores.

"—and Jian, her twin. Both are children of the Jade Emperor. A fox demon and a witch-doctor, respectively."

"Fascinating, well met." Galyn nodded, placing one hand against his sternum and inclining his head to each twin. "Will you both be accompanying us to Titan's Fen?"

"Not me." Kari waved a hand dismissively.

"I will," Jian said.

Slate whipped his head to both of them. "Excuse me?" He scowled. "Doing what now? No." He shook his head. "No, I already told my father, I'm not going anywhere."

"It is of the utmost importance that you journey with us back to Titan's Fen," Galyn pressed calmly. "We must get you away from Faerloch. Zeyphar and his soldiers still stalk the city, and he will wait you out until you leave the district. He *will* make another move on you." Galyn's dove-soft eyes were suddenly sharp.

Huh. Not a spineless advisor then.

"I'll fuck him up this time," Slate growled, stubbornness gripping him in a chokehold. "I'm not afraid." The new magic inside him rustled. It needed to go *somewhere*, and he'd be *happy* to blow Zeyphar to smithereens.

Galyn shook his head. "I urge you, my lord, to approach this from a logical angle."

"Look." Slate held up his hand. "No disrespect, but I don't know you. And I'm not in the business of letting people boss me around. I found out I'm fae *yesterday*. Logic would be not making impulsive decisions like *leaving my whole life behind* to go on a field trip into the Forest of L'el."

Galyn seemed to be nodding in all the right places, but instead of speaking to Slate, he turned to Ebisu. "Fiery and stubborn as his mother."

"Imagine being his father."

"Goddess bless you." A dry voice with a hint of amusement grated on Slate's nerves.

"I'm *not leaving*." Slate's voice was icy and acerbic now, rising a little in volume.

A sense of hesitation tickled him. He recognized it as coming from Jian. "What?" he snapped at his friend, willing his heart to stop thundering against his ribs.

Jian rubbed his face and cupped his chin. "We should go. Today."

Slate went still, breath freezing in his lungs. "Are you kidding me right now? I can't leave!" His voice was definitely escalating. "I have this school, my people, Dani... I can't just uproot my whole life, everything I've known. Are you for real?"

"You need help, Slate." Kari's voice was soft, but deadly serious. He flashed her a dirty look and she sighed. "I mean, like, you need guidance. You got this gigantic aura and all this power just flooding out of you... you can't control it. What are you going to do, wait for it to explode out of you?"

"I feel fine now. The magic is just there."

"Fae magic is different, though," Jian said with a little shake of his head. "It needs to be used, that's why Faerie Dust Glamours are dangerous. You'll overflow with magic and it'll find its own way out of you, when you're most vulnerable." He glanced at the fae in the room for confirmation. All three of them nodded in agreement.

"What's going to happen when you lose your temper? Are you prepared to risk being around *her* when that happens?" Kari's eyes glittered with knowing.

Ice crept over his skin. He didn't have an answer for that. Self-control was not his strong point when he was upset.

A violent instinct inside him roared to the surface—he'd *never* hurt her. But intention was a fickle mistress. Just because he didn't *intend* to hurt her didn't mean that he *wouldn't*. Accidents happened.

The idea stilled him.

God, he'd really fucked up her whole life, hadn't he? Dragged her straight into this fae hellscape with him, put a target on her back by mere association with him. All because she did him a solid and saved his ass from being kidnapped in the spring.

"... you are inviting trouble to Daniella's doorstep, whether she knows it or not."

It was a shot to his pride, but he had to admit that Roger was right. Slate was trouble for Dani. All around.

"That's why it might not be a bad idea for you to just... go for a while." Jian tipped his chair back again, rocking it on two legs. He was watching Slate closely—too closely—for Slate's current mood. "Like, train in controlling the magic inside you. It's only something you can learn from the fae."

Slate stared at Jian for a long moment, processing. The twins were serious. They thought he should go. Leave. He shifted his eyes to his father, who was also watching him with an even steadiness. Lastly, he glanced towards the three fae—members of his mother's *court*—and found they were watching him intently as well.

Waiting to see what his choice would be.

Which meant... he could say no, if he wanted to.

Did he want to?

Dani's face flashed in his mind. Risk her safety? He'd never.

"Plus..." Jian hedged. "I'm gonna guess the fae need you. As funny as it is that your dumb ass is a fae prince, it remains a fact."

"Crown prince. *Tatya*," Galyn amended graciously. "You are to be king someday. *Titania*."

Slate rubbed his hands down his face, overwhelmed. "I'm not king material, seriously."

"That's the whole point, isn't it?" Kari tacked on. "You have to learn how to be fae, Slate. You have to learn how to use your magic, and learn how to be a king."

Slate peeled his hands away from his face. The magic thrummed a little harder inside him, and it was an effort to steady his voice. "Zeyphar tried to recruit me." His voice was hoarse.

A collective fury bled out of Saida and Galyn, and Slate hissed. "Please don't do that," he snarled, stuffing his hand into his eye again.

Instantly, the emotional wave eased off. "Apologies," Saida pressed a hand to her sternum. "I assume... you have your mother's magic."

"Yeah. And it's really fucking new and everything hurts," Slate snapped. He sighed. "Sorry. Listen, listen..." He tried to pull his thoughts together, his brain scattered into the four corners of his skull. "I'm not an idiot. If I come back to Titan's Fen, it's a declaration of war against Zeyphar, right?"

"We have been fighting a war long before you were born, my lord," Galyn said softly.

"You declared war when you blew up the arena last night," Kari added in a dry quip.

Slate tugged his hair out of the tie and shuffled his fingers through it. "This is madness. This would be a massive undertaking. And I know *nothing*. I don't... I don't even *want* this. I just want to teach at my school and date Dani. I didn't *ask* for this."

"Sometimes," Ebisu said, "it's a choice. Sometimes, it's fate."

"Yeah, well—" It was on the tip of his tongue to say *fuck fate*, but that sounded wrong. Fate always had a way of coming back around. There was no dodging it. If the red thread of fate had woven this path for him, he'd never escape it.

"This is craziness," he muttered. Could he do this? Could he somehow find balance between a martial arts school and fae king? Could he have everything he wanted, while still being the thing he *needed*? He wasn't a king... or *Titania*, whatever. He didn't know how to fight a war. He was just *Slate*. Just a guy who taught martial arts and fought in the fight circuit some nights.

Apparently not, not anymore.

"Let's say I go with you..." Slate started. He crossed his arms over his chest. "What's... what would I be walking into, here?"

"The climate is tense among the fae," Galyn said slowly. "We've been without leadership for a few years now."

The sadness in the room was so thick, Slate could taste it like poison in his mouth.

"Many are hesitant of new regime. And yes, it will likely be a full-scale war," Galyn added.

Fucking fantastic.

"This seems real involved... and beyond dangerous," Slate mused darkly. "I mean, I'd be happy to take out Zeyphar for you. Can't I just take out the head of the snake and be done with it?"

"Just because you kill the snake that poisoned you does not make the venom disappears from the vein..." Ebisu said softly.

"Zeyphar knows you exist now. He will stop at nothing in order to eliminate his competition to the throne. He craves absolute power, and it seems to me as if he's deluded himself into believing what he wants is what's best for the fae." Galyn's voice was hard now. "He is drunk on power and suffering from an unchecked madness, one that is known to fester in males with strong empathy magic."

Slate's stomach bottomed out at that, and Galyn's gaze was grim on his. "With proper training and discipline, it can be managed, but Zeyphar has always thought himself above those needs. He sees those of us who followed his sister as a threat not only to himself, but to our people, and while we were considered an annoyance to him once, with the threat of the true heir to give our cause fuel, he will undoubtedly seek to eliminate us once and for all. Our resources are mighty but small. Without proper leadership, it is only a matter of time before he tramples our wards and razes Titan's Fen to the ground. Males, females, babes—he will not discriminate. Thousands of fae will die."

Slate took a couple of deep breaths, his mind processing rapidly. A large part of him wanted to stay put, to preserve the way of life that he knew. But another, larger part of him couldn't do that. His father hadn't raised a selfish, self-serving man. He'd always been told that if there's something to be done, do it yourself. Help others. Part of being a master in the martial arts wasn't about being an expert; it was about being a servant to those underneath you, to help them rise up.

"If I go... *if*," he added when Galyn's expression lit up. "I want certain conditions. I want to come back whenever I want."

"Of course, my lord. We will make arrangements. One of your first lessons in magic will be portal creation, so you can return here whenever you wish." The council-fae gestured to Kallen. "Kallen can teach you himself."

"Fine," Slate conceded. His mind waffled for a moment, and he flipped his eyes to Jian. "You wanna come with me? Seriously?"

"Yep." Jian nodded. "You still aren't right from the glamour. I'll keep an eye on you. Just for a few days, then I'll come back."

Slate kept his overwhelming nerves and gratitude to himself. Jian wanted to be a part of this madness, wanted to stand by Slate, in order to help him weather this potential shitstorm, and Slate was endlessly grateful. He didn't know if he'd be able to handle all this on his own. He turned to Kari. "Kari, can I... can I borrow your phone?"

Kari gave him a long look full of too much knowing before she handed her phone over to him. "You're calling Dani, *ne*?"

He nodded. Once.

She gave him a thin smile. "You got this."

"Who is *Tani*?" Galyn inquired, his lilting accent softening the D of her name.

His father said something to the council-fae in a low whisper, spoken in that melodic, foreign language.

A gasp hissed out of Kari, followed by a squeak. Slate glanced over to see the *kitsune* curse as she looked down at the tea she'd been drinking, now spilled across the table. When she looked up, her widened thundercloud eyes pinged back and forth between Ebisu and Galyn, cheeks pinking and brows high.

"Sorry..." she whispered, rising from her seat and darting away to fetch a towel.

"What?" Slate demanded.

Galyn's eyes were wide too, but he simply waved a hand. "Can Tani-*tana* not simply come with us? That would be simpler, I should think."

Slate's chest tightened in a burst of protective fury, maddening in its intensity. "No," he said flatly. "She's... no, that's not possible." Slate gave a tight shake of his head.

Galyn's brows rose, and he glanced at Ebisu before he nodded solemnly. "I understand... these things take time."

Slate turned on his heel and stalked out of the waiting room and into the office, shutting the door behind him. He supposed privacy was not really a thing, but the shut door gave him a little sense of security as he pulled up Dani's contact information.

Breathe, Melisande. This is for her. This is for the best.

He heaved a fortifying breath and held the phone to his ear. It rang... and rang. Each trill sent a vibration of icy agony through him. He had to work to keep his breathing even as her voicemail picked up.

"Hi! This is Dani, I'm not here right now, so please leave a message after the beep."

Beep.

A heartbeat of silence. "It's me," he nearly whispered into the phone. "I uh, I lost my phone, but... I have to tell you something." He faltered for a moment, gumption failing. "I'm... I'm done." It sounded choked in his own ears. "I'm done. We're done. I can't see you anymore." He let out a shaking breath. "I'm sorry I dragged you into all this. I just—" He shook his head. "Never mind. I gotta go. I'm sorry."

And he hung up before he could make a complete fuckery of himself.

He stared at the blank phone screen, everything inside him frozen solid. He didn't breathe. He didn't think.

A different kind of fear edged over him. Not the survival type, but one that was a close cousin to grief. Fear of emptiness, of unknown, of trying to backfill the void she was about to leave in his life.

Fear of the finality of it.

What did he just do?

The urge to dial her number again and take every word back pounded through him. An insanity to reclaim what was *his*.

But she wasn't. She couldn't be.

They were as he'd always thought they'd be—a quick burn, bright and vibrant and over before it even began.

Slate pulled in another shaking breath and shook himself out. This was better. This was how it had to be. He was fae. She was afraid of fae. He was a fae *prince*, which meant a lot more fae would be in and about his life. He couldn't put her through that. Worse yet, he would *not* allow her to remain a tool that his psychotic uncle could use against him.

He'd rather die.

He stalked out of the office and back into the waiting room, the light chattering a strange cacophony to the hum inside his head, punctuated by cracking that he supposed was his heart. He handed the phone back to Kari. "Please—" The word came out hoarse. He tried again. "Please be friends with her, still."

Kari nodded, a sadness in the lines of her face. "I was planning on it."

Slate turned to Galyn. "Are we going or not?" He didn't bother to keep the bite out of his voice.

Galyn nodded and turned soft gray eyes to Slate's father. "Old friend, shall we?"

Ebisu stood from his chair with a groan. "One moment. I shall fetch Old Tom."

"That rascal Familiar is still around?" Galyn chuckled. At Slate's questioning frown, he waved a hand. "Old Tom was your mother's Familiar. She had him as a kitten, a gift for her birth. He was sent to keep your father company when he was returned to the city."

Ebisu disappeared for a moment. Slate heard him open the door to the apartment and call gently up the stairs. Heard the feather-light footfalls of the cat coming down the stairs.

Slate glanced around. A shot of anxiety spiked through his blood, "So... so this is really happening?"

Ebisu returned, the jet black cat perched on his shoulder. His chartreuse eyes blinked eerily at Slate. "Are you ever gonna talk to me, *neko-baka*?" Slate asked.

Those ears pressed flat to Tom's skull and he sulked behind Ebisu's head, wrapping his tail around the older man's neck. Ebisu chuckled, stroking the cat's sleek tail.

"Familiars are so *fickle*," Jian teased. He slammed his chair down on all fours and stretched. He tracked his eyes to Kari as she sauntered over to him and flicked his nose. Slate's heart did a little squish as the twins touched foreheads, an intimate gesture that made so much more sense with the context of their deep empathy. Slate could feel the nerves and concern flowing and twisting between them. Kari and Jian didn't like to be apart for many days. Slate remembered Jian studying abroad during University—a very short stint in Japan—and Kari hadn't been herself.

She'd booked a plane ticket by the end of the first week and spent the semester with Jian.

For one wild moment, Slate wondered if he'd be able to reach that level of intimacy with someone now, with the scope of his magic. He'd always envied that between the twins. To be so intune with another person...

He shut down that line of thinking fast. Instead, he turned to the fae standing in his waiting room, looking out of place, as if they'd jumped out of a high fantasy novel. "Do I need to bring anything?"

"Everything you could ever desire will be provided for you."

"You guys don't have wi-fi or anything, huh?"

"I am afraid not," Galyn chuckled. "Time moves differently for the fae, *mai tatya*. Our kin in Titan's Fen are not quite caught up with our brethren within the city limits."

"Gonna have to change that first thing..." Slate muttered.

Kari kissed his cheek. "You can send word with the faeries if you need to talk. I speak Faerish well enough."

He drew in a deep breath. "I'm not loving this, I'll say that much," he confessed. "What about the studio?"

"I'll handle everything. Maybe I'll take on more interns to help. Ronin would *love* to quit school and teach full time."

"Don't let him do that. It's his senior year. His parents will flay me."

She laughed and flicked his nose. "Come back often. You'll miss me."

He grinned. "You sure about that?"

"Everyone misses me. It's a fact." She flashed a sly grin.

Jian laid a steady hand on Slate's shoulder. Instantly, his best friend's emotions raced through Slate's mind. He inhaled sharply, feeling Jian's nerves, cautious excitement, a painful ache of missing Kari already blooming. "We're leaving now, *baa-chan*."

A portal appeared, right in the center of the waiting room. Slate hesitated for a moment. Was he really going to do this? Was this not all just a long, elaborate dream? He was going to pass through the portal and wake up and discover the last two months were nothing but a fever dream?

"What's it feel like?" he asked, instead of dwelling on Dani's freckled face.

"Like jumping into a hot, narrow drain." Ebisu smirked, Tom perched on his shoulder. "We will have to portal-skip. One cannot portal across ward borders."

Kallen and Saida stepped through first. His father gave him a heartfelt smile, before he stepped in, disappearing in a flash of golden light.

"After you, my lord." Galyn gestured for Slate to enter.

He stepped up to the edge of it and took a fortifying breath. He closed his eyes. Jian's hand squeezed his shoulder, and once again, Jian's emotions circulated and churned through him.

They could come back any time they wanted. This wasn't forever. This wasn't a kidnapping.

"Three, two, one..." Jian counted softly.

Slate stepped into the portal.

In an instant, he vanished.

CHAPTER · 四十四 · FORTY-FOUR

TOO FARAWAY

... known as the Tuatha De to those Lorekind
that live to the north...

– Gherald Schmidt, Faerloch Historical Archives

"Daniella, *ma chérie*, where are you? *Ah, bonjour, mademoiselle Selene. Comment va notre fille?*"

A melodic, sweet voice drifted through the fresh morning air, and Dani's eyes scrunched tightly shut when sunlight hit her face along with a rustling of plush feathers. Blinking past the sunspots, she peered up to find Sellie had lifted her wing away to expose her to the sun, nestled in a blanket against the flank of the griffin.

A tinkling laugh. "*Mon dieu!* Don't tell me she slept like this last night?" Maddie's lovely voice was fraught with amusement, her steps light as she came to a stop a few feet from where the girl and griffin were curled up on the flat roof above Loraine's warded 'safehouse.'

Sellie clicked her beak, angling her head upward in a clearly regal fashion, and Dani didn't need to use her magic to read what the griffin was impressing upon Maddie at that moment: *As if anyone would mess with my chick with me here.*

She still didn't know how she'd gone from being the 'mother' of a baby griffin to the 'chick' of that same griffin, but it was useless to argue with Sellie. Completely and utterly useless. Sellie made up her own mind, and that was *that.*

Sellie clicked her beak again, soft now, and angled her head to preen at Dani's loose hair, the way she'd done over and over throughout the night. Caring for Dani in the only way she could.

Dani's heart squeezed, and she reached up to thread her fingers through the downy soft feathers and fur that mingled at the base of her neck, giving the griffin a scratch that had her cooing and purring at the same time—a mesmerizing sound.

"You'll never be alone with Selene by your side, *n'est-ce pas?*"

Dani's eyes flashed away from Sellie and over to Maddie, heart dropping into her stomach. Those words again, or close to them—*you're not alone.* The words that she'd held tight to her chest all through the night, curled up under a griffin's warm wing and cocooned in the wards of Loraine's place—wards that extended about ten feet above the roof, according to Roger.

Naturally, she hadn't made it five minutes on the roof before he'd shown up, with a protective glint in his eyes, but he'd kept his distance, brought some food, then departed.

Dani blinked her eyes and focused on Maddie. The witch's full lips were pulled into a bright smile, her dark curls cascading over one shoulder from the slight tilt of her head. Her heart-shaped face was like a balm over Dani's bruised heart, and the knot in her chest loosened, just a fraction. The witch was wearing a dark gray babydoll dress that came to just above her knees, soft white lace trimming it along with small silken bows down the midline.

An utterly adorable outfit that was absolutely her.

Dani let her lips tug up in a smile, but didn't sit up from where her head was pillowed against Sellie's soft side. "*Bonjour,* Maddie. How was the recital?"

A soft laugh, and Maddie's skirts rustled as she folded her legs beneath her to kneel on the edge of the blanket that edged Sellie's nest. "You, *ma chérie*, are always worrying about everyone else first, you know that, right?"

Dani rolled her eyes and snuggled deeper against the spotted fur that was better than any silk sheets. She'd come up for fresh air last night, and also because she'd wanted to escape the temptation of her phone. She wanted to call Slate, but... she also wasn't ready. Her world was still reeling, and he had been at the center of that vortex. She needed to hear his voice, and yet she was dreading hearing Zeyphar in that voice.

Essentially, she was being cowardly.

"Roger filled me in on some of the details from two nights ago," Maddie offered softly, her gaze gentle.

Dani didn't want to look at her face. "Which parts? The part where everyone almost died, the part where a homicidal fae king is now out to get me and my friends, or the part where my... my... where Slate is now a *fae prince?*" Her voice might have pitched, just a little. Sellie's wing rustled, then settled back to curve around Dani's middle. Dani let her hands lie flat over the soft white feathers over her lap, and let out a soft breath as she struggled with the roiling emotions inside her.

Terror. Worry. Panic. Desperation.

But worse of all was the *ache*. The emptiness she hadn't known she'd been carrying in her chest until Slate had slipped inside it and lit it up.

The man whose very eyes now reminded her of heart-pounding moments of terror like those that chased her in her nightmares.

It was kind of messed up, and she had no idea how to handle it. Not when forgetting about Slate didn't feel like an option.

She'd given it some serious thought. Wash her hands of him and walk away. It had always been Plan B, and now seemed like the kind of time that called for Plan B.

But Plan B made her lungs stick to her ribs. Made the chills in her veins over Zeyphar seem insignificant.

"Do you want to talk about it, *cherie?*" Maddie reached out to cover one of Dani's hands with her own. She felt a soothing ripple, up her arm, felt her fluttering heart ease a bit. Maddie's water-aspect, the healing element for witches.

Well, as far as most people knew. Dani knew better, knew that Maddie was powerful enough to use it offensively, but the public image of the Silver Grace Coven wouldn't fare well if they knew the Covenleader could control people's bodies with the very blood in their veins.

Not when Maddie had worked hard to push the coven image around her strong healers, as opposed to battlewitches.

"I don't... know," Dani confessed honestly, letting Maddie's magic ease her tight muscles as she relaxed back against Sellie. The griffin gave a soft trill, and reached her snow-owl head over to preen at one of Maddie's curls, before clicking her beak softly.

"*Je vous en pris, Selene.*" Maddie smiled, then looked back at Dani. "You do not have to do anything you don't want to do, yes. Roger, Loraine, and I will keep you safe."

Dani nodded, biting at her lower lip. Despite the nightmares that haunted her every time she closed her eyes, she did *feel* safe here. Safe, but...

Caged. She was in a gilded cage, with Zeyphar on the outside.

With Slate on the outside.

Sellie's feathers puffed up, reflecting Dani's thoughts about cages. She pulled in her thoughts, not wanting to distress the griffin, but Sellie crooned at her, preening her hair once more. Maddie chuckled, reaching out to mirror Dani as she scratched at the griffin's neck.

The purring started again.

"Daniella," Maddie murmured, and she angled her head to catch Dani's eyes, holding them with an effortless show of power that had nothing to do with actual magic. It was impossible to look away from her nutmeg brown eyes, but she knew she wasn't being enchanted—Maddie could hold anyone's attention, a necessary trait for being the coven leader of the largest coven in Germany. Even the aggressive were-Alphas tended to listen when she spoke.

"I want you to consider something. I know Roger will not tell you this, because he thinks he is protecting you, but you need to hear this." The last of her kind smile faded from Maddie's lips, and Dani's gut tightened.

She didn't want to hear this.

But she couldn't look away. "Daniella, you have lived in fear for a long time. I know that fear is justified given the experiences of your past, not all of which I am privy to. But you need to know that by living in fear like this...?"

Maddie cocked her head, and Dani realized she wasn't breathing, couldn't breathe past the panic wedging its way up her throat. Sellie's feathers ruffled again, and she gave a low, warning snap of her beak, but the look Maddie shot at the griffin had Sellie pulling her head back and muttering darkly.

Her eyes, richly framed in thick lashes, slid back to Dani. "You are letting them win, *ma cherie*. You are letting your fears drive your narrative, and you are stronger than that. You take whatever time you need, but when you are finished pulling yourself back together, you need to stop letting fear dictate what you do with your life. Neither of those two fears, do you understand?" Hard eyes from a sweetheart face, such a startling contrast that it shocked the panic out of her throat, and Dani inhaled sharply.

Two fears.

When had Maddie become so perceptive? Dani squirmed under her gaze, feeling like a butterfly trapped under a pin. Face her fears? Or walk away from them?

The task seemed so monumental that Dani's lungs shriveled, but still, Maddie wouldn't release her. "You can have a life, or you can have a life led by fear. Make your choice, Daniella."

The witch finally blinked, and Dani was free. She slumped back against Sellie, feeling like her skin was too tight. A life without fear?

It was a dream.

To stop jumping at shadows, thinking someone was following her. To stop watching the fae at the Den, as if they would swoop her up again. To stop keeping her friends at arm's reach, dreading that they would dig into her as deeply as Kat or her parents had.

A dream that seemed terribly far away.

Maddie leaned forward and brushed her lips over Dani's cheek, one of her fragrant curls brushing Dani's jaw. "I believe in you, *cherie*. Believe in yourself too."

As the scent of lilies of the valley retreated with Maddie's light steps across the roof, Dani's thoughts drifted back towards that dream.

A life without the shadow of fear?

Impossible.

Yet...

The lingering warmth of Maddie's kiss suddenly made it feel... perhaps not *too* far away.

TITAN'S FEN

... the ward around the Silver Valley. The project was headed by Bran Ewyt, an authority on warding and portal magicks, along with his vampire counterpart, Ludovic Vasiliev...

– Gherald Schmidt, Faerloch Historical Archives

Slate and Jian sprang into being deep in the Forest of L'el, surrounded by trees so dense, it was as though night had come early. The thick canopy drowned out even the smallest sliver of remaining daylight. Despite that, Slate found—after a minute of adjustment—that he could see perfectly well.

The magic this deep in the Forest was pressing. Slate could feel it against his bones, a depthless, ancient magic that called to the deepest heart of him. It was in his mind, in his heart, a thousand pairs of eyes watching him, voices whispering against him. Perhaps there was some truth to the old superstitions within the city—the Forest was, in fact, *whispering*. And eyes were, in fact, *watching*.

"Pay no mind to the whispers of the Forest, *mai tatya*," Galyn offered. "It's a magic deeper and older than living memory. You will grow accustomed to it, once it settles within you."

"Do you feel that?" Slate asked Jian.

Jian shook his head with a light shrug. "Mysticfolk don't feel Lore magic the same way. It's hardly more than a pressure against my senses. Like, I *know* it's magic, but it's probably not to the degree you feel it."

"Come," Galyn beckoned them.

Ebisu slipped a strong, weathered hand around Slate's bicep, guiding him to follow the fae male. Jian stayed at Slate's back, eyes darting around, taking everything in with a keen alertness. This part of the Forest was devoid of any distinguishing features, aside from dense trees, shadowed darkness, and an ancient, crumbling stone bridge layered with moss and lichen.

The other two fae—Saida and Kallen—brought up the rear. As Slate stepped onto the bridge, the male, Kallen, said, "This bridge is a static point. So long as one could portal to the bridge, they might find Titan's Fen."

"What's stopping Zeyphar and his soldiers from just... storming in here and laying waste to your village?" Slate asked as they crossed the stone bridge. He felt a shimmer over his skin, and suddenly, the landscape in front of him shifted slightly. No longer was it a generic forest landscape, but instead, a narrow mountain pass appeared, with insurmountable rocky cliffs on either side, as if some great god had cleaved an ax straight down the middle of a mountain, creating a wedge and a passthrough. The narrow opening was divided by a sweeping stone wall—30 feet high with parapets. Fae soldiers stood along the top. Archers, from what Slate could discern.

"Oh... I see..." Slate nodded, a shiver of nerves flavoring the marked appreciation in security measures.

"I have a... certain proclivity with warding magic," Kallen offered, not a hint of arrogance in his words. Only bald fact and zero bullshit. Slate found himself warming up to this dark-haired, stoic fae. "Because Titan's Fen was once a summer retreat for the royal family, Zeyphar knows about it. It *is* possible he could teleport to the bridge. I've personally set up certain protections that disguise the bridge. But if that were to happen... we are prepared. In addition to the archers, there are several wards between the stone bridge and the village, and one cannot portal across ward barriers, forcing any enemy to approach on foot."

"And how far apart are the wards?" Slate asked.

"About a dozen paces or so. Just enough to force a team of intruders to slow down."

"I'm assuming the same security measures surround the Silver Valley as well?" He wondered why this war was lasting as long as it was. Why didn't the fae just... go after each other?

"Correct. And the magic of the Forest itself both helps and hinders. It will often shuffle the locations of any settlement located within its magical boundaries," Kallen explained.

"I'm sorry, what?" Slate blinked, incredulous. "*Shuffle the location?*"

"Correct. It is magic far older than any Lorebeing. But it is exactly as it sounds. Imagine the Forest like a giant ocean, and every settlement, a raft. The natural flow of the Forest shifts the locations of settlements in the same way the tide does on the ocean. The stone bridge is the only location that is part of the raft that is Titan's Fen which is not within our wards, which makes it the static location to allow for teleportation. If you ever wish to return to Titan's Fen, simply portal to the bridge; the archers know your face now."

Digesting this information, Slate followed as they passed through the gate in the stone wall. Beyond the wall was a gatehouse built right into the wall. They passed probably half a dozen fae soldiers; distinguishable by their leather armor and weapons. Slate felt eyes boring into him, watching him as he walked. He kept his chin up, meeting the eyes of every fae. Each met his gaze; some hesitated a moment before placing a hand to their sternum and inclining their head in his direction.

Right. He was a prince. What the *fuck*.

Jian chortled behind him, the sound muffled by a hand. Slate flashed a look back at his best friend. "I hate you," he hissed.

Jian laughed. "Dude, you are *never* gonna live down this royalty shit, I'm telling you right now."

"How does portalling work, exactly?" Slate asked, changing the subject away from himself. "Is it by visual or memory or...?"

"By memory," Kallen responded. "It's difficult at best to portal to a location you haven't visited. Some skilled in such dimensional magicks can portal on visual alone, such as from a photograph, but those individuals are few and far between. Even less can portal to people, unless they have a deep attachment to that person through a bond of some sort."

Slate nodded. "A bond like...?"

"A *mayt* bond or a blood bond, typically. As I said, it's difficult at best. And many fae do not possess the magical reservoir to teleport anyway. It requires a good deal of skill and a fairly large amount of magic."

"But I can learn to do it?" Slate asked, his mind hashing through the merits of being able to simply disappear from one place and reappear in another.

"I don't see why not. You come from a strong line of magic, and your aura feels strong."

The path shifted and the steep sides of the mountains dropped off as the path wove along the very edge.

"Ah, there it is." Galyn gestured.

Slate stopped dead in awe. Jian swore colorfully.

Below them was a sprawling valley, deep and steep, surrounded by the tall cliffs and mountains. The setting sun had disappeared behind the mountains, casting the valley in deep, bruising shades of purple. A river cut a slow, swathing path right through the center, with a roaring, multi-tiered waterfall on the other end. And there, surrounding the pool and creeping up the mountain sides was a town. Far larger than Slate's imagination had sketched it for him. It was a far cry from his expectation of a dusty little village with no sophistication.

He'd been dead wrong. It was breathtaking.

Lights danced through the cobbled paths, sprinkled like faerie lights over the houses. Tiered pockets of land rose up, yielding space for small farms and gardens. Markets and stores and homes of varying sizes and a few mills, and on the side of the pool that bled into the river, a dam had been built, presumably to create energy from the flow of the water.

The image of it crawled through his brain like a long-forgotten dream, a tickling sense of deja vu pricking his skin, his mind, his memories.

Jian whistled. "I feel like I've jumped into a fantasy novel..."

"Welcome home." Galyn touched Ebisu on the shoulder with a smile.

Ebisu smiled, and Slate felt his father's intense joy so profoundly, his own chest tightened.

"That manor there?" Galyn pointed out a much larger building than the rest that climbed the side of a cliff, one side hugging the waterfall. Bridges and elegant stone stairs connected the manor to the rest of the town. "That is your home, my lord. Eas Manor."

Slate nodded, taking in the information with a grain of salt. His home wasn't a lavish manor with stunning views. His home was a small apartment on the second story of a warehouse. His home was a training floor made of blue puzzle mats that always smelled a little like feet and old foam with a fresh undertone of tatami.

The fae continued along the narrow path that hugged the cliffside. Anxiety pitched through Slate. "Dad... I don't know..." he muttered to his father. All the foreignness of the situation was pressing into him. His magic thrummed against his skin in response, and Slate wondered if he was on the verge of a meltdown.

Ebisu tightened his hold on Slate's arm in a reassuring squeeze. "Take everything in slowly. At face value. There will be time to adapt later."

Slate sucked in a deep, steadying breath and made quick eyes at Jian. His best friend nodded once in solidarity.

They progressed down the narrow path until they came to a large gate with twin watchtowers. Saida called to them in a different language—Slate assumed Faerish—and slowly, the gate split open. Another shimmer over Slate's skin as they passed through yet another clever ward.

The village streets were quiet as they walked through the town. Sensation began to creep in over Slate. He could *feel* the public, even if they were all tucked into their homes. A beating hope, astonishment, joy to the point of sadness. There was a touch of distress, of hesitation cloaked with trembling anticipation. Even beyond what his magic was telling him, he could feel *eyes* on him, watching him from windows and cracked doors. He rubbed his eye with his hand, the pulse uncomfortable in its unfamiliarity. He silently focused on his own breathing, thankful in that moment no one tried to front load any more information at him.

A firm hand on his nape, and Slate felt the cooling tingle of magic slither through him. It beat back some of the discomfort. He tossed a grateful look at Jian.

They ascended a set of wide, sweeping stone stairs inlaid along the edge of the waterfall and crossed another stone bridge, elegantly carved and spotless, before entering the manor. Nothing but a large stone archway denoted the entrance.

The foyer was large and minimalistic, with curving, organic carvings in the smooth marble walls and rich wooden furnishings. The floors were also marble, smooth with hints of gold and silver flecks. A sweeping spiral staircase curved along the far wall. There looked to be a large gathering room to one side, and the other side yielded wide halls that twisted and disappeared into deeper parts of the manor.

Three people waited in the foyer. An older fae female—though it was hard to tell with the fae—and two younger fae, a male and a female. From the look of them, Slate could instantly tell they were related. Not siblings, but perhaps cousins.

All three of them placed both hands to their sternum and inclined their heads in his direction. The older female turned her cloud-gray eyes to Slate's father. "Ebisu-*tana*," she greeted. "It's been a long time."

"Indeed it has, Frieda." His father smiled.

Those pale gray eyes turned to Slate and gave him an assessing glance. "The last time I saw you, Zlaet, you were as high as my knee and more trouble than all of us could handle."

"I'm willing to bet I'm still quite a bit of trouble." He grinned, pulling up a bit of charm to deflect away from the sheer sense of being overwhelmed. He had no memories of this woman.

The female—Frieda—blinked at him, then burst out into light laughter. "I should say! Welcome home, princeling. I am Frieda, the major-domo to this estate. Whatever you need, come see Frieda, darling, and it will be done."

"Thanks." Slate nodded. "This is Jian, my best friend."

Frieda sniffed in Jian's direction. "You smell like trouble too, though not any kind I know."

"He is mysticfolk, Frieda," Ebisu said with a calm smile.

Frieda's brows rose, and her frank assessment became sharper. "You must be the witch-doctor I have heard of then. Definitely trouble," she mused. She pointed a stern finger between the two of them. "I have little patience for trouble in this house. Behave."

"Yes, ma'am," the boys said in unison.

The she-fae gestured to the two people next to her. "Rhylan." She waved a hand at the male. He was blond, hair neatly secured at his nape, with a wiry figure. "He was a personal attendant to *mai titania* Aredhel. He will gladly continue those duties, if you desire, Zlaet."

Words froze on Slate's tongue. "Personal... what now?" he stuttered out.

Ebisu squeezed Slate's arm. "He would be like an assistant to you, basically." His father smiled at Rhylan. "We were good friends in a past life, *ne*, Rhylan?"

Rhylan inclined his head to Ebisu. "We still are, Ebisu-*tana*."

Frieda gestured to the younger she-fae. "Autymn," she introduced. "Rhylan's cousin. She too, was a personal attendant to Aredhel."

Slate cocked his head at the younger fae female. She was *young*, he was certain. And she couldn't have been more than five feet tall, and a hundred pounds soaking wet, with an incredibly slight build. He'd have easily mistaken her for a teenager if she didn't have a distinct yet youthful maturity to her face and figure. "Do I know you already, too?" Slate asked.

She shook her head and tucked a strand of honey-blonde hair behind her pointed ear. "No, *mai tatya*," she stammered. "I've just seen twenty summers. But I spent a great deal of time with your mother." She flashed caramel brown eyes to Ebisu. "She said my magic and love of plants and gardening reminded her of you, Ebisu-*tana*."

His father nodded, a telling sheen to his eyes. "Did she, now? Perhaps we can garden together, child, and you can regale me with stories."

She smiled, young and dazzling in its innocence. "I'd like that very much."

Slate pinged his eyes back and forth between the cousins. "No offense, but I don't personally need *two* attendants or whatever."

Frieda waved a hand at him. "It is tradition to have two—a male and a female. If the Goddess blesses you with a *queen consort* some day, Zlaet—"

"Two is fine." The words came out a little ragged as his brain instantly zeroed in on a certain woman. He didn't want to think about her and the aching hole she left inside him.

Frieda gave him a cunning look. "Come," she continued after a tense moment. She gestured with her hand. "A tour, and I shall show you to your chambers."

Galyn, Saida, and Kallen said good-bye to them. Galyn informed them he would be at the home he'd pointed out earlier, the one he shared with his *mayt* and child. Saida, also, had her own home in the village. Kallen had a bedroom deeper in the manor.

"I will call upon you in the morning, *mai tatya*," Galyn said upon his departure.

Frieda took Slate, Jian, and Ebisu on a walk-through. Autymn and Rhylan disappeared to attend to different duties. Slate still didn't know how he was gonna handle having a *personal attendant*, let alone two of them, but he supposed it was as his father had said. Being a prince—or a king, whatever—couldn't be much different than being a master instructor in the martial arts world, right? He had assistants and instructors he managed in the studio. How different could this be?

The manor was as breathtaking as the town, winding halls, sweeping rooms with stunning views of either the village or the waterfall, graceful arches that opened right out into the air. Trees and stone coexisted side by side, as though the manor were not an interruption to nature, but rather a part of it.

Jian took a marked interest in a room on the top floor, overlooking the waterfall. It was modestly sized, with a large balcony and a stunning fireplace. There was even a small wine cellar attached that had no wine, but Jian thought it would make a wonderful personal apothecary.

"Kari can use the fireplace," he said, studying it. At Slate's cocked brow, he clarified, "She can travel by fire. Like, teleport."

Slate's brows rose. "That's pretty cool."

Finally, they were shown the suites of the *Titania*. Located at the top of the manor, it was beautiful; large, spacious, bigger than his whole apartment, with an open floor plan. They stepped into a large sitting room, with cozy chairs and subtle elegance. The entirety of the wall to his right was lined with great arches like doors that opened right out to a stunning and expansive balcony. Soft white curtains of a sheer, weightless material danced mildly in front of them. Beyond a set of open double doors, Slate could see what looked like a bedroom.

He wandered through the suites silently, touching everything. A deep sense of belonging resonated with him, and a piece of him hated it. This room... something about the energy of this room felt *right*, and Slate didn't want to *want* such luxury.

Through the bedroom doors, a large bed sat in an intricately carved bed frame, with four posters and more of those sheer curtains and open archways to the balcony. Tree branches spread and snaked across the ceiling, and if Slate looked closely, he would see faeries flirting among the leaves. Another doorless archway on the other side of the room led into an expansive bathroom. A large, deep stone tub set against an open, glassless window. A toilet. Sinks, sprawling marble countertops. A large mirror.

"It looks different than I remember..." Ebisu said, moving through the rooms with mild interest.

Frieda nodded. "We had the rooms renovated and redecorated. We had the foresight that perhaps Prince Zlaet would not enjoy resting in his mother's exact bedchamber."

Slate's eyebrows rose and he looked at his father. "No way, I'm not sleeping there if that's the bed I was conceived in."

Ebisu laughed. "No, no, it was different, I remember."

Slate glanced at Frieda for confirmation. The she-fae nodded sagely.

"Where will you stay?" Slate asked his father.

"If my memory suits me, there is a lovely room downstairs that faces the waterfall," Ebisu said. "The energy feels smooth there. I shall make that my residence."

"Of course. I shall have it prepared for you," Frieda agreed. She turned to Slate. "My lord, if you'll excuse me, I shall guide your father downstairs and leave you. Please feel free to explore the manor as you wish. It is all yours."

"Sure. I appreciate it."

His father patted his cheek, and he and Frieda made their way out of the room and down the spiral stairs, leaving him alone with Jian in the suite of rooms. Slate could hear them conversing breezily in Faerish.

Slate took in the surroundings. He still couldn't believe this was happening. He let out a huge breath and linked his fingers over the top of his head and paced. In a matter of hours, he'd gone from Slate Melisande, martial arts school owner, to Zlaet Titania, prince of the fae. His eyes took in the rooms, and how nature seemed to have elegantly and seamlessly blended with civilization, from the rich wooden furniture carved with nature's motifs to the tree branches that intertwined in a serpentine pattern along the ceiling. He cocked his head as a few little faeries peeked out to look at him, before giggling lightly and retreating behind branches and leaves.

He wandered through the space, pulling open dresser drawers, and opening the large and elaborate wardrobe. Empty. At some point, it would probably be filled with clothes and belongings as pieces of him settled here.

If he decided to settle here.

He couldn't do this. He couldn't...

He was aware of Jian watching him, perched in one of the lush armchairs, idly fidgeting with a leaf, presumably from the tree above their heads.

"Jian... I can't do this..." Slate finally said, standing in the middle of the sitting room and staring out the archways. Beyond the balcony, the town of Titan's Fen's glimmered in the dark, lights sparkling, refracting off the water, off the white cobblestone streets. To the left, a curve in the balcony overlooked expansive gardens. "I can't... you hear the way these people talk to me? Like I'm some... I'm some..."

"A royal prick?" Jian offered with a sardonic grin.

Slate rolled his eyes in Jian's direction, pegging him with a long-suffering look.

Jian sighed. "I think beyond the fact that some of them aren't sure about you yet, for many of them, you give these people a lot of hope, Slate," he admitted quietly, tipping his head back and gazing at the ceiling. "Their long-lost prince has returned to help them fight a war that's been going on since before you were born."

"I don't know the first thing about war," Slate said, choking on the words. "Or being a king."

"I dunno." Jian shrugged. "Doesn't sound any different than you being the master instructor at the studio. You give a direction, we all say 'yes sir' and jump to follow your lead. You have some people who you bounce ideas off of, there's a ranking system... I dunno. How is that different here? Except you aren't a master, but a crown prince. Future *Titania*. Still a leader. And anyone who isn't sure about that yet? They'll come around when they meet you, when they see your skills."

Slate chewed that around in his head. When it was phrased like that, he couldn't argue about the similarity between this and what he'd grown up doing, he supposed. But this king shit probably had a steeper learning curve. And with larger consequences than just his little martial arts school.

"This is a fever dream, isn't it?" Slate finally said after a few long, silent moments. "This time yesterday I was gearing up for a title fight. Now I'm a fae prince."

Jian chuckled. "From one adventure right to the other. Never a dull moment with you, brother."

Slate said nothing, mind whirling. Gingerly, because he didn't quite know what he was doing, he sent out a feeler of magic towards Jian. Emotion poured back into him—wariness, but excitement and thirst for something new and interesting, cautious concern, blazing hot loyalty, and the barest ache from missing his twin.

Not quite sure what he was doing, Slate fed him a wobbling sense of deep gratitude. Jian's thundercloud eyes whipped to Slate's. "Are you feeding me emotions?" he asked.

"Just... just mine." Slate swallowed hard. "Nothing weird. Just stuff I don't know how to word."

The fact that Jian was here, beside him, taking in this strangeness with him, made this entire situation easier to grasp. It hadn't been lost on him as well, the fact that Jian claimed an empty room in the manor, claimed it like he was going to make the most of this place. Slate's emotions choked up his throat—Jian was making a choice to be here because Slate couldn't. Slate's choice had been stolen from him.

"Wanna see what kinda trouble we can get into before Freida gets mad at us?" Jian asked, a wicked mischief about him.

Slate chuckled, anxiety easing a bit. "Absolutely."

CHAPTER ⟨四十六⟩ FORTY-SIX

OUT OF TOWN

... *the magic is extinct, with the only surviving user having vanished in the late 18th century. The far weakened ability of animal sensitivity, and the occasional talent of mental communication, has popped up occasionally in lorekissed individuals over the centuries, but seems to have vanished entirely from the general fae population...*

- Gherald Schmidt, Faerloch Historical Archives

The sun hadn't yet reached its zenith when Dani finally peeled herself from Sellie's side. The events of two nights ago had been a heavy lump that seemed to squish her guts down to her pelvis and force her lungs up into her skull, but after Maddie's visit a few hours earlier...

That lump didn't feel quite so big anymore. Didn't feel quite so insurmountable.

Yes, her... boyfriend?—her mind still shied away from the word, but she found words like *friend* or *boy toy* to be lacking now—her *boyfriend* was half-fae.

Yes, her boyfriend was also the *prince* of the freaking fae.

Yes, her boyfriend's uncle was the freaking *king* of the fae, and a cruel bastard who caused a riot of nerves under her skin.

It was all terrible. But worse than that?

Slate stood, poised over her heart with a shovel in hand, ready to dig deeper than Kat or her parents or Roger and Maddie. Ready to dig deep enough into her heart that if he disappeared like so many of her loved ones had? Nothing and no one would be able to fill that gaping hole.

And when she looked at the situation with only the negatives in mind, her mind quailed and all she wanted to do was forget that Slate—along with the twins—had ever existed. It would be much easier. Just walk away.

Perhaps not *easy*, really, with Zeyphar possibly still hunting for her, but it would certainly be easier than standing up to all of the things that made panic a living beast under her skin.

And yet...

And *yet*...

Slate's face, with the sharp grin on his face, a wickedness there, and the way his eyes softened just a little, but only when he was looking at her. His *face* and his *scent*, that first breath of winter with a hint of a storm, they wouldn't leave her alone. Neither would the memory of his warm hands sliding over her exposed skin.

Like she had a million times in the last few days, her fingers brushed idly at the mark at the juncture of her neck, the one that was starting to form a small scar.

She couldn't seem to drop those memories, to hurl them to the ground and stomp on them before walking away, walking back to her normal, easy life.

All those new terrible things about Slate suddenly became small and insignificant when she thought of never seeing Slate again—never seeing Kari or Jian again. Her fears weren't gone; they continued to swirl inside her and poison her blood if she let herself linger on them, but when she focused on *just* Slate? Just Slate and his sharp smirk and his laughter and his deep well of emotional capacity?

They didn't seem to matter as much.

You are not alone.

I believe in you.

Roger and Maddie's words swirled through her as she stepped away from the comforting shelter of Sellie's wing. Both of those sentiments resonated inside her—Roger's was an assurance that he would stand by her regardless of her choice, and Maddie's was an urging to do what *Dani* needed for herself.

To be brave.

Dani turned to face the griffin, and Sellie let out a series of soft whistles and clicks as she leaned her majestic head down for a scratch. Dani ran her fingers through the griffin's feathers, and murmured, "Do you think I should be brave?"

Sellie's answer was a haughty blink with an imperious tilt to her enormous snow-owl head: *Will that make you happy?* Words that weren't words, but came across that way to Dani nonetheless from the series of impressions she'd pass to Dani.

Dani hesitated. Would it make her happy to be brave?

Before she could answer, Sellie said, in clear, crisp words that rang out in her head, so unusual when Sellie preferred images and feelings to convey her meaning: *What is more important to you? Being happy, or being safe?*

The question was posed with the utmost innocence, the kind only animals seemed to possess. Sellie was *truly* curious as to which one mattered the most to Dani. Sellie herself couldn't care less which one she chose, so long as it was *Dani's* choice.

Dani blinked at her griffin, amazed at how this creature had taken the tangled mess of fear and anxiety in her gut and smoothed it out to two simple things.

Happy... or safe?

She knew it was possible to be both, absolutely. But she had a feeling her griffin saw right through to Dani's phobias—if she gave in to her fears, she would be giving up some of her happiness too.

Happiness, or safety. Suddenly, it was as easy as that. Would it erase her fears? No. But did those fears suddenly seem... *manageable?*

Manageable enough to be worth a try.

"Sellie, I need you to take me somewhere... is that okay?" Her heart was racing faster than a galloping stallion. Her hands flew to her hair—she'd showered the night before, the only time she'd left the bed after waking up to the news that Slate had survived and that Zeyphar was gunning for her—but she'd fallen asleep with it still wet. It was likely a mess—

Sellie had just gotten to her feet when the door to the roof opened behind her.

"Going somewhere?"

Dani looked over her shoulder to find Loraine standing in the doorway of the exit, thick arms crossed over her chest with one shoulder leaning against the doorframe. One silvery brow was perked over her brown-gold eyes.

"Loraine... what's more important? Safety... or happiness?" Dani stepped toward Sellie's flank, and the griffin bent one foreleg for her. Dani didn't take her eyes from Loraine, fingers delving into the thick white and gray fur at Sellie's side.

Loraine barked a laugh and shook her head. "So you finally listened to someone with some sense, then?" She jerked her chin at Sellie, who gave an appreciative hoot and began to preen with self-satisfaction.

"I thought you hated Sellie?" Dani said with a half-grin, glancing between her griffin and the owner of the building that had been her sanctuary for a day and a half.

"No, cub. She and I have fierce wills, and sometimes we don't get along. But you can respect someone without always agreeing with 'em." Loraine gave another casual shrug, and her entire demeanor said she couldn't care less about the griffin, but it was probably the longest sentence Dani had ever heard from the were-bear. She gaped at the woman, then wanted to gape some more when a hint of red filtered into Loraine's golden cheeks.

"Off with you now, cub. I'll relay to the vampire where you're off to," Loraine said gruffly, scowling now.

"How do you know where I'm going?" Dani blinked.

"It's written all over your face, girl. You're off to see that troublesome fae boy." Loraine was already turning away.

The roof-access door slammed shut before Dani could utter a reply.

Dani didn't know why she'd been worried about her hair—riding a griffin over a busy city would have messed up even the most carefully constructed hairstyle. By the time Sellie took them to the garden on the roof of Slate's home, she had so many tangles it would have taken forever to comb through them with her fingers.

So she simply tugged her hair-tie from the knot she'd made at the top of her hair, and let the red-gold tangles hang loose down her back.

Whatever.

Hair was the *last* thing she should be worrying about. Even if the normality of it seemed to help her through the anxiety that was trying to cut off the oxygen to her lungs.

Dread. Dread was a bitter shiver beneath her skin, but she drew in a deep breath and reached for those words, the mantra that had somehow come to replace *casual and fun* where Slate was concerned.

Happiness or safety?

She clung to them, standing on the roof of the garden. She heard the faint giggles of faeries, the even fainter sounds of people on the street far below, and realized her feet were stuck to the floor beneath her.

Happiness. She had to cling to that—she didn't want to become one of those people who never lived their lives because they were always *afraid.*

It had to be happiness. She had to choose that.

A smooth but hard beak nudged her between her shoulder-blades, and Dani started. Another firm nudge, one that had her stumbling forward a step, and Dani whipped her eyes over her shoulder to see Sellie's exasperated silver-blue eyes blinking at her. The griffin clicked her beak, then ruffled her feathers until she looked almost twice her usual size.

"No, I can't do that to look bigger, and I don't think the things I'm afraid of would even care if I could, but I appreciate the thought," Dani said with a strained laugh. Then, she sighed.

She could do this.

Dani approached the roof-access door, but she floundered when she got to it. She'd never come here from the sky—would anyone even be able to hear her knock? She didn't think Ebisu kept the door locked, but it seemed... wrong to barge on into their home.

She'd just swiveled on her heel to march back to Sellie—with every intention to ask to be set down in the alley next to the studio, rather than brave the fire-escape stairs attached to the side of the building—when she heard the distinct catch of the roof-access door being opened.

Dani froze, heart slamming against her sternum.

Turn around, turn around, her mind wailed, but it was like she had one of those golden circles under her feet that glued the soles of her shoes to the rooftop.

"Dani?"

And just like that, the glue under her feet vanished, and she nearly fell over. Trying to get her racing heart under control, she pivoted back around.

Kari's smile was bright, but concern pulled the corners of her almond-shaped eyes into crinkles, and a hint of spectral blue flickered over her gunmetal-gray irises. The initial surprise in Kari's face gave way to a wary happiness. It wasn't the face Dani had been expecting, but somehow it still made a hint of that fear curl a cold finger up her spine.

Not *at* Kari. No, it was a fear of what she'd last encountered when she'd been with the fox-woman. Piercing blue eyes assessing her with far too much maniacal interest. The sound of the arena exploding. The pressure of magic...

Dani forced herself to swallow the lump in her throat that was trying to crawl out her mouth, and forced a smile. "Hi, Kari. I... uh... I guess I'm here to see Slate," she blurted the words out before her courage could abandon her.

If she just *saw* him, maybe some of her anxiety would go away. The anxiety that whispered he might *become* like his uncle now that he had this power.

Kari's smile faltered. "Oh... well... Did you not get Slate's message?"

Dani's stomach hit the floor, then continued down past the apartment and studio below her, plunging into the earth.

"What?" She hardly dared to breathe. The sight of her phone, deliberately abandoned in the safehouse, flashed in her mind. Slowly, she shook her head. "N-no, I... I haven't checked my phone."

Kari was watching her closely. She took a tentative step toward Dani, and offered a half-smile. "Slate's... well, actually..." She seemed to be tasting each word as it came out, and Kari's hesitancy to talk straight to her made her heart plunge right to the floor with her stomach. "He's going to be... out of town for a bit."

"Out of town?" she repeated numbly.

We're goin' outta town, the words echoed through her memory, a memory so deep she'd buried it. A memory of the night she'd moved away from Ireland.

The night her parents had simply packed them up and left Ireland, leaving behind friends and relatives... or perhaps not. She'd been so young, and everything was so hazy—she'd never been certain whether the impression of people was real or a dream. Her parents had insisted they had no family but each other.

And yet, for much of her youth, she'd felt like she'd been missing someone, or many someones...

But those *words*... spoken in her father's brogue, were as crisp and clear in her mind as if she'd heard them just now. *We're goin' outta town.*

Leaving. Leaving. Everyone always left.

And never came back.

Her gut twisted painfully, and the blood drained out of her skull. The world swayed a little in front of her.

Slate *left*.

Kari's eyes flared with alarm. "Dani? You okay?" She stepped close enough now that she could feather one slender hand up Dani's arm.

Dani sucked in a breath. Another. Nodded.

"Yeah, sorry, just... just..." She shook her head minutely. "Out of town... where?" Dani forced herself to ask, to stay in the present, in the right here and the right now.

Kari hesitated, then let out a sigh. "He's with the fae. Members of his mother's former court came and collected them yesterday. Not... not Zeyphar's fae. He's not in any danger or anything. But he's not here. And it's *just* for a little while."

Dani's head spun. Behind her, she heard the rustling of feathers from where Sellie roosted behind her. Kari's fingers were now clutched around her upper-arm, ready to catch her if she slid to the ground. "Dani, he's not *gone, gone*, you know. He'll come back."

Dani's head jerked up, and she locked eyes with Kari. So much *knowing* in that gaze. More than Dani wanted to know.

She gave a little jerk of her chin. "Of course." She dislodged her arm with a gentle tug, then fell back a step towards Sellie. "I'll... I have to go."

Out of town. Never coming back, that's what that meant. Just like she'd never gone back to Ireland. Her parents had gone 'out of town' on a ski trip when she was sixteen and never came back. Kat never came back. No one ever *came back*—

"Dani, are you sure you're—"

"Will you let me know if he comes back?" Dani asked, finally rallying the smile she needed, rallying the energy to force her shoulders to ease from their unnatural tenseness. She hoped her smile would be enough to ease the concern that was in every line of Kari's small, curvy body.

Kari stopped her approach, but her fingers twitched before she hid her hands behind her back in a casual shifting of her stance. "Yeah, sure, of course. Do you... do you want to get some tea sometime this week?"

Dani faltered for a heartbeat. Still be friends with Kari, even though Slate... left her?

It was on the tip of her tongue to come up with an excuse, any excuse, but the look on Kari's face...

The *kitsune* rarely revealed any vulnerability, but just the barest hint of it had flickered in her gaze.

"It's just... Jian's with him, you know? I thought we could get together." Kari rocked on her heels, just once, then she flipped her hair over her shoulder. "It's fine if you're busy! I'm flexible for whenever." Kari recovered swiftly with a breezy smile.

For that one moment, it struck Dani crystal clear that she'd just watched Kari slip into one of her many masks.

Dani swallowed, and shook her head. "I'm not busy." A pang in her heart for this woman in front of her, who'd literally saved her life two days ago.

Despite the trembling in her throat, she didn't know if she had it within herself to abandon Kari. Kari, who'd dragged her out of the arena, who near-carried her through the streets, stuffed her in a taxi, and had taken her to the safest place she knew.

The trembling increased slightly, a crushing tightness settling on her.

But Kari's smile became more *real*, and she patted her pocket, where her phone was likely tucked away. "Whenever you want, *tori-chan*. No pressure."

Dani gave a nod, trying to look cheerful as she pulled herself onto Sellie's back. The griffin let out a series of clicks with her beak, and turned to peg Kari with an unblinking stare.

Kari rolled her eyes, and held up a hand in farewell, but Dani had the distinct impression the fox-woman was anxious about her leaving.

Dani's own anxiety had nothing to do with her own departure from the Eastern District, and had everything to do with *Slate's* departure.

He'd *left* her.

People didn't *return* from the fae, even if they weren't Zeyphar's fae. People just... didn't.

By the time Sellie landed back on the roof of the Den, Dani found she was having trouble breathing. It was difficult to get the oxygen past the sobs she was trying to shove back down her throat. Sellie let out a sound of distress as Dani slid off her.

She couldn't breathe. Drawing air in felt like breathing through a wet washcloth, a pressure on her lungs—fear, anxiety, desperation, anger, hurt—she didn't know, but whatever cocktail thrummed inside her, it paralyzed her. The ground swayed under her feet, coming up to greet her.

Arms were suddenly around her, catching her before her knees hit the rooftop.

Roger guided her toward the roof-access door, and his shadows slithered over her with each step—shadows that were protecting him from the *sun*.

"Roger," she gasped, the sound wet and ragged as she struggled to pull herself together. "Wait, Roger, you'll *burn*." It was a little past one or two in the afternoon—the sun was hot and bright above them.

"Nonsense, Daniella. Come now, let's go watch a terrible movie with some popcorn. Madeline is arriving in an hour." Roger's voice was smooth, and had no hint of the pain he must be enduring in the force of this sunlight. A glance up showed her that shadows writhed around him like thick, affectionate snakes, obscuring much of his face.

She still hadn't found the words past the tempest in her chest when he'd tugged her into the doorway leading down to the apartment below. She let Roger usher her inside, let him guide her down the steps and into the small but neat living room of the safehouse. She didn't resist when he nudged her down onto the couch, and tugged the quilt over the back of it into her lap. He did all of this with quiet efficiency, with only light touches to guide her where he wanted.

Never overbearing, not Roger.

She used that moment to attempt to pull herself together, to pull all those little shards back into herself, the ones that had cracked outward when Kari had said Slate was gone.

Slate was gone.

Gone.

It hit her in a rush that he'd already dug a hole inside her. Dug the hole and took the shovel, leaving her with nothing but her bare hands to try and backfill the aching gap he'd just left in her life.

"Daniella." A soft murmur, coupled with a brush of fingers as the vampire tucked her hair back from her face. She looked up at him, and he offered her a small, sad smile. It was enough to break through her spiraling mind, and she pulled in a slow breath. He watched her for a moment, and she managed to corral her lips into a wobbly smile. With a nod of approval, Roger moved out of her field of vision, and the gaping hole of thoughts yawned open before her once more.

She teetered on the edge.

Small sounds distracted her from that maw of self-doubt—the clatter of a plastic bowl against the counter, the crinkling of a wrapper, then the distinctive beeps of a microwave.

A vampire of an unknown age, but likely *old*, was in the kitchen behind her making *microwave popcorn*.

It was enough to let her step back from that hole, to look away—for now—and forget Kari's words. She shut down all of her thoughts save for those reserved for popcorn time.

She curled her fingers into the quilt in her lap, and hoped her voice didn't sound as hoarse as it did to her own ears.

"What movie?"

It was late in the middle of the night when Dani found herself staring at her phone. She'd been doing her best to avoid it all night, had allowed Roger and Maddie to distract her with terrible movies, popcorn, and eventually, margaritas that Maddie had whipped up. But now, as the clock on the nightstand ticked past three in the morning, she couldn't sleep, and she couldn't stop staring at her phone.

"Did you not get Slate's message?"

Kari's words curled sinuously through her mind. On one hand, she was so *mad* that he had left her that she didn't want to listen to it. On the other, she craved the sound of his voice, craved the small hope that his message would soothe all of her fears. She wanted to hear that he would come back for her, and that he cared for her, that he was still *him*, any kind of sweet words as a balm to the hurt inside her.

3:11am

No longer able to resist, Dani's hand slipped out from the covers. She reached toward the nightstand, and curled her trembling fingers around the cool case of her phone. The screen came alive in a blast of glaring light, forcing her to blink several times before she could see clearly. The notification for a voicemail flashed across the screen, and her thumb hovered over the button to play it.

Dani froze, thumb still hovering, as a sense of creeping panic curled through her. What if...?

"Stop being a coward," she whispered to herself, and pressed the button.

"It's me," Slate's voice came out of the phone's speaker in a whisper. *"I uh, I lost my phone, but... I have to tell you something."* There was a pause, and Dani's heart started pounding against her ribcage as icy fingers slipped down her spine. Something about his tone...

"I'm... I'm done. I'm done. We're done. I can't see you anymore. I'm sorry I dragged you into all this. I just—Never mind. I gotta go. I'm sorry."

Dani couldn't breathe. The air in her lungs had turned to stone, becoming a heavy block that was a pressure against her chest and spine alike. The phone fell from her numb fingers, the sharp light stuttering out as it landed screen-side down, plunging her into darkness.

We're done.

I can't see you anymore.

We're done. I can't see you anymore.

He'd left her. Totally. Completely.

He was gone. Evaporated from her life.

The tears were a sudden and sharp sting against her eyes before she was even able to wrestle in another breath. More stones lodged in her lungs as wetness flooded her eyes, then ran in rivulets down her cheeks to soak the pillow beneath her head.

Then it was like a dam broke inside of her, and Dani buried her face in the pillow as sobs wrenched from around those heavy stones inside her. She pulled her knees to her chest as she curled into a ball, clutching at herself as if afraid she might simply fly apart if she wasn't careful. She swallowed hard, tried to swallow past the heaviness in her chest, the heaviness that crawled up her throat to choke her. Pain was a living, twisting creature inside her, raking at her insides with claws that left bloody furrows of misery in its wake.

As the witching hour wrapped her in darkness, Dani cried.

Alone.

CHAPTER · 四十七 · FORTY-SEVEN

ADAPT AND OVERCOME

... healers and scholars alike hypothesize that the higher concentration of magic in males who inherit this unusual magical ability has led to the development of an oftentimes unstable psychosis...

- Gherald Schmidt, Faerloch Historical Archives

Slate was lonely.

And his loneliness made him restless, a thrumming stir under his skin.

Jian had stayed with him for the better part of a week. An entire week to settle into this manor, this life, this culture. An entire, chaotic week. Every new aspect of this life, Jian had been right there, taking it all in with Slate.

And there was a lot to take in. A lot to process.

But now Jian was gone. Back to Faerloch. Slate sat on the banister of his balcony, feet hanging precariously over the dizzying drop. From here, he had a sprawling view of the town—particularly the center of the town, with a large open area he'd graciously call the town square. Lining the perimeter were markets and stalls, vendors, and artisans. He watched as throngs of faerfolk meandered around, calling out to each other in greeting, to sell their wares, to wrangle the rare child—according to his father, the fae were unable to reproduce as often as mortals, which made sense, he supposed, given their incredibly long lifespans.

He hadn't been able to bring himself to go into the town yet. He had a hard enough time with half a dozen people in the same room as him, their emotions pressing on his mind and magic like a swarm of bees. He'd probably faint or something if he tried to go into the town square. Even from here, he could feel the press of the people, the range of emotions a swelling wave through him—

Slate stitched together his nascent mental shields—and shut out of his head the little voice in the back of his mind that whispered he probably could and should work harder to make them stronger faster, but...

That restlessness stirred in him. That weight in his gut since Zeyphar had claimed to be his uncle and changed his life so utterly. He tapped his fingers against the banister, suddenly agitated. He was lonely; he wanted to mingle with people. He *liked* people. He liked to socialize and charm and watch and interact...

But they weren't exactly... *people*.

Not the kind of people he'd socialized and charmed and watched and interacted with all his life. They weren't *mortal*. What did they expect from him? What could he expect from them?

Was that why he hadn't pushed to train his shields more? He growled at the thought—he'd never backed down from a challenge in his life. And yet... his entire sense of *self* felt like it had been flipped upside down and shaken like some kind of drink tumbler.

Trapped in this stupid situation he didn't even ask for.

A distant part of his mind kept assuring him that this was temporary. That someday, he could go back to his normal, boring mortal existence...

But it wasn't temporary, was it? This was his life now.

The driving desire to return to his normal life took the shape of a woman he couldn't get out of his dreams. She haunted his daylight hours as much as his nighttime ones. Even in this wholly unfamiliar place, he still found her tucked into the corners of his life; she was the empty space in his bed, the other side of the bath, the second armchair in the sitting room. As if everything around him had been designed with her in mind as an extension of him, some other unknown half in the creation of this life.

He couldn't have her, though. That stupid fucking voicemail he'd left her kept repeating over and over again in his head. *We're done, we're done, we're done.*

A constant, icy reminder that there were so many things he couldn't have anymore. Less than a week of this life and he was already angry and bitter and exhausted by it.

Slate flipped his body around and stormed off the balcony and through his rooms. Out into the hallway. Down the winding spiral staircase. Across the foyer, his flip flops snapping in an angry staccato across the stone.

Down the stairs in front of the manor, across the smooth white stone that reached out to the bridge to the town. His feet hit the thicker, heavier stones of that bridge, long, purposeful strides, and then....

Emotion crashed at him like waves against the rocks of a shoal, shredding his shields and flooding him with an overwhelming sea of feelings. A thickness in his throat, tightening on him until he could hardly breathe—

Back inside. Back inside and every step up the spiral stairs, his anger swelled and swelled like a hot, tight balloon of buzzing energy inside him. *Child.* Hiding from the world like a *spoiled, royal child.*

He hated this.

One level down from his suites and across the manor was a gorgeous and brand new martial arts space. It was the first thing Slate had asked for, something comfortable and familiar. Somewhere to train—the normal kind of training, with fist and foot, none of the magic shit that was suddenly a part of his life. A training room that was *normal* to him.

And somehow—by magic or manipulation—Frieda had made it happen. Slate and his father now had a gorgeous and fairly traditional martial arts training space, overlooking the waterfall, with fresh foam mats, gear, heavy bags.

Slate stormed into this space, a hurricane wrapped in skin, feeling the familiar scent of the foam mats soothe the agitation in his soul.

But only a little. Not even the familiar feel of a studio could temper the storm inside him.

His father was there, sitting on the balcony overlooking the waterfall. Ebisu had taken to Titan's Fen like a fish took to water. Slate hadn't failed to notice that his father was markedly healthier, more spry, less *weathered*, as though the mere magic of this place breathed new life into him.

Slate ignored his father as he dragged out a heavy bag—conveniently shelving the fact that he had some kind of telekinetic magic that could help him manipulate the weight—and he placed it in the middle of the floor.

He kicked it as hard as he possibly could.

It slid across the floor by several feet.

He dragged it back and did it again. And again, and again, something inside him winding up.

It was the fifth time of him shoving the bag back to the center of the room before Ebisu drifted into the space, dark eyes studying Slate.

"You are unsettled," his father commented.

"No shit," Slate growled. He kicked the bag again. Dragged it back to its spot. He idly processed that his hands were shaking, the veins looking a little darker than usual. He laid them on the top of the heavy bag, splaying his fingers out. "I don't want this."

His father cocked his head minutely. "What is 'this'?"

"*This!*" Slate gestured around him. "All of this." He kicked the heavy bag again. As he was dragging it back, he continued, "I don't want to be a prince. Or fae. Or whatever. I just..." He just wanted to be *him*. "I miss the school. I miss Dani. I miss the twins. I miss my normal life."

"Normal is abstract," Ebisu said. "What is normal to the fox is chaos to the hens."

"And which one am I, *oyaji*?" It came out in a snapping whip.

"Who do you wish to be?"

"I *wish* to be *me*. Slate."

His father nodded. "And who is Slate?"

"*I don't know.*" *Not anymore.* Another hard thump on the bag, the material caving around his foot before the base went sliding once more. "I feel like a stranger in my own skin."

"You will adapt and overcome. Once you are settled, you will feel less like a stranger and more at home—"

"This is *not my home!*" The words burst out of him in a loud, angry shout, his breathing ragged with every syllable. And he felt it, every word like a bullet to his heart.

His father blinked at him, a firmness settling over his expression. Slate could taste his father's concern, his vigilance, his patient assessment. It was just more fuel to the fire, a reminder he had this *thing* called *magic* inside him that he didn't want and he didn't need and he didn't ask for.

"Home is where you make it," Ebisu replied with endless, infuriating patience.

"I'm not making it here! I'm not—I don't *belong* here. I am not a *prince*. I don't want to be here. This manor is a fucking prison." He felt the words sting his father. Unintentionally, but a sting nonetheless. The one place his father had found freedom, Slate now found a prison. "I don't know these people, and they don't know me—a lot of them don't even like me." Something he'd picked up easily whenever one of the Titan's Fen's guards was in range. "And I can't leave or else my brain explodes."

"If you took care to work on your mental shields…"

"I don't *care*!" Slate blazed forward, the words leaping from his mouth as if they'd been waiting for this moment, and surging, spiraling emotions shot through his bloodstream. "I don't care and I don't want it."

His father's eyes narrowed slightly. "You do care," he stated, "or else you wouldn't be feeling so much."

"I don't *want* to care! I don't…" he floundered and found the words choking out of him. Fuck, his father was right. Of course he was right—Slate did care and that was the fucking problem. "I don't know who I am here! I don't know who I am and what I'll be and I don't want to be here and I don't—" He was sobbing now, everything just pouring out of him. "I don't know how to be what these people expect me to be. I'm not a prince or a king. I'm not *Zlaet Titania*! I'm not even *Slate Melisande* anymore."

He gestured wildly around him. "I'm just… I'm just… I'm *drowning*."

His father was watching him, taking him all in. Slate could feel him processing, could feel Ebisu's own emotions choking him, even if outwardly, he was calm as a smooth ocean at midnight.

"Perhaps if you settled into the idea of staying here…" Ebisu started calmly, gently.

"I don't want to stay here."

"This is where your life is now, Slate. This is where you were always meant to be. Clear it from your mind that this is a temporary situation. You being here is not a choice. It is fate." His father continued, and it was a reprimand, from master to student. The logic of it, the familiar tone from a father who was quick to correct his mistakes… All of it made something snap inside him.

"I'm leaving." Slate stormed toward the door, wiping his face with his hands.

"Where will you go?"

"I'm *going home.*"

He stormed out. He was a disaster, a crippling mess. Out of the manor, across the bridge, and the whole town pressed in on him. Pushing and pushing and *pushing.* Tightening over him, tightening his skin to his skeleton, tightening his throat, his lungs...

He didn't care. He nearly flew down the road that connected the manor to town, hitting the cobbled street and *running.* People moved out of his way, startled by the sight of him. He didn't stop to think about it, didn't pause to listen to the *whispers* that his *damned fae ears* could actually *hear.* Shock and alarm pressed in on him from the people, people who also looked at him with this mixture of tentative, budding hope, distrust, and swirling apprehension.

He didn't want this. He didn't want this kind of responsibility, but at the same time, he couldn't bring himself to truly abandon it either. These people needed a leader, and for many, he was supposed to be this... messiah to them, their 'long lost prince returned' and he didn't know how to be that.

He charged up the path, through the gates. The guards on the other side started, hard eyes and weapons shifting in his direction. Slate was overwhelmed by their alarm, their instant animosity to a potential threat, then confusion, then caution—feelings slapping at him like physical blows.

He burst through and into the gatehouse. Inside, there were several small round tables. Fae guards loitered here and there. They all whipped around at his sudden arrival, their emotions spiraling through him. But Slate didn't pay attention to them. Instead, he pushed through to another room and into the back, ignoring the guards calling his name. *Titania. What do you need?*

Titania. He *wasn't* a king, couldn't be. Their words were frigid gusts in an already swirling blizzard inside him.

He slammed open the door to Kallen's office. The fae male was at his desk and his purple eyes shot up to lock on Slate's face.

Unlike the guards, Kallen's emotions were held closer to his chest. Only a hint of alarm on his face.

"Take me back," Slate growled.

Were those ragged breaths his? He swiped the blood that trickled from his nose. Around him, objects in the room shook and trembled—books danced on their shelves, pens and parchment shivered across the desk. The door vibrated on its hinges. White energy skipped over Slate's skin like tiny dancing lights, swirling and shimmering over his skin like delicate snow.

Kallen gently placed his book on the desk, violet eyes assessing the room before settling back on Slate. He glanced over Slate's shoulder at the guards who lingered by the door, watching them, and Slate didn't have to look over his shoulder to know some of them had their hands on their sword hilts.

He could *feel* their uncertainty, some even had a hint of animosity towards him, others a sense of caution, though none acted in any way disrespectful.

They were sizing up this young half-fae royal prince who was just dumped on them and now was supposed to somehow guide them to a magical solution to this war.

A fae prince who'd just spent the last week *hiding* in the manor. The disgust in his chest belonged solely to *him* now.

"Back where?" Kallen asked carefully.

"To the city," Slate said, pressing his hands into the desk. The wood underneath his fingers groaned, and not from the weight of his upper body. "Take. Me. *Home.*"

Kallen watched him with an inscrutable look, then waved a casual hand at the guards by the door, dismissing them. He heard the soft treads of their retreat as much as his magic—*magic*—sensed their emotions drifting away, no longer insistent knocks against his psyche.

"Of course." Kallen nodded, still watching Slate with an unreadable expression. Slate could feel some sense of edgy observation around the fae male, but not much else. "You are allowed to return to the city whenever you please."

"Now," he bit out. "Please."

Without waiting for an answer, Slate stormed back out of the office, out of the gatehouse, hearing the almost-silent footfalls of the purple-eyed fae behind him. Slate didn't look back, and only stopped when he was on the other side of the ancient stone bridge that functioned as the static point for portalling.

Kallen said nothing, creating a portal with a smooth gesture of his hand. Slate didn't hesitate—he stepped into it. The crush of the magic squeezed him with a warm gentleness completely at odds to his swirling emotions.

They repeated that several more times, portal-skipping from Titan's Fen, through the ward in the Eastern District, and then finally, to the garden on the roof of his apartment. Slate stumbled out of the portal, catching his balance.

"Send word with the faeries when you wish to return, my prince," was all Kallen said. He pressed his hand to his sternum and in a blink, he was gone.

Slate twisted around violently, eyes bouncing around, taking in his surroundings.

The garden. He was in his father's garden.

He was *home*.

The weight of the last week crushed him. His knees collapsed underneath him and he hit the roof hard on his ass. He could feel the swirl of thunderous emotions pouring in; so many more people here in the city than in Titan's Fen. Slate wove his mental shields around him, wove and wove and wove and wove until he could barricade his mind from the rest of the city.

And still, emotion leaked through.

Fuck. Avoiding those shielding lessons with Saida was biting him in the ass today. Apparently, the building of mental shields was a skill taught at infancy to *faelings*. And Slate was desperately lagging.

He wasn't sure how long he sat there. Eventually, he shifted until he could press his back against the chilly metal of the roof access door, pulling his knees to his chest and pressing his forehead into them. He just sat. And he listened. The endless traffic in the distance; cars honking, motorbikes revving, the low horn of big trucks. He could hear so much more now, with his fae senses. He could hear the chatter of people in the district, the laughter of children.

This was his home. This was where he belonged. Fuck choices. Fuck fate.

Even as emotions that weren't his own continued to slip inside his mind and twist it up with confusion.

The sun was setting when Slate felt tiny little wisps of touch against his hair and face. He snapped his eyes open, startling the faeries who'd drifted close. Gently, he lifted his head and held out his hand. They danced across his palm, flitting around his hair.

One bold thing chattered at him in high, fast-paced Faerish, excitable, gesturing madly. Slate gave her a half-grin. "I don't understand," he said in halting, broken Faerish. It was pretty much the only phrase he knew how to say at this point.

The faerie huffed at him, her tiny hands on her tiny hips, the picture of attitude. She tried again, one miniscule hand brushing at her neck, while the other flapped in the air like a bird as she chattered.

Slate shook his head, but the faerie just giggled, pulling a chuckle from him.

So tiny and fragile, and yet undaunted by this being who was a hundred times her size. It struck home.

Adapt and overcome.

Slate peeled himself off the roof and headed inside the apartment. The faeries followed him, clinging to his hair and shoulders, flitting about.

His home was quiet, with the distinct feeling of emptiness. He welcomed the silence, the stillness on his mind, his mental shields holding out better here than they had outside, as if being in such a familiar place had added another shield against the onslaught of emotions of the city. Slate moved on silent feet through the apartment and down into the studio, which was decidedly more lived in than the apartment above.

There were no classes tonight, the studio dark. He stood in the middle of the training floor, darting his eyes around, taking it all in. Faeries danced around, checking out all the new sights and smells. Slate's earliest memories were right here on this floor. He remembered helping his father assemble the puzzle mats, walking along the seams to press them down. He couldn't have been more than four years old. He remembered testing for every rank, right here, pouring blood, sweat, and tears into this floor, this space.

He'd worked hard for his rank. There'd been something about being the instructor's kid that had been a hard mold to break out of. He'd had to prove he deserved his spot here. Worked hard to prove he belonged here with everyone else, even when they whispered behind his back that he was a *gaijin*—a foreigner, someone too other to truly fit in here, in a community that valued the group over the self.

"People think I'm strange." Slate, six years old, sitting in a hot bath, his long, dark hair a tangled mess around his face.

His father stilled. So young, in Slate's memory. "Tell me more."

Slate's little face screwed up in thought. "They think weird thoughts about me. I just... know. They say I'm too smart. And that I talk funny. And my eyes are a weird color. Teachers say I'm 'gifted'."

His father laid a large hand on Slate's head. "Lots of kids talk funny. And your eyes are blue."

"Yeah. Weird blue. Not normal blue."

"They are your mother's eyes. And they are a beautiful blue."

Slate was quiet for a long moment, running his fingers through the water. "Am I strange?"

Ebisu shifted his hold and cupped Slate's little face in his hands. "No," he said, his words a little thick around the edges. "No, you are perfect. Just as you are. People don't always trust things that are different than they are. But once they see you for who you are, they will like you more."

Slate wandered into the office, and stopped dead in the doorway. There, on the floor, was his gear bag. The one he'd lost in the arena. Or thought he'd lost.

Kari. He knew it was her. She'd gone back and found it for him.

He snatched it up and rifled through it. Inside, everything was there. His uniform, his wallet, his cell phone...

He scrambled around the desk for a charger, finding one tangled in the middle drawer. He plugged it in with shaking hands, and waited with growling impatience for his phone to reboot and power on. His heartbeat thrummed in his ears as the phone came to life. He waited... waited.

No new messages.

He had his thumb ready to dial Dani's contact before he realized he'd even gone through the motions to pull up her information. He stopped.

We're done.

She was the one thing he couldn't have.

The self-control it took him to lay his phone face down on the desk should've earned him some sort of award from the very gods themselves. Everything north of his heart tightened in bitter, icy agony.

But he'd not jeopardize whatever tentative safety Kari and Roger had managed to pull over her. Not for something as selfish as a relationship.

Slate left his phone alone and turned his attention back to his bag. Tucked into the side, secured beneath one of his heavier uniforms, was his martial arts belt.

He pulled out the worn black belt. It was graying in many places, especially where the knot would tie. Loose and flexible, fraying in places. Sure, it was a material item, and probably most people thought it was a silly thing to attach sentimental value to, but it mattered to him. This belt was proof of his accomplishments, the worn bits proof he'd not just been handed his title, but rather that he'd earned it.

Adapt and overcome.

"Doesn't sound any different than you being the master instructor at the studio..."

"I don't know who I am!"

"Who is Slate?"

He gripped that belt, strangling it in his fist. Of course he didn't know who he was... this new version of Slate was starting at the bottom again. A white belt. He had to figure out who and what he was all over again. Magic, madness, and everything. *Adapt and overcome.*

But if there was something Slate understood with absolute certainty—it was how to earn his rank. He'd never been handed a title in all his life. He wasn't about to start now. He *knew* how to be a leader, knew how to earn that rank too.

"People don't always trust things that are different than they are. But once they see you for who you are, they will like you more."

Slate turned on his heel and strode off the training floor and through the studio, pounding up the stairs and back into his apartment.

His bedroom was exactly as he'd left it. Neat, if not a little stale from lack of use. On the wall above the bed was a belt rack, displaying all his rank belts from white belt to black belt. Each was looped and tied into a knot and hung on a peg.

He studied them, then plucked the tiny white belt off its peg. The belt was a little dusty and worn from age. He fingered the knot in the center. Tradition in his school was to tie the old belts into a knot after each promotion, to symbolize that that rank, that belt, and all the experience tied to it was henceforth retired.

"What happens if you untie this knot?" His father's words—eventually parroted by Slate—said to every kid at every promotion.

"You untie the knot, and you become that rank again, sir."

Slate worked his fingers into the knot, loosening it, a touch of conditioned anxiety crawling up his throat.

The little white belt loosened and came untied, draping over his hands. He let out a long breath.

He held out his palm for a faerie. One of them danced into his hand.

"Go find Kallen," he said to her, "and tell him I want to come back."

It was time to start over.

EPILOGUE

Slate woke up with the sun in his bedroom in Titan's Fen. Dawn was creeping her first glowing fingers over the mountains, turning his bedroom into shades of gray and violet and navy.

He didn't move right away, feeling a tightness settling over his body. A physical tightness. And he was hesitant to move and discover how much his body hurt.

But it was a good hurt. A hurt that soothed his wild, temperamental soul.

He'd come back from his father's garden and marched right onto the training grounds.

"I want to fight," Slate demanded, giving Saida a hard look.

The small she-fae cocked her head at him. "Fight?"

"Yes. I want to fight through the ranks of your militia. And don't let me win. Honest fighting."

She'd regarded him steadily for a long, breathless moment. A mischievous grin pinched her face. She gestured with a hand. "By all means, my lord—"

"Stop. Don't call me that. Slate is fine. I want to start at the bottom."

She nodded slowly, glancing around at some of the guards around her, some grinning with her, some stoic, all of them uncertain about him. Slate attempted and failed to construct mental shields to block them out. He'd live with the overwhelming headache. "Fine then, Slate. After you."

And he'd gotten his *ass* handed to him. Several times.

And he fucking loved every second of it. It settled something unhinged inside him, the restlessness dissipating. It gave him a purpose. *Adapt and overcome.*

Slate rolled over, stifling a groan, when he heard the sitting room door open. The bedroom door was ajar, and through the crack, he spied Autymn carrying a tray ladened with fruits and sweet homemade breads and tea. He was still getting used to the idea of personal attendants, but the thing he appreciated the most about Autymn and Rhylan was their discretion. It took a couple of days, but now Slate was used to them ghosting through his chambers on silent feet, bringing tea and food or fresh towels and clothing.

He rolled out of bed gingerly, hissing through his teeth, and snatched a robe, cinching it to cover his boxers. He wandered into the sitting room, every step absolute agony, his knees buckling a little as his muscles protested. Autymn's caramel eyes flicked in his direction, and she smiled brightly and pressed her hand to her sternum in greeting.

"*Fayr dahyn*, my lord, good morning," she said. "The strawberries are fresh. Your *tatkyr* and I picked them not an hour ago."

"Thanks," Slate rumbled, rubbing his eyes.

Running a hand through sleep-mussed hair, he wandered out onto the expansive balcony. Below him, the village was already awake. It was a goal of his to venture out into town this week, maybe early morning or late night, when there were less faerfolk in the streets. He wasn't going to *settle in* if he didn't try to make an effort, even as anxiety fluttered against his pulse. Titan's Fen might not ever feel like *home*, but he could belong here, someday. He could make this place feel less temporary.

He had mind-magic training this morning with both Saida *and* Kallen. To work on his 'mental shields'—so he didn't *feel* everything all the damned time.

He might not know shit about being a prince, but he definitely wasn't going to be a very good one by hiding in this stupid manor all the time. He needed to get out or he'd go crazy, shields or not.

Right now, it looked like the town was gearing up for a celebration.

"Did I miss something?" Slate asked, beckoning Autymn with a tip of his chin.

She joined him on the balcony and handed him a cup of tea. A smile graced her youthful face. "Oh! No, my lord, not particularly. Some of the townsfolk are gathering for a *mayting* celebration." She sighed dreamily.

"A *mayting* celebration? Is that like a wedding or...?" He was still desperately unfamiliar with the culture here. He'd heard the term '*mayt*' several times now, and he still didn't fully grasp it.

"Oh, well," she hemmed for a second. "It is and it isn't. The act of *mayting* is private, and a celebration is held afterwards to congratulate the two. Finding your *mayt* is very special, more than simply being *together* with someone, yes? I don't know how to explain it..."

"Like a soulmate or something?"

She lit up. "Yes! That's right. Two people who are meant to be together. The fae believe it is the person the Goddess chose for you at the inception of magic in the world. Two people who fit together seamlessly, as though they were woven from the same cloth. Two halves coming together to create a whole."

"I see," he mused. "I take it it's... rare... to find a *mayt*?"

She nodded. "Perhaps not *rare,* but it's not as common for fae as other species, no. It can take decades or even centuries to find a *mayt*. Some folk don't at all. We have many *mayted* pairs in Titan's Fen." She sounded proud of that fact. "I would say our percentage of non-*mayted* to *mayted* is much better than you'd find in the Silver Valley."

"Why's that?" Slate asked with honest curiosity.

"*Titania* Aredhel always spoke of love. She believed love was the most powerful form of magic. She was *mayted* with your *tatkyr*, a mortal. The act showed her people that one could find love regardless of station or even species. It is my belief it made our people braver in matters of the heart." Her lovely face was soft at the thought, almost dreamy. "*Mayts* need each other. It's a very deep bond. Worthy of celebration."

Slate nodded and watched the faerfolk busy themselves around the square, preparing for the celebration. "How does it work? Like, do you just look at someone and *know*?"

Autymn laughed, a breezy sound. "I cannot know, my lord. I hear it is different for everyone. Some folk do simply know, some discover the feeling over time. But *mayts* are always marked."

"Marked? How?"

"It is a scar, from a bite. It is most commonly seen on the neck or shoulder, but not always." Her fingers absently brushed at her own neck, the muscle that joined shoulder to neck, and Slate couldn't stop from zeroing in on the spot she indicated.

Slate blinked at her, his mind going still as stone. "A... bite?"

"Yes." Autymn flushed a little and looked away from him, eyes trained on the view of the village, and he wondered if he was being rude in asking about a topic that was obviously very private to most fae. "A bite. Two crescent-shaped scars, coming together to form a complete circle. As I said, I do not know how it is in detail, but folk say it's usually a..." She fished for the right word. "A need? A want? A..." She mumbled under her breath in Faerish, then snapped her fingers. "An instinct? Yes! An instinct. Generally, the more dominant of the pair starts the *mayting*."

Slate stopped breathing, alarm pinging through his mind.

Sinking his teeth into Dani's shoulder.

Listening to the power of her orgasm.

Feeling the power of it.

Dani's words: "*It doesn't hurt...*"

Zeyphar's delight over the bruise. Those long-fingered hands tipping Slate's chin. *You cannot be without her. She belongs to you.*

"What..." Slate swallowed, clearing his throat, clearing his mind. His hands strangled his mug. The ceramic creaked under his fingers. "What happens after the dominant person starts the *mayting*?"

"The less dominant *mayt* has to accept the *mayting*," she responded with a half-shrug. "There's always a choice, yes? *Maytings* are..." Once more, she floundered for the right word, before giving up with a smile and a wave of her hand. "It is a choice. I do know if the *mayting* isn't completed, the initial mark will fade. However, that is incredibly rare, from what I've come to understand. Most people would not be able to resist the call in their soul to their other half."

Another dreamy sigh from her as she leaned on the railing, cupping her chin in her hand. "To find the one person in your life you are *meant* to be with... it is beautiful and fortunate, to be so blessed by the Goddess." She straightened and dusted off her simple periwinkle dress. "If you are concerned, you are not expected to join the celebration, my lord. I'm sure you would be welcomed, but there is no expectation—the people will understand you are still learning how to shield your mind," she said with a smile.

"Okay..." Slate unstuck his suddenly dry throat. "Thanks. Maybe... maybe we can send them a gift or something? Is that... normal?" He grasped for anything to talk about, anything to distract his mind from what he was very rapidly drawing some *alarming* conclusions about.

Autymn nodded. "Yes, my lord, of course."

She took his empty mug from him and strolled back into the room. Slate white-knuck-led the banister, suddenly starving for air. The ache in his body flew out of his mind.

That bath. That *bite*. His discomfort at his own strange attachment to the mark. That bastard Zeyphar's near-maniacal joy in it. *She belongs to you. Your instincts chose well...*

Not to mention the insane sexual chemistry between them, the casual intimacy they both readily slipped into, and how insane he felt about her, going so far as to tell his father he'd *marry* her if given half a chance.

The door to his bedroom eased closed, indicating Autymn's departure.

Slate knees gave out. He sank to the floor of the balcony.

Goddess above.

Dani was his *mayt*.

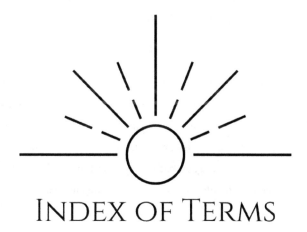

INDEX OF TERMS

Definitions:

Aura: Magical output, what others can sense on any magical being. Most magical beings—with skill and practice—can learn to mask their auras either partially or entirely.

Chi: *(Origin: Mystic Magic)* Life energy. Different than magical aura, chi is the amount of life energy in any living thing, magical or non-magical.

Dryad/Nymph: *(Origin: Lore Magic)* Creatures of nature who inhabit a tree or stream, tying them to the land. They are protective of nature, especially of their particular tree or stream, but otherwise nonaggressive. These women are sometimes mistaken for female fae, as both are often lithe and willowy in stature.

Dwarf: *(Origin: Lore Magic)* Lorefolk with strong ties to mountains and the underground, with the unique ability to handle silver and iron, which is harmful to many in Lorekind.

Fae: *(Origin: Lore Magic)* A race of beings prone to magic with a close tie to nature, like most beings in the Lore. They consider themselves the most refined and cultured of Lorefolk. Fae are often distinguished by their pointed ears, sharp, clever faces, large eyes, and uncanny grace. Fae magic is varied but includes such abilities as telekinesis, plant-based magic, portals, warding, empathy magic, and more. Fae react badly to pure iron, making city-dwelling difficult. Fae have an exaggerated life span of up to a thousand years.

High Fae: A term used by the fae to refer to those whose bloodlines stem closely to the original 13 Houses, and has since come to mean fae nobility. It is a contested term by those fae who oppose the idea of classism among their race.

Faeling: *(Origin: Lore Magic)* A fae child, or young faerfolk.

Faeries: *(Origin: Lore Magic)* Tiny winged humanoid beings who stand no higher than three inches. Though they have no gender, their inherent grace is reminiscent of the goddess and so the pronoun "she" or "her" is often used when referring to a faerie. They are drawn to flora and shiny things alike, and are frequently mistaken for dragonflies by mortals. They are well known for their child-like innocence and love of mischief and gossip that sets them beyond the control of even the strongest in Lorekind, though they share a unique relationship with the fae.

Faerloch, Germany: A (fictitious) city set in Western Germany, about two hours north of Zürich, Switzerland. It is a sprawling metropolis with many sub-sections and districts. It is sometimes called the City of Wonder, due to its heavy roots in Lore magic.

Faerish: *(Origin: Lore Magic)* The language of the fae.

Familiar: *(Origin: Lore Magic)* A witch's companion, often a cat or a crow, sometimes a snake or even a fox. Familiars are sentient, capable of mortal speech, and often have extended lives.

Four Gods of Creation: Children to the Mother of the Cosmos, four gods who were given the power to breathe life into the world. They are as follows:

> The Tribal Father, who was the first among them and who favored the vast continent of Africa, and created Tribalistic Magic.

> The Jade Emperor, who made his mark in the vast lands to the East, and created Mystic Magic.

> The Goddess of the Wood and Wild, who favored the middle lands of Europe, creator of Lore Magic.

> The Great Spirit, the youngest of them, who favored the Americas and created Shamanistic Magic.

(The) Forest of L'el: A large forest that spans the western border of Germany, sometimes called the Black Forest by mortals. The Forest of L'el runs parallel to Germany's western border, north to south, and bleeds over into parts of France. The trees are ancient, thick, and towering, and magic soaks the land. It has survived when other forests fell to the modern logging industry because of this magic, which makes mortals forget their intentions upon crossing L'el's boundary. Magicfolk believe the Forest is alive and sentient, and it is thought to be the birthplace of the Lore, particularly the fae.

Goddess of the Wood and Wild: *(Origin: Lore Magic)* The mother of the Lore. She created all beings of European magic. She is one of the Four Gods of Creation.

Kitsune: *(Origin: Mystic Magic)* A female-exclusive race of fox spirits. Rare, extremely powerful, and capable of great magic, it is thought that *kitsune* are the right-hand females of the Jade Emperor himself, the Father of Mystic Magic. They are renowned for knowing a great deal about the world due to their innate curiosity and highly observant natures. They can take the form of a fox, mortal, or a combination of both, and are masters of fire, illusions, tricks, and other sleight of hand magicks. Upon reaching a certain age, they are also capable of intense regenerative magic, essentially making them immortal.

Lorefolk: *(Origin: Lore Magic)* A general term for beings all belonging to the magic of Lore—the European branch of magic.

Lorekissed: *(Origin: Lore Magic)* A human with a drop of magic in their blood from some distant Lorefolk ancestor. Some manifest a weak talent for magic, others gain physical advantages, but most never become aware of their ancestry.

Manyeo (witch-doctor): *(Origin: Mystic Magic)* An Eastern witch with the ability to see and manipulate the *chi* in living things in order to create potions, medicines, and healing poultices. Most *manyeo* become witch-doctors by trade, but some prefer to deviate from the art of magical medicine and pursue careers in enchantment work. Enchantment work involves manipulating a being's *chi*, often through tattoos or other permanent markings, to keep an enchantment active. Enchantments can be attached to non-living objects—such as in the creation of wards—but each enchantment still requires a *chi* signature from either the *manyeo* or the client. Manyeo have exaggerated lifespans, upwards of several hundred years. *Manyeo is a fictitious being created for this world/book series.*

Miko: A priestess of a Japanese Shinto Temple. They typically wear a traditional red *hakama* (top) and white *kosode* (pants).

Mysticfolk: *(Origin: Mystic Magic)* A general term for all beings belonging to the magic of the Mystics—Eastern magic.

Shintoism: A Japanese religion in which the core belief revolves around gods (kami) and spirits inhabiting the world around us.

Silver Valley: A large fae city whose location within the Forest of L'el shifts constantly with the magic of the forest. It is considered the seat of power for the fae, and is overseen by the High Fae Council and the *Titania*—the leader of the fae.

Taekwondo: A Korean martial art that developed in the 1950s in Korea, during the Japanese occupation. It takes many of its movements and foundations from Karate, once being called "Korean Karate." It's known for its aerial kicking and recognition in the Olympics for its full-contact and point-based fighting.

Tamashoko *(tama - soul, sho - together, ko - heart) (Origin: Mystic Magic)*: In the Mystics, the idea of a soulmate exists. The red thread of fate binds two people together forever.

Tei Enaid: *(Origin: Lore Magic)* This is what the witches refer to as a soulmate—the person they are meant to be with. Witches often tie their life energies together if they are Tei Enaid. In the case of non-witches, tying life energies together through witchcraft results in the partners sharing the combined lifespans. Because of this, beings with shorter lifespans, including mortals, gain extended life and youth.

Titan's Fen: A small town in the Forest of L'el. It was once the summer retreat for the royal fae family.

Witch: *(Origin: Lore Magic)* A race whose magic favors the females of their lineage, with only rare cases of males born of witches developing magic. Their magic stems from their ability to control one or more elements: water, fire, earth, and air. Witches practice their magic in covens and peddle their enchantments to any with the coin to pay for them. Witches have an exaggerated life span of several hundred years, but also possess the ability to tie the lifespans of two beings together through a blood-tie, allowing species of dissimilar lifespans to mate.

Were (werefolk): *(Origin: Lore Magic)* A race of beings who have two skins, one human and one animal. They can shift between their animal form and human form at will (despite human superstitions involving full moons), and boast the fastest regenerative abilities in the Lore. Their lifespans differ based on the species of their inner beast, from a few hundred years to over a thousand, but all share a weakness to silver, as silver interrupts the regenerative magic.

Vampire: *(Origin: Lore Magic)* Thought to be the first among the Lore created by the Goddess, vampires are creatures of the night. Their solitary nature and low reproductive rates mean they are the rarest beings in the Lore, especially after a bloody civil war decimated their numbers centuries ago. They are the longest-lived, and prone to an arrogant and secretive nature that has done little to bolster their waning numbers. It is unknown if they can die from old age. They consume food as well as blood, and are sensitive to fire, silver, and the sun.

Yokai: *(Origin: Mystic Magic)* A demon from Japanese mythology.

Languages:

Japanese:

Ai: Love.

Domo: Thank you.

Gaijin: Foreigner, or anyone who isn't strictly Japanese.

Happi: A Japanese short sleeved short robe, usually open in the front. Like a short house coat.

Hajimemashite: Nice to meet you.

Inari: Fox deities, often depicted in shrines.

Izakaya: A traditional Japanese bar.

-chan: A Japanese honorific and term of endearment, usually reserved for children or between female friends. It's also a diminutive term, used for anything small and cute.

-kun: A Japanese honorific usually reserved for younger boys and men, added to the end of their name. It has a certain level of familiarity to it, meaning the two people know each other well.

-san: A Japanese honorific which roughly translates to "Mr." or "Miss/Mrs."

Ohayo: Good morning.

Oyaji/Oto-san: Father.

Ossan: Old man.

Okaa-san: Mother.

Ojii-san/Jii-chan: Grandfather/old man.

Obaa-san/baa-chan: Grandmother/old woman.

Ototo-kun: Little brother.

Okaeri: A phrase said in response to *tadaima*, loosely meaning "welcome home".

Oyasuminasai: Good night.

Ne: A word that denotes a question or a confirmation. English equivalent of tacking on a "ya?" to the end of a sentence.

Noren: A tapestry.

Kampai: Cheers!

Kami: God/gods. Lowercase *kami* is many gods or minor gods, and uppercase *Kami* is larger deities.

Kotatsu: A low, heated table commonly found in Japanese houses.

Sayonara: Good bye.

Torii: A red arch that denotes an entrance to a sacred space.

Tadaima: A phrase said when someone returns home from being out.

Faerish:

Mayt: The Faerish term for soulmates. The fae believe that mayts are destined to be together, chosen by the Goddess at the inception of magic in the world. Mayts are often marked by a scar from a bite, typically found on the neck or shoulder.

Titania: Leader of the fae. This term is not gendered—male and female leaders have used the same term over the centuries.

Tana: Consort to Titania. This term is not gendered. It is simply an honorific reserved for the partner of the Titania.

Tatya: Prince/Princess (non-gendered).

Fayr Dahn: Good morning.

Irish:

Iníon: Daughter

German:

Dirndl: A feminine dress native to countries in the Alpine region. A dirndl consists of a close-fitting bodice featuring a low neckline, a blouse worn under the bodice, a wide high-waisted skirt and an apron. It's typically worn by barmaids in Southern Germany.

Herr: Equivalent to "Mister".

Frau: Young woman.

French:

N'est-ce pas? A french phrase that translates to "is it not?" or "isn't it?"

Mon garcon: My boy.

ACKNOWLEDGMENTS

It's crazy that two little girls who used to say: "Someday we will publish a book!" have turned into two adult women who can now say: "We HAVE published a book!"

Publishing a book never happens in a silo, so there is a veritable team of people who deserve our unending gratitude for their help in getting this book into the hands of readers.

Sierra's Acknowledgments:

I'll admit, writing acknowledgements is a little overwhelming to me. Because of this, and despite the fact that there are so many people who have helped to support our writing throughout the years, I'm going to limit my acknowledgments to only two: my amazing co-author and my husband.

Jessica, thank you so much for not only your support, but for you. Thank you for being you, for being my best friend for life, for being the wind beneath my writing wings, the oil of our two-part engine. Without you, this book would never, ever have happened, because you poured so much of your time and energy into making our writing more than just something that happens in a Google doc. I will always be grateful to you for many things, but this particular thing is dear to my heart. You've made a dream of mine come true, to physically hold a book that *we* wrote. More than that, you've filled my life with fantastical ideas and moments of magic that are truly priceless. Thank you, thank you, *thank you*.

To my husband Michael: thank you for always being a pillar of support and love for me. Your taste in books runs far from the romance genre, and yet you took your time to read our book and offer your sincere advice on improvements, especially with our villain. I know that you will always support my writing, and I will always be endlessly thankful for that and for you. You've brought more joy into my life than anything or anyone else, and I'm so glad you've been a part of this literary journey with me. I love you.

Jess's Acknowledgments:

First… to Sierra. My coauthor. But more importantly, my best friend.

Nearly 25 years of friendship. And over 20 years of it has been writing together. It started by accident—you were trying to teach Alicia how to role-play-write with you, and she just wasn't getting it. I shooed her out of the way, cracked my fingers, and finger-pecked my first paragraph to you.

It was history after that. Making characters. Diving into chatrooms that my mother would have surely expired to know we were in. Notebooks and notebooks and *notebooks* of world building and characters. The words *I posted* became our love language. Reading romance novels that we definitely should not have been reading. Watching anime and eating pizza and taco pie and talking late into the night about scenes and ideas and plots. It became our entire existence. Bound together by wild imaginations and words.

Over 20 years we've been doing this thing. This writing back and forth thing. It has a name now—coauthoring. But even before there was a label, you were always my partner. None of my ideas were ever too crazy for you. You always handled my brain dumpings with grace, never judged a single garbage word I wrote. You challenged everything I ever thought with ideas, pushing us both to think about plots and characters and scenes differently. We fought viciously (these things happen when an Aries and Leo are best friends) but somehow, we still managed to come out with something better, stronger, more refined, more creative. You were always right in the mess right with me.

Even outside of writing, you were always right in the mess with me. When my health failed, you literally picked me up. When my parents divorced, you were somewhere I could run away to. When I needed a boost of confidence, you were my cheerleader. You assured me that I needed no one's approval to be exactly and unapologetically who I was. I was a Goddess, you'd say, handcrafted by the the Grecian artists of old themselves.

We are really different people since you first stuck you hand out at me at 10 years old and declared us friends, but somehow... just like with our writing, we are better, stronger, more refined, more creative... more everything. Because we've always been better together.

I will never stop writing with you. Even though I plan to take this writing thing down the career track, I will never stop. Creating stories with you is so deeply embedded into my identity now that I don't know how to be without it. You are my best friend, my coauthor, my partner in crime, my sounding board, the ground to my sky, the cheese to my pizza, the Jian to my Kari.

I love you to a depth my being that cannot even be explained with something as simply as love. It's every emotion. It's something too deep to be boiled down to words. It's the stuff universes are made with, the threads of fate themselves.

I hope you love the feel of this book in your hands. Because there would be no book without you. No Jessica as she stands today without you. You and I... we are forever, girl.

Next, to my husband, Fred.

There is so much to encapsulate here. Because while there would be no book without Sierra, there would've been no publishing a book without you.

Thank you for listening to my endless prattling about my book, for nodding in all the right places, for being a sounding board when I needed one.

Thank you for making sure that there was always *just enough* money to fund this silly little publishing dream.

Thank you for choosing to play video games for nights on end when I needed to write, to edit, to create content for social media for marketing. Thank you for giving me the time and the space to do that.

Thank you for listening to me cry as I tried to finagle and navigate the complexities of this self-publishing thing. As I poured hours and days and late nights into research.

Thank you for all the nights we didn't have together as I tried to get this book off the ground, and thank you in advance for all the time we still won't have as I continue to make dreams into realities. You've never complained, not once, and you alone understand the sheer amount of energy it takes to get a book from its draft form into something that can be consumable by others, in addition to marketing, social media, newsletters, websites, staying relevant, setting up logistics, hiring professionals, buying programs, consuming media, etc. And so much research.

Thank you for the constant, quiet, nonjudgmental reminder that life does exist outside of the story, outside of the screen, outside of the book. It's so easy for me to get sucked into it, to become consumed by the next thing and the next thing and the thing after that. Thank you for allowing me the space to be consumed and also to be freed from it.

Thank you for hashing problems out with me, not allowing me to be gaslit by either myself or others, and constantly, endlessly, reminding me that *yes, Jessica, you are on the right track. You are doing the right thing.*

Thank you for being an endless, rock-solid, unwavering support pillar. You are my biggest, most understated cheerleader, my main male character in this book of life, my corner coach. There is no other person I ever want in my corner with me. I love you.

Some people like to take the time to thank their family. My family doesn't even know I write books, so instead I'm going to take this space to thank some very special friends who helped me get this book out of its draft and into its final evolution.

Liza: The first alpha reader. Obviously, your initial perspective of this book was invaluable for shaping the book everyone now sees, but our friendship is so much deeper than that. Always by my side, always supportive, in everything. I hope you know without a shadow of doubt that you are one my best friends, and I'm forever grateful for you.

The Beta Readers: Abigail, Charity, Amber, Laura, and Char. I'm endlessly grateful for all your support, your insight on this book, and of course, your friendships. The universe has truly blessed me with incredible friends and community. I share such special friendships with each of you. I hope you all know that there is a space in my heart reserved just for you. Thank you for everything.

The Street Team: Ashley, Bethany, Britt G, Britt L, Erin, Rachel H, Bree, Sam, and Tia... I am BLESSED to know each and every one of you. Thank you so much for helping with the promotion and exposure for this book. Self-Publishing can't be successful isolated in a bubble. Without your support, Frost and Sunshine would just be another dusty book lost among the algorithm of Amazon. Thank you for bringing us so much joy during Launch Season.

Alex (AP Walston): My chaos goblin. What is there to say that hasn't already been said? You have been an incredible friend to me. I'm so so grateful that I met you. Being able to crawl into your DMs with every single thought in my head has been... refreshing. Every garbage thought, every little grievance, every personal thing, anytime I needed someone to just talk to, you were right there. Our chats give me so much life. Someday, we will be the greats.

MJ (Miranda Joy): Sweet but so spicy. Thank you endlessly for... well, everything. From DMs about books and LLCs, to talking about health, to spilling a little innocent tea here and there... everything. You've taught me so much, and you've helped me so much on this journey. I'm so happy we are friends.

Tia (TM Ledvina): My baby Tia. I'm so glad I saw a fellow anime girl and clicked that follow button. I'm so grateful for your friendship. Your support, your hype, your constant cheerleading. You can't know how much I crave your energy in my life. Thank you for absolutely everything.

To all the others—if I wrote individual posts for all of you, this acknowledgement section would be longer than the book. But know that you all played a huge part in my drive and motivation to be an author, to help show me that it was possible to do this thing. Every time you've popped into my DMs, every tagged post, every tagged Story, every reshare of my content, every reaction to the regular life shenanigans I share on Instagram. I've never had writing or book friends other than Sierra. I sometimes still can't believe any of you even exist. The culture of community is a powerful creature. Thank you, truly, for including me. Alexa, Sarah, Britt Corley, LB, Raeanne, Sam, Lindsey, Briana, Talia, Rachel R, Lauren... and others that I'm probably desperately missing. With an extra special shout-out to Melissa, who is still with me from my early makeup Instagram days. Supporting me through all of my social media identities.

And finally... to the readers. We would still write books without an audience, but the audience helps, doesn't it. The power of the community is heady. Never ever underestimate how much power you hold, both as a collective and as a small piece of the collective. You are not insignificant. Every page read, every review, every recommendation... it culminates into something incredible. You are part of something incredible, and We are grateful to you, reader.

We are grateful to *you*.

ABOUT THE AUTHORS

Surprise! J.S. Alexandria is actually TWO people—Jessica and Sierra. They are best friends and coauthors. They've been writing books together for over 20 years.

Sierra lives in Philadelphia with her husband and three guinea pigs. When not writing, Sierra can be found playing video games, watching anime, or cooking. She loves to listen to audiobooks. She speaks three languages fluently—English, French, and Japanese—as well as a smattering of other languages as well. Sierra prefers to be more of the 'silent partner' of the writing duo, so you won't find her on many social media sites.

Jessica lives in New England with her husband and two cat children. She's a special educator by day and a martial artist by night. She currently holds a 3rd degree black belt in traditional Taekwondo. She's often the point of contact for anything related to J.S.

Alexandria. You can find her on Instagram @jess.alexandria.books where she posts sneak peeks and teasers for upcoming novels. She also is the founder of Shadow Rain Publishing LLC, which can also be found on Instagram @shadowrainpublishing.

CPSIA information can be obtained
at www.ICGtesting.com
Printed in the USA
BVHW051225090123
655885BV00007B/27/J

9 798987 418611